JENNIFER ESTEP

*To all the readers who wanted more
Galactic Bonds books—this one is for you.*

To my mom—for everything.

*To Kitty Boodle—for reminding me how much fun,
joy, and love pets bring into our lives.*

*To myself—for trying something different
and writing a book of my heart.*

*Enemies are like stormswords.
Even if you defeat them, they still
end up stabbing you in the heart.*

—AUTHOR UNKNOWN

PART ONE

UNWANTED CONNECTIONS

ONE

VESPER

Sometimes in life, you have to do unpleasant things to get revenge.

Like sit through a boring corporate meeting in the morning, train until your muscles scream at noon, and let yourself be bribed before midnight.

Unfortunately, my day was just getting started, and my revenge, well, it was quite far off, maybe even on the other side of the galaxy—assuming I could get it at all.

". . . sales of Lady Vesper's new brewmaker are up forty-three percent from the previous Kent model . . ."

A thirty-something man waved his hand, making spreadsheets, earnings reports, and other documents flicker and spin over the holoscreen embedded in the long wooden table in the center of the conference room. The holograms' glow added a silvery sheen to his dark brown eyes and skin, and an errant curl of black hair drooped over his forehead. He absently shoved the stray lock back into place, making the spreadsheets spin again.

Raul Xanxado was the best sales analyst at Quill Corp, but his presentations were as dry and precise as the numbers he tracked, calculated, and projected. He'd been talking for almost ten minutes, and I bit my tongue to stifle a yawn.

I looked past Raul, staring out the permaglass windows at the neighboring chrome skyscrapers, which were studded with green solar panels, as though they were sleeping dragons waiting to be recharged so they could spring into motion. I might be physically looking at skyscrapers, but in my mind's eye, I was seeing another building entirely—a dark stone structure with towers and turrets that sprawled across one end of a busy street.

Was Kyrion Caldaren on his home planet of Corios? Was he relaxing in his old-fashioned castle on the Boulevard, the wide avenue lined with the ostentatious homes of the rich and powerful Regal lords and ladies? Or had he been sent to some distant planet on a dangerous Arrow mission to track down the Techwave? Did he ever think about me the way I so often thought about him—

Under the conference table, out of sight of the others, the woman sitting next to me jabbed the sharp, pointed toe of her black stiletto into my calf. Once again, I bit my tongue, this time to keep a hiss of pain from escaping my lips.

I glared at the woman, who wore a sleek, tailored pantsuit that was both professional and fashionable. The shimmering gold fabric brought out her ebony skin, while gold shadow and liner accentuated her dark brown eyes. Her dark brown hair was pulled back into an elegant twist, and chandelier earrings shaped like gold stars brushed the tops of her shoulders.

Tivona Winslow, my best friend, skilled corporate negotiator, and second in command at Quill Corp, tilted her head at me in a chiding motion, making her earrings tinkle together like tiny wind chimes. Tivona turned her attention back to Raul. I sighed and did the same.

". . . given these projections, brewmaker sales should continue to rise . . ."

Raul spouted a few more figures, then finally, mercifully, wrapped up his presentation. He waved his hand, and the spreadsheets flickering over the table disappeared.

Tivona gave him a warm smile. "Thank you for that very thorough report, Raul."

Raul blinked a few times, clearly surprised that Tivona had been paying attention and not staring into space like everyone else. He shyly smiled back at her.

At the opposite end of the table, a fifty-something woman loudly harrumphed. Unlike everyone else, she hadn't bothered to hide her disinterest in Raul's presentation, and she'd been swiping through screens on her tablet the entire meeting, despite Tivona's dark glowers.

The woman's blond hair was pulled back into a high bun, and obstinance glinted in her light brown eyes, which were the same color as her coveralls. Even though I had sent out numerous memos telling workers they could wear whatever they wanted, many folks still sported the brown, beige, and gray colors of House Kent, the previous owners of Quill Corp. Loyalists to the old regime were among my many, many headaches.

"Burgeoning sales won't matter as long as we keep using more expensive materials," the woman said in a snide voice. "The astronomical increase in production costs is decimating profit margins."

Under the tabletop, my hands clenched into fists, and I bit my tongue again, this time to keep from sniping back at her.

Millicent Tobani was the head foreperson of the Quill Corp production plants—and the proverbial thorn in my side, questioning my every decision. I didn't know if Millicent kept lashing out because she was worried about losing her job, because she was still devoted to House Kent, or because she just enjoyed annoying me. Knowing my bad luck, it was probably all three. But Millicent excelled at her job, and the production plants ran safely and smoothly under her watch. It would take me months to find a suitable replacement, which was why I hadn't fired her for insubordination—yet.

Millicent took my silence as encouragement and kept right on chastising me. "Rowena Kent was always happy to use the cheapest materials the production plants could procure."

Raul had been about to sit down, and he shot bolt upright again, his gaze snapping back and forth between Millicent and me. All around the table, the other department heads did the same thing, wondering how this latest tug-of-war would play out.

Three months ago, everyone in this room, myself included, had worked for Kent Corp, which had belonged to Rowena Kent and her daughter, Sabine. The Kents had been among the most powerful Regal families in the Imperium, and they had ruled Kent Corp with an iron fist.

They had also been traitors.

Rowena and Sabine had secretly equipped their new space cruisers with faulty navigation sensors that were designed to make the ships crash on command. Like the *Velorum* cruiser, which had gone down on its maiden flight, killing everyone on board, as well as many others on the ground in the spaceport below.

Thousands of innocent people had died.

At the time, I had been a lowly lab rat, someone who worked in the research and development lab at Kent Corp, and I had been among those assigned to investigate the *Velorum* crash. Rowena and Sabine Kent, along with Conrad Fawley, my supervisor and ex-boyfriend, had blamed the tragedy on pilot error, but I'd discovered the real culprit was the navigation sensor.

When I'd brought my findings to Conrad and the Kents, I'd

learned the horrifying truth: the faulty sensor wasn't a design flaw, an overlooked safety hazard, but rather a deliberate, calculated part of the design. The Kents were secretly in league with the Techwave, a powerful terrorist group that wanted to destroy Imperium military cruisers and kill all the soldiers on board, along with the elite fighters known as Arrows.

When I'd suggested that the Kents could quietly fix their mistake, Rowena had ordered her corporate mercenaries to knock me out in this very conference room. I had woken up conscripted on an Imperium ship and had been forced to take part in a battle against the Techwavers, who had seized a Regal-owned metal refinery on a Magma planet.

My seer magic surged up. In an instant, the conference room vanished, and I was standing in a field of shiny black rocks and staring out over the bodies of the other conscripts that littered the ground like dead, tattered leaves. Smoke and ash swirled through the air, and the oppressive heat sucked the moisture out of my body, as though I was slowly being roasted alive inside an oven—

"Well, Vesper?" Millicent demanded in a loud, obnoxious voice. Unlike everyone else at Quill Corp, she refused to address me by my Regal title. "Are you finally going to come to your senses and revert to the cheaper materials like I suggested in *my* report?"

I blinked. The rocky field and broken bodies vanished, and I snapped back to the here and now, although the sulfuric stench of smoke lingered in my nose. My hands clenched into even tighter fists, and I struggled to keep my breathing slow and steady. Thanks to my seer magic, I never forgot anything I saw, heard, or experienced, no matter how much I might want to.

Tivona cleared her throat. Everyone was staring at me, including Tivona, whose forehead was crinkled with worry. Raul remained standing, awkwardly hovering over the table, while Millicent smirked at me again.

I forced myself to relax my hands. Then I sat up straighter and lifted my chin, striking a haughty pose befitting a Regal lady. "No. We will keep using the more expensive materials and continue to produce the new, improved designs—*my* designs."

Millicent opened her mouth to keep protesting. Annoyance bubbled up in my chest, and I leaned forward and speared her with a hard look.

"The Kents are dead, and this is Quill Corp now. The days of churning out shoddy brewmakers and other junky appliances to turn a quick profit are gone. *My* company will produce high-quality brewmakers, blasters, and space cruisers using the finest materials and most advanced designs available."

I leaned back and gestured toward the door. "Anyone who doesn't like that is free to find employment elsewhere."

A tense, heavy silence dropped over the conference room. No one spoke or moved, not even Raul, who was still on his feet. I kept staring at Millicent. Anger stained her pale cheeks, but her arrogant smirk melted into a sour, petulant expression, as though I had taken away her favorite toy. She harrumphed again, but she slowly wilted down into her seat. As the head foreperson, Millicent earned a hefty salary, and she wouldn't find a better, more lucrative job on Temperate 42. She might not like the way I did business, but she was stuck with me, the same way I was stuck with her.

"Raul, thank you for that very detailed report. I want to see the updated sales numbers and projections again next week."

His head bobbed in quick, nervous agreement, and he finally sank down into his chair.

"That's the last item on the meeting agenda," Tivona chirped in a bright voice. "Everyone, please enjoy some refreshments before you return to work."

She gestured toward a table along the wall that was filled with fresh fruits, cheeses, and pastries—real, organic food that had cost me a small fortune. Everyone eyed the impressive spread with hungry interest, even Millicent.

I got to my feet, and everyone else stood up as well, except for Millicent. I marched over to the refreshment table, piled one plate high with food, and placed a single blueberry scone on a second plate. Then I went over and set the second plate in front of Millicent, who still hadn't moved.

"You should try a blueberry scone," I replied in a syrupy-sweet voice. "They're *so* much better than what the campus food carts sell. Like the one I saw you eating on your way into work this morning."

Millicent crossed her arms over her chest, but her stomach let out a telltale rumble, and she snuck a longing glance at the tempting pastry.

Still clutching my own plate of food, I left the conference room, trying to ignore the tension gathering at the base of my neck. The day had barely begun, and I was already fighting one battle after another.

I headed down the corridor and stepped into a permaglass elevator. Tivona joined me, also holding a plate of food.

"That went well," she drawled.

I ignored her sarcastic tone and sank my teeth into a blackberry tart. Sweet, juicy fruit. Creamy vanilla-bean custard. Buttery, flaky crust. All of it topped with a sugary glaze that melted in my mouth. Mmm-mmm-mmm. The new Quill Corp executive chef was worth every credit it had taken to convince her to leave Corios and come work for me.

The elevator dropped, and my mood along with it, despite the delicious pastry.

"Have you figured out why Millicent dislikes me so much?" I asked. "Have I done something to personally offend her, or does she just enjoy being difficult?"

Tivona nibbled on a raspberry tart. "No one likes radical change, especially someone like Millicent, who has been in a position of power for several years. Everyone at Quill Corp is worried about what you'll do next. You can't really blame them, given everything that's happened over the past few months."

I grimaced and gobbled down the rest of the tart, but the sweet treat couldn't drown out the bitter taste in my mouth. A few months ago, I had been the most famous—or infamous—person in the Archipelago Galaxy. A lowly little lab rat who had managed to expose a Techwave plot, take down a traitorous Regal family, and seize control of their corporation. Sometimes I couldn't believe all those things had happened to *me*—and that I had survived them all.

Naive, foolish, stupid me had thought the attention would fade after a few weeks and that the gossipcasts would move on to something else, *someone* else. But no fresh scandals had arisen, and the gossipcasts kept replaying my interviews, along with video clips from a ball that had been held in my honor at Crownpoint, the Imperium palace, where I had been officially elevated to Regal status. Lady Vesper Quill, media darling. My stomach soured, and the light, airy tart was suddenly as heavy as a brick in my belly.

The elevator slowed, then stopped. The door slid open, revealing a subterranean corridor, and I dumped the rest of my uneaten food into a recycler. Tivona followed me, still nibbling on her own treats.

I stepped onto a mat that sanitized my boots with UV light, then swiped my ID card through a nearby reader. A couple of permaglass doors hissed open, and I strode through to the other side.

The Quill Corp research and development lab was located three stories underground, and white tile stretched out in all directions, covering the floor, the walls, and even the ceiling high above. Folks wearing long white lab coats huddled over clear polyplastic workstations, tinkering with vacuum cleaners, self-stirring spoons, and other household appliances large and small. I used to be one of them, and in many ways, I still was.

As soon as I entered the sterile space, a sense of calm swept over me, as though I had trudged out of a hot, scorching desert into a cool, soothing oasis. In the lab, I wasn't burdened with being a Regal lady in name only, or people in my own corporation questioning my every decision, or all the other enemies who were plotting my downfall. No, here I was just Vesper, a lab rat working on her latest project and hoping to use her brilliance to make people's lives a little better and easier.

Feeling lighter, I moved forward, with Tivona still walking alongside me.

Several folks looked up at my footsteps. Some people's eyes widened in surprise, and they ducked their heads and focused on their projects again. Others studied me with shrewd, calculating gazes, silently scrutinizing everything from my wrinkled lab coat to my dark blue shirt and matching cargo pants to my worn black work boots. A few even shook their heads in disbelief at the fact that I still toiled in the lab with everyone else.

I stepped into a large shadow, and my gaze flicked upward. Enormous models of Kent Corp spaceships used to hang on thick cables that were embedded in the ceiling, but I'd had the maintenance workers remove all the ships, except for the model of the *Velorum* that now hung over the center of the lab like a dark gray storm cloud. I didn't want anyone to forget what the Kents had done, and it was also my way of honoring my cousin Liesl, who had been on board the doomed ship and died along with all the other passengers.

I stopped and stared at the spot below the observation deck windows where Rowena and Sabine Kent had installed their faulty navigation sensor. This model was an exact replica of the original *Velorum* cruiser, complete with the safety hazard. My seer magic kicked in, and a silver light flared around the sensor, just as it had when I had first studied the ship's schematics, trying to figure out why it had crashed. The Kents' plan had been extremely sly, subtle, and clever, and if not for my magic, then I too would have overlooked the faulty sensor, along with everyone else.

The longer I stared at the sensor, the brighter the silver light became, and the more my stomach twisted with worry. I had already exposed the Kents' scheme, so why was my power flaring up? Why now, when looking at the ship again? What was my magic trying to tell me?

"Vesper?" Tivona asked in a low voice. "Are you okay? Are you . . . seeing something?"

Thanks to the gossipcasts, everyone knew that I was a seer, although my magic was reported as being extremely weak. Tivona was one of the few people who knew how strong I really was. She also knew about the odd flashes of light I saw as part of my psionic abilities—and how difficult it could be for me to figure out what they meant.

I blinked, and the silver flare faded away. I shook my head. "Nothing important."

I stepped out of the *Velorum*'s shadow and headed over to the far side of the room, where the ceiling dropped down, and the white tile floor and walls gave way to a gray concrete bunker that housed the weapons lab. I stopped and peered into the space, where folks were tinkering with blasters, hand cannons, and other weapons, both offensive and defensive.

Everything was perfectly normal, but one by one, the workers disappeared until all I saw was an empty lab—and the woman I had killed in there.

A few months ago, Julieta Delano, an Imperium Arrow, had kidnapped me from Corios and brought me to the main Kent

Corp building as part of Rowena Kent's plot to frame me for the *Velorum* crash. Eventually, I had ended up here in the R&D lab, where I had hidden a copy of the original *Velorum* files in a tiny model of the ship.

I'd swiped the plastic model from my workstation and had been trying to escape when Julieta had forced me into the weapons lab. I'd gotten hold of a stormsword and used it to fight back against the Arrow, who had her own stormsword. Julieta had almost killed me—she *would* have killed me—if I hadn't used my seer magic to remember the weapons training and lessons that Kyrion Caldaren had drilled into me while I'd been staying at his castle.

". . . rumored to be dispatching Kyrion Caldaren to track down the Techwave . . ."

The low murmur of Kyrion's name snapped me out of my dark memories. I spun around, and my gaze landed on a worker who was staring at his terminal instead of fiddling with his latest project. Bodie often watched gossipcasts when he thought no one was paying attention. On the screen, a man wearing a dark helmet was holding a glowing sword and striding down a metal hallway on some spaceship.

It was old footage of Kyrion, something I had seen dozens of times before, but my heart still squeezed with longing. I hadn't contacted him since I had left Corios after the last Regal ball, but he was in my thoughts far more often than he should have been, even with our truebond lurking in the back of my mind like a shark about to break through the surface of the water and take another bloody bite out of me.

Or maybe it was my heart that was more affected by Kyrion. Maybe it always had been. Because I doubted any psionic connection, any galactic bond, no matter how strong, could account for all my feelings for the Arrow. Feelings that had not dimmed, despite the time and distance that had separated us these past few months.

". . . along with Zane Zimmer, another member of the Arrows . . ."

The image of Kyrion vanished, replaced by that of a blond man who was preening at the camera. Even on a terminal screen, Zane Zimmer still managed to be a pompous, arrogant jackass. Ugh.

I walked on and ended up in the very back of the appliances lab, which had been cordoned off into a large private office. I swiped my ID card through another reader and submitted to retinal, fingerprint, and DNA scans. The permaglass doors hissed open, and I stepped inside, with Tivona still following me.

The center of the office featured a long, rectangular work-station cluttered with projects in various stages of develop-ment—brewmakers and other food fabricators, self-propelled mops, even books made of real paper that dusted and sanitized themselves without losing their delicious musty-paper scent. A wooden desk stood in the back right corner, next to a couch that folded out to make a serviceable bed for nights when I was working late and didn't want to bother going home. More nights than not, lately.

Another area in the back housed a bathroom, while a small kitchen off to the left featured drinks and snacks for when I didn't want to bother leaving the lab to get lunch. More days than not, lately.

I hit a button on the wall. The doors closed behind Tivona, and an opaque sheen frosted the permaglass. We could still see out of my office, but no one in the R&D lab could peer inside at us now.

Tivona set her plate of food down on the one clean corner of my cluttered workstation. "How bad is it today?" she asked, jerking her chin at my hands.

I froze. I hadn't realized it, but I had been using my right thumb to massage my left palm, which was aching. It almost always ached these days, right along with my heart.

Tivona raised her eyebrows, but I ignored her questioning look, went over to my workstation, and stopped in front of a multidimensional printer. Then I pressed in on what looked like a button-size freckle on the inside of my left wrist. A soft *hiss* sounded, and I hooked my right index finger under a thin layer of polyplastic, which I peeled off my hand. I tossed the thin flesh-colored glove into the printer, which whirred to life, recycling the used plastic. A few seconds later, a chime sounded, and the printer spit out a new glove.

"Vesper," Tivona said. "How bad is it today?"

I sighed and held my hand out where she could see it. "Not too bad. No blood, just the cuts."

Tivona blanched, clearly not sharing my assessment of the gruesome injury.

Several deep cuts adorned my left palm. At first glance, they seemed like random, haphazard marks, but a closer look revealed that they formed a very distinctive shape: an eye.

Kyrion had carved the same marks—the same eye—into his own hand during the last Regal ball. Lord Callus Holloway, the ruler of the Imperium, had ordered Kyrion to cut his hand in hopes of proving that a truebond existed between the two of us. When such a bond was first forming, one person would often exhibit physical signs of the other person's injuries. So if Kyrion cut his hand and the same marks appeared on my hand, it would have definitively proved the bond between us. Ironically enough, that was how Kyrion had proved the bond's existence to me, by cutting his hand when we'd been trapped on a blitzer together.

During the truebond test, I had felt the hot, stinging pain of every line Kyrion had carved into his skin as though he was slicing my hand instead of his own. But thanks to my flesh-colored glove, one of my many inventions, my hand had appeared injury-free, and I had fooled Holloway and everyone else into thinking that Kyrion and I weren't bonded—including Kyrion himself.

At least, I thought I had fooled Kyrion too, but I had no way of knowing for sure. We hadn't been in contact since I'd left Corios, although Daichi Hirano, Kyrion's chief of staff, often messaged me, since we were friends.

I had no idea if Kyrion realized the truebond was intact, despite all our attempts to break it. Maybe he didn't realize we were still connected. Or worse, maybe he did, and he never wanted to see me again. Either way, it was yet another situation in which I had only bad options.

Tivona opened a cabinet along the wall, rummaged around inside, and then handed me a metal tin. "Put some ointment on the cuts. This is a new kind of skinbond, made by House Gonzalo. Supposed to be the best on the market."

Skinbonds did just what their name implied—they bonded skin together to heal cuts, scrapes, and other injuries. The House Gonzalo ointment had a strong, menthol scent that made my eyes water and my nose twitch, but I dutifully slathered it on my palm. A tingling sensation spread through my skin.

"Is it working?" Tivona asked in an eager voice.

Before I could respond, the pleasant tingle morphed into a hot burn, and the marks widened and reddened, as if they were angry that I'd tried to get rid of them and were fighting back against the skinbond's healing properties, just as Kyrion and I had fought back against having a truebond.

I grimaced, grabbed a nearby rag, and wiped off the ointment. The burning sensation faded away, although the eye-shaped marks remained wide, red, and angry. Sometimes the marks were as thin, white, and invisible as plastipaper cuts, as though they were on the verge of healing completely, but they always flared up again. On rare occasions, the marks would even split open and drip blood, as though Kyrion had cut his hand—and by extension, mine too—just a moment ago.

There didn't seem to be any rhyme or reason as to how, when, or why the cuts fluctuated, although I'd started keeping track of their whimsical severity and dull, aching pain. For science, of course. My theory was that the pain, intensity, and vividness of the marks correlated with whatever moods Kyrion and I were in, along with the physical and mental stresses we might be experiencing, but I had no way of proving my hypothesis. Not without asking Kyrion, which I was *not* going to do.

I tugged on the fresh skin-colored glove, molding the open ends so that the polyplastic stopped just short of my fingertips. Then I smoothed the whole thing out, front and back, until the glove seamlessly adhered to my skin, once again hiding the eye-shaped cuts. Tivona was the only one who knew that Kyrion and I were still bonded, and I wanted to keep it that way.

A truebond might make two people stronger and able to share thoughts, emotions, skills, and psionic abilities, but it also made them targets. Callus Holloway would love nothing more than to siphon off our magic for his own, just as he had done to Kyrion's parents for years, while the Techwave would experiment on us to try to unlock the secret of our psionic connection. The Erzton, a powerful group that controlled minerals, wood, and other raw resources, would probably treat us the same way. More bad options that made me shudder.

I handed the tin back to Tivona. "Best on the market, eh?"

She sniffed. "Clearly, House Gonzalo is engaged in false advertising. I should report them to the gossipcasts. Think of the headlines. *Ointment oozes fraudulent claims! House Gonzalo stuck in a sticky situation!*"

I laughed at her grandiose, gossipcaster voice, and Tivona chucked the tin of ointment onto a pile of similar products I had tried over the past several weeks. The sharp motion rattled another item resting in a clear plastic holder on my workstation: a stormsword.

Unlike the brewmakers and other appliances Quill Corp mass-produced, the stormsword was a single, unique object of dangerous beauty, an artifact crafted long ago by a spelltech, someone who could infuse psionic power into weapons and other objects. Anyone could pick up a stormsword and cut someone with the sharp blade, but supposedly, only a powerful psion—someone with mental abilities like telekinesis, telepathy, and telempathy—could wield a stormsword to its fullest, deadliest potential.

My sword had a silver hilt studded with three eye-shaped sapphsidian jewels, which were such a dark blue they almost looked black. Smaller pieces of sapphsidian adorned the cross-guard, which also featured two prongs of silver that curved out in opposite directions, although their end points perfectly aligned, as though they were two halves of a yin-yang symbol. More prongs of silver curved up to touch the opalescent blade, which was made of lunarium, a rare, precious mineral that amplified psionic abilities.

The stormsword had been sitting on a workstation in the weapons lab when Julieta Delano had chased me in there, and I'd grabbed the blade on a desperate impulse. Somehow I had managed to use the weapon, along with my seer magic, to kill Julieta, something that still amazed me.

I traced my index finger over the sigils carved into the sword's hilt. I hadn't noticed it while I'd been fighting Julieta, but symbols had appeared in the silver after I had touched the weapon—several arrows that clustered around the sapphsidian eyes, almost as if they were protecting the larger jewels.

Supposedly, the sigils that appeared on a stormsword's hilt were a reflection of that psion's power. The eyes were an obvious sign of my seer magic, but I thought the arrows had more to do with my bond with Kyrion, especially since they were shaped like spades from an old-fashioned tarot or playing card—the sigil for House Caldaren.

A few crescent moons and stars also adorned the hilt, along with another sigil on the bottom of the pommel—a large *N*. An unwanted reminder of Nerezza, my biological mother, who had abandoned me to chase after Regal riches and power. Disgust filled me, and my fingers twitched with the urge to grab a laser cutter and melt the mark out of existence. But I couldn't do that without damaging the sword, so the *N* would have to remain on the pommel, just like the hurt from Nerezza's actions would always linger in my heart.

"It's a good thing you left your sword in here like I suggested," Tivona said in a light, teasing tone, oblivious to my sudden sorrow. "Otherwise, the janitors would still be mopping up Millicent's blood in the conference room."

I huffed at her bad joke. "You're not entirely wrong about that."

Thanks to the biometric locks and other safety measures, my lab office was one of the most secure places in the main Quill Corp building, which was why I'd left the weapon in here instead of wearing it to the meeting. And so I wouldn't be tempted to use it on Millicent Tobani and everyone else who either doubted me or was secretly plotting against me or both.

I dropped my hand from the stormsword. "Are you sure Millicent isn't going to be a problem?"

"According to the gossip I've heard, Millicent is worried about getting laid off," Tivona replied. "Hence all her talk about using less expensive materials and keeping costs down. Everyone knows the quickest, easiest way for a corporation to save money is by firing senior staff and replacing them with younger, cheaper employees."

Given my position as the head of Quill Corp, people no longer spoke freely in front of me, but Tivona had a warm, innate charm that made everyone like her, and she often gathered information that I couldn't.

"Where did you hear this gossip?"

Tivona gave me a sly smile. "I went out clubbing with some of my negotiator friends this weekend. Millicent was there with some folks from the production plants. I bought a round of chembond cocktails for everyone and convinced Millicent to share all her worries with me."

I let out a low, appreciative whistle. "Downing a chembond with the enemy? That's going above and beyond. I should give you a raise."

There were all kinds of bonds, but chembonds were among the most common, and they were used mostly for sex. Go to a club, find a willing partner, down a chembond with them, and supposedly you would have the most amazing sex of your life.

"Don't worry. We danced, we drank, we had a good time. It wasn't too much work, and I didn't go home with her." Tivona winked at me. "Although I will still take that raise."

I laughed at her teasing tone. My friend loved to shake off the rigors of her high-stress negotiator job by going clubbing. Sometimes I went with her, although no amount of dancing could make me forget everything that had happened recently, and I never, ever downed a chembond with anyone. I'd had enough problems with bonds over the past few months that I would never willingly ingest a chembond now, even if it would burn out in a few hours.

Tivona's teasing smile vanished, replaced by a thoughtful look. She picked up a small blue plastic eye from a tray on my workstation. Two similar jewels adorned my thumbs, along with sparkling silver polish.

"You're still planning to plant these trackers on the Techwavers?" she asked. "And then follow them back to one of their secret bases?"

"Yes."

The eyes were another one of my recent inventions. They might look like manicure accessories, but the plastic jewels contained a variety of sophisticated electronics, including high-powered trackers that could access local wireless networks and broadcast location information across the galaxy.

Tivona chewed on her lower lip. "When do you think the Techwave will approach you?"

"I don't know, exactly. But soon. Maybe even later today."

She blinked. "*Today?* Are you sure?"

That was the problem with being a seer. I wasn't always *sure*, especially when it came to other people's schemes, schedules, and agendas. But over the past couple of weeks, I'd had vivid, recurring dreams—nightmares, really—of being surrounded by Black Scarabs, the Techwave troops known for their black armor and being more machine than man. More than once, I'd woken up in a cold sweat, certain my magic was trying to tell me something, and the most obvious interpretation was that the Techwave was targeting me.

"All I know for sure is that the Techwave is going to approach me sooner or later. Rowena, Sabine, and Conrad aren't around to help them anymore, and according to the information I found in the Kent Corp mainframe, the Techwavers need my expertise to finish the weapons they have in development, especially if they want to figure out some way to kill Callus Holloway."

In addition to being a cruel, clever, wily ruler, Holloway was also a siphon who could absorb energy from other people, machines, and even the weather, if the rumors were true. An energy bolt from a typical blaster or hand cannon would only add to Holloway's own psion power, rather than injuring him the way it would a regular person.

When she had kidnapped me, Julieta Delano had said that the Techwave was searching for a way to kill Holloway—and so was I. Because if Holloway ever discovered that Kyrion and I were bonded, the Imperium ruler would stop at nothing to get his hands on us. But right now, the Techwave was the bigger threat. Once I figured out a way to destroy them, then I would worry about Holloway—and the unwanted connection I still shared with Kyrion.

"I could increase security," Tivona offered. "Have some guards shadow you. Then, when the Techwavers move in, the guards can apprehend them."

I shook my head. "No. We can't risk it. The Techwave might have already bribed some Quill Corp guards to work for them. Even if we knew that all the guards were loyal to us, I still wouldn't want innocent people getting hurt. This is my fight, and I'm going to finish it."

Tivona kept chewing her lip, worry written all over her face.

"Instead of wasting weeks or months trying to find their current base, I'll let the Techwavers approach me, pretend to be open to whatever they suggest, and plant as many trackers on them as possible." I gestured at the eye jewels. "When they leave, the Techwavers will take my trackers along with them. I'll send the location information to Daichi so he can pass it along to Kyrion. With any luck, the Arrows and Imperium soldiers can raid the base and eliminate the Techwavers once and for all."

Tivona stabbed her finger at me. "But if things don't go the way you expect, you'll use an emergency beacon to alert me and the nearest guards?"

I drew an X over my heart with my finger. "Promise."

She nodded, and a more speculative look filled her face. "What are you going to do when Kyrion realizes that the Techwave has approached you? He'll contact you, especially if the truebond is still as strong as you think it is."

Eagerness, wariness, and other conflicting emotions churned in my chest like comets circling around and around, but I blew out a breath and forced myself to relax. Then I shoved all those pesky feelings into a box and buried it in the bottom of my brain, although I couldn't quite get rid of the fragile hope that clung to the corner of my heart like a sticky cobweb.

"Kyrion won't sense anything," I said, struggling to keep my voice light and even. "He thinks the bond was broken when we drank those chemicals in Touma Hirano's workshop, and he has no reason to believe we are still connected in any way, shape, or form."

A hard knot of regret clogged my throat, but I swallowed it down. "Besides, Kyrion *never* wanted the bond. Even if he realized that we are still connected, he wouldn't contact me. The best thing for him would be if I went somewhere far, far away where no one could find me, especially not Callus Holloway."

"Is that really what you want, Vesper?" Tivona asked in a soft voice. "To never see Kyrion again?"

My gaze strayed out through the glass into the lab. Bodie was still watching the gossipcast, and the image of Kyrion striding down that never-ending hallway was back on the screen.

"It doesn't matter what I want," I replied, my raspy voice betraying me. "Only what is. I told Kyrion, Holloway, and the rest of the Regals a good lie during the last ball. That's the story they believe, so that's the one I'm going to keep telling them."

Tivona stared at me. After a few seconds, she pulled her tablet out of her pocket and started scrolling through screens. "Well, if you are still determined to go through with this, let's review the plan again. I've got guards stationed at all the campus exits monitoring the security feeds. They have standing orders to rush to your side the second they see anything suspicious . . ."

Her words washed over me. I nodded along and listened with half an ear, but once again my gaze locked onto the gossipcast still playing on Bodie's terminal.

I had been wrong before. I might have lied to Kyrion about us not having a truebond, but it hadn't been a good lie.

No, the only good lies were the ones you believed yourself.

TWO

VESPER

Tivona and I went over the plan again, then she headed to her own office. After I had taken control of Kent Corp and rebranded it Quill Corp, I had installed Tivona as my chief operating officer to help me run the company. She handled most of the meetings and paperwork, while I toiled in the R&D lab and dreamed up ways to improve old Kent Corp products, as well as coming up with my own new designs.

I switched the permaglass back to clear, then stepped outside my office and took a seat at my old workstation in the lab. It was important for folks to see that I was working just as hard as they were to make Quill Corp a success. Most people still regarded me with a mixture of wariness and curiosity, but a few folks, including Bodie, came over to show me their projects and ask for my advice. Small progress, but I would take it.

Lunchtime rolled around, and I grabbed my stormsword from my office, then left the lab, got into an elevator, and returned to the hundredth floor. Instead of going into the conference room, I went to the far corner of the building. My corporate office lay on one side of the corridor, while Tivona's office was on the other side.

Flirty laughter drifted out of her open door, and I knocked on the wood and stepped inside. Tivona was perched on the corner of her desk talking to a thirty-something woman who was standing a few feet away, her hands clasped behind her back.

The petite woman was quite striking, with hazel eyes and glossy black hair that was cut into a sleek, severe bob that just brushed her chin. Pale, rose-pink gloss stained her lips, while shimmering powder accentuated her light brown skin. Like Tivona, the woman was wearing a crisp, tailored pantsuit, although hers was a deep, vibrant pink trimmed with gold buttons shaped like roses, and a lunarium sword with a gold hilt was dangling from her thin gold belt.

"I see you've stolen my lunch date yet again," I teased.

Tivona grinned. "That's because she is such a lovely date to steal."

Leandra Ferrum glanced at a clock on the wall. "You're three minutes late," she replied in a light, musical voice with just a hint of the crisp Corios accent. "That's three more times I could have already killed you."

Unlike many of the other Regal Houses, which mass-produced appliances, blasters, and spaceships, House Ferrum was known for its small, handcrafted batches of lunarium-studded staffs, crossbows, and other old-fashioned weapons. House Ferrum would also lend out its members to teach you how to use their weapons—for the right price.

Leandra was among their strongest psions and most skilled warriors, and so far, she had been worth every credit it had cost to bring her to Temperate 42. Learning how to better use my stormsword was one of my top priorities, which was why I spent every lunch hour training with Leandra. Or rather, why

I spent every lunch hour getting my ass repeatedly, ruthlessly kicked by her.

"Nice to see you again too, Leandra," I drawled. "Have you and Tivona been having a pleasant chat?"

I might be paying her for the privilege of beating me to a pulp, but I was never one to back down from a challenge. Leandra arched an eyebrow at my sarcasm, then sauntered through an open door into the next room.

"You're going to pay for that," Tivona whispered, still grinning.

I followed Leandra into the gym that connected Tivona's office to mine across the hall. Rubber mats covered the middle of the floor, while racks of hand weights lined the walls. Treadmills, elliptical bikes, and rowing machines squatted in the corners, all equipped with headsets that would let you run, bike, or row your way through virtual landscapes.

Like everything else at Kent Corp, this gym used to belong to Rowena and Sabine Kent, although the two of them had rarely used it, preferring to bolster their fitness with chemical, surgical, and other enhancements.

Leandra had already taken off her pink heels and removed her suit jacket, revealing the tight gold tank top she wore underneath, along with her toned arms and sculpted shoulders.

My muscles were already grumbling that this was not a good idea, but I removed my work boots and socks and shrugged out of my lab coat. Then I stepped onto the mat and pulled my stormsword out of the slot on my black leather belt. The hilt was cool, smooth, and solid against my palm, and the lunarium blade glimmered a faint pale blue in a reflection of my seer magic.

Technically speaking, I was a psion, a catchall term for seers, spelltechs, siphons, and others with extraordinary mental powers. But no one had ever been able to figure out exactly where those abilities came from—or to scientifically replicate them on a consistent basis—which was why so many folks, myself included, referred to those abilities as magic.

Leandra drew her own stormsword, which featured a gold hilt adorned with sapphsidian vines and thorns that curled around a large piece of rose quartz that was shaped like an actual rose. The lunarium blade glimmered the same soft pink as the quartz.

Tivona strolled into the gym and plopped down onto a couch that ran along one wall. She deposited several containers of fresh fruits, cheeses, crackers, and pastries onto a small table, along with an oversize mug, then dragged the whole thing over in front of her.

"You brought snacks?" I groused.

Tivona toasted me with her mug, and the rich, dark scent of chocolate espresso wafted through the air. "Of course. There was plenty of leftover food from this morning's meeting. Besides, I need a lunch break too, and watching Leandra kick your ass is always highly entertaining. Then again, watching Leandra do anything is *always* highly entertaining."

A hint of pink streaked across Leandra's cheekbones, and her stormsword glowed a little bit more brightly. My seer magic stirred to life, and a silver light flared around each woman, growing larger and stronger the longer they looked at each other.

Tivona loved to flirt, but my friend had been yearning for a more meaningful relationship for a while. Despite her reserved nature, Leandra seemed just as interested. Her hazel eyes sparkled, her lips twitched, and she slowly grinned back at Tivona. I hid my own grin. No one could resist Tivona's warmth and charm for long.

Leandra turned toward me, lifted her sword, and settled into a fighting stance. All the good humor was snuffed out of her face, replaced by cool, professional detachment, as though I was a lump of metal that she was determined to hammer into a weapon no matter how many blows it took.

I resisted the urge to groan, even as I raised my own sword. I didn't need my seer magic to know that today's sparring session was going to be even more painful than usual.

Forty-six minutes later, I was flat on my back on the mat, desperately trying not to whimper. Sweat poured down my face, and I gasped for breath, despite the fact that I had an oxygen optimization—or O2—enhancement. A special liquid had been injected into my lungs that greatly increased their capacity and functionality. Basically, I didn't need as much oxygen to breathe as other people, but my lab-rat enhancement was no match for Leandra's warrior stamina, and she had pummeled all the air right out of me.

Exhaustion crashed over me in waves, and every single part of my body was bruised and battered. Hands, arms, legs, feet. Even my blasted hair hurt, mostly from my ponytail poking into the back of my head from where I was sprawled on the mat.

Leandra towered over me, twirling her sword around and around in her hand at a dizzying pace. In addition to her psion power, she had a speed enhancement, and the rapid, blurring motion of the shimmering pink blade made me slightly nauseated. I had landed several solid hits during our last bout, but Leandra had shrugged them off as though they were as light as butterflies brushing up against her blade. She was neither sweating nor gasping, and she looked as serene as a freshly cut rose.

"Again!" Leandra barked out. "Your hour is not up, and you're not paying me to stand around and look at you."

I stifled a groan and staggered to my feet, my stormsword still clutched in my hand. I was so tired that the psionic blue sheen on the blade was barely more than a flicker, like an old-fashioned light bulb desperately sputtering to stay aglow.

"You managed to last almost two minutes that time," Tivona piped up from the couch. "That's progress, right?"

My friend had finished her lunch and was now nibbling on some leftover pastries. My stomach rumbled. I should have eaten the food from the conference room earlier instead of dumping most of it in the recycler. The blackberry tart I'd had for breakfast was long gone, and the bite-size strawberry shortcake in Tivona's hand looked delicious.

She noticed my hungry gaze, winked, and popped the treat into her mouth.

"You're a terrible friend," I grumbled.

Tivona licked a dollop of whipped cream off her fingers. "I am an *excellent* friend. I'm eating all this flour, sugar, and butter so you don't sully your own body with it."

I shot her a sour look and started to snark back when a blur of pink caught my eye. On instinct, I spun around and lifted my sword.

Clang!

My sword met Leandra's, stopping the other blade three inches from my face.

"Be aware of your opponent at all times," she intoned in a cool voice. "Even when you think you've defeated them."

"A sneak attack?" I groused. "Really?"

She lowered her sword and stepped back. "You're paying me to train you, not coddle you. People who are coddled wind up dead, Lady Vesper."

A faint sneer crept into Leandra's voice as she said my title, and despite the fact that she was a couple of inches shorter, she still somehow managed to peer down her nose at me. I'd heard that same sneer and seen that same condescension on the faces of other Regals. Callus Holloway might have dubbed me Lady Vesper Quill, but none of the other Regals truly respected me.

Anger pulsed through me. I had *earned* that blasted title, sweat and bled and almost died for it. I was a Regal now, whether the others liked it or not, and no one was going to disrespect me without suffering the consequences. More anger pulsed through me, even stronger than before, and I surged forward and lashed out with my own sword.

Clang!

Leandra snapped up her weapon, easily blocking my blow. "Now who's resorting to sneak attacks?"

Her mocking tone further angered me, and I swung my sword back and forth in a series of quick moves, driving her across the mat. I wasn't quite sure where this anger was coming from. Leandra Ferrum wasn't the first Regal to dismiss me. She wasn't even the first person today to challenge me, to think that I had lucked into running Quill Corp and was unworthy of everything I had worked so hard for. But more and more anger kept boiling up in my veins, and I kept attacking her.

Leandra's eyes narrowed, and her stormsword glowed an even brighter pink, humming with power. Sharp crackles of wind erupted out of her blade and zipped over me, scraping across my skin like thorns and tearing my hair out of its ponytail, but the stinging sensations were nothing compared with the anger still pulsing through my body.

Leandra darted in, but I spun away and shoved her in the back. She tried to recover her balance, but I was already coming up behind her. Leandra lifted her sword and whirled back around toward me. Too slow. I snapped my own sword forward.

Leandra froze. She stared down at the glowing blue blade that was three inches away from her throat, then up at me. "Better. Much better."

A bit of grudging respect filled her eyes. Somehow that made me feel even worse, and my anger evaporated as quickly as it had boiled up.

I hissed out a tense breath, lowered my sword, and stepped back. "Sorry. I lost control."

Leandra lowered her own sword. "Never apologize for being a good enemy."

I frowned. "A good enemy?"

She nodded. "Yes, a good enemy. Someone who pushes you to dig deeper, work harder, be stronger, fight smarter. The only good enemies are the ones who have a chance of defeating you, which makes your victory over them even more satisfying." Her face grew thoughtful again. "Although I do find it interesting."

"What?"

Her gaze sharpened. "How you can flip some sort of switch deep inside you and suddenly become so much *better.* Faster, stronger, more fluid and precise with your strikes. Like you've been fighting with that stormsword for years instead of just a few months."

My heart stuttered. Leandra might not realize it, but she was talking about my truebond with Kyrion. Certain high-level, military-grade chembonds let soldiers, scientists, and academics share strength, skills, and thoughts, but what she was describing went much, much deeper than that. Once again, without meaning to, I had somehow tapped into my connection to Kyrion and used his fighting prowess to help me defeat Leandra, just as I had when I'd been battling Julieta Delano in the weapons labs a few months ago.

I carefully examined the place in my mind where the bond was. The sticky little cobweb of Kyrion was frozen and still, and no warmth or alertness rippled through the connection. I breathed a quiet sigh of relief that I hadn't disturbed the bond, hadn't disturbed *him*, with my unconscious floundering.

Just like the eye-shaped cuts on my left palm, Kyrion's presence in my mind fluctuated with no apparent rhyme or reason. Most of the time, all I felt was that cold cobweb, as though a tiny shard of ice was buried deep in my mind.

Sometimes the ice vanished altogether, and I couldn't sense Kyrion at all. I often wondered if physical distance was a factor, if his presence dimmed the farther away he was, but it was yet another unanswered question I had about truebonds. Temperate 42 and Corios were fairly close to each other, but the fact that I could sense Kyrion even though we were on different planets was a painful reminder of how deep and strong our connection seemed to be—and how very one-sided it was on my part.

Regardless of however distances and emotions might affect things, I needed to stop reaching for the truebond like a child jabbing their finger into what they knew was a particularly painful bruise and making it hurt even worse.

Leandra kept studying me with laserlike focus, so I shrugged off her words. "Maybe it's simply your excellent training, finally sinking into my mind."

"Mmm." Her noncommittal reply was full of both disbelief and judgment.

A sharp chime rang out from the clock on the wall. My hour of misery was officially over. I bowed to Leandra, who returned the gesture. Then I plucked a towel off a rack, shoved my wayward hair aside, and wiped the sweat off my face. Leandra daintily patted her own face, although not so much as a sheen of sweat glistened on her skin, and her black bob of hair was still perfectly in place. I envied her stamina and especially her poise.

I dropped my towel onto the rack, then picked up my tablet and hit a couple of buttons. A few seconds later, a soft beep erupted from Leandra's tablet. "The funds for today's lesson have been transferred to your account."

Leandra pulled the tablet out of her jacket pocket and checked the screen. "Thank you."

"I could pay you in advance for the rest of the month," I offered, not for the first time.

She shook her head. "Thank you, but I prefer to be paid for the work I complete. Not for things that might never come to pass. It's something of a House Ferrum policy and motto."

"Things that might never come to pass? What does that mean?"

She shrugged. "Not to look beyond the battle in front of you. Because you never know what unexpected thing might crop up and ruin your best-laid schemes."

Leandra grabbed a bottle of electrolyte water and drank deeply from it. Then she wandered over to Tivona, who smiled and handed her a strawberry shortcake. Leandra gobbled it down, along with some more water, and the two of them started talking in soft voices.

A fresh wave of sweat popped out on my skin, but this sensation was cold and prickly, and my seer magic stirred to life, jabbing into my body like hundreds of tiny, invisible needles. Leandra's words had been innocent enough, but a chill swept down my spine all the same.

Whether she realized it or not, I had a sinking feeling she had just jinxed all my careful plans to find and destroy the Techwave.

THREE

VESPER

Tivona and Leandra flirted for a few more minutes. Leandra agreed to return tomorrow for another training session, and then she left to visit with some cousins who were currently staying on-planet.

Still smiling, Tivona returned to her office, while I headed into the bathroom attached to the gym. I took a shower to stave off as much muscle soreness as possible, then donned a fresh long-sleeved blue shirt, along with matching cargo pants. It was a small thing, compared with the excessive privileges many Regals had, but being able to shower at work was one of my favorite perks about running Quill Corp, especially since I'd tweaked the nozzle settings to make the water pressure as hot and hard as possible.

Thirty minutes later, I was back in the R&D lab. I ate some snacks from my office for a quick, unhealthy lunch, then spent the rest of the afternoon tinkering with my latest brewmaker design and dealing with crises large and small. Everything from the amount of solar wiring Quill Corp needed to procure this month to use in our appliances to the number of food carts allowed on campus to what kind of organic artisanal tea was stocked in the breakrooms. Finally, around nine o'clock galactic time, long after everyone else, including Tivona, had gone home, I turned off my terminal, locked my office, and left the lab.

I rode an elevator up to the lobby, which was deserted except for a few security guards. Judging from the music drifting out of their tablets, the guards were watching a gossipcast, although they switched off the sound and snapped to attention at my approach. I nodded to them, pushed through a perma-glass door, and headed outside.

The main Quill Corp building was nestled in the heart of a sprawling campus in the center of Stahl City, one of the most populous cities on Temperate 42. Many Regals situated their corporate headquarters on Temperate planets because they were, well, *temperate*, with four mild seasons of winter, spring, summer, and fall. No Regal wanted to close their production plants because of weeks-long blizzards, floods, or other prolonged hostile weather events, which often occurred on more extreme planets.

Lawns covered with real green grass rolled out in all directions, along with red-clay tile paths that snaked by rust-colored polyplastic fountains. Matching benches lined many of the paths, along with tall solar lights that gleamed brightly against the growing summer twilight. High above, the twin suns were setting, streaking the sky in dull, dim swaths of orange and pink, given the haze of smog and exhaust that always cloaked the city.

Reducing waste and pollution at Quill Corp was another one of my top priorities, although I hadn't made much progress with it yet, just like I hadn't made much progress with many of my other projects. Running a Regal corporation was akin to maintaining a fussy, complicated machine that constantly threatened to break down, and it had been much harder and far more time-consuming than I'd expected. Not because I couldn't, wouldn't, or wasn't smart enough to do the work but because I grew tired of dealing with the overbearing personalities and convoluted politics between departments. I had no idea how Rowena Kent had juggled it all, much less found the time, energy, and ambition to engineer a massive criminal conspiracy on the side.

As I stepped onto one of the paths, a woman wearing brown maintenance coveralls swept up around a food cart, even though the area was already clean and the cart was locked and closed. My seer magic flared to life, gilding her in a telltale silver light. And she wasn't the only one.

A man drinking from a water fountain. A woman peering at her tablet while she waited for the campus transport to circle back around. A landscaper snipping his shears at a hedge that had already been trimmed. Even a woman ambling through the grass and taking a cute corgi puppy for an evening stroll.

The farther I walked, the more people I spotted, and the more my magic surged up. But even without my magic, I still would have known they didn't belong here. Oh, they were dressed like Quill Corp employees and had all the tools and props to match their personas, but their eyes were watchful, and their bodies were tense.

These people weren't workers. They were spies.

I'd first spotted the spies about a month ago when I'd ventured outside for a quick dinner. The woman sweeping up around the food cart tonight had been doing the same thing to another closed cart. The glaring lack of trash had caught my attention, and it hadn't taken me long to figure out that she was watching me, although I had no idea if she was working for the Techwave, Callus Holloway, or someone else.

So far, the spies had been content with tracking my movements from Quill Corp to the apartment I shared with Tivona and back again, but maybe that would change tonight.

I reached out with my right hand and fingered the blue plastic eyes that circled my left cuff like jeweled buttons instead of the spy tools they really were. Similar eyes also circled my other cuff, along with moons and stars. I'd coated the eyes with a magnetic glue, another one of my recent inventions. A rip and a flick of my fingers would remove the jewels from my clothes and send them spinning through the air. Then the magnetic glue would seek out whatever metal was nearby—like a zipper on a jacket—and attach the eyes to someone else's clothes.

That was my plan, but I had other options to fall back on, namely, the stormsword belted to my waist.

The Techwave's most logical course of action was to approach me with a business proposition the same way they had Rowena Kent—offer me an insane amount of credits to help them, solidify my wealth, and further bolster my status as a newly appointed Regal. But I could always be wrong, and the Techwave could have something more sinister in mind. Either way, I had a weapon to defend myself, and thanks to Leandra's training, I was much deadlier with the blade than I had been a few weeks ago.

I reached a branch in the path and headed to the right toward the main transport station at the edge of campus. My watchers held their positions as I walked past them. The path curved around a large fountain shaped like a crescent moon that was shooting water down over a cluster of bubbling stars. In the distance, the bright lights of the transport station appeared. Disappointment flooded me, along with more than a little frustration. Nothing was going to happen tonight after all—

A man stepped out from behind the fountain. Surprised, I stopped short. Even though I'd been searching for enemies, I hadn't seen or heard him approach.

The man was around my age, late thirties, and roughly six feet tall with a muscled body that was poured into a tight suit.

At first glance, his jacket, tie, shirt, and pants all seemed to be a simple, boring black, but he shifted on his feet, and a nearby solar light revealed the shiny dark green iridescence in the sleek fabric. The same iridescence glimmered in the coating on his chunky black polyplastic boots.

His eyes were as black as his suit, while his dirty-blond hair was slicked up into short spikes, and his skin was unnaturally pale, as though he spent most of his time indoors.

"Hello, Vesper," the man drawled. "So nice to finally meet you in person. Although I've been following your exploits on the gossipcasts for several weeks."

His voice was low, with a faint accent that indicated he had spent some time on Corios or one of the other posh planets where the Regals played, partied, and schemed. Thanks to my seer magic, I never forgot a face, but I didn't recognize him. Whoever the man was, he didn't show up on *Celestial Stars* or any of the other Regal gossipcasts that Tivona loved to watch.

"My name is Harkin," he continued. "I'm here to collect you."

I tensed. "For what?"

"Oh, I wouldn't want to spoil the surprise." He grinned, showing off a mouthful of perfect, blindingly white teeth.

Harkin raised his hand and made a circular gesture with his index finger. Despite the summer heat, he was wearing thick, shiny black gloves.

Footsteps slapped on the path behind me, and I glanced over my shoulder. The woman sweeping around the food cart, the man drinking from the fountain, the woman reading on her tablet, the landscaper pruning with his shears. All my usual watchers were gathered around, and the only one who was missing was the woman with the puppy. She must have been someone else's spy.

These people weren't here to bribe me. They wanted to kidnap me.

I clasped my hands behind me and surreptitiously used my

right fingers to press in on a small star-shaped jewel on my left cuff. The star grew warm and vibrated against my skin, and the emergency beacon hidden inside would alert Tivona and the Quill Corp guards that I was in trouble and tell them to converge on my location. I might have wanted to face my enemies alone, but this situation was rapidly spinning out of control, and I needed reinforcements.

"Why go to all this trouble?" I asked, my mind whirring as I thought of and discarded possible plans of attack and escape. "You could just schedule a meeting. In case you haven't heard, Quill Corp is open to new business."

Harkin chuckled. "Unfortunately, I don't have the time or patience to wait for a meeting."

So he was on a schedule. Interesting. "Well, since you refuse to go through proper channels, I must politely decline."

I stepped to the side to skirt around him, but Harkin matched my movement, once again blocking my path.

"And I must insist." He grinned at me again, still playing the part of the proper gentleman, instead of the hired thug he truly was.

I lifted my chin, mimicking the haughty expressions of the Regals on the gossipcasts. "I am a Regal lady. No one dictates terms to me, especially not some random stranger."

Harkin's amiable grin cracked, then dropped off his face. "You shouldn't be so bloody arrogant. Everyone knows you're a Regal in name only, *Lady Vesper*."

I bristled at his derisive tone, but I tilted my head, acknowledging his point. "Maybe. But I *am* still a Regal, so get out of my way."

His eyes gleamed with anticipation. "I was hoping you would put up a fight."

Harkin snapped his fingers. The watchers behind me rushed forward. I yanked my stormsword off my belt and whirled around to face them.

The fake sweeper jabbed a shock baton at my chest, but I spun to the side and sliced my sword through the end of the weapon, making white-hot electricity shoot through the air. The woman yelped in surprise and dropped the rest of the useless baton, then pulled a blaster out of her coveralls pocket. Before she could aim it, I darted forward and shoved my sword into her chest. She screamed, but I yanked the blade free and shoved her aside. She stumbled forward and flopped to the ground at Harkin's feet.

The other woman and the two men were also equipped with shock batons, and I swung my sword back and forth, battling first one enemy, then another, then another. Leandra's training, combined with Kyrion's lessons, made a real difference, and despite being outnumbered, I killed them just as I had the first woman. A minute later, the watchers were dead on the ground, and I was facing Harkin again.

"Impressive," he drawled. "You're stronger and more skilled than we thought. Pity it won't make a difference."

I growled and charged forward, determined to skewer him like I had his underlings. Or at least wound him badly enough to make him scurry away with one of my trackers attached to his clothes.

Harkin clenched his right hand into a fist. Bright white veins of energy appeared in his polyplastic black glove, streaking all the way up his fingertips. He punched his fist forward, and an invisible blast of power rolled off him and slammed into my body, sending me flying. I hit the ground hard, pain spiking through my ass, back, and legs, but I scrambled to my feet and brandished my sword at him again.

"Your gloves," I snarled. "They emit some sort of kinetic energy. How?"

Harkin flexed his fingers, making the white veins ripple in ominous waves. "Oh, you're not the only one who likes to invent things, Vesper. Psion power is easy enough to mimic, if you know how."

He punched his fist forward again. More kinetic energy rolled off him and hammered into my hand, trying to knock my stormsword away, but I tightened my fingers and held on to the weapon.

Harkin's eyes narrowed, and he punched even more power at me. This time, I braced my feet, letting the windy sensation flow over me rather than knocking me sideways. The instant his power blew past me, I hurried forward.

For the first time, a bit of concern flitted across Harkin's face. He backed up and snapped his fingers in rapid succession. Heavy footsteps sounded, and someone rushed up on my left side. I spun in that direction.

Unlike the other watchers in their Quill Corp uniforms, this person was encased in a suit of plated black armor, making them practically invisible in the growing shadows. I stared up at the smooth helmet, and two eyes snapped open, glowing a bright, electric green, like the compound orbs on some massive insect.

Not a person—a Black Scarab.

My seer magic surged up, and memories exploded like stun grenades in my mind. The smoke and ash swirling through the air on the Magma 7 battlefield. The loud *clank-clank-clank-clank* of the Black Scarabs marching forward. The shrieks and screams as the mechanized troops ripped arms and legs off Imperium soldiers and then tossed the appendages aside like pieces of bloody trash.

I sucked in a breath and staggered back, shoving the memories away. Before I even had time to lift my sword, the Black Scarab surged forward and jabbed a silver injector into my left shoulder.

A needle punched deep into my skin, making me yelp in pain and surprise. I jerked away, then spun around, swung my sword, and lopped off the Scarab's head.

Hot green sparks showered over me like raindrops, and

the Scarab crumpled to the ground. The helmeted head rolled away, but there was no blood, no bones, no body, because no one was inside the armor. It was an empty suit, a hollow metal shell, being controlled by someone in a different location.

I stared down at the helmet, looking directly into the green eyes, which were still glowing, despite being removed from the rest of the armor. Someone was on the other side of those eyes, watching me. I shuddered and turned away from that bright, unblinking gaze.

More Black Scarabs scurried out of the shadows like oversize cockroaches. One of them darted forward and chopped my stormsword out of my hand. I lunged for the weapon, but it skittered out of reach. My shoulder throbbed from the injector, and a cold rush of chemicals flooded my body.

"There's no use fighting it, Vesper," Harkin called out. "You belong to us now."

I opened my mouth to respond, but my tongue was numb and heavy, along with the rest of my body. My legs crumpled, my head hit the ground, and the world winked to black.

FOUR

VESPER

My body might be cold, numb, and unconscious, but my seer magic was not. I blinked, and from one heartbeat to the next, I was standing in a dark stone hallway in an old-fashioned castle.

A relieved breath hissed out between my teeth. At least whatever chemical the Black Scarab had injected me with hadn't disrupted my power. A small favor, but I was going to need every single one I could get to survive.

Since I had no idea when—or where—my body might wake up, I strolled along the hallway. A few months ago, the castle had been shrouded in dust and cloaked in cobwebs, from the thick rugs underfoot to the silver-framed mirrors on the walls to the stained-glass chandeliers that dangled from the high, vaulted ceilings. But the dirt and grime had slowly vanished over the past several weeks, as though someone was taking care of the fine furnishings again. I trailed my fingers over the wooden case of a grandfather clock, listening to it chime the hour. I'd fixed the clock myself when I had been in this castle in the real world a few months ago.

Eventually, I stepped into a library with floor-to-ceiling shelves filled with real, paper books instead of the more common plastipaper versions. I squinted, but I couldn't make out the glimmering foil titles on the book spines. No matter how hard I tried, I had never been able to do that, even though I had been visiting this library since I was a child.

But I could see one thing clearly: the large portrait hanging over the fireplace.

The portrait featured a handsome man with black hair and eyes and tan skin, along with a beautiful woman with blond hair, blue eyes, and pale skin. In between them was a boy with black hair over dark blue eyes and pale skin. Lord Chauncey and Lady Desdemona Caldaren and their son, Kyrion.

My gaze snagged on Desdemona's face. For some reason, I felt like I had seen the lady somewhere before, somewhere *other* than on the gossipcasts. Even though Desdemona and Chauncey had been dead for roughly twenty-five years, the gossipcasts still frequently mentioned the couple and their storied truebond.

Desdemona's gaze bored into mine like a cold laser. I shivered and moved away from the portrait and over to an open space along the wall beside the fireplace. At my approach, a door appeared in the stone, beckoning me to venture even deeper into this dream world.

I went down a tight, spiral staircase with sigils carved into the dark stone banister. Just like the book titles in the library, I had never been able to decipher the symbols, although some of them pulsed with light and heat and shimmered with cold and frost at my touch. Many of the sigils also murmured, although I couldn't make out whatever words of wisdom or warnings they might be whispering.

I reached the bottom of the staircase and stepped into a large round room—my mindscape, the space in my mind, heart, and body where my seer magic resided.

Black vines snaked along the floor, along with pale blue flowers that perfumed the air with a sharp, slightly sweet scent, like the sticks of spearmint candy I had loved as a child. The vines and flowers climbed all the way up to the ceiling before dropping back down to curl around the many doors that were set into the wall.

And then there were the eyes.

Dozens and dozens of eyes stared at me from their spots on the doors, the wall, and even the low ceiling. At first glance, the eyes seemed to be a dull, flat black, but a closer look revealed that they were a deep, dark blue with specks of black sparkling and swirling like comets trapped inside them. The glittering, faceted eyes were eerily similar to the sapphsidian jewels embedded in the hilt of my stormsword, although I didn't know what, if any, connection they had to the weapon. When I was young, the unblinking eyes had creeped me out, but now they comforted me, as though they were some higher power watching out for me, although that was just a wishful fairy tale on my part.

Many of the doors were open, and images flickered on the other side of the archways, as though I was watching different movies on a plethora of holoscreens. In a way, I *was* watching movies—all the little snippets of my life, good, bad, and decidedly ugly.

Useless child . . . My mother's angry voice floated out of one of the doors.

I stopped in front of a child-size archway and watched a twenty-something Nerezza argue with our cousin Liesl. This was the day the Imperium academy instructors had told my mother that my seer magic was too weak to bother training me to use it properly. The memory played out just as it had happened in real life, with my mother storming away and seven-year-old me clutching a plastipaper book to my chest and silently crying on the stairs above. That night, Nerezza had abandoned me and returned to Corios to seek the posh Regal life she had always wanted.

Even now, thirty years later, seeing exactly how little my mother thought of me made nails of pain hammer through my chest. Nerezza had never viewed me as a child, as someone to love, but merely as a tool she might employ in her climb up the Regal ladder. No matter how many times I came in here, I could never ignore this door, no matter how much sharp heartache it reignited.

The scene started again, caught in the endless loop of my mind and my magic, but this time, I focused on Liesl, who could have been my mother's twin with her dark brown hair, blue eyes, and pale skin. After Nerezza had left, Liesl had placed me at a different Imperium academy so I would receive an education, and she had even visited me from time to time.

We had lost touch over the years, and I'd been shocked to find her name on the passenger manifest for the *Velorum* cruiser. Liesl's death had been one of the reasons I had been so determined to expose the crash conspiracy. I had wanted to get some sort of justice for my cousin, along with everyone else who had died.

Over the past few months, I had discreetly looked into Liesl, but I hadn't been able to find any information about her, much less why she had been on the *Velorum*, which had been bound for Corios. Did she have business on the planet? Was she working for one of the Regals? It would probably be yet another frustrating mystery among all the other unanswered questions in my life, most of which revolved around my mother's cruelty.

In the doorway, Nerezza stormed away. Liesl looked up and grimaced when she realized that I had heard my mother's harsh words. Liesl opened her mouth and raised her hand, as if to try to soothe me, but I scrambled to my feet, darted into my room, and slammed the door. Liesl scrubbed her hands over her face, and her shoulders drooped with weariness.

Surprise flickered through me. I had never seen Liesl's reaction before, as I had already been in my room. So why was I viewing it now? Was my seer magic expanding in some way?

The memory rewound and started playing yet again. This time, I moved away from it, although my mother's words—*useless child*—echoed out of the archway and chased me across the room.

I stopped in front of another door, which was closed. Instead of an eye, a sapphsidian arrow streaked upward through the stone—the sigil for House Caldaren. Kyrion's door, as I had come to think of it, although I wasn't sure if it led to his mind, his magic, our truebond, or something else entirely.

I was tempted to find out, though.

My hand itched with the urge to twist the knob and fling the door open, but I curled my fingers into a tight fist.

No. Kyrion hadn't wanted the bond—hadn't wanted *me*—and I would *not* worm my way into his mind or magic, not even subconsciously, or however the blasted bond worked.

I spun away from his door and stalked over to the one in the very back of the room. Intricate carvings of crescent moons and stars adorned this door, along with an upside-down sapphsidian eye embedded deep in the stone. I waved my hand. The jeweled eye turned right side up, a soft *click* sounded, and the door opened. Unlike the other archways, only soft curls of black smoke drifted out of this opening, and nothing but night lay beyond.

A few months ago, after the last Regal ball, I had finally found the courage to walk through this door and embrace the darkness within myself. The cold, hard, ruthless part of my mind, heart, and magic that had let me survive all the awful things that had happened. The cruel, calculating, villainous piece of myself that I hoped would give me the strength, tenacity, and wits to exact revenge on my enemies and keep myself—and Kyrion—safe from their deadly schemes.

I strode through the opening, and darkness flowed over me like a cool, misty fog. My boots scraped against solid stone, but the blackness swallowed me whole, and I couldn't see anything, not even my hand in front of my face. Still, my magic whispered that *something* was lurking in this blackness, something I needed to discover, something I desperately needed to find to endure all the horrible things that were coming my way—

A needle jabbed into my shoulder, and a hot rush of chemicals flooded my veins. I sucked in a breath, and the darkness vanished. My eyes snapped open, and a bright light stabbed into them, making me wince. I shut my eyes and jerked upright, even though the motion made my brain slosh around in my skull, as though I were on a spaceship rocketing through the atmosphere.

After a few seconds, my mind settled back down into place, and I slowly opened my eyes. Early morning sunlight warmed my face, indicating that I'd been unconscious for several hours.

I was sprawled across a fancy green velvet settee in front of permaglass windows that overlooked a barren landscape of shiny black rocks and a hazy sky filled with smoke, soot, and swirling ash. Despite the building's ventilation and filtration systems, a whiff of sulfuric smoke lingered in the cool, recycled air, bringing a cavalcade of memories along with it.

Dying conscripts. Screaming Imperium soldiers. Advancing Black Scarabs. All of them being swallowed up by plumes of red-hot lava that kept spewing up out of the jagged cracks and fissures under their feet.

I shuddered. I was on another blasted Magma planet. Who thought it was a good idea to build anything on what was essentially a giant volcano that could erupt at any moment?

"Hello, Vesper," a familiar voice purred.

I froze. My breath caught in my throat, my chest tightened, and cold sweat slicked my palms. Just like the memory in my mindscape, the voice triggered spikes of pain, misery, and anguish.

My heart pounded, the sound roaring in my ears like a shrill alarm warning of extreme danger. I slowly turned my head to the left, looking away from the windows, knowing and dreading what—*who*—I would see.

Harkin was standing in the corner of this large office. A silver blaster dangled from his gloved hand, and he had one shoulder propped up against the wall in a casual, relaxed pose. My stormsword was hanging off his belt.

But he wasn't the one who had spoken. No, that low, sultry voice belonged to the woman lounging on another green velvet settee a few feet away from me.

The woman was simply stunning, with long dark brown hair and pale, flawless skin that made her look much younger than her fifty-some years. Her subtle makeup highlighted her dark blue eyes, along with her high cheekbones, while glossy bloodred lipstick accentuated her heart-shaped mouth.

Her fashionable dark blue pantsuit outlined her toned body to perfection. The jacket's deep V showed off her cleavage, along with a wide diamond choker that ringed her neck. A large solitaire diamond glowed on her left index finger like a miniature moon, while much smaller diamond chips glittered on her dark blue painted nails.

My kidnapper was Lady Nerezza Blackwell, infamous Regal climber, the current head of House Blackwell, and my biological mother.

FIVE

KYRION

A fist slammed into my left shoulder, bringing a spike of pain along with it. A vicious curse spewed out of my lips, and I staggered back. For some reason, that blow had hurt far worse than it should have.

I wiggled my arm, trying to shake the sting out of it. The sharp, immediate pain faded away, leaving behind a dull, hollow ache. I cracked my neck from side to side, then circled around, my bare feet sinking into the rubber mat as I stalked around my enemy.

Zane Zimmer was roughly my height, a couple of inches over six feet, with a body that was all hard, rippling muscle. Like me, he was stripped bare to the waist, exposing his tan shoulders, chest, and stomach. His mane of longish, wavy blond hair gleamed brightly underneath the lights, but his blue eyes were as cold and hard as the ice on a Frozon moon.

"Aw, what's the matter, Kyr?" Zane taunted, bouncing up and down on his feet like a rocket about to shoot up into the sky. "Did that hurt?"

Kyr. No one had ever called me that except Vesper. When she had said it, the nickname sounded like a musical endearment. Zane spat it out like a mocking epithet.

The two of us were sparring in my training ring in the bottom of Castle Caldaren. The few other Arrows currently on-planet were gathered around, along with Daichi Hirano, my friend and the chief of staff for House Caldaren. At first, they had offered encouragement to Zane and me, but as our sparring had progressed and it had become apparent the two of us wanted to tear each other apart, the cheers had died down, and a tense, watchful silence had dropped over the training ring.

Zane and I had been fighting for the last ten minutes, neither one of us able to knock the other down. And I really wanted to knock him down—and then grind his face into the mat until he choked on his own blood.

"You're slipping, Kyr," Zane said, taunting me again. "What's the matter? Distracted by wistful thoughts of your little conquest? Even though she left you months ago?"

The hot anger bubbling in my chest crystallized into a tight knot of icy fury.

The other Arrows shifted on their feet. Many were psions and had sensed the abrupt change in my mood with their telempathy. Daichi shook his head and huffed out an exasperated sigh.

"What did you say?" I asked, my voice a low, dangerous growl.

Zane grinned, amusement crinkling his face. He always delighted in annoying me. "I see that stick is firmly lodged up your ass again now that Lady Vesper is gone. Let me guess. She finally realized what a broody bastard you are and decided to get as far away from you as fast as possible. Is that about right?"

That knot of icy fury in my chest grew colder and tighter, like a moon wyvern coiling its long, spiked tail around my body and squeezing all the warmth out of it. First, Zane mocked me with that nickname, and then he claimed *I* was the reason Vesper was no longer on Corios with the other Regals. But the thing that rankled the most was that he was *right*.

I had done everything in my power to get rid of Vesper, including breaking the truebond between us. I could hardly complain now, since her absence was the very thing I had wanted all along. But every sneering word from Zane made me want to punch him again and again, until I knocked every one of his perfect teeth out of his bloody mouth.

"Uh-oh! Looks like I hit a nerve." Zane smirked. "Guess I was right about you fucking your weapons consultant after all. Or did you go and catch some actual feelings for her, Kyr? Wouldn't that be something, for a coldhearted bastard like you?"

The ice in my chest cracked wide open, and unchecked fury shot through me like cold arrows skewering me from the inside out. I snapped my right hand down and reached for my psion power. A dark blue light exploded in my palm, and it only took the smallest thought to shape all that raging, pulsing energy into a long, glowing sword.

I twirled the psionic blade around in my hand, and it spat, hissed, and crackled with cold in a perfect mirror of my emotions. "I told you before not to insult Lady Vesper," I snarled. "But I guess you need a reminder."

Zane arched an eyebrow and snapped his hand out to the side the same way I had. Energy surged, and a pale blue hammer appeared in his fingers. He grinned, then darted forward, lifting his psionic weapon high. I growled and rushed forward to meet his charge.

Zane swung his hammer at me time and time again, but I countered his hard blows and lashed out with my own sword in return. Blue sparks shot off both our weapons, showering over us as though we were fighting on the surface of an exploding star, but the light, heat, and stinging sparks were nothing compared with the icy fury still zinging through me.

I was angry at Zane for being an arrogant dick who challenged me at every turn, but mostly, I was furious at myself, and I wasn't quite sure why. Or perhaps I knew exactly why and just didn't want to admit it to anyone, especially not myself.

Zane and I exchanged several more quick, hard blows, but neither one of us wounded the other. Psi-blades were hard to create and even harder to maintain. They required an immense amount of energy, willpower, and concentration, and even the strongest psion usually couldn't form one for more than a few minutes. So I bided my time and waited for the right moment to strike.

Slowly but surely, Zane's hammer started to dim. The second his weapon flickered out of existence, I dropped my grip on my own power. My sword also vanished, but I surged forward and punched him in the face, putting all my fury into the blow.

Zane's nose broke with a loud, deeply satisfying *crunch*, and blood spurted up like a fountain, spattering all over his face and dripping down his bare chest. Some of the warm, sticky drops hit my own chest, but I relished the sensation. Thanks to my telempathy, I could feel every sharp throb of his nose, along with the pain radiating out through his face. My inner monster growled with approval.

"You're going to pay for that!" Zane snarled, his hands curling into fists.

I shifted my weight onto the balls of my feet and snapped up my own fists to punch him again—

"Enough!" Daichi barked out, stepping into the ring. "That is enough!"

He shot Zane a disgusted glare, then gave me one as well. My chief of staff was normally calm, cool, and collected, but his dark brown eyes glimmered with anger.

Zane stalked forward so that his bloody nose was inches away from mine. "You're going to pay for that," he repeated in a lower, more sinister voice.

"For what? Getting the better of you?" I sneered at him. "I've been doing that for *years*. Go sit down, Zane. Before I *make* you sit down."

Rage flared in his eyes, making them burn more silver than blue, and the same emotion blasted off him, as hot as lava spewing into my face. His emotions mixed with my own, until I couldn't tell where his anger ended and mine began. My fists tightened a little more, and I shifted forward again.

Daichi shoved his way in between us, using his tablet to push me back, then doing the same thing to Zane.

"That is *enough*!" he snapped, his voice even louder and more irritated. "You two barbarians need to get cleaned up. I have a message from the palace. Holloway wants to see you both."

Zane kept glaring at me. "This isn't over."

"I never said it was," I growled right back at him.

Zane glared at me a few seconds longer, then whirled around and stalked over to one of the stone benches that lined the training ring. The other Arrows stepped forward and started talking to him in low, hushed voices, but Zane ignored them and yanked a shirt on over his head. He didn't bother doing anything about the blood still pouring down his face, even though it had already ruined his clothes. Unflappable bastard.

Zane grabbed his bag, along with his stormsword, and left the ring. The other Arrows murmured their good-byes and quickly followed him.

I waited until the door had clanged shut behind them all before heading over to another bench. I picked up a clean white towel and wiped Zane's blood off my chest. I started to toss the towel into the recycler, but a thought occurred to me, and I held it out to Daichi instead.

"Here. Run this against the other samples."

His black eyebrows shot up in surprise. "You want me to run Zane's DNA against Vesper's to see if they're related?"

I nodded. "Yes. Just like you have all the other samples."

During the spring Regal ball, Vesper had told me that Nerezza Blackwell was her biological mother but that she had no idea who her father was, just that he was most likely some Regal lord Nerezza had dallied with once upon a time. Ever since then, I had been quietly poking around, trying to uncover her father's identity.

It was in my own best interest to know, as I needed to avoid whoever Vesper might be related to so that I wouldn't accidentally form a truebond with them the way I had with her. But even more important, I wanted to give Vesper that missing piece of information about herself. Although she might be better off not knowing who her father was, especially if it was someone as conniving as Callus Holloway.

I might be a Regal lord and the leader of the Arrows, but even I couldn't go around asking people for their DNA. Over the past few months, I had become quite an adept thief. Every time I was around another Regal, I did my best to get a sample of their DNA. A cup a lady used to sip her tea. A comb a lord swiped through his hair. Or in Zane's case, his blood.

Daichi gave the samples to his uncle, Touma Hirano, a spelltech who dabbled in all sorts of illegal things. Together, Daichi and Touma discreetly hacked into the Regal archives that recorded the families, bloodlines, and psionic abilities of all the Houses, big and small, old and new, and compared the samples with Vesper's DNA. Some Kent Corp mercenaries had injured Vesper while trying to recover the original files about the *Velorum* crash, and she had bled all over the blitzer we had used to escape from Magma 7 after the Techwave battle.

Daichi took the towel and carefully folded it, so that he wouldn't contaminate Zane's blood with his own touch DNA. "You should tell Vesper what you're doing."

"That I'm secretly trying to find out who her biological father is? How do you think she would react to that?"

He shrugged. "Probably quite poorly. She told you that she didn't want to know who it was. Assuming you can even find him, of course. Vesper's father might not be a Regal. He could be a servant or a guard. Someone who left Corios or died long ago. You might never discover who he is."

"And that's why I'm not going to tell her that I'm looking until I have some concrete information. I don't want to get her hopes up, or down, or however she might feel about learning who her father is."

Daichi let out another aggravated huff. He clearly thought I was making a mistake. He was probably right about that.

After the last Regal ball, I had finally told my friend everything that had happened between Vesper and me. How she had saved my life on the Magma 7 battlefield. How we had each plotted to kill the other when we'd been trapped on a blitzer together. How we'd snuck on board a Kent Corp ship to gather evidence of Rowena Kent's sabotage. How Vesper and I had shared a truebond. How we had drunk some chemicals in Touma's workshop to get rid of it. How the cold concoction had frozen and then shattered the bond between us.

The only thing I hadn't told Daichi was how . . . concerned I had become about Vesper's safety and how breaking the bond had . . . bothered me more than I'd ever thought possible. How I almost . . . missed being connected to her and knowing that she was safe, well, and thriving in her new life as a Regal lady and the head of Quill Corp.

"Is something wrong with your arm?" Daichi asked, breaking into my thoughts.

I hadn't noticed it, but I was massaging the spot in my left shoulder where Zane had hit me. For some reason, it was stinging again.

I dropped my hand. "It's nothing. What's this about a meeting with Holloway?"

Daichi swiped through a few screens on his tablet, the white glow highlighting his golden skin. "You've been summoned, along with Zane. I'll try to find out more details while you get cleaned up."

I nodded. "Thank you, Daichi."

He nodded back, then left the training ring, still carrying the towel with Zane's blood.

I gathered up the practice swords, staffs, and other items the Arrows had trained with and returned them to a weapons locker along the wall. I blinked, and suddenly, Vesper was there, grabbing blasters out of the locker and carrying them over to a bench.

A few months ago, she had done that in real life, hot-wiring the weapons together to create a new, better blaster which she had used to fry Zane's clothes after he had insulted her. A smile lifted my lips. That was one of my favorite memories of Vesper, and I thought about that moment every time I opened this locker, although I wasn't quite sure why. Or perhaps that was something else I knew, deep down inside, but simply didn't want to admit to myself.

I stared at the spot where Vesper had been a moment longer, then left the training ring. Even though I couldn't see her anymore, the ghost of her still lingered in the air all around me and, even worse, lurked in the bottom of my heart.

I went to my chambers, took a shower, and changed into an Arrow uniform—a long-sleeved tactical jacket over a shirt, cargo pants, and knee-high boots, all in a dark blue that bordered on black, the color of House Caldaren. The sigil of an arrow streaking upward through a cluster of stars was threaded into my jacket, right over my heart.

I slid a blaster into a holster on my right thigh and threw a silver bandolier studded with daggers, injectors, and other small supplies across my chest. Then I picked up my stormsword.

A few tiny stars and arrows were carved into the silver hilt, surrounding a single sapphsidian jewel shaped like a much larger arrow that matched the House Caldaren sigil on my jacket. Curls of silver stretched out in opposite directions, forming the weapon's crossguard, while other curls of silver snaked up and wrapped around the base of the lunarium blade. I had always liked the relative simplicity of my sword, especially compared with some of the other Arrows' weapons, which were practically dripping with jewels. Or Zane's sword, which was covered with tiny carved Zs in a reflection of House Zimmer and his enormous ego.

I traced my index finger over the other sigils carved into the hilt: eyes. I had never known what to make of the eyes that adorned the sword, until I had met Vesper. After we'd broken the bond, I'd expected the eyes to sink into the silver and disappear, but they hadn't. Perhaps it would just take more time. Or perhaps they would never fade away, just as the memories of Vesper would never fade from my mind.

I added the sword to my weapons belt and went downstairs to the library. With its thick rugs and comfortable chairs, the library was the coziest room in the castle, despite all the terrible things that had happened in here.

The kitchen servants had set out some refreshments. I wandered along a table against the wall, popping fresh berries into my mouth before filling a plate with cheeses and bite-size roast beef sandwiches slathered with a delicious, tangy onion-and-bacon jam. I poured some iced apple tea, took everything over to a low table in front of the cold fireplace, and started eating.

The refreshments look like they've been ravaged by wolves. My own voice whispered through my mind, and a rueful smile stretched across my face. I'd said that to Vesper a few months ago, and now here I was, gobbling down food just as she had.

I finished my meal, then sank deep into the chair, leaned my head back against the cushion, and closed my eyes. Zane Zimmer was a highly skilled, dangerous enemy, and fighting him always took a toll. Using a psi-blade for that long had further drained me, but breaking his nose was worth the resulting exhaustion.

Zane had always thought he should be the leader of the Arrows, although he had become much bolder about usurping my authority and being a pain in my ass over the past few months. Zane had also threatened Vesper during the last Regal ball, something I was determined to make him pay for, one way or another.

Eliminating Zane was the smart thing to do. In addition to not wanting his sword to end up in my gut, I also needed to make sure that he never learned about the truebond between Vesper and me. Zane would run straight to Callus Holloway with the information, which would be more than enough to convince Holloway to make Zane the leader of the Arrows— and for me to wind up in one of the palace labs.

Ever since I was a boy, Holloway had eagerly wanted me to form a truebond with someone so he could siphon off the resulting power from whoever was unlucky enough to be shackled to me, just as he had done to my parents.

My head lolled to the side, and I opened my eyes and stared up at the family portrait over the fireplace. It was the last happy moment I remembered between my parents. The portrait had been painted shortly before Holloway had taken too much of my mother's power at once and caused her wasting sickness and eventual death. After that, my father had spiraled so far down into his grief that nothing could rouse him out of it. One night, Chauncey had too much to drink and became so enraged that he'd attacked me, shouting that we could both be with my mother again if we died.

I'd retaliated by shoving my stormsword into my father's heart.

To my utter shock, Chauncey had given me a beatific smile, as though I'd released him from the horrific prison of his own body. *Thank you, my boy*, he'd whispered, then dropped to the floor beside the fireplace, right in the shadow of our family portrait.

I had always hated the bloody painting, as it always reminded me of everything I had lost. But ever since Vesper had come to Corios, I had been reevaluating my views about my parents and their truebond. Vesper was right. It would be nice to be . . . connected to someone, to *her*, despite the enormous danger it would put us both in.

I sighed and started to look away from the portrait, but a faint flicker of light caught my eye, a weak silver glow that snuffed out as suddenly as it appeared. What was that?

I surged to my feet, went over to the fireplace, and stared up at the painting. I'd studied the portrait a thousand times, but for some reason, my mother seemed to be in a slightly different position than before. Instead of lovingly staring into Chauncey's eyes like usual, Desdemona was peering at something past my father's smiling face. I tracked her gaze down and over to the right . . .

A door appeared in the wall beside the fireplace.

Startled, I jerked back. Had Zane hit me harder than I'd realized during our sparring session? Did I have a concussion?

But this didn't feel like a concussion or a hallucination. No, this felt strangely . . . *real*.

Curious, I studied the stone door, but there was nothing overtly unusual or sinister about it, except for the fact that it had suddenly appeared in my library.

Powers could vary wildly among psions, and I had a strange affinity for being able to open doors, even when I couldn't physically see or touch them. A skill I'd used to get Vesper and myself onto a blitzer so we could escape the lava on Magma 7. Although I still had no idea why *this* door would appear. Why here and now? What was so special about it?

Even more curious, I stepped forward and twisted the knob. It didn't move, so I put some more force behind it, using my own physical strength as well as some telekinesis. With a low *creak*, almost like a resigned sigh, the knob turned, and the door opened, revealing a staircase that curled down like a tight, twisted ribbon.

This kept getting stranger, but I eased down the staircase. Intricate sigils were carved into the banister, and they glowed as I passed, like lamps lighting my way. Pale blue flowers also appeared—blue-moon peonics, the same flowers that grew in my mother's garden. The servants used the spearmint-scented petals to perfume House Caldaren soaps, shampoos, and other cleansers. Odd but not threatening, so I kept going.

I reached the bottom of the staircase and stepped into a large round room. Even more peonies bloomed in here, their black vines snaking up to form crude trellises over the doors that were set into the wall. My gaze zipped from one door to the next, many of which featured dark, jeweled, sapphsidian eyes that watched my every movement.

I drew in a shaky breath, although shock punched it right back out of my lungs. I had been in this room once before. Back on the blitzer when Vesper had been injured and I had been flying us both to Corios.

I was in a mindscape—Vesper's mindscape, the heart of her psion power.

As I stood there among the flowers, doors, and eyes, a hard truth erupted in my mind and settled in my heart. One I had known all along but hadn't wanted to admit to myself until right now.

Vesper and I were still bonded.

SIX

VESPER

Nerezza lifted her chin and peered down her nose at me, looking every inch the Regal lady. Poised, polished, and utterly elegant. But the longer I studied her, the more everything about her *sharpened*, from the line of her nose to the point of her chin to the shardlike diamonds glittering on her fingernails, as though they were razors that would slice me to pieces if I dared to touch her.

I remained frozen in place on the settee. Just as I had during the Regal balls on Corios, I waited for recognition to flood Nerezza's features as she realized that *I* was the unwanted daughter she'd abandoned. But just like at the balls, that recognition never came.

Equal parts cold relief and hot fury surged through me. Nerezza knowing who I really was would make this situation even more difficult and unpleasant, but it would also be oddly, darkly satisfying to watch the shock spread over her face, especially for her to realize that her useless child was a

Regal lady now, just like she was.

Nerezza and I continued our silent staring contest. My pounding heart slowed, but sweat continued to slick my palms, and I resisted the urge to swipe my cold, clammy hands against my pants. Nerezza had never been my mother in any way that truly mattered, and now she was only an enemy.

A good enemy, as Leandra would have said. Maybe even my best—or worst—enemy.

I finally looked away from Nerezza. We were in a large office filled with overstuffed green velvet chairs and settees, like the ones we were sitting on. Gold-framed portraits of Nerezza in various gowns and jewels covered the walls, and delicate white orchids perched in fluted crystal vases on tables made of real wood. An elaborate blue porcelain tea set patterned with white orchids rested on a silver serving platter on the low table in front of Nerezza. Not an office but a luxurious suite befitting a proper Regal lady.

"Vesper, how lovely to see you again," Nerezza said, her voice a low, silky purr. "Sorry for all the theatrics, but my associate said that you refused to come along quietly."

My gaze cut to Harkin. "I told him to make an appointment. He drugged me instead."

Nerezza picked up a cup and took a dainty sip of tea, and the strong, cloying scent of lavender drifted over to me. "Forgive me, but I didn't have time to wait for an appointment. Besides, from what I've been told, your schedule is quite full these days as befitting a newly appointed Regal lady and the head of a corporation. What is it that Quill Corp specializes in?"

"Brewmakers." I jerked my head over toward a table in the corner. "Like that one. That's an older version, though. You should replace it with a new model. I've made several improvements to the previous Kent Corp design."

"Mmm." Nerezza made a noncommittal sound, then took another sip of tea. "I'll be sure to have someone do that."

Empty words and an empty promise, although she delivered them with a smooth face and a pleasant tone. With that excellent acting ability, she should have been starring in one of the romantic serials instead of plotting to overthrow the Imperium.

"I figured it was you."

Nerezza peered at me over the rim of her teacup. "What do you mean?"

"I figured that you were working with the Techwave."

Her eyes narrowed. "Did your seer magic tell you that?"

"No."

"Then how did you figure it out?"

"I saw you talking to Rowena Kent during the spring ball when the new Kent Corp ships were put on display for the Regals. The two of you were very friendly."

Truth be told, I hadn't thought much of their friendship at the time. But when Rowena, Sabine, and Conrad had been poisoned inside their cells at Crownpoint, I'd remembered just how chatty Rowena and Nerezza had been. Plus, as a Regal lady, Nerezza had easy access to the Imperium palace and more than enough money to bribe someone to poison the prisoners' water.

Maybe my seer magic had subconsciously clued me in to Nerezza's involvement, or maybe it was my own prior experience with her. Either way, I knew that she would do whatever it took to achieve her goals, including killing her co-conspirators to protect herself.

"I'm friendly with lots of people. After all, I *am* the head of House Blackwell. Being friendly is part of being a Regal, something you should know by now."

Nerezza set her teacup aside, then waved her hand over the holoscreen embedded in one side of the table.

"Vesper Quill." She flicked her fingers, and one hologram after another hovered over the table. "Age thirty-seven. Toiling away in obscurity as a lab rat in the R&D department at Kent

Corp until a few months ago, when you ran afoul of Rowena Kent and she conscripted you onto an Imperium military cruiser. Somehow you managed to survive a battle with a Techwave squad of Black Scarabs on Magma 7. Then you journeyed to Corios where you helped Kyrion Caldaren expose Rowena Kent's conspiracy to sabotage Imperium ships. Lauded by the gossipcasts and given the title of Lady Vesper Quill by Callus Holloway for your bravery and heroism."

She paused and flicked through a few more documents. "Nothing of note before that, though. Parents died when you were a youngster, so you grew up in an orphanage on Temperate 44, then attended an Imperium academy and later a university on that same planet. Several lab-rat jobs at smaller companies until you started working for Kent Corp about five years ago."

She shrugged and leaned back, dismissing the lack of information about my existence as unimportant. "But it doesn't matter exactly where you came from. Like so many other people in the galaxy, you were leading an exceptionally boring life. Until a few months ago, you, Vesper Quill, were completely ordinary and utterly useless."

I flinched. There was that damn word again. *Useless.* Maybe the one word I hated above all others. Her cold, clipped condensation of my life also bothered me, but for a surprising reason.

Nerezza's information was wrong—it was *all wrong.*

I had grown up on Temperate 45, not Temperate 44, and scores of records chronicled my childhood, along with my progress through the Imperium academy and university. Nerezza's name was even listed on my birth certificate, although my father was unknown.

I studied the holograms floating over the table. All the documents boasted official seals, which added to my confusion. Someone had deliberately erased all traces of who I really was from every single record they could access. But who would do that? And why?

Nerezza waved her hand again, and the holograms vanished. This time, I leaned forward and stared at her.

"Lady Nerezza Blackwell. A notorious Regal climber who is famous—some would argue infamous—for getting what you want out of one House and relationship and immediately moving on to your next conquest. The current head of House Blackwell, thanks to the death of your husband, Giorgio, several months ago, although his nieces and nephews are trying to wrest control away from you, along with the Blackwell fortune. Some of the gossipcasts claim that you are currently trying to align yourself with Callus Holloway, and a few folks even whisper that you have your eye on the ultimate prize—the Imperium throne. But unfortunately for you, Callus Holloway is not *nearly* as gullible as the other Regals you've used and discarded, and so far, he has resisted all your attempts to ingratiate yourself with him." I recited the facts of her existence just as coldly and calmly as she had mine.

Her eyebrows lifted in surprise. "You've been studying me."

"Something like that."

I would never admit that I had seen her swanning about on the gossipcasts for years, despite my best efforts to avoid hearing anything about the woman who had abandoned me. Even now, knowing she didn't care about me—that she had *never* cared about me—still stung, like a sharp, throbbing splinter I could never quite pluck out of the deepest part of my heart.

"What else do you know about me?" Nerezza asked.

I sat back against the settee cushions, mimicking her relaxed pose. "The most important thing of all—that you are a ruthless, coldhearted bitch who will do whatever is necessary to get what you want."

Nerezza threw back her head and laughed. Her merry chuckles splattered all over me like acid rain. "A fair assessment."

"What do you want?" I growled. "I might be a newly appointed Regal lady, but we both know that mine is a title in name only. I don't see what *use* I could be to you."

Nerezza stood up. "Let's take a walk, and I'll show you just how useful you can be, Vesper."

Harkin pushed away from the wall, grinned, and aimed his blaster at my left ankle, a clear indication that he would be happy to shoot me if I didn't comply.

Worry filled me, but I had no choice but to get to my feet and trail Nerezza out of the suite.

Nerezza went down a short hallway, and Harkin followed along, his blaster pointed at my back and my stormsword still hanging off his belt. The cool suite air vanished, replaced by a growing, stuffy heat that made sweat gather in the small of my back.

I glanced down at my sleeves, but all the eye, moon, and star jewels were gone from my cuffs. They must have fallen or been ripped off while Harkin and his Techwave buddies had been transporting me here. My heart sank, but I checked my hands. The polyplastic glove still covered my left hand, hiding the cuts in my palm. The two eye jewels were still attached to my thumbnails, although they contained other electronics and not the tracking equipment and emergency beacons that I needed right now. I swallowed a frustrated growl.

Nerezza opened a door, and we stepped onto a metal landing that overlooked the floor of a massive factory. Noise slammed into my ears—*clangs, cranks,* and *bang-bang-bangs* of heavy machinery so loud that I ducked my head and scrunched up my shoulders to try to block out the overwhelming roar. Magma planets were often home to metal refineries, chemical labs, and other enterprises that required immense amounts of heat, and here enormous machines stretched out as far as I could see, along with conveyor belts that rolled, rolled, rolled at a dizzying pace.

Their product? Suits of Black Scarab armor.

On the closest machine, a robotic arm laid a black metal breastplate on a conveyor belt. The breastplate zipped along the assembly line, and more robotic arms danced all around it, attaching arms and legs and then hands and feet. No head, though. Would this Black Scarab be fully automated? Or would an actual person be stuffed inside the metal shell?

Nerezza glided down a set of stairs, then ambled along the assembly line, unconcerned by the rapidly moving equipment and roaring noise. Harkin jerked his blaster, ordering me to follow her.

I scanned the area, looking for a terminal, a server room, or anything else that would let me contact Tivona and call for help, but all I saw were conveyor belts and robotic arms assembling one Black Scarab after another. The acrid stench of hot polymetal flooded the air, along with clusters of sizzling sparks.

Nerezza punched a code into a keypad, opened a door, and stepped into a corridor. I followed her, and Harkin shut the door behind us, cutting off the overwhelming cacophony of the factory floor. I sighed with relief and shook my head, trying to get the ringing sensation out of my ears.

Nerezza strode along the corridor, making a few twists and turns before climbing a set of stairs. I memorized the route the same way I had memorized the keypad code and added them both to my growing mental map of the facility.

A minute later, Nerezza stopped and gestured at a long permaglass window. "I know that you specialize in brewmakers, Vesper, but I thought you might like to see our weapons lab."

I peered through the glass. The Techwave lab was eerily similar to the one at Quill Corp. Clear polyplastic workstations marched down the center of the room, while the floor, walls, and ceiling were all made of thick gray concrete so that no stray energy bolts or other deadly pulses of light and heat could escape.

Weapons techs wearing dark green lab coats tinkered with half-assembled blasters and shock batons, while others sorted through tubs filled with solar batteries, sparkers, and other parts. A couple of supervisors wearing black coats moved from one workstation to the next, tracking the workers' progress and typing notes on large tablets. A few test dummies were also leaning against one of the walls, waiting to be shot to pieces.

My eyes narrowed. No, wait. Those weren't polyplastic dummies like the ones we used at Quill Corp.

Those were actual *people.*

Two men and a woman dressed in tight white jumpsuits were positioned at the far end of the lab. Their necks were anchored to the wall with thick, clear plasticuffs. So were their arms and legs, which were spread out wide, contorting their bodies into five-pointed stars.

For a moment, I thought they were already dead, but then the woman's dark gaze flicked in my direction, her eyes wide with panic. *Help me . . . please . . .*

Her thought rasped through my mind, along with her terror, which scraped against my skin like broken glass. I ground my teeth to hide a grimace. Kyrion's psion powers included telepathy and telempathy, and thanks to our truebond, I too could sometimes hear other people's thoughts, as well as sense their emotions, especially when they were particularly loud, pointed, or desperate, like this woman's.

"Why did you bring me here?" I snapped.

Nerezza ignored my question and rapped her knuckles on the glass. Inside, one of the supervisors nodded, donned a pair of safety goggles, and plucked a hand cannon off a workstation. He came over to the window and held the weapon up and out where I could see it.

Once again, I froze. "That's . . . that's *my* design."

Rowena and Sabine Kent had used my ideas to create a hand cannon, which Julieta Delano had fired at Kyrion and me during the Techwave battle on Magma 7. That weapon had only contained bits and pieces of my work, but this cannon was practically a mirror image of my original design.

"Oh, yes," Nerezza purred. "That's the design you submitted to try to get promoted to the Kent Corp weapons lab several months ago. Rowena and Sabine both saw its potential, although they tried to put their own stamp on it. Their modifications actually weakened the weapon, so my Techwave friends scrapped the Kents' cannon and went back to yours. It took a few iterations, but they have greatly improved upon your original design."

She rapped her knuckles on the glass again. A grin spread across the supervisor's face, and he marched over to the far side of the lab. My chest tightened. I knew *exactly* what he was going to do, but the knowledge didn't make it any less horrifying, especially since there was nothing that I could do to stop it.

The supervisor positioned himself about twenty feet away from the three people cuffed to the wall. The two men were already dead, but the woman's eyes darted from side to side, as though that small motion would somehow help her escape.

The other workers scurried back out of the line of fire, then raised their tablets and started recording the proceedings as though this was a scientific experiment and not calculated murder.

The supervisor nestled the butt of the hand cannon in the crook of his shoulder, then took aim. The lab was soundproofed, but I could have sworn I heard the soft, distinctive *click* of him pulling the trigger.

A green blast of energy shot out of the cannon and slammed into the woman's chest. Maybe it was some quirk of my magic, but I could *see* everything that was happening, all the brutal damage the weapon was doing to the woman, as though I were watching a movie one frame at a time in super-slow motion.

The pulse of light and heat tore through her jumpsuit, vaporizing the thick, heavy fabric. Burns bloomed like crimson roses on her skin, then abruptly wilted, and chunks of her muscles disintegrated like dry, blackened petals, revealing the white curve of her ribs. But the energy didn't stop there. An eerie, intense glow spread over the woman like she was dappled in rays of radioactive sunlight, and each shimmering green prism ate through even more of her skin, muscles, and bones.

I blinked, and time snapped back to its normal flow. The woman's eyes were already fixed in death, her mouth sagging in a silent scream.

Most people could survive a bolt or two from a regular blaster or cannon, depending on where it hit them, and many psions like Kyrion could absorb such energy and add it to their own mental power. But this was no normal weapon, and the green glow kept eating and eating at the woman's body like a chemical fire that refused to be extinguished. Somehow I knew that it would keep right on burning until every single inch of the woman was destroyed. Or maybe *consumed* would be a better word to describe the sickening destruction.

The supervisor flashed Nerezza a thumbs-up, then placed the weapon on a workstation and started running a diagnostic scan on it.

My gaze snagged on a row of similar cannons lined up in a nearby locker. One, two, five, ten . . . I stopped counting after the first dozen.

When I had first sketched the cannon, it had been a mental exercise, a way to flex my skills and do something a little more intricate, creative, and challenging than design yet another brewmaker. Later on, I had hoped to use the design to get promoted so I could escape from Conrad and his sneering condescension in the R&D lab. To me, the cannon and its uses had been abstract theories, and I had never *dreamed* it would be put into production at Kent Corp or anywhere else.

Even though Rowena Kent had bragged that she'd used my ideas in several special projects for the Techwave, I'd still thought that I could stop them from hurting anyone. But the Techwavers had made dozens of cannons—deadly weapons they were going to deploy against Arrows and Imperium soldiers and weapons they had already tested on innocent people, like the dead woman still cuffed to the wall.

I had been such a naive fool.

My heart dropped, my stomach roiled, and I fought the urge to vomit. I had just wanted to work on things that would *matter*, that would *help* people protect themselves. I had never wanted any of *this*.

"That woman was a powerful psion." This time, Harkin spoke, his voice excited and eager, like a kid with a marvelous new toy. "The drugs we gave her immobilized her body but not her power, and she was still capable of creating impressive psionic shields. She blocked all the blaster fire we shot at her, but one bolt from your cannon, Vesper, and, well, you saw what happened. You should be proud. You created a truly impressive weapon."

I swallowed the hot, sour bile in my throat, although it took me a moment to unlock my clenched jaw. "That's not *my* weapon. I designed my cannon to incapacitate, not incinerate. What did you do to it?"

"Harkin and his techs gave your cannon a little more *oomph*." A sly smile spread across Nerezza's face. "That was my idea. I'm no designer, but I have a talent for . . . social engineering. For figuring out how to make things work to their full potential, especially when it comes to people and institutions. In this case, I simply applied my little skill to your weapon."

Social engineering? That sounded eerily similar to my own

ability to fix things, to figure out how to make objects better, stronger, and more efficient. Was Nerezza a seer like me?

"Come," Nerezza said. "There's someone I want you to meet."

Once again, Harkin waggled his blaster at me. My hands clenched into fists, but I resisted the urge to try to grab the weapon and smash it into his smug face. He would shoot me before I took two steps toward him. So instead, I peered through the glass again.

The techs and supervisors had returned to their previous projects, but my gaze skipped over them to the far side of the lab. By this point, the intense green glow had eaten almost all the way through the woman's torso, as though her chest had been made of soft wax instead of solid muscles and hard bones.

Once again, despite the lab's soundproofing, I could have sworn I heard the sizzle of her skin cooking and could smell her fried flesh, along with the electric stench of the energy blast. More bile rose in my throat, but I forced myself to study the woman and memorize every little thing about her.

I *never* wanted to forget this. Never wanted to forget how Rowena, Sabine, and Conrad had stolen my idea. Never wanted to forget how the Techwavers had twisted my design from something meant to protect people into something meant to annihilate them.

Leandra Ferrum had been right in the gym earlier. The only good enemy was one who had a chance of defeating you, and I was going to do everything in my power to destroy the Techwave.

"Let's go," Harkin ordered, jerking his blaster at me again.

I stared at the dead woman a moment longer, then headed down the corridor, wondering what other horrors were hidden in the Techwave base.

SEVEN

VESPER

The farther we walked, the more guards appeared. They were all wearing the same sort of black armor that I'd seen on the Black Scarab assembly line, but these metal plates were sculpted to each person's body and adorned with small, sharp, retractable spikes that jutted out from their elbows, knees, and feet—vicious weapons they could use to further wound an enemy. Similar spikes also jutted up from the tops of their black helmets.

Opaque green visors covered the guards' faces, blurring their features, but the fact that they were real people instead of hollow shells made them even more frightening and monstrous than the Black Scarab I had cut down at Quill Corp. Each guard clutched a silver blaster, and shock batons dangled from their belts.

Nerezza stopped and knocked on a door flanked by four guards. A deep voice barked out for her to enter. She twisted the knob, and I followed her inside, with Harkin and the four guards bringing up the rear.

Unlike Nerezza's luxe suite, this office was spartan in the

extreme. The floor, walls, and ceiling were the same dull gray concrete as the weapons lab. No rugs or paintings softened or brightened the hard surfaces, and the few pieces of furniture were made of cold, functional chrome. The only thing even remotely colorful was a large plastipaper map of the Archipelago Galaxy that was hanging beside a metal shelf bristling with military history books. A long window off to the side overlooked the factory floor, where robotic arms were still assembling one Black Scarab after another.

In front of the window, a man was sitting behind a desk and typing away on a large terminal. He looked to be in his mid-sixties, with dark brown hair that was cropped so short it was little more than a sheen of stubble covering his scalp. Wrinkles grooved harsh lines into the ruddy skin around his mouth, as though he scowled on a constant basis. His eyes were the same deep, bottomless black as Harkin's, and his nose sliced the same sharp line down his face, indicating that the two of them were related. Father and son, most likely.

A short, formal, military-style jacket stretched across the older man's shoulders, and a sigil of a scarab made of pale lunarium was embedded in the stiff, shiny black fabric over his heart. Emeralds glittered as the scarab's eyes, while thread-thin veins of lunarium spread out from the scarab's legs and formed the jacket's seams. I would bet every credit in the Quill Corp accounts that the lunarium gave the jacket some sort of energy and ballistic shielding.

"Vesper Quill, may I present General Orion Ocnus," Nerezza said.

And just like that, things went from bad to worse.

Not much was known about the senior members of Techwave, but Orion Ocnus was one of the few public faces of the terrorist organization and rumored to be its leader, according to the gossipcasts. Ocnus used to be an Imperium general, but after a falling-out with Callus Holloway, he had defected to the terrorist group several years ago. From the videos I had seen, the general was a ruthless tactician who would use any soldier, weapon, and spaceship at his disposal to win a battle, which made me even more curious—and wary—about what he wanted from me.

General Ocnus got to his feet and jerked down the bottom of his jacket, even though it was already perfectly crisp and straight. The four guards remained on the fringes of the office, but Harkin went over to the general, plucked my stormsword off his belt, and handed it to the older man.

"Look, Father," Harkin said, excitement creeping into his voice. "Now that we finally have a stormsword, we can run even more tests to see how these sorts of weapons amplify psionic abilities—"

The general tossed my sword down into a nearby trash can like it was an oversize paper clip. The clanging echoes of the weapon rattling around inside the metal drowned out Harkin's voice.

"Forget it," General Ocnus barked out. "How many times do I have to tell you? Such antiquated weapons are of no consequence. Your job is to figure out how to ensure our superior firepower, something you have failed to accomplish."

Harkin jerked back as though his father had slapped him. An angry flush stained his cheeks, and he opened his mouth, but a sharp look from his father made him clench his jaw and swallow his words. Looked like I wasn't the only one in the room with a shitty parent.

General Ocnus turned toward me. "This is the weapons expert?"

"Yes," Nerezza replied. "She designed your new hand cannons."

Ocnus studied me, his gaze cold and critical. I resisted the urge to shift on my feet like a wayward schoolchild summoned to the headmaster's office.

"We've had great success repurposing your design," he said. "Although we've had some difficulty fully adapting the cannon to our needs."

More wariness filled me. "What needs?"

Nerezza stepped forward, drawing my attention. "We have a proposition for you, Vesper. One that will make you extremely wealthy. All you have to do is fix a small flaw in your own design. Why, if you figure it out fast enough, you might be back on Temperate 42 in time to enjoy a nice, leisurely lunch."

I laughed. "Really? That's your sales pitch? Do what the Techwave wants, and you'll pay me off and ship me back home?"

Ocnus's eyes glittered like black holes about to swallow up everything in their path, including me. "You don't have any other options, Vesper. You would be wise to keep your mouth shut and do as you're told."

He was wrong. I *did* have other options—they were just exceptionally bad ones. Then again, that was the story of my life.

The general gave me another cold glare. No doubt he was used to such icy glowers making his underlings quake in their boots, but I had survived a battle against the Black Scarabs, a fight to the death against an Arrow, and being trapped on a ship with Kyrion Caldaren, the most notorious killer in the galaxy. Dirty looks didn't faze me anymore.

Ocnus turned his cold gaze to Nerezza. "You assured me that she would be ready to cooperate by the time you brought her to my office."

She shrugged off his harsh accusation. "It's not my fault she has more stubbornness than common sense."

I ground my teeth. The two of them were talking about me like I wasn't even in the room, like I didn't have a *choice* about any of this.

"I don't know what you need me to fix, but I will *never* help you." I spat out the words. "I have no love for the Imperium, but you're worse. *This* is worse."

I stabbed my index finger at the window. Down on the factory floor, robotic arms continued to assemble one Black Scarab after another.

Ocnus rolled his eyes, as though my refusal was expected but still annoying. "I don't have time for this. Take her to the lab and break her—quickly. It won't be long before someone notices that she's missing, and we need to be on to the next phase by then."

He brushed past Nerezza, whose fingers twitched, as though she wanted to grab one of the thick military history books off a nearby shelf and bludgeon him with it. Nerezza noticed me watching her and smoothed out her expression.

General Ocnus swept out of the office. Two of the guards followed him, and they all strode down the corridor and vanished from view.

Harkin snapped his fingers. "Seize her."

The two remaining guards headed toward me. I couldn't afford to let them take me to any lab, or I would end up like that poor woman in the weapons bunker, paralyzed and shackled to a wall. I had to escape *right now*, so I went on the offensive, just as Kyrion and Leandra had taught me.

I shoved the first guard back into the second one, sending them both staggering to the side. I had to get my hands on my stormsword, which was still sitting in the trash can several feet away, but to do that, I was going to have to actively tap into my bond with Kyrion and deliberately use his telekinesis, assuming I could even reach his power. I still didn't know how, when, or why the bond worked, but it was my only option.

I lunged forward and stretched my hand out, but Harkin stepped up beside me, whipped up his hand, and stabbed an injector into my left shoulder.

I yelped and staggered back, but that cold, inevitable rush of chemicals once again flooded my veins. My entire body went numb, my legs buckled, and my ass hit the floor. I tried to get up, move, fight back, but the chemicals blasted over me like a Frozon blizzard, making my arms and legs feel like chunks of ice that were disconnected from my mind.

Harkin tossed the used injector into the trash can. It rattled around my stormsword, and each metallic *tink-tink-tink* sounded like a soft laugh, mocking my failure to escape.

Harkin towered over me, a sinister smile spreading across his face. "Take her to the lab."

Harkin must have given me a smaller dose of chemicals than the Black Scarab had on Temperate 42 because I didn't pass out this time. No, this time, I was fully conscious and painfully aware of the two guards stepping forward, grabbing my arms, and hauling me upright. The guards dragged me out of the office, down several corridors, and into another room.

Try as I might, I couldn't move my arms and legs, couldn't wiggle a single finger or twitch a solitary toe in protest. The guards hauled me up onto a metal slab and plasticuffed my wrists and ankles to the cold, hard surface. Then they tilted the table so that my body was upright, and my boots were on a footrest. The abrupt motion made my head spin, but I blinked away the dizziness.

Unlike the gray concrete bunker of the weapons lab, the floor, walls, and ceiling here were made of pale green tile. Several metal slabs were spaced throughout the room, while scalpels, forceps, drills, and other surgical tools were resting on nearby trays. Defibrillators, IV stands, and other, larger medical equipment were lined up against the walls, all of them on wheeled carts so that the objects could be easily moved to any spot in the room. The chilly air smelled of a lemony antiseptic that couldn't quite mask the coppery tang of blood lurking underneath the sharp, stringent scent.

My stomach clenched with dread. This was so much worse than a weapons lab.

This was a medical lab.

Harkin left the room, along with the two guards. Nerezza remained behind, examining her perfect nails as though contemplating whether she needed a fresh manicure.

Some of the numbness had left my body, and I struggled against the cuffs, but the thick, strong polyplastic didn't give a single inch. Anger and frustration pounded through me, along with more than a little fear. Despite my seer magic and all my plans to outwit the Techwave, I had badly miscalculated how this would play out, and now I was going to pay a painful price for my arrogance.

Nerezza clucked her tongue in mock sympathy at my weak, flailing moves.

Even more anger pounded through me, but I stopped my pointless struggling. "You don't have to do this. I saw how much you hate working for General Ocnus back in his office. Let me go, and we can escape this place—together."

An amused laugh rasped from Nerezza's red lips. "You must be truly desperate to try to play on my sympathies, Vesper."

She glanced through a permaglass window set into the wall. Out in the corridor, Harkin was pointing at the guards, giving them instructions. Once she was certain he was distracted, Nerezza strolled over to me. Given the upright position of the slab, my face was level with hers.

Up close, she was even more beautiful than I remembered from when I had last seen her in person at the Regal balls. Her dark brown hair formed a shiny, lustrous frame around her face, every lock a perfect wave that curled exactly the right way, while her eyes glimmered like dark blue moonstones. Even without her light makeup, her flawless features would be the envy of any model who graced the gossipcasts' fashion shows. Oh, yes. Lady Nerezza Blackwell was a diamond that had been hardened over time and then cut and polished until it reached the peak of its beauty, just like the solitaire that adorned her finger.

"You're right. I *am* sick and tired of working for Ocnus. He's a blustering fool who is more interested in mass-producing his toy soldiers and preening for the gossipcasts than he is in truly toppling the Imperium." A conspiratorial smile curved Nerezza's lips. "But I won't have to suffer him for much longer. I have my own plans for the Techwave."

"You're the head of House Blackwell and one of the most powerful Regals in the Imperium. What do you need with the Techwave?"

"Oh, the Techwave is merely a means to an end. Although I was rather shocked when my first husband, Johann, secretly aligned himself with them. Back then, the merest *hint* that you might be in league with the Techwave was enough to get you executed for treason, but I saw how useful the group could be in getting what I want."

"Which is what, exactly?"

"What does any Regal truly want? To have everyone in the mighty Imperium bow down to them, bow down to *me*." Her chin lifted, and her eyes brightened, as though she was picturing that glorious scene in her mind.

"Why do you hate the Imperium so much?"

Nerezza studied me, as if debating whether to reveal her secrets. After a few seconds, she shrugged. "As a teenager, I had so much psionic potential that I was invited to attend a prestigious academy on Corios. I excelled in my classes and my psionic training, and I positioned myself to catch the eye of a young Regal lord. Everything was going exactly the way I wanted."

"Until what?" I asked the obvious question.

Her nostrils flared with disgust. "Until one of the Regals

decided that I wasn't good enough for their precious son."

I scoffed. "You mean they saw you for the manipulative bitch you really are and didn't want you to poison their House and family."

"Something like that," Nerezza agreed. "I thought I had enough leverage to accomplish my goals, but my enemy had far more money and power, and they banished me to a backwater Temperate planet."

I should be back on Corios. I should be part of the Regals, not rotting away on a useless planet trapped in a useless life with an utterly useless child.

Her voice whispered through my mind, and my magic roared to life. Suddenly, I was seeing a much younger Nerezza telling Liesl how useless I was, standing right alongside this older, even crueler version of my mother.

"But you went back to Corios," I said, trying to distract myself from the eerie, unwanted double vision. "And somehow you weaseled your way into a Regal House."

"It wasn't hard. All you have to do is tell people what they want to hear, and they think you're their best friend. It's always been very easy for me to make friends."

Social engineering. That was what she had called her ability to charm and manipulate people until they no longer served her purposes, just as she had done to me.

Heartache rippled through my chest, and I struggled to keep my voice steady and even. "The gossipcasts always mention what a remarkable climber you are, especially since you don't have any magic of your own."

Nerezza laughed again, and the light, tinkling sound pelted me like icy sleet. "You're right. I *have* done an excellent job convincing everyone that I'm just a regular person with no psion power. The other Regals always underestimate me because they think I'm not as strong as they are, but they're wrong about that."

A sneaking suspicion filled my stomach. "What do you mean?"

She leaned a little closer and smiled, but her eyes remained as cold and hard as the metal slab against my back. "I *never* lost my power."

Nerezza waggled her fingers. Telekinetic power surged off her, and a scalpel floated up off a tray, zipped across the lab, and landed in her outstretched hand. My breath caught in my throat. Not only was Nerezza a psion, but her magic was *strong*, and she seemed just as powerful as Kyrion, Zane Zimmer, and the other Imperium Arrows.

She waggled her fingers again, and the scalpel zipped back over to its tray. "Losing my power was just a nasty rumor my enemy circulated to get me kicked out of the Regal academy. Of course, I have to keep my abilities hidden from my Techwave friends, lest Harkin gets ideas about sticking me in his charming lab."

She jerked her chin toward the window. "Harkin is one of the Techwave's top lab rats. He's obsessed with studying psions and trying to translate their powers into weapons. He thinks if he comes up with something strong and clever enough, he'll finally win his father's approval. Fool."

I thought of the black gloves he'd been wearing on the Quill Corp campus, which had emanated enough kinetic power to knock me down. What other weapons had he invented? And how many psions had died for his research?

Harkin strode out of view, along with the Techwave guards. Worry twisted my stomach. At least when he had been in sight, I could keep an eye on what he was doing.

I dragged my gaze back to Nerezza. "Why reveal your psion power to me? Why talk to me at all?"

She gave me a thoughtful look. "I'm not sure, exactly. Maybe it's because you remind me of myself. Focused, driven, ambitious, determined to bend other people to your will."

I wanted to protest that I was *nothing* like her, but I couldn't, because I was all those things. I'd been so confident in my own abilities and so determined to get my revenge on the Techwave that it had blinded me to how big a threat they truly were. I'd tried to bend them to my will, just like Nerezza had said, and now they were going to break me in return.

"At first, people admire my ambition, drive, and determination," Nerezza continued. "But once they realize that I will always put myself first, no matter what, they become *much* less enamored. Servants, friends, lovers. It always ends the same. Anger, tears, desperate pleas and blustering demands about why I can't change, why I can't be different. As if *I* should ever sacrifice *my* happiness for someone else. Or worse, conform to what someone else *needs*." Her lips curled back in disgust, and her shoulders shuddered with revulsion.

A bitter laugh burst through my lips. "So you're talking to me because you're selfish and love hearing the sound of your own voice."

"One person's selfishness is another person's happiness," she countered. "But no, those aren't my only reasons for indulging in this conversation. It's refreshing to talk to someone I can be completely honest with. Besides, you've been on my mind lately, Vesper."

I frowned in confusion. "How so?"

"My plans for the Techwave were proceeding exactly as intended—until you came along," Nerezza replied, anger creeping into her voice. "I was quite surprised when Rowena told me that one of her little lab rats had figured out that the rigged navigation sensor had caused the *Velorum* crash. Ever since then, you've caused me nothing but problems."

"What sort of problems?"

"For starters, I had to send Harkin to make sure that the security footage in and around the spaceport before the *Velorum* crash was erased."

Why would she care about the footage being erased? Unless . . .

Shock and horror spiked through me, as though one of the Techwave guards had skewered me with his armor. "You were there when the *Velorum* went down."

Nerezza's dark eyebrows lifted in mild surprise. "You really are quite perceptive. Too bad your seer magic didn't warn you about Harkin's lab. Then again, I've never thought seer magic was good for much of anything. Visions and whatnot. How *useless*."

She slapped her hands together, as if wiping something unpleasant off them. I couldn't stop myself from flinching at the curt, dismissive motion, along with her sneering, mocking tone.

"People should make what they want a reality, not rely on others to reveal if their secret dreams, desires, and destinies are ever going to come to pass. Weak, simple-minded fools."

My shock faded, although horror kept spiking through my body at all the ugly truths hidden inside her words. "*You* crashed the *Velorum*. *You're* the reason all those people are dead."

Nerezza pushed her long hair back over one shoulder, completely unconcerned by my accusation. "Of course I did. Rowena gave me a prototype of her hand cannon. As a Regal lady, it was easy to access a private part of the spaceport, then wait for the *Velorum* to take off. I fired the cannon, hit the navigation sensor a few times, and down it went, like a mammoth butterfly with a ripped wing. *Boom*."

My magic rose up again, and suddenly, I was *there*, standing right beside Nerezza and watching everything from her point of view.

The cannon's green energy blasts hitting the navigation sensor on the ship's hull. The sensor turning yellow, then orange, then a bright, warning red as it overheated. The *Velorum* plunging into a steep dive and slamming into the spaceport below. Metal shrieking, glass smashing, and then a stunned silence, as if the *Velorum* itself couldn't believe that it had crashed. And maybe worst of all, Nerezza's cold satisfaction flooded my heart like an ocean of ice as she watched the ship burn . . .

I shook my head, and the vision vanished, although disgust kept churning in my stomach.

"*Why?*" I demanded. "Why did you crash that cruiser? None of the people on board the *Velorum* did anything to you."

Fury flashed in her eyes, making them smolder like blue flames. "Oh, I knew someone on the *Velorum*. Liesl. A cousin of mine."

Once again, shock spiked through me. "You killed your own cousin?"

Nerezza pushed the rest of her hair back over her other shoulder. "Oh, please. Liesl was no innocent victim. She served as my lady-in-waiting and helped me climb the Regal ladder for years. Gathering gossip, spreading rumors about my enemies, taking videos of other Regals in compromising situations. But eventually, I didn't need her anymore, so I paid her off, and she disappeared until about six months ago."

"What happened then?"

"Liesl sent me a message that she was out of money. She threatened to tell the gossipcasts about an old mistake unless I paid her off again. Fool. I told her to meet me at the spaceport on Temperate 33. As soon as the *Velorum* took off, I canceled the credits transfer and shot the ship out of the sky—and that arrogant bitch right along with it." Pride rippled through her voice, and a serene smile stretched across her face. The red gloss on her lips made her look like a predator that had just taken a big, bloody bite out of some helpless prey.

I frowned again. "What mistake?"

Nerezza's gaze flicked over to the window, but the corridor

was still empty, so she focused on me again. "Back when I was young and stupid, I had a child. A girl."

I ground my teeth to keep from flinching again. *Girl*. Nerezza had always called me that, instead of giving me a real name. I hated that blasted word almost as much as I hated *useless*.

"I left the girl behind on that backwater Temperate planet when I returned to Corios," Nerezza continued. "Liesl took care of her for a while."

"You abandoned your own daughter?" My voice was barely above a whisper, but I croaked out the question that had haunted me for the last thirty years. "Why?"

"At first, I was thrilled to discover I was pregnant. I thought a child would guarantee my place in the Regal House I had chosen." Her face darkened with fresh fury. "But I had underestimated my enemy, and the child wasn't enough leverage after all."

Once again, she was talking about *me*—her own daughter— as a commodity, a tool to further her Regal climb, instead of an actual person. Anger sizzled in my chest like a shooting star streaking across my heart, and I seized onto the emotion, letting it burn away my shock and horror and especially my hurt and bitterness.

"Let me guess. You tried to force that Regal lord into marrying you, and he refused."

Another low laugh tumbled from her lips. "Oh, no. Before I could even get to my darling lord, his family shipped me off-planet. I don't think they ever told him about the child, but it doesn't matter now."

"Why not?"

"Because the girl died long ago." Nerezza shrugged again. "Some accident in one of the student labs at her academy."

She thought that I was dead? More shock spiked through me, even as a tiny bit of unexpected hope sparked in my heart. Maybe I'd been wrong about her. Maybe *that* was the reason she'd never come back for me. Maybe she did care about me in some small way.

"It's a shame, really. The Regal who exiled me still needs to pay, and the girl would have been a useful tool in getting my revenge." Nerezza flicked her fingers again, as though tossing a bit of dirt off them. "But she's dead, so that avenue is closed to me."

My shock vanished, and that warm spark of hope dimmed and died, just like I supposedly had. Icy numbness sank into my bones, and my entire body ached from the chill. I had always known that Nerezza was cruel and calculating, but the depths of her depraved determination astounded me. She had killed Liesl to keep her secrets and make sure the Techwave's plans remained on track, and now she was going to do the same thing to me.

I opened my mouth to tell her the truth, to reveal that *I* was the daughter she'd abandoned. If she knew who I really was, Nerezza would get me out of this lab. I *knew* she would. I could *feel* it with my seer magic.

But at the last instant, I clamped my lips shut. I might want to escape, might want to survive, but I would not help her destroy more lives.

I would *not* be like my mother in that way.

Nerezza continued talking, oblivious to my inner turmoil. "My personal business aside, the *Velorum* crash convinced General Ocnus to move forward with Rowena's sabotage of the new Imperium ships. We were getting ready to launch our attack, and then you came along." She shook her head. "Because of you, Vesper, I had to kill Rowena, which cost us months of work. But now we're finally back on track."

"How did you poison Rowena and Sabine?" I asked.

Another smile played across Nerezza's lips. "I got some incriminating footage of an Imperium guard with an underage girl and blackmailed him into letting me into the Kents' cell.

Rowena thought I was there to help her escape. She was another fool, just like her daughter and that insipid man who worked for them at Kent Corp."

I had no love for Conrad Fawley, but I still grimaced at her harsh words. He too had been a Regal climber, although he hadn't played the game nearly as well as Nerezza. Conrad had gotten far more death than he had bargained for by aligning himself with the Kents.

"Why are you telling me all these secrets? Aren't you worried that I'll go to the gossipcasts like . . . Liesl?" I stumbled over her name.

Nerezza laughed again, and the look she gave me was almost pitying. "Oh, Vesper. You really don't know what's going to happen next, do you? How quickly and thoroughly Harkin is going to dismantle you." She shook her head again. "Useless seer magic."

The door opened, and Harkin entered the lab. A long green medical gown now covered his body. A green cap hid his spiky blond hair, and matching gloves covered his hands. More horror shot through me. He looked like a surgeon strutting into an operating suite—and I was going to be his patient.

Nerezza clucked her tongue in mock sympathy again. "Now you understand. Too little, too late."

Once again, I considered telling her the truth, but once again, I squashed the urge. *No.* Nerezza might save me now, but she would only hurt me again later, and I wasn't going to give her the satisfaction of dreaming up further ways she could use, abuse, and discard me.

Nerezza leaned forward, her gaze on mine. "Let this be a lesson to you, Vesper. The last one you'll ever learn. You can only count on yourself to do what needs to be done. And when other people offer to help you, don't believe a word they say."

She straightened up and looked down at me, calmly examining me the way a scientist would examine an experiment they were about to conduct. "Don't damage her too badly. We still need her mind, eyes, and hands intact."

"Of course," Harkin murmured.

Nerezza left the lab. I tracked her through the window, but she didn't slow down or look back, not even for an instant.

Harkin plucked a scalpel from a nearby tray and stepped forward, his body blocking out the bright overhead lights. Two faint *clicks* sounded, like he had just taken my picture with an old-timey camera. Instead of their usual black, his eyes were now a bright, unnatural green. Not only was the color wrong, but his eyes also looked odd, as though they were made of tiny prisms that had been fitted together.

Maybe it was my imagination or some quirk of my magic, but I could see my own reflection in every one of those prisms. More horror flooded my body. I was staring into the face of a man-size insect that wanted to dissect me.

"Do you like my contacts, Vesper?" Harkin asked. "They're one of my newer inventions, able to record everything I see and do. In the lab, I prefer to have my hands free so I can focus on my subjects."

Harkin smiled, although the expression twisted his handsome features into a grotesque mask. "I could tell you this won't hurt a bit," he purred. "But I don't want to lie to you, Vesper."

He leaned down a little closer, and when he spoke again, his words were a warm whisper against my cheek. "And even more important, I *want* it to hurt."

Harkin shoved the scalpel into my left forearm to punctuate his point. Fire flared, pain erupted, and I screamed.

EIGHT

KYRION

I slowly turned around in a circle, struggling to come to terms with the fact that I was in Vesper's mindscape. That the bond wasn't broken, that it had *never* been broken.

During the last Regal ball, Holloway had ordered me to repeatedly cut my hand with a dagger during the truebond test in hopes of the same marks appearing on Vesper's hand, but her skin had remained injury-free. How had she fooled Holloway and all the other Regals? And why had she fooled *me*?

An avalanche of icy anger plummeted through me, along with a few hard boulders of regret that bounced around inside my chest and bruised my heart. She should have told me the bond wasn't broken. I deserved to know. I deserved the chance to . . . consider my options, even if only bad ones were available when it came to Holloway and truebonds.

But Vesper's deception didn't explain why I was here. Why now, at this moment? What had drawn me into her mindscape again?

I could tell you this won't hurt a bit. But I don't want to lie to you, Vesper. And even more important, I want *it to hurt.*

A man's voice filled the room. I whirled around. Images flickered in one of the open doors like a video playing on a holoscreen.

Vesper was strapped to a metal table that was positioned in such a way that she was almost standing upright. A man in green surgical scrubs was standing beside her. I recognized him from Imperium intelligence reports. Harkin Ocnus, son of General Orion Ocnus, one of the Techwave's top scientists who was tasked with creating weapons strong enough to kill Arrows and other powerful psions.

Harkin grinned, leaned over Vesper, and shoved a scalpel into her forearm. A small sting erupted in the same spot on my own forearm. My jaw clenched at the psionic echoes of Vesper's pain.

Vesper opened her mouth. I tensed, expecting her to scream, but a soft, resigned sigh sounded instead. A flutter of movement caught my eye, drawing my attention away from the open door, and I glanced over to the right.

Vesper was sitting on the floor of her mindscape, propped up against the wall and staring at the archway where she was being hurt. Several sapphsidian eyes had migrated down the wall to where she was, forming an odd unblinking outline around her body. Blue-moon peonies curled in between the eyes, almost as if the flowers and vines were trying to shield her from what was happening in the archway, out in the real world, wherever she was.

"Vesper!" I hurried over and dropped to my knees beside her.

She kept staring at the archway, as though she couldn't see anything else, not even me looming right in front of her. Vesper didn't move, didn't blink, didn't even breathe. Her skin was pale and sweaty, her clothing cut and covered with blood. But perhaps worst of all, her eyes were fixed and still, the silver flecks in her dark blue irises dull and dim like stars about to wink out of existence.

She looked . . . *dead.*

Icy dread flooded my veins, freezing me in place. My inner monster roared with denial, and I kept staring at her, willing her to move, to twitch, to do something that would indicate she was still alive.

Vesper blinked. Another soft sigh escaped her lips, although her gaze remained focused on the archway.

A tidal wave of relief rushed through my body, the sensation so strong it sent me listing to one side and almost knocked me down to the floor. I exhaled and steadied myself. I would examine my emotions, whatever they were, later. Right now, I needed to help her.

"Vesper," I said, my voice louder and sharper. "Vesper, wake up."

I started to grab her shoulder to shake her out of whatever daze she was in, but I hesitated. A few months ago, when I knew we were bonded, I had avoided touching her, not wanting to strengthen our unwanted connection, although I hadn't been able to stop myself from brushing my fingers against hers a time or two. Then, when we had been hiding from the guards in the supply closet on the Kent Corp ship, the two of us had been plastered up against each other, and I'd wanted nothing more than to lower my lips to hers and sink into her warm, solid curves.

In the archway, Harkin made another vicious cut with his scalpel. Vesper's mouth opened, but instead of a scream, all that escaped was another sigh.

More anger filled me, along with a fair amount of disgust— at *myself.* Vesper was in trouble, she was being tortured, and I was worried about the truebond and my own bloody fragile *feelings.* Zane was right. I really was a coldhearted bastard.

I scooted even closer to her, then leaned down and placed

my hand on her shoulder. The moment I touched her, a jolt of . . . *something* shot through me, as though an electric arrow had plunged deep into my chest and shocked my heart back to life. Despite the intense, almost painful jolt, I curled my fingers around her shoulder, not wanting to let go of her, not wanting to let her go. Not like I had before when she had left Corios.

"Vesper," I repeated in a firmer, calmer voice. I also jiggled her, just a little bit. "Wake up."

Vesper blinked once, twice, three times. The silver flecks in her eyes slowly brightened, like tiny crescent moons rising in dark blue skies, and her gaze finally focused on my face.

"Kyr?" she asked in a low, raspy voice.

Kyr. When Zane had called me that in the training ring, I had wanted to rip his arms off his chest and force-feed his bloody fingers to him. But coming from Vesper, that one simple word soothed something deep inside me. It just felt *right*, as if it was the name I should have had all along.

Vesper let out a small chuckle, although she winced, as if the motion hurt. "All the drugs must be catching up with me."

"What do you mean?"

She fluttered her hand at the archway where Harkin was still torturing her, but it was a weak gesture. "I keep passing out from the pain, and he keeps giving me adrenaline injectors to wake me up. He wants me to feel every single slice so he can record my reactions to his *experiments*."

Her face scrunched up in thought. "He's given me five injectors so far. Or maybe six? It's hard to keep count. Not to mention all the other chemicals he used when he kidnapped me and then woke me up for Nerezza."

A dagger of worry stabbed deep into my gut. "Nerezza Blackwell is working with the Techwave?"

"Yep," Vesper replied. "She tried to recruit me to join their little evil cabal. General Ocnus needs my help fixing the

Techwave's new hand cannon, the design Rowena Kent stole from me."

That made sense. Vesper was the smartest, most talented person I had ever met when it came to fixing things. With her seer magic, all she had to do was look at an object, and she could figure out how to make it better, whether it was something as simple as a broken clock or something as powerful as a hand cannon.

In the archway, Harkin grinned and sliced the scalpel along Vesper's right shoulder, and a line of fire burned in my own shoulder. Now that I knew we were still bonded, I would probably feel more of her wounds. Vesper's intense pain might have even been the thing that had drawn me back into her mindscape. My mother and father had often been able to sense when the other was severely injured, even when they had been on different planets.

"Come on, Vesper," Harkin crooned. "All you have to do is cooperate, and this can all stop . . ."

Vesper shuddered and focused on me again. After a few seconds, her face softened, and her lips curved up into a smile. "It's good to see you, Kyr, even if you are a drug-induced hallucination."

"Why do you think I'm not really here?"

She tried to shrug but couldn't get her shoulders to move. "Because I tricked you into thinking the bond was broken. Even if you realized that we were still bonded, you would never willingly come here."

"Why not?"

She sighed again, and the soft, sad sound cracked something deep inside my chest. "Because you hate truebonds more than anything else."

My inner monster sputtered in denial. "You're wrong about that."

As soon as I said the words, I realized how true they were.

Before Vesper, I *had* hated the thought of being bonded to anyone. But now . . . now I wasn't quite sure how I felt about it—or her.

Vesper snorted in disbelief. "See? Hallucination. The real Kyr would *never* say something like that."

I stabbed my finger toward the archway. "Right now, I hate that bastard more than anything else. I'm going to find Harkin Ocnus, and I'm going to eviscerate him with my sword," I growled. "Slowly and deliberately and with great bloody pleasure."

She laughed. "Well, you certainly sound like Kyrion Caldaren, proper Regal lord, ruthless Arrow, and the most notorious killer in the galaxy. Then again, my imagination has gotten very good at conjuring you up these past few months."

My inner monster roared again, wanting to prove her wrong, and I carefully took her hand in mine. Her fingers were cold and clammy, but her soft skin sliding against mine sent another electric arrow of awareness shooting through me.

I lifted her hand and pressed her palm to my chest, right over my heart. "Does this feel like your imagination?"

Confusion creased her face, although her eyes sharpened. "Kyr?" she whispered. "Is that really you?"

A shake jerked my body. I lost my grip on her hand, and her fingers fell away from my chest. I reached for Vesper, to hold on to her, to stay with her, but that bloody shaking wouldn't stop. From one instant to the next, Vesper's mindscape vanished. I drew in a breath, opened my eyes, and lashed out with my fists, ready to fight my way back to her—

"Kyrion! What are you doing?" Daichi asked, leaping out of the way of my wild swings.

My fists fell to my lap. I was still in the library. I had been so tired from my fight with Zane that I must have fallen asleep in my chair after I'd eaten.

I glanced over at the wall where the door to Vesper's

mindscape had appeared, but it wasn't there. According to a clock on the fireplace mantel, only about thirty minutes had passed since I had sat down, although it felt like a lifetime. I scrubbed a hand down my face.

"You were muttering," another voice rumbled. "Bad dream?"

A seventy-something man was sitting in the chair across from mine and nibbling from a plate of food. His golden skin glowed underneath the lights, as did his thick tufts of white hair that were sticking straight up. The man was shorter than Daichi, with a stocky body, although he had the same dark brown eyes as the younger man. Touma Hirano, Daichi's uncle.

"Kyrion?" Daichi asked. "What's wrong?"

"Vesper is in trouble."

I told Daichi and Touma about everything I had seen in Vesper's mindscape, including her being tortured by Harkin Ocnus. Daichi started typing on his tablet, while Touma drummed his fingers on his plate. Restless energy surged through my body, and I got to my feet and started pacing back and forth in front of the fireplace.

After a few seconds, Daichi's tablet chimed. "I've contacted Tivona Winslow, Vesper's friend and her second in command at Quill Corp."

"And?" I asked in a sharp voice.

Daichi read for a few more seconds. "Vesper suspected that the Techwave might approach her about the weapons designs they stole from her. Tivona says that Vesper was hoping to plant some trackers on the Techwavers that would reveal the location of one of their secret bases."

My pacing quickened. That was exactly the sort of bold, risky thing that Vesper would do. Part of me admired her courage and cleverness, even as another part of me wanted to throttle her for putting herself in danger. If she had just told me what she was planning, I would have . . . Well, I didn't know *what* I would have done. No, that wasn't true. I knew *exactly* what I would have done: killed anyone who was a threat to Vesper in even the smallest way.

The depths of my icy, murderous rage should have surprised me, perhaps even alarmed me, but they didn't. Not anymore. Not when it came to Vesper.

But the inevitable question nagged at me, the way it always did. Were these really *my* feelings? Or some psionic quirk triggered by the truebond? I might have . . . softened toward Vesper, but I would *not* be anyone's puppet, not even if the strings were connected to my own power.

I whirled around and stabbed my finger at Touma. "Did you know your chemicals didn't work? That the bond wasn't broken?"

He nudged a strawberry around on his plate. "I had my suspicions. To my knowledge, no one has ever been able to break a truebond once it has formed, especially not a bond as strong, deep, and intense as the one between you and Vesper."

My eyes narrowed. "What do you mean, *intense?*"

Touma gestured over at the portrait of my parents. "Chauncey and Desdemona met, they fell in love, and *then* the truebond formed between them. It was a slow, gentle, gradual process."

"But?"

He shook his head. "But you and Vesper are not gentle people, and you did not meet under gentle circumstances. You saved each other's lives in the middle of a volatile battle. Your truebond is a reflection of that." A speculative look filled his face. "As is the psionic power that comes along with it."

"You're saying what, exactly? That my bond with Vesper is even *stronger* than the one my parents had?"

Touma shrugged. "Some people theorize that the circumstances of a galactic bond greatly impact its strength, as well as the power it might bestow. You and Vesper are both strong psions in your own right. Who knows what you might be capable of together?"

I frowned. "If you thought the bond couldn't be broken, then why let us come to your workshop and drink those chemicals? Or let Vesper and me believe the bond was broken afterward?"

Touma set his plate of food aside and looked at me with a serious expression. "Because you and Vesper both wanted to break the bond. Because you were both struggling with how you felt about it—and each other. Because it would be much safer for the two of you if the bond was broken. And especially because you don't want to end up like your parents, Kyrion." He shrugged. "I wanted to give you both some options, some time and space to figure things out."

My gaze zoomed up to my parents' portrait again. No, I had never wanted to end up like them. Never wanted Callus Holloway to take my power for his own. Never wanted to be his bloody battery the way they had been. But now . . . now I wanted . . . something different.

"Eventually, you are going to have to make a choice, Kyrion," Touma said in a soft voice. "To either accept the bond or reject it."

My entire body tensed at his words. "And then what will happen?"

A grim smile curved his lips. "That depends on what you choose."

Before I could tell him to stop talking in riddles, Daichi's tablet chimed again. "Holloway has moved up the meeting. He wants you and Zane at Crownpoint as soon as possible."

I dragged a hand through my hair. The last thing I wanted to do was waste time meeting with Holloway when I could be searching for Vesper. I had opened my mouth to tell Daichi to make some excuse when his tablet chimed for a third time.

He reared back in surprise, then looked up at me. "Apparently, the meeting is about the Techwave."

I tensed again. "Do you think Holloway has information about Vesper's kidnapping?"

"It's possible," Daichi replied. "Holloway has spies everywhere, and he probably has someone planted inside the Techwave, despite how elusive they've been. I would bet every single credit I have that he's already bribed someone at Quill Corp to keep an eye on Vesper, especially since he recently appointed her as a Regal lady."

He was right. Those were exactly the calculated things Holloway would do, but perhaps the Imperium ruler's deviousness would help me find Vesper.

"Very well," I replied. "I'll go to Crownpoint and see what I can find out. In the meantime, prepare my ships. I want to be ready to leave Corios the second my meeting with Holloway is finished."

I asked Daichi and Touma to check on a few more things, then left the library, exited from the back of Castle Caldaren, and hopped into a waiting transport. The vehicle lifted off the ground and zoomed away.

Down below, more castles lined the Boulevard, the broad, cobblestone avenue where so many Regals lived, worked, and schemed. Some of the castles were tall and narrow, while others were short and wide, but they all bristled with towers and turrets, and they were all painted in bright, vibrant colors that made the structures resemble pink, purple, and orange flowers pointing their spiky petals toward the sky.

Horse-drawn carriages rolled along the Boulevard, conveying Regal lords and ladies to their appointments, while servants hurried along the sidewalks, going about their morning chores. The far side of the Boulevard opened into Promenade Park, and people clutching lace parasols ambled along the pink cobblestone paths that crisscrossed the rolling green lawns.

I looked past the park, my gaze locking on the much larger structure in the distance—Crownpoint, the Imperium palace.

Crownpoint's massive shadow engulfed all the colorful castles below, and its chrome-and-glass façade was an ugly, metallic contrast to the whimsical, old-fashioned charm of the Boulevard and the soft, pastoral peace of Promenade Park. Cruisers, blitzers, and transports hovered around the palace's many towers, which soared several miles into the air and glittered like oversize swords that were thrusting up to stab the bright blue armor of the sky.

My thoughts turned back to Vesper, and I yanked up my jacket and shirt sleeve. A thin red welt slashed along my left forearm in the same spot where I'd seen Harkin cut her. I hadn't sensed any more of Vesper's pain since leaving her mindscape, but it was just a matter of time before Harkin started hurting her again.

My gut twisted with disgust, even as my inner monster roared with helpless rage, but I straightened my sleeves and tamped down my emotions. The last thing I needed was for Holloway to realize I was upset. That would lead to all sorts of questions I didn't want to answer and further delay finding Vesper.

A few minutes later, the transport landed inside an enormous docking bay. The door hissed open, and I stepped outside, still wearing my Arrow uniform, stormsword, bandolier, and blaster. I nodded at the flight directors, cargo unloaders, and fuel technicians, but they all dropped their gazes and concentrated on their tasks and tablets. Vesper was right. I was the most notorious killer in the galaxy, and none of these people wanted anything to do with me.

My jaw clenched, and I strode over to the closest elevator and jabbed the button that would take me to the top level. Right before the door would have closed, Zane slithered inside.

His broken nose had been healed, and he too was dressed in an Arrow uniform, although his was the ice blue of House Zimmer. Such an impractical color for anyone to wear, but especially an Arrow, given all the blood, guts, and grime we were exposed to on missions. I had often wondered how many thousands of credits Zane spent each year replacing his uniforms. Probably more than most people, including Regals, spent on clothes in their lifetime. Then again, Zane Zimmer was as vain and arrogant about his appearance as he was about everything else.

Impatient, I jabbed the button again. The door slid shut, and the elevator started to rise. I was content to endure the ride in angry silence, but Zane opened his mouth. I tensed, bracing for yet another insult, either to myself or to Vesper.

"The last time we were in an elevator together, Julieta was here," Zane said in a low voice.

His face was tight and pensive, and he slumped against the wall as though he didn't have the energy to stand up straight. Even more surprising was the longing that washed off him and scraped against my skin like a broken razor.

"Julieta is dead," I replied in a flat voice. "Even if she wasn't, she still wouldn't be here. She was a traitor. If Rowena Kent's scheme had succeeded, Julieta would have smiled, clapped us both on the back, and told us to have a safe flight right before her Techwave friends shot our bloody spaceship out of the sky."

Zane shoved away from the wall, anger flaring in his eyes. "I know this is hard for the great Kyrion Caldaren to fathom, but the galaxy does *not* revolve around you. Everything is not about *you*. She didn't just betray *you*, Kyrion. Julieta was *my* friend, my *best* friend—or so I thought."

I didn't know what to say to his confession. I was so used to arguing with Zane that I didn't know how to have a normal conversation with him.

"I am sorry that Julieta was a traitor," I said in a gruff voice. "I liked her too. Her betrayal . . . stings."

A low, bitter laugh rasped through Zane's lips. "*Stings*. Yeah, that's a good word for it."

He brooded for a few seconds, then looked at me again. "But you didn't like Julieta *nearly* as much as you like Vesper Quill. I still don't understand why you keep insisting that you killed Julieta, when you and I both know that Vesper did it."

My hands tightened into fists. Somehow I resisted the urge to punch him in the throat just to get him to shut his mouth. "I've told you a dozen times. *I* killed Julieta. I don't know why you think otherwise."

Zane tilted his head to the side, leaned his shoulders back against the wall, and crossed his arms over his chest. Despite his seemingly lazy, unconcerned pose, his gaze was sharp and searching. "You're protecting Vesper. Why?"

Before I could answer, pain erupted in my left wrist, so sharp it made me wince. I glanced down. Another red welt peeked out of the end of my jacket sleeve. No blood appeared, but my arm throbbed. Harkin had cut Vesper again. Fury shot through me, drowning out the pain. The bastard was going to pay for hurting her.

Zane's golden eyebrows drew together in confusion. He opened his mouth, but the elevator chimed, cutting off his question. I yanked down my sleeve, hiding the mark, then stepped outside. Zane followed me.

We strode along the corridor, our boots cracking as loudly as bones breaking against the marble floor. Supplemental oxygen hissed out of vents in the walls, adding a soft, sinister white noise to this entire level.

Zane and I reached a set of double doors that soared more than a hundred feet into the air. We stopped and waited while six guards, three for each door, took hold of bronze rings and tugged the stone slabs open. I drew in a breath to steady myself, then stepped through to the other side, with Zane still walking beside me.

An enormous throne room took up most of this level of the palace. Just like the corridor outside, the floor, walls, and ceiling were made of white marble, although tiny veins of red shimmered through the stone in here, making me feel as though I was striding across a person's pale skin instead of solid stone. Even worse was the sensation that emanated from the marble, as though it was a gigantic white leech that was sucking the life, energy, and vitality out of me one heavy footstep at a time. Perhaps it was. Holloway would do anything to increase his own power, even surreptitiously stealing it from others with a booby-trapped floor.

All around the room, orange-red flames flickered in clear hoverglobes that bobbed up and down in midair like miniature suns rising and falling, while the copper chandeliers high overhead burnished the room with more light. Even bigger pieces of copper shaped like crooked fingers and grasping hands adorned the walls, but the display was more functional than artistic. Copper was good at blocking signals from spy cameras—like the one embedded in my jacket.

The miniature camera was hidden inside the House Caldaren arrow right over my heart. It was the latest tech from House Zimmer and one of the few devices capable of circumventing the copper sculptures and other countersurveillance measures. I'd been wearing the spy camera for several weeks and analyzing the resulting footage, trying to figure out some way to assassinate Holloway.

Several guards clad in bloodred armor were spaced around the throne room, each boasting a sigil of a large bronze hand on his chest. Bronze helmets with a pebbled texture covered their faces, and only the faint glitter of their eyes was visible through the wide horizontal slits in the metal. Bronze-colored mesh gloves covered their hands, and they were all clutching long bronze spears with glowing, diamond-shaped tips.

The Bronze Hands were Holloway's personal guards, loyal to him alone, and they were just as dangerous as Zane and I were. Electricity crackled through their spears, which could be used to either shock or stab someone to death.

Holloway was paranoid about his own safety, but several more guards than usual were spaced around the room. Unease trickled down my spine like cold water.

Something was wrong.

Zane and I stopped in front of a dais with three wide, flat steps that was topped with a white-marble throne. Sharp spikes of stone jutted up from the throne's arms, while the back was a mirror image of the Crownpoint towers. We both went down on one knee and bowed our heads to the man lounging on the throne.

"Rise," Callus Holloway called out in a smooth, silky voice.

Zane and I rose to our feet and looked up at the Imperium ruler. Despite my intense hatred of him, even I had to admit that Callus Holloway had a dignified air. His wavy brown hair gleamed under the lights, and only a few strands of silver glinted in the thick locks, despite the fact he was in his mid-sixties. His skin was surprisingly tan, since he rarely ventured outside, and his bronze eyes shimmered as brightly as the hoverglobes.

Holloway was clad in a long bronze-colored jacket over matching pants that made him look much taller than he really was. Bloodred thread twisted together to form the jacket's thick seams, which reminded me of the veins of red running through the floor.

Holloway studied us in silence, and the only sound was the faint drumming of his fingers on the right arm of the throne. Even more unease filled me. Holloway was only silent when he was plotting the best, most painful way to ensure someone's destruction.

His hand stilled, and he got to his feet and glided down the dais steps like a bronze viper slithering over the white stone. He strode right in between Zane and me and went over to a table that had been set up on one side of the room.

"Come," he barked out.

Zane raised his eyebrows at me in a silent question. He too had realized that the Imperium ruler was in a foul, dangerous mood. I shrugged back. I had no idea what was bothering Holloway. It could be something as inconsequential as his morning tea being the wrong temperature or something as important as a thwarted attempt to seize more power and resources.

Zane and I took our usual positions at the table. Holloway waved his hand, and a hologram appeared: Vesper lying on the ground, clearly unconscious.

My gut clenched with fresh dread, even as more pain sliced through my body, this time on my right thigh. Harkin was still hurting Vesper.

"Yesterday evening, Vesper Quill was kidnapped from the Quill Corp campus on Temperate 42," Holloway said. "One of my spies captured some footage of the incident. They were not able to identify the people who took her, although the Techwave is involved."

In the hologram, figures wearing black plated armor appeared out of the shadows. The Black Scarabs hauled Vesper upright and carried her away.

"Where did they take her?" I asked, keeping my voice calm and even, despite the dread still twisting my gut and the slices of pain crisscrossing my body.

Holloway waved his hand, and another image appeared, showing a group of buildings. "To this production plant on Magma 3."

Zane frowned. "Why did they take her? She's just a lab rat who lucked into being a Regal lady. No one important."

My fingers curled into fists, but I smothered the urge to break his nose again for insulting Vesper.

"From what my spies have discovered, the Techwave is hoping to make Vesper Quill engineer some weapon they plan to use against the Imperium, against *me*."

Anger blasted off Holloway and hit my telempathy like a red-hot axe slicing into my chest. His intense emotion blotted out everything else, including the psionic stings of Vesper's wounds. Despite his calm façade, Holloway was seething inside, although for some strange reason, his ire seemed to be directed more at Vesper than at the Techwave. Why would he be upset with her?

"What do you want us to do?" Zane asked. "Rescue Lady Vesper?"

"Something like that," Holloway replied. "But the two of you don't have to go it alone. I've brought in reinforcements."

He clapped his hands together. Footsteps sounded, and two people stepped out from behind the dais.

The thirty-something man who came around the left side was roughly my size, a few inches over six feet, with a heavily muscled body. His short dark red hair glimmered under the lights, as did his ruddy skin. His Arrow uniform was the same light gray as his eyes, and a stormsword with a gold hilt and a long, curved lunarium blade was belted to his waist.

In contrast, the woman who stepped around the right side of the dais was several inches shorter, with a curvy body. Her long, wavy hair was more strawberry blond than true red, and her skin was a rosy flush compared with the man's more mottled tone, but her eyes were the same light gray as his. The woman was clad in the same pale gray Arrow uniform, and the stormsword on her belt was a smaller version of the man's curved one.

Beside me, Zane tensed. *What the fuck are they doing here?*

His thought whispered through my mind, echoing my own

worry and surprise, although I didn't know if he was asking himself the question, or directing it at me, or both.

Dargan Byrne swaggered over and clapped Zane on the shoulder. "Hello, Zane. You're looking as pretty as ever."

Zane's icy eyes grew even frostier, and he shrugged off the other man's hand. "Dargan." He tipped his head to the woman. "Adria."

Adria Byrne glided to a stop beside me. "Zane. Kyrion."

I murmured a greeting to her, although I tensed, just like Zane had.

Adria was a couple of years older than Dargan, and the sister and brother both belonged to House Byrne. Theirs was a relatively small, poor House, but Adria and Dargan had something no other Regal siblings did.

A truebond.

Despite what the gossipcasts claimed, truebonds didn't have to be romantic in nature. They could form between any two people—friends, lovers, siblings, even complete strangers like Vesper and me. Bonds between family members were somewhat common, especially among the Byrnes. In just about every other generation, a truebond formed between either two siblings or two cousins in House Byrne. Dargan and Adria were the latest iteration, which made them among the most powerful and dangerous people in the galaxy.

Dargan was the muscle, both physically and mentally, since he was a psion who was particularly talented in telekinesis. Adria wasn't quite as physically or mentally strong as her brother, but she was much smarter. Dargan was a blunt hammer, while Adria was a focused laser, and Holloway employed them both to brutal effect.

Even among the Arrows, Dargan and Adria were known—and feared—for their ruthlessness. They killed people as casually as I brushed lint off my jacket, and they didn't care whom they had to hurt to complete their missions. Men, women, children, animals. The Byrnes cut through them all like robotic scythes slicing through a field of wheat and leaving nothing behind but death and destruction.

Adria moved to stand beside her brother, the two of them almost looking like twins, given the strong genes in the Byrne family. Holloway eyed them with a hungry expression, although he didn't touch either one of them. Not the way he would have acted if my parents had still been alive and in this room.

"How was your mission on Frozon 16?" Holloway asked.

Adria shrugged. "We destroyed the facility as you requested. The Techwave won't be mining any more minerals there."

"Neither will anyone else," Dargan said, a grin creasing his face. "We imploded the mine with all the workers trapped inside. It's nothing but a giant tomb now."

I tensed again, as did Zane. Both of us might be stone-cold killers, monsters through and through, but the Byrnes were another species entirely. Adria and Dargan had no interest in politics or preening for the gossipcasts and no loyalty to anyone except each other and their few other family members. The only reason they obeyed Holloway was because he paid them extremely well and let them continue their indiscriminate slaughter.

Zane glanced over at me. *Vesper Quill is in even more trouble than I thought.*

This time, he was directing the thought at me, although in such a soft, subtle way that no one else could sense it. He was right. Vesper being held by the Techwave was bad enough, but Holloway bringing in the Byrnes put her in even more danger.

Holloway turned to me. "Kyrion, my boy, your mission is simple. Go to Magma 3, infiltrate the Techwave facility, and find Vesper Quill. I want to know exactly what weapon the Techwave wants her to engineer."

Relief flooded me. I could do that. I *wanted* to do that. "Understood. Anything else?"

"Oh, yes. I want you to do one more thing after you find Vesper Quill."

Even more unease filled me. "What's that?"

A sly grin spread across Holloway's face. "Kill her."

NINE

KYRION

Everything inside me seized up, as though I were a volcano about to erupt and spew rage everywhere. I had to work very hard to keep any emotion from showing, although my fingers clenched around the edge of the table, hard enough to make my knuckles turn white from the strain.

Never, the thought blazed through my brain. I would *never* hurt Vesper, and I would destroy anyone who tried, including Callus fucking Holloway.

Beside me, Zane tensed yet again, while Adria and Dargan studied me with curious expressions.

"You want me to kill Vesper Quill?" I asked. "Why? You just made her a Regal lady a few months ago."

Holloway flicked his fingers in a dismissive motion. "Bah! That was simply a show for the gossipcasts. Vesper Quill being a Regal lady is a laughable notion. As if I would ever make a poor, unknown orphan a true member of Regal society."

He chuckled. Adria and Dargan joined in with his mocking laughter, but Zane remained quiet.

"But why do you want her dead?" I gestured at the image of an unconscious Vesper that was still floating over the table. "She's not conspiring with the Techwave. They are clearly kidnapping her."

Holloway flicked his fingers again. "I don't care whether she is working with them willingly. Vesper Quill needs to be eliminated."

"Why?" Adria asked, echoing my question. "She's just some nobody with a meaningless title."

Holloway stared at the image of Vesper, anger slowly filling his face like water seeping into a sponge. "Over the last three months, Vesper Quill has managed to salvage what was left of Kent Corp. Even worse, she's made it profitable again. Sales of her new brewmaker are astronomically good, and my spies indicate that she's working on space cruisers that will be even more profitable."

"So she's making too much money?" Dargan asked, a puzzled note in his voice. "Just raise the Regal tax on her corporation like you usually do."

A shrewd smile spread across Holloway's face. "Why tax her when I can take over her company? I was going to wait a few weeks for the dust to settle before I quietly seized control of Kent Corp, but Vesper Quill swooped in ahead of me." He shook his head. "Even worse, she actually *believes* she is a Regal now. Foolish woman. I'm going to make sure she remembers her proper place—under my boot."

Jealousy colored his words. Vesper had outwitted—out-smarted—Holloway by making a success out of Kent Corp, and he was going to retaliate by killing her.

I had to stop this—I had to stop *him*.

Once again, I studied Holloway just as I had a thousand times before, and once again, I couldn't come up with a way to kill him. As a siphon, he would easily absorb an energy bolt from my blaster, and he could always leech away my own psion power, along with my physical strength, and make it impossible for me to even lift my stormsword, much less gut him with it.

Even if I could somehow assassinate Holloway, I wouldn't leave the throne room alive. Not with the extra Bronze Hand guards lining the walls and Adria and Dargan standing nearby. The siblings would cut me down before I took three steps toward the door.

If Vesper had been here, she would have said this was an OBO—a situation with only bad options—and she would have been right.

Holloway turned to me, his face as cold as the copper sculptures adorning the walls. "I don't *have* to give you a reason to kill Vesper Quill. I gave you an order, Kyrion. Your job is to follow it." He arched an eyebrow. "Unless you wish to relinquish your position as head of the Arrows?"

Dargan grinned again, and Adria's hand drifted down to her stormsword. They would be happy to slice me to ribbons for Holloway and their own amusement. Beside me, Zane tensed yet again. He too clutched his stormsword, although his gaze remained on the other Arrows.

I gritted my teeth and bowed my head, once again playing the part of the obedient weapon. "Of course. Do you require anything else?"

Holloway must have been satisfied by my calm, steady words, because he faced the table again. "Do whatever you want to any Techwave troops and Black Scarabs you encounter." He waved his hand again, and the image of a different facility popped up over the table. "While Kyrion is securing Vesper Quill on Magma 3, Adria, Dargan, and Zane will investigate another suspected Techwave facility on Magma 4. Once the three of you have destroyed this secondary facility, you will rendezvous with Kyrion on Magma 3."

Holloway looked at Dargan. "Question Vesper Quill about

her interactions with the Techwave, then take her back to Temperate 42 and force her to give you access to the Quill Corp servers. I want every single schematic and potential design she has ever dreamed up. Pay special attention to the weapons and ships, but I want *everything*, right down to those new brewmakers."

Dargan's grin widened. Anticipation pulsed off him and stabbed into my chest like a red-hot poker. Disgust churned in my gut, but it was quickly drowned out by icy determination. No matter what happened, what I had to do, whom I had to kill, or what I had to sacrifice, I would *not* let Dargan hurt Vesper.

"Get the information first. Then you can play with Vesper Quill as long as her mind and body last. Bring her back to Corios and that charming basement workshop in your own House, if you like. I don't care." Holloway stabbed his index finger at Dargan. "But if you kill her before you get what I want, then I will be most displeased with *you*, along with the rest of House Byrne. Am I clear?"

The grin dropped from Dargan's face, replaced by a flicker of worry. He might be cruel and dangerous, but Holloway could still kill him, along with his sister and every single member of their House.

Adria stepped up beside her brother. "I'll make sure he behaves, my lord. I won't let him damage your prize too badly."

Her eyes gleamed, and anticipation surged off her the same way it had done with her brother. Dargan might enjoy inflicting pain on others, but Adria enjoyed watching it just as much.

"Oh, I know you will, my girl," Holloway purred. "You always follow my orders to perfection. That's one of the things I appreciate the most about you."

Hunger filled his face again, even stronger and more obvious than before. He hesitated, then reached over and patted Adria's hand. I recognized the simple touch for what it truly was—an attempt to take her psion power.

Holloway kept patting Adria's hand, his bronze eyes brightening with every soft stroke of his skin against hers. In contrast, Adria's skin paled, and her shoulders slumped as the energy flowed out of her body and into his, like sand trickling through an hourglass. Zane shifted on his feet beside me, as though he could also feel it with his own telempathy.

Adria drew in a weak, raspy breath, squared her shoulders, and lifted her chin. Dargan stepped closer to his sister, hovering right behind her, and an invisible wave of . . . *something* rolled off them both and crashed into Holloway.

Surprise shot through me. What in all the bloody stars was *that*?

Even though it hadn't been directed at me, the psionic echoes of that energy scraped across my skin, and I had to resist the urge to scrub the phantom sensation away. Zane also tensed.

Holloway jerked his hand away from Adria's and started coughing, as though he'd taken too big a bite and a piece of food was lodged in his throat. He plucked a red handkerchief out of his pocket and coughed into the silk.

My surprise vanished, replaced by curiosity. I had never seen Holloway try to siphon any energy from the Byrnes' truebond, and I had often wondered why he didn't use them the same way he had used my parents. From the rumors I'd heard, Holloway's scientists had been studying the Byrnes' blood for years. I'd thought they had been trying to replicate the truebond, the same way they were always studying my blood, but perhaps the scientists were simply trying to figure out how Holloway could take the Byrnes' power.

This was completely different from the memories I had of Holloway draining my parents. It almost seemed like Adria and Dargan had used their truebond to . . . fight off Holloway and that their power had actually made him . . . ill.

But how was that possible? Holloway was one of the most

powerful siphons in the galaxy, able to absorb energy from people and machines and even the chandeliers blazing overhead. So why was Adria and Dargan's truebond so different from the one my parents had shared?

Adria arched an eyebrow, clearly amused by Holloway's attempt to drain off her power. How could she be so calm about that? How could Dargan? Surely, they had been frightened, as my parents had always been. A sword of jealousy stabbed deep into my heart.

Holloway stopped coughing and wiped the sweat off his forehead with the handkerchief. He shoved the red silk into his pocket, but it slipped free and floated to the floor. Holloway didn't notice the wayward fabric, and a flick of my fingers and a trickle of my telekinesis made the handkerchief fly up off the floor and into my hand. I discreetly shoved it into my own pocket.

"Kyrion, you are dismissed," Holloway said, his voice weak and raspy. "Zane, Adria, Dargan. Here are some more schematics of the Techwave facility on Magma 4 . . ."

Holloway kept talking, while the other three Arrows focused on the images hovering over the table. I bowed my head to Holloway, then headed for the exit. The Bronze Hand guards turned their heads, watching me, but I walked slowly and steadily, as though this was just another day, mission, and order.

The second I was out of the throne room, I quickened my pace, each step a little faster and more urgent than the last. One thought pounded through my brain, keeping time to my long, hurried strides.

I had to get to Vesper before anyone else did.

TEN

VESPER

I screamed for a long, long time.

Harkin would cut me one, two, three, four times in rapid succession, slicing his scalpel across my shoulders, arms, thighs, and shins. Next, he would wiggle the blade around and around in one of the wounds as though it were a screw that he was twisting deeper and deeper into my flesh. Sometimes he would even release the scalpel, leaving it in the wound and watching it vibrate in time to my screams.

When I grew accustomed to the pain and my screams died down, Harkin would deliberately blink his eyes to make sure his green contact lenses had recorded every second of my agony. Then he would ram an injector into my shoulder. Skinbonds, adrenaline, and other chemicals would flood my system, healing the worst of my injuries. He'd let me recover and catch my breath for a few minutes, then blink his eyes, start a new recording, and cut me again.

Cut, heal, wait . . . Cut, heal, wait . . . Cut, heal, wait . . .

Harkin repeated the vicious cycle again and again until I

lost all sense of time. He could have been torturing me for minutes, hours, days . . .

Sometime later, I finally, mercifully, passed out.

When I opened my eyes, I was in my mindscape, too exhausted to do anything but slump on the floor and stare through the open door that showed Harkin torturing me out in the real world. The silver flash of his scalpel and the red spray of my blood blotted out everything else . . .

A shadow fell over me, and I welcomed the darkness. Maybe it was death coming to claim me . . .

"Vesper . . . Vesper, wake up." Death had a surprisingly familiar voice, low, rich, and deep, with the crisp Regal accent of Corios . . .

I blinked, and suddenly, Kyrion was in my mindscape, kneeling on the floor and talking to me, as though he was really here and not just a figment of my imagination.

He looked just as I remembered. Sharp cheekbones, straight nose, strong chin. Not traditionally handsome, but something about his features made him infinitely fascinating, at least to me. His skin was pale, due to all the time he spent in space, and his midnight-black hair was wavy and just a bit too long, as though he couldn't be bothered to get it cut on a regular schedule.

His dark blue Arrow jacket stretched across his broad shoulders, while a silver bandolier sliced across his muscled chest. His stormsword was belted to his waist, and a silver blaster glinted in a holster on his right thigh. Even kneeling on the floor, he was still tall and strong and looked every inch like the deadly killer he was.

If this was the end, then at least I had a good view.

Kyrion kept talking, although his voice still seemed faint and far away. He gently shook my shoulder, and I started babbling, my fragmented thoughts pouring out of my mouth. It was so good to see him again, to talk to him again, even if he was just a figment of my imagination.

Then Kyrion laid my palm against his chest. His heart beat hard and fast under my fingers, matching the quick rhythm of my own racing heart. He stared at me, his eyes such a dark, inky blue that they bordered on black, much like the sapphsidian eyes here in my mindscape.

Kyrion tightened his grip on my hand, and a wave of *something* surged through me—hot, intense, and electric. The sensation snapped me out of my fugue state, as though Kyrion had flipped a switch and restored the power to my brain just like I would fix a faulty engine. Fresh strength and energy flooded my body, my breath came much more smoothly and easily, and the dull fog cleared from my mind.

"Kyr?" I rasped.

His eyes brightened, burning like dark blue stars, and his heart quickened under my fingers. The shard of ice buried in the bottom of my brain cracked away, and the sticky cobweb that was Kyrion shimmered with heat. More energy flowed through me, as though he was sharing his strength with me, but that was a ridiculous notion. Even if he had really been here, Kyrion would *never* do that, would never use our bond in any way.

I opened my mouth to repeat his name, but a needle stung my shoulder, and more chemicals zipped through my veins. I tried to fight them, tried to stay in my mindscape with Kyrion, but my hand fell away from his chest, and the drugs dragged me back to consciousness . . .

I sucked in a breath. My eyes snapped open, but instead of Kyrion, Harkin was leaning over me, still clutching the injector he had just shoved into my skin.

"What was that?" He cocked his head to the side. "What did you say?"

I bit my tongue to keep from repeating Kyrion's name. The injector must have contained some truly marvelous hallucinogens for me to dream that Kyrion was in my mindscape. That he was talking to me. That he was touching me of his own free will. Or maybe it wasn't the chemicals but the foolish longing in my heart that had conjured up such soft, pleasing images of the Arrow.

"You've lasted much longer than I anticipated," Harkin said. "Usually, one or two rounds of cuts is all it takes for people to start begging to do whatever my father wants, but you've managed to go seven rounds without a peep of concession."

Curiosity and eagerness colored his voice, as though I was an experiment that had produced an unexpected, but delightful result. Harkin blinked at me, activating his eerie green contacts yet again. He was a fucking mad scientist in every sense of the term, and if I could have gotten my hands free, I would have punched my thumbs into his eyes and shoved those recording lenses all the way back into his brain.

I cleared my throat, which was raw and hoarse. "I've always been an overachiever."

He laughed and tossed the spent injector aside. It clattered onto a nearby tray with the others he'd used. "Well, I didn't expect you to last this long, and I'm out of skinbonds. Don't go anywhere, Vesper. I'll be right back."

Harkin gave me an evil grin, then left the lab. Relief rushed through me, and I wanted to weep as the door hissed shut behind him, but I pushed all that fear down, down, down into the bottom of my brain and locked it up tight. Then I glanced around, searching for something that would help me escape. Despite my bravado, I was on the verge of breaking, and I wouldn't make it through another round of cuts.

The lab was full of defibrillators, IV stands, and other big, bulky medical equipment, but I needed something small, sharp, and thin. Something that would cut through the cuffs that secured me to the table. Something like . . . a scalpel.

My gaze dropped to the table by my right elbow. The scalpel Harkin had been using glittered like a bloody needle in the middle of the used injectors. Hope erupted in my heart, along with an equal amount of confusion. Why would he leave that in here? Why not take it with him?

Then I remembered all the documents Nerezza had shown me when she had recapped the wrong story of my life. She, Harkin, and all the other Techwavers thought that I was a low-level seer with limited magic. They didn't know how strong I really was or, more important, about my truebond with Kyrion and the fact that I could sometimes tap into the psion's magic, including his telekinesis, and wield it as though it were my own power.

The last time I had used Kyrion's telekinesis, I had been desperately trying to kill Julieta Delano in the Kent Corp weapons bunker. I hadn't even realized what I was doing back then, and I still wasn't sure how I had managed it, but I needed to do the same thing again right now if I had any chance of escaping.

I stretched my hand toward the table and flexed my fingers wide. Then I reached for the corner of my mind where Kyrion had been, the sticky little cobweb of his presence. I hadn't deliberately reached for that place, for those silky, knotted threads of power, since I had left Corios. I hadn't wanted Kyrion to realize that we were still bonded. I wouldn't have reached for those threads now, but it was my only option.

I carefully searched for that spot, but it was like fumbling for a light switch in a dark room. Kyrion's faint, icy presence had been there back in my mindscape, but now all I sensed was empty nothingness. Had Harkin's drugs finally drowned out the bond? Or had something else disrupted it?

I tried again and again, but I still didn't sense anything. Not Kyrion, not his psion power, not my connection to him.

Nothing.

Hot tears stung my eyes, and I swallowed down a frustrated scream. Leandra was always chiding me to control my breathing while we were sparring instead of sputtering for air like an engine out of fuel, so I focused on filling my lungs with air and then releasing it. Thanks to my O2 enhancement, the simple act of breathing flooded my body with far more oxygen than normal and helped me—settled me—far more quickly than it would do for other people.

When I was calm, I reached for that spot again. At first brush, all I sensed was empty nothingness, but I forced myself to go deeper inside my own mind and stretch out toward Kyrion's at the same time . . .

The softest sliver of silk wisped through my fingers.

Relief rushed through me, and I carefully took hold of that tiny, fragile strand that connected me to Kyrion. I wanted to reach for more strands, to feel even more of him, but I forced myself not to do that. All I needed was a tiny thread of his power, and then I would let the connection go, I would let *him* go—for good.

I tightened my grip on that one thin strand, and power slowly trickled into my body—magic similar to and yet completely different from my own. I wanted to weep as that power, that strength, that energy flooded my body, but once again, I pushed my emotions down.

There was no time for feelings, only time to escape, kill, survive.

Still holding on to that thread of power, I stared at the scalpel and curled my fingers, as though the blade was a skittish Frozon fox that I was beckoning to come closer. Over on the table, the scalpel slowly wriggled around, trying to worm free of the injectors clustered around it. My muscles clenched, and sweat gathered at the nape of my neck, but I kept staring at that scalpel, even as I tightened my grip on Kyrion's power.

Come on! I thought. *Just a few more inches! All I need is a few more blasted inches!*

A second strand of power joined that first one, and the

scalpel flew up off the table and zipped over into my right hand. A grin spread across my face, and I sawed the scalpel into the plasticuff around my wrist.

My arm trembled, my hand shook, and my fingers cramped from the awkward position, but I kept sawing. Harkin could return at any moment, and I needed to be far away from the lab before then.

Snick.

The plasticuff snapped, and I punched my free hand into the air in triumph.

I got a better, more natural grip on the scalpel and used it to cut through the cuff around my left wrist, then the ones around my ankles. The instant I was free, I stepped down off the metal footrest and staggered forward. My legs threatened to buckle, and I clutched the table for support. It skidded back a few inches, making the used injectors rattle around together. I shuddered at the noise and forced myself to stand upright.

The first part of my escape was complete. Now all I had to do was get my stormsword, access a terminal, call for help, and download all the Techwave's deep, dark secrets. Getting kidnapped and tortured might not have been part of my plan, but I wasn't leaving here without finding some way to destroy these sadistic bastards.

Still clutching the bloody scalpel, I staggered over to the door, shoved it open, and left the lab.

I stumbled into the corridor, holding the scalpel out in front of me like a dagger, but no alarms blared. No one was guarding the lab, and even better, no security cameras were mounted to the ceilings so no one could track me.

I kept going, moving from one corridor to the next. Every once in a while, armored footsteps would sound, and I would have to duck back around a corner or slide into an empty room to avoid the roaming guards. Stealth was the key to my survival right now.

Eventually, I ended up back at the weapons lab. I cautiously peeked through the window in the wall, but the concrete bunker was empty. Maybe it was some meal or break time, or maybe the weapons techs were gathered somewhere else, dreaming up new horrors to inflict on other people.

Unlike the other rooms, the lab was locked with a keypad that required a retinal scan, so I couldn't go inside and steal a blaster. I cursed my bad luck and started to move on, but then I stopped and stared through the glass again.

The gooey remains of the woman's body were still shackled to the wall, her wide, sightless eyes staring down at the empty space where her chest had been as if she couldn't believe it wasn't there anymore. I shuddered and hurried on.

I was just about to move into the next corridor when a familiar voice sounded.

". . . surprisingly resistant to all the usual methods so far . . ."

I stopped and peered around the corner. Harkin had removed his green scrubs and contact lenses and was showing a tablet to Nerezza and General Ocnus. Some human guards in spiked black armor were lurking around them.

". . . quite a high tolerance for pain . . ."

Harkin's voice drifted over to me, and I froze, listening to him cheerfully explain how many times he had cut and healed me. With every statistic he spouted, my fingers curled a little tighter around the scalpel, and my rage flared a little bigger, brighter, and hotter.

I blew out a breath and forced myself to loosen my grip. As much as I longed to charge forward and bury the blade in the sadistic scientist's chest, retrieving my stormsword, accessing the Techwave files, and escaping were much more important.

A tablet blared out a high-pitched warning. General Ocnus

pulled a device out of his pocket and swiped through a few screens. "We have company," he growled. "An unauthorized ship has landed nearby."

Harkin frowned. "Does it belong to the Imperium?"

"Unclear," General Ocnus replied. "It doesn't have any of the usual Imperium markings. Some guards are going to check it out right now—"

Staticky crackles erupted from the tablet, along with the distinctive *pew-pew-pew* of blaster fire. "Under attack!" a voice yelled through the device. "We are under attack—"

The voice died off in a garbled scream. General Ocnus cursed, shoved his tablet back into his pocket, and snapped his fingers at a couple of the Techwave guards. "Trigger the evacuation procedures."

The guards saluted him and ran off.

Ocnus looked at Nerezza. "This facility is compromised. Get to your ship and return to Corios as we planned. I'll signal you when the weapons are finished and we are ready to proceed."

Nerezza nodded, spun around, and hurried away. Disgust rolled through me. If there was one thing she excelled at above all others, it was walking away.

General Ocnus looked at his son. "Return to the lab and secure Vesper Quill. She's coming with me."

Harkin's eyebrows shot up in surprise. "You want to take her to the primary facility?"

Orion nodded. "Yes. Her design skills are far too valuable to waste by putting a blaster bolt through her head. Get her, and meet me on the roof. As soon as we're clear, activate the self-destruction sequence. I'm going to the launchpad right now."

"What about the information on the servers?" Harkin asked.

Ocnus shrugged. "It will be destroyed in the explosion, along with everything else."

The general hurried away, flanked by a couple of guards.

Harkin muttered a soft curse, then jerked his head at the remaining guards. "You three. With me."

He spun around and went in a different direction from Nerezza and General Ocnus.

I bit my lip, considering my options. I could slip out of the facility before it exploded and risk running into potential enemies outside. Or I could stay in here a little while longer, get my stormsword, try to access the information I wanted, and then slip out of the facility before it exploded.

Neither option was ideal, but it would take General Ocnus at least a few minutes to evacuate. It was worth the risk to find out more about what he was plotting to do with my designs.

Since General Ocnus was heading toward the roof, he wouldn't be returning to his office. I called up my mental map of the facility. Then I set off down the corridor, moving in the opposite direction from Nerezza, Ocnus, Harkin, and the Techwave guards.

To my surprise, no lights flashed, no alarms blared, and the corridors remained quiet and empty. Unless I was mistaken, General Ocnus's evacuation procedures only involved himself and whatever other higher-ups might be on-site, and he wasn't going to alert the weapons lab techs and other workers. Disgust surged through me. People were as disposable to him as his Black Scarab machines were.

I quickly moved from one corridor to the next, but I didn't encounter anyone, and I didn't hear any blaster fire or other signs of a battle. Whatever was happening, whoever was here, they were still outside the facility. Maybe it was a group of Imperium soldiers. Maybe Zane Zimmer and some other Arrows were with them.

Maybe Kyrion was here.

Maybe he really had been in my mindscape.

Maybe he had come to help me.

No. I derailed that runaway transport of thought. I'd had a drug-induced hallucination of Kyrion, nothing more. Even if he realized that we were still bonded, he wouldn't come here. Not for me.

Nobody ever came back for me.

As loath as I was to admit it, Nerezza was right about one thing. I was on my own. I had *always* been on my own, ever since the day she had abandoned me. A bone-deep weariness crashed over me, but I kept trudging forward, the way I always did.

I reached the corridor that led to General Ocnus's office. Two guards were posted outside the door as though everything was normal. More disgust surged through me. Ocnus didn't even have the decency to tell his own guards about the evacuation, and they would probably stand here until the building exploded around them. Still, they were standing between me and my stormsword, along with Ocnus's terminal, and I had no choice but to go through them.

I held the scalpel down by my side, hiding it from sight, and shuffled forward as though I was more injured than I was. It wasn't hard to do. The drugs from the last injector Harkin had given me were wearing off. The skinbonds had closed most of my shallow injuries, but I was still leaving drips, drops, and smears of blood behind from the deeper wounds.

One of the guards spotted me, and they both whirled in my direction. Unlike the plated, spiked armor that most of the other Techwave guards wore, these two were clad in tactical fabric uniforms, along with black helmets with clear visors. I gritted my teeth. This would have been so much easier if they were Black Scarabs, faceless machines, but they were still my enemies.

The first guard aimed his blaster at my chest. The second man also raised his weapon. I held up my left hand in mock surrender.

"Help me," I rasped. "Please, please help me."

I kept repeating those words as I shuffled toward the guards. They eyed me with suspicion, but they didn't start firing. Both men were wearing the same bright green contact lenses that Harkin had worn in the medlab, and their eyes resembled the compound insect orbs in the mechanized suits of Black Scarab armor. The eerie effect made the guards seem like something more—or maybe less—than human. I couldn't quite decide which one, but the sight still made me shudder with revulsion.

"Stop right there!" the first guard called out.

"*Please*," I put an extra bit of helpless pleading into my tone. "Please, help me . . ."

I let my voice trail off, then staggered into the first guard. He cursed, but he lowered his blaster and instinctively lifted his other arm to catch me. I dug my left hand into the top of his jacket, yanking the tactical fabric down as far as I could. Then I snapped up my right hand and buried the scalpel in his throat.

Blood spurted over me like a hot, sticky fountain. The guard gurgled, stumbled back against the wall, and slid down to the floor, the scalpel still stuck in his throat. I wrested the blaster out of his hand and spun around.

The other guard yelled and aimed his own weapon, but I was still standing next to his buddy, and he hesitated for one precious second.

Pew! Pew! Pew!

I put three blaster bolts into his chest. They cut right through his uniform, and he too gurgled and slid down to the floor.

More weariness crashed over me, but I straightened up and looked left, then right. No footsteps pounded in this direction, and the corridor remained deserted, so I fired the blaster at the keypad on the wall. The energy bolt fried the electronics, and the door let out a loud, startled chirp and popped open.

I hurried through to the other side, sweeping the blaster back and forth. The office was empty, so I went over to the terminal General Ocnus had been typing on earlier. I set the blaster down on the desk, then peeled the skin-colored glove off my left hand and stuffed it into my pocket. Next, I pried a blue plastic eye jewel off my left thumbnail, revealing a small microdot drive hidden underneath. I'd used a similar jewel and hidden drive to smuggle the *Velorum* crash files out of Kent Corp, and I'd thought the items might come in handy on the off chance I ever needed to download sensitive information again.

I placed the drive on the appropriate terminal slot, then tapped a few keys. The drive's software started downloading the general's files, although they were all heavily encrypted. I grumbled at the delay, but right now, the important thing was getting the information. I could find someone to decrypt it later.

While I waited for the files to download, I plucked my stormsword out of the trash can General Ocnus had dropped it into earlier. The second my fingers closed around the silver hilt, I felt better, stronger, and more in control, and the lunarium blade began glowing with a pale blue light.

Next, I prowled around the office, searching for more information. Other than the military history books lining the shelves, the rest of the room was empty. No tablets, no servers, not so much as a stray piece of plastipaper in the recycler. No wonder General Ocnus wasn't worried about leaving information behind. His office was like a skeleton, all bones and no meat. The chrome furnishings gave the entire place a dull, drab look, and the only thing with even a hint of personality was the map of Tropics planets that was hanging on the wall near Orion's desk.

My eyes narrowed. Now, *that* might be something.

Curious, I went over and stared at the map. The bright colors and cutesy graphics made it look like something on a travel site, but someone—probably General Ocnus—had marked it with gelpens. Black *X*s covered several planets, as though they had been scratched off a list, while green question marks adorned others. But only one planet was circled in red: Tropics 33.

Why would General Ocnus mark that planet? It wasn't even the largest Tropics planet, and its main industry was tourism. No metal refineries, no production plants, no chemical factories, just resorts, beaches, and rain-forest tours. So why was it highlighted in a different color? What was so special about Tropics 33?

I stared at the map, memorizing every single detail so that I could recall it later with my seer magic. The terminal chimed, indicating that the download was complete. I grabbed the microdot drive and dropped it into a zippered pocket on my cargo pants—

Snick.

A soft sound rang in my ears, almost like a key turning in a lock, and an electrical awareness rippled through my body that hadn't been there before. I whirled around, thinking someone had crept into the office, but the area was empty. I exhaled, but strangely enough, the awareness remained, as though a shadow was looming over my shoulder. Weird.

I shrugged the odd sensation aside, turned away from the door, and focused on the general's desk again, wondering if I had missed anything.

"I knew you would come back for your stormsword," a snide voice drawled behind me. "Psions like you always do. You're as dependent on those archaic weapons as a baby with a bottle."

Once again, I whirled around and whipped up my sword.

Harkin was standing in the office, cradling a silver hand cannon—the same sort of hand cannon that had killed the woman in the weapons bunker. He hefted the weapon a little higher. "You saw what your cannon did to that other psion in the lab. Let's see what it does to you, Vesper."

He grinned, aimed the weapon at me, and pulled the trigger.

ELEVEN

KYRION

After leaving the Crownpoint throne room, I went directly to the private spaceport where my blitzer was housed. Daichi was waiting for me there. I gave him the handkerchief with Holloway's DNA and told him about my latest Arrow mission and Holloway's orders to find, question, and kill Vesper.

Daichi frowned. "Why would Holloway want you to kill someone he just appointed as a Regal lady? Vesper is still all over the gossipcasts. Her death will raise a lot of questions."

I started pacing back and forth. "I don't know. Holloway mainly uses Adria and Dargan Byrne to hunt down people who anger him, not to raid Techwave bases. Holloway is playing some game, which means that I need to find Vesper before the other Arrows finish their mission and catch up with me."

"And what will you do once you find her?" Daichi asked in a soft voice.

I jerked to a stop. My body tensed, and my hands clenched into fists. I had been asking myself that same question ever since I had gone to Vesper's mindscape and realized that she had been kidnapped. Right now, all I wanted to do was kill Harkin Ocnus and every other person who had dared to hurt Vesper. After that happened, well, I didn't know what I would do—or how to deal with the fact that she had been lying to me for months.

"I have to bloody find her first," I growled.

Daichi's eyebrows lifted at my harsh tone, but he nodded. "I'll keep digging and see if I can find out exactly why Holloway is sending you after Vesper. I'll also contact Tivona Winslow in case she has any new information."

"Were you able to take care of the other thing I asked about?"

Daichi hit some buttons on his tablet. An answering chirp erupted from my own device. "Touma was able to set it up. You can see and control everything from your own tablet." He hesitated. "Are you sure you want to do this, Kyrion? If Holloway finds out, he'll know that you have some . . . regard for Vesper. He'll use that against you."

Yes, he would. Holloway was always pulling all the levers at his disposal to keep me as close as possible.

Icy rage surged through me at the thought of Holloway using Vesper the same way, but I gave my friend a nonchalant shrug. "I'll think of some excuse for Holloway. I always do."

Daichi and I made a few more plans and contingencies, and then he left the spaceport to return to Castle Caldaren while I boarded the blitzer.

This fighter ship was an older model produced by House Zimmer that was shaped like an old-fashioned wooden arrow. I strode up the ramp and stepped into the cargo bay, which spread out like a tuft of feathers at the very back of the blitzer before narrowing and flowing into a long, shaft-like corridor with various rooms branching off it. Instead of heading to the flight deck, which formed the front tip of the ship, I stopped and stared at a blue button on the wall.

Vesper and I had used this same ship to escape from the lava field battle with the Techwavers on Magma 7. Back then, I'd thought Vesper had been an enemy plant sent by Holloway to force me into a truebond, and she had used that blue button—and the permaglass barrier it controlled—to trap me in the cargo bay when I had threatened her. Suddenly, I could see her standing on the other side of the barrier, demanding to know why I had menaced her.

I shook my head. The phantom image vanished, but fresh anger erupted in my chest. Why had Vesper hidden the bond from me? Didn't she realize how much danger she had put herself in?

Let me guess. She finally realized what a broody bastard you are and decided to get as far away from you as fast as possible. Zane's mocking voice whispered through my mind.

As much as I hated to admit it, perhaps Zane was right. Perhaps Vesper had realized how villainous I truly was. Perhaps she had been desperate to escape from me. My anger vanished, and sharp spears of worry stabbed deep into my chest, skewering my inner monster.

I shoved the unwanted feelings aside. Emotions were as useless as speculation. Right now, I needed to find Vesper before the Techwave eliminated her. No matter what she thought of me, I didn't want memories to be all that I had left of her.

I marched to the front of the ship, dropped into the pilot's chair, and started the thrusters. I also pulled out my tablet, accessed the new program Touma had created, and sent it several sets of instructions. A minute later, the blitzer took off from the spaceport.

As soon as I cleared the Corios atmosphere, I entered the coordinates for Magma 3 and engaged the blitzer's pinpoint drive. Pinpoint drives poked wormholes in space, like sticking a pin through a piece of fabric to create a tiny opening, and let people cross the galaxy in days, sometimes even hours, depending on which planets they were traveling to and from. Magma 3 was relatively close to Corios, so it wouldn't take me long to get there.

While I waited for the Magma planet to come into view, I reviewed all the information Tivona Winslow had sent Daichi about Vesper's kidnapping. Only a few cameras had captured the abduction, and the footage was roughly the same as what Holloway had shown in the Crownpoint throne room. Once the Techwavers had left the Quill Corp campus, there had been no trace of them, which made me even more curious about how Holloway knew they were on Magma 3. The Techies were usually much better at covering their tracks, but this time, Holloway's spies had found them in a matter of hours.

"Approaching destination," a mechanized female voice chirped out. "Please be advised of active, ongoing volcanic activity in your selected location."

I groaned and peered through the flight deck windows. The surface of Magma 3 came into view, looking like every other Magma planet—dark gray clouds, black mountainous volcanos spitting out thick plumes of smoke, surrounding slopes and fields covered with jagged black rocks half-buried in a thick layer of snowy ash. I eyed the volcanos, but no streams of lava oozed down their sides like ribbons of molten red glass. A small mercy, although the Techwavers would happily bomb the volcanos and trigger the lava to cover their escape and try to kill me, just as Julieta Delano had done on Magma 7.

Despite the current lack of lava, the last thing I wanted was to set foot on another bloody Magma planet, but I would do it to rescue Vesper. Bond or not, I was starting to think there was nothing I wouldn't do for her, which worried me far more than I cared to admit.

While the surface grew closer, I reviewed all the information Daichi had been able to dig up, along with some reports from Holloway's spies. A couple of weeks ago, the Techwave had quietly taken over an abandoned Regal production plant and made it operational again. I swiped through a few photos. From the outside, the facility looked run-down, but inside, it would probably be teeming with Black Scarabs, along with human guards with speed, strength, and other physical enhancements.

A loud, clanging chime sounded, and the landing gear engaged. I'd picked an out-of-the-way spot half a mile away from the facility, close enough to set the blitzer down without drawing too much immediate attention. The ship's scanners swept the surrounding area, but there was no movement, other than the smoke and ash drifting through the sky. I armed the blitzer's defensive systems and shields, then left it behind.

The second I stepped outside, the planet's intense heat blasted over me, sucking the moisture out of my body, and a sulfuric stench invaded my nose.

"Bloody Magma planet," I muttered.

I moved from one pile of rocks to another, using them for cover as I quickly made my way toward the facility, which sprawled across a flat field in the shadow of a nearby volcano. Bits of ash rained down like gray snowflakes, coating the facility's walls, while exterior pipes spewed out steam that flooded the air with another layer of suffocating heat.

I was still a hundred feet away from the facility when a series of loud, metallic *clanks* rang out, and two Techwave guards rounded a corner of a building and headed in my direction. I crouched down behind a spindly tree that had managed to grow out of an outcropping of rocks. I had no idea if the guards were on a regular patrol or if they'd spotted my blitzer on a scan and were coming to check it out.

Either way, they were dead men walking.

I peered around the side of the tree. Instead of Black Scarab armor, these guards were clad in tactical uniforms similar to my own, although their boots were polymetal, hence all the clanking. Good. The lack of armor would make them much easier to kill. They were both carrying hand cannons, which was no surprise, although the weapons were sleeker, smaller, and more compact than other Techwave cannons.

I slid my blaster out of its thigh holster and waited for the guards to march closer. They weren't even trying to be quiet, and their armored boots kept clanking across the loose rocks. Their voices also drifted over to me.

". . . don't see why *we* have to check out the ship . . ."

". . . why not send a squad of Black Scarabs . . ."

". . . what kind of idiot lands on a Magma planet . . ."

The guards moved past me and headed up the rise so they could get a look at my ship parked in the shallow valley below. I got to my feet, moved out from behind the tree, and aimed my blaster at the guard on the left—

Crunch.

One of my boots had cracked through a brittle rock, and the guards whirled around.

Pew! Pew! Pew!

I shot the first man with my blaster, and he toppled to the ground.

The second man raised his cannon to fire at me. "Under attack!" he yelled. "We are under attack—"

Pew! Pew! Pew!

I shot him as well, and he too toppled to the ground.

I spun around, scanning the landscape, but no more guards appeared. I didn't know if the second man had managed to warn his friends inside the facility, but it wouldn't be long before more guards came looking for these two. Once their bodies were discovered, whoever was in charge would probably decide it would be better to be somewhere else, and they might take Vesper with them.

I needed to stop that from happening, so I exchanged my

blaster for my stormsword and hurried toward the facility—
and Vesper.

It only took me a few seconds to sprint the last hundred feet
and plaster my back up against one of the outer walls. Despite
my killing the two guards, the facility remained oddly quiet,
and the only sound was the steady hiss of steam escaping from
enormous pipes high above. The lack of noise worried me even
more than if alarms had been blaring.

This side of the facility featured a series of buildings, along
with a loading dock. All the doors were closed, except for
the one on the loading dock, which was standing wide open.
I ignored that area. Such an easy, obvious access point most
likely led into a room filled with guards waiting to blast me
into oblivion.

One of the perimeter buildings connected to an even larger
structure deeper in the facility, so I climbed a set of exterior
metal stairs to the second level and sliced my sword through
a keypad. A door buzzed open, but no alarms sounded, so I
cautiously stepped through to the other side.

A metal catwalk stretched out in front of me, and I crept
along it, my steps soft and silent. Rickety scaffolding and
steaming pipes zigzagged through this level, but the area
below was wide open. Machines and robotic arms filled the
factory floor, although they were all quiet and dormant, as
though they were slumbering giants waiting to be woken up
so they could return to work. Conveyor belts also crisscrossed
the factory floor, revealing long lines of half-assembled Black
Scarab armor. A faint green sheen gleamed on the arms, legs,
and torsos, as though they had been dipped in some iridescent coating. Curious. I had never seen that kind of luster on
Techwave armor before.

The catwalk split left and right, and I stopped, not sure which way to go. In the distance, the faint murmur of voices sounded, along with the echoes of quick footsteps, although I couldn't tell how many guards were in the facility or exactly where they were. I also couldn't tell where Vesper was. Not like this, anyway.

But there was another way I could find her—through our truebond.

Touma had said that ours was a strong bond—a galactic bond—but it seemed to vary wildly, and I had no idea what, if any, limits it might have. Back on Corios, I'd felt the physical effects and psionic echoes of Vesper's pain, although I hadn't had a clue to where she was. But now that I was on the same planet, in the same area, perhaps the bond would let me home in on her exact location. My only other option was to search the entire facility, which would take hours. I needed to find Vesper right now, before something worse happened to her.

I needed to use the bond.

Before I had met Vesper, the mere idea would have filled me with revulsion, but now it seemed like a much-needed lifeline. So I closed my eyes and reached for the space in my mind where the truebond had been. For the last few months, I'd thought that space had been cold, hollow, and empty, like the rest of me, but now that I was examining it more closely, I could sense the thinnest of ribbons curled up into a tight little spiral, as if Vesper had made her presence as small as possible to further hide the bond from me. I gently took hold of the end of that velvety ribbon, then slowly, carefully uncurled the spiral . . .

With a soft *thwang*, almost like an arrow releasing from an old-fashioned bow, the ribbon straightened out of its own accord, and my connection to Vesper roared back to life, like a blue moon rising and flooding my mind with its pale, beautiful light.

She was over . . . *there.*

My eyes snapped open, and I headed in that direction.

I hurried along the catwalk, moving from one section to another, and getting closer and closer to Vesper. Even though I was deep in the facility, no guards appeared, and I didn't encounter any resistance or countermeasures as I crept down a set of stairs to the factory floor. The lack of activity made me even more wary. Was this a trap? If so, for whom? Me? Vesper? Someone else?

Footsteps sounded, moving in my direction. I stopped and slid behind a piece of machinery. On the conveyor belt, the armored head of a Black Scarab peered at me with its oversize green eyes. I tensed, ready to skewer the bloody bug with my sword, but the head wasn't attached to a body, and it remained still and inanimate.

". . . make sure our plans are not compromised . . ."

I eased forward and peered around the side of the machinery. In the distance, a man wearing a black military-style jacket was talking to a couple of guards. Short dark brown hair, black eyes, ruddy skin, stern features. General Orion Ocnus, the supposed leader of the Techwave. Ocnus was cut from the same cruel cloth as Callus Holloway, and each man thought the galaxy should bow down to him.

". . . a squad going there to make sure everything proceeds as planned . . ."

Ocnus kept talking, and the guards nodded in response. My hand clenched around my sword. A couple of rows of machinery stood between us, but General Ocnus was less than a hundred feet away, and I could probably kill his guards and capture him before he sounded an alarm. I could force Ocnus to take me to Vesper, and then I could kill the general and end the threat he represented to her, along with the Imperium—

BOOM!

Green cannon fire erupted, and a window on the level above my head shattered with a thunderous roar. A shadowy figure grabbed hold of the windowsill and leaped through the jagged opening. The figure dropped more than ten feet to the factory floor below, and the jolt of their landing spiked through my legs as if I had done that abbreviated swan dive right along with them.

The figure stumbled forward several feet, then whirled around, revealing their face, although I already knew exactly who it was.

Vesper.

My hungry gaze swept over her from head to toe. Her dark brown hair was wild and tangled, and her face was much paler than usual. Her clothes had been cut to shreds, and blood stained the dark blue fabric in a dozen different places. Despite the distance between us, my telempathy let me sense the pain and exhaustion cascading off her.

Another figure leaped through the shattered window and dropped to the factory floor. A loud, distinctive *clank* rang out, and the man easily stood up, his balance perfect, since his reinforced armored boots had absorbed the jarring impact. Blond hair, black eyes, tan skin, smug smirk. Harkin Ocnus. The man who had been torturing Vesper in her mindscape.

"Going somewhere?" Harkin called out in a mocking voice, hefting the cannon in his hands.

Vesper spun around and snapped up her stormsword like it was a shield that would protect her from Harkin and his weapon.

More footsteps rang out. I glanced back over my shoulder. Ocnus and his guards had also spotted Vesper and Harkin. The general was swiftly moving in the opposite direction, although he was still close enough that I could catch him.

Now I had a choice to make: kill Ocnus and the threat the Techwave posed to the Regals and everyone else in the galaxy or save Vesper.

No choice at all.

I spun away from Ocnus and started running around the machinery that separated me from Vesper.

TWELVE

VESPER

I scrambled away from Harkin, making more pins and needles explode in my body. I'd landed awkwardly when I'd leaped out of the shattered window to escape the office, and I'd badly twisted my left ankle. The broken permaglass had also sliced into my left forearm, and blood dripped down my fingers and spattered onto the concrete floor.

Harkin tilted his head to the side, studying me as though I was still a specimen in his lab. "I'm surprised you're still on your feet, Vesper. And that you made it out of the lab and all the way across the facility. Most people would have either given up or passed out by now. What's your secret?"

"Just my burning desire to kill you," I growled.

Harkin nodded. "Rage and hate are powerful motivators." He lifted the cannon in his arms. "But unfortunately for you, I have the superior weapon. Surrender now, and I won't blow your leg off. I just need your brain intact. The rest of you is expendable."

I tightened my grip on my sword, and the blue glow on the

lunarium blade flared a little brighter and hotter. "I'd rather be dead than go back to your lab."

Harkin shrugged. "Suit yourself."

He pulled the trigger. Another blast of green cannon fire shot out, and I threw myself down and to the right. I hit the floor, and pain spiked through my shoulder, although not as much as I expected. The throbbing in my twisted ankle must be drowning out everything else. Terrific.

I gritted my teeth and staggered back up and onto my feet. Harkin strode toward me, the green glow on the end of the cannon intensifying as the weapon revved up for another blast.

"You know what, Vesper?" he called out. "I didn't get the chance to tell you what's wrong with your design, from one inventor to another. Isn't the curiosity killing you?"

It was, actually, and I couldn't help but ask the obvious question. "What's that?"

"For one thing, your cannon takes too long to recharge." Harkin stopped and gave me another evil grin. "But I'm in the process of fixing that."

He pulled the trigger. Another blast of cannon fire erupted, although it wasn't quite as strong as the previous ones. Still, it was powerful enough to scorch the machinery I'd ducked behind, and the acrid stench of hot metal filled the air.

"But with what we have planned, the lack of quick, consistent sizzle won't really matter," Harkin continued. "In the end, overwhelming numbers always beat raw force. My father taught me that."

How many hand cannons were the Techwave planning to make? And what did they intend to do with the weapons?

Boom!

Harkin fired the cannon again, and another blast slammed into the machinery in front of me. Parts and pieces flew everywhere, and bits of metal *ping-ping-pinged* across the floor.

Boom! Boom! Boom!

Harkin fired the cannon again and again, obliterating the machinery one chunk at a time. I staggered to the side, trying to duck behind a conveyer belt, but my boots slipped on some loose screws rolling across the floor. My feet flew out from under me, and I hit the concrete hard, pain spiking through my ass before spreading out into my back and legs. The blow also knocked the air out of my lungs, and it would have completely stunned me if not for my O2 enhancement.

Footsteps clanked, and I looked up. Harkin was rapidly advancing in this direction, his cannon glowing with sinister green energy once again.

Despite my many aches and pains, I scrambled back up onto my feet. I could barely stand on my twisted ankle, much less run away, and I was tired of Harkin hunting me like a deer through a metal forest, so I held my position.

Harkin stopped about twenty feet away. Behind him, more clanking footsteps sounded, and several Black Scarabs appeared, their eyes glowing like green fireflies trapped in black metal jars.

Harkin jerked his head, and the Black Scarabs spread out, forming a semicircle around him. I glanced back over my shoulder, but I was pinned up against a wall, and there was nowhere to run. I gritted my teeth and snapped up my stormsword. I was so weak from the cuts and blood loss that the lunarium blade wasn't glowing anymore. It wouldn't protect me from another cannon blast, and I barely had the strength to hold it upright.

Harkin was going to blow my leg off like he'd promised. Then the Black Scarabs would haul me off to another horrific Techwave lab to be tortured yet again until I finally broke and did whatever General Ocnus wanted.

Fear punched into my stomach, and bitter bile rose in my throat, but I choked it down. I'd meant what I'd said before. I would rather be dead than let Harkin get his hands on me again.

The thought of my own death didn't fill me with dread, though, just red-hot anger that Harkin had gotten the better of me for a second time. That Nerezza had escaped. That General Ocnus was probably already on his way to another planet to keep plotting against the Imperium.

But most of all, I was angry at myself for not telling Kyrion that we were still bonded. It had been stupid and selfish on my part, and now I just had to hope that my death wouldn't affect him. But maybe it was better this way. Maybe since he thought we weren't bonded, he wouldn't feel any psionic echoes of my death. Maybe he wouldn't feel a thing, although that thought angered me for other reasons.

Harkin swung his cannon back and forth. "Which leg should I take off, Vesper? Right or left? Ah, I suppose it doesn't really matter."

He focused on my left leg and pulled the trigger.

Boom!

I tensed. My seer magic surged up, and for a moment, everything slowed down just as it had when I'd been watching the woman in the weapons lab earlier. The green energy erupting out of the cannon. The sneer twisting Harkin's lips. The sick satisfaction rolling off him in palpable waves. In an instant, all those sights and sensations were burned into my brain, and I wondered if this would be the last thing I ever saw.

Then, in the next instant, everything snapped back to its normal speed. The cannon fire streaked toward me, and I tensed again, ready to throw myself to the side to avoid the blast—

Someone stepped up beside me, their body engulfing mine in a tall, familiar shadow. A dark blue blur sliced through the air, and the cannon fire hit a lunarium blade and bounced away, slamming into one of the conveyor belts instead of my body. Something exploded, and fire erupted in that part of the factory, but I only had eyes for the man beside me.

"Kyr," I whispered.

He stiffened, although there was no way he could have possibly heard me over the roaring explosion. He turned his head, and our gazes locked. His voice didn't sound in my mind, and I didn't whisper any words to him, but an ocean of sensations flowed between us. My surprise, his determination, my relief, his anger.

Harkin pulled the cannon's trigger again, but something in the weapon shrieked in protest, like a brewmaker boiling over and shooting hot water everywhere. Harkin growled and pulled the trigger again. Another blast of energy erupted out of the cannon. It was much weaker than the previous attacks, but the bolt still streaked through the air, heading straight toward Kyrion.

"Kyr!" I screamed.

I lunged forward and thrust my left arm out, as if I could stop the blast from slamming into his chest with my bare hand. Energy sizzled up against my skin, scorching it, even though the bolt wasn't even close to me. I screamed and flung my hand aside. I wasn't sure what happened, but the bolt veered off course the tiniest bit, giving Kyrion enough time to slap the energy away with his stormsword.

Harkin pulled the trigger yet again, but only a few weak green sparks sputtered out of the cannon. Even more telling, acrid smoke was wafting out of the weapon, a clear sign of fried circuitry. What had he done to my design to make it malfunction so badly?

Harkin growled again and tossed the broken weapon aside. "Kill them!" he screamed. "Kill them both!"

He backpedaled, and the Black Scarabs surged forward. Kyrion stepped up to meet them, whipping his sword back and forth in quick, furious motions. Every time he hit an enemy, dark blue fire zinged off his stormsword, along with shards of ice and sharp crackles of wind. The lunarium blade was amplifying Kyrion's own psionic abilities and transforming that energy into physical elements that were further damaging the Black Scarabs, along with his actual blade strikes.

His wrath was beautiful to watch.

One after another, Kyrion sliced his way through the Scarabs, and they toppled to the floor like black dominoes he was casually knocking aside in a game.

The last of the Scarabs dropped. Kyrion whirled around, his sword up and ready, but Harkin had vanished. Once he was sure there were no more enemies to kill, Kyrion turned toward me. His face was as hard as the icy shards still shooting off his sword, and the sticky cobweb of him in my mind vibrated with cold fury, although I wasn't sure if it was directed at Harkin, the dead Black Scarabs, me, or all of us.

"Can you walk?" he growled.

"Yes," I lied, even as my ankle throbbed in protest.

Kyrion's gaze skated over my body, flicking from one cut and injury to another. Some of the ice in his eyes thawed, although even more fury vibrated off him. A muscle ticked in his jaw, and he jerked his head to the side. "Let's go. Before more Scarabs show up."

He spun around, then strode forward, stepping over the bodies of the machines he had just destroyed. I let out a tense breath, shoved my stormsword onto my belt, scooped up Harkin's broken cannon from the floor, and followed him.

Kyrion led the way, cutting down one Black Scarab after another. Arms, legs, even heads sailed through the air and clanged off the surrounding machines and conveyor belts in an odd, harsh symphony of death. I hobbled along behind him, watching his back and using the broken hand cannon to bludgeon any human guards that rushed up behind us.

We reached a door that led outside. Guards were pouring

out of the facility, but instead of running over to attack us, they were heading in the opposite direction.

"What are they doing?" Kyrion muttered. "They should be converging on our position."

"General Ocnus is going to destroy the facility. The guards must have finally realized that they need to get out or risk getting blown up."

"How long do we have?"

"No idea. Probably not more than a few minutes."

Kyrion glanced up at the factory, then at the surrounding volcanos in the distance. "If the plant goes, the volcanos will probably blow as well. Bloody Magma planet." He held out his hand. "Give me the cannon."

I did as he asked, and he secured the weapon to his bandolier, then spun the whole thing around so that the cannon was strapped to his back. Kyrion plucked the blaster from his thigh holster and shoved it at me.

"Here," he growled. "Shoot anything that tries to stop me."

I nodded. "What are you going to do?"

Instead of answering, he moved forward, bent down, and scooped me up into his arms.

"Hey!" I protested. "What are you doing?"

He gave me a cold look. "Your ankle is severely twisted, and you're slowing us down. I can bloody *feel* your pain through the bond, like hundreds of tiny swords stabbing into my psionic shield with every step you take. It's annoying and distracting, and I'm not going to be blown to bits or incinerated by lava just because you stubbornly keep trying to walk."

Arrogant Arrow. I glared at him, but he gave me another cold look.

"Fine," I muttered, and flapped my hand. "Carry me to safety, oh great and mighty Arrow."

Kyrion rolled his eyes at my sarcasm, but he hefted me up so that I fit a little more snugly against his chest.

His firm, solid, deliciously warm chest.

I hadn't realized the chill that had crept into my bones until this moment. I wanted to sigh at the warmth and strength of him surrounding me, but I clamped my lips shut. He was doing this out of necessity, not choice.

"Here we go," Kyrion said, his voice lower and rougher than before.

I looked up at him, and he stared right back down at me, his eyes dark and unreadable. I lifted my blaster, ready to defend us both. He nodded and drew in a deep breath.

Then he started running.

THIRTEEN

VESPER

Kyrion set off at a swift jog. He showed no visible strain from carrying me, and I could have been as light as a piece of plastipaper for all the effort he seemed to expend.

I got the sense he was trying to be as gentle as possible, given the circumstances, but every one of his quick, pounding footsteps sent a fresh wave of pain spiking through my body. If Kyrion could feel my misery through the bond, he wasn't showing any signs of it. He kept his gaze fixed straight ahead, while I glanced around, keeping an eye out for any enemies—

BOOM!

BOOM! BOOM!

BOOM!

I jerked around in Kyrion's arms, causing even more pain to spike through my many cuts and bruises and my twisted ankle. Sweat popped out on my forehead, and I ground my teeth to hold back a scream.

Behind us, one explosion after another ripped through the

Techwave facility, and plumes of orange fire and black smoke shot up into the air like phoenixes taking flight. Screams and shouts sounded, and even more people started pouring out of the buildings. The weapons techs and other workers had finally realized that something was wrong, and they were scrambling to get to safety.

Several guards also ran out of the facility. Some of them caught sight of Kyrion and me and gave chase. I propped my arm on Kyrion's shoulder and took aim with his blaster.

Pew! Pew! Pew!

One after another, I shot the Techwave guards. My aim wasn't great, given all the running and jarring on Kyrion's part, but I took down everyone who approached us. Eventually, the last of the guards dropped.

"We're clear!" I yelled.

"Good!" Kyrion replied. "Hold on!"

Somehow he increased his speed. I dug my hand into his jacket while he sprinted up a rise. In the distance, a blitzer was half hidden behind some small trees and bushes that looked more like brittle gray glass than actual vegetation.

Kyrion approached the blitzer's cargo bay, and the image of a green button popped into my mind. Telekinetic power rolled off him, and I felt him punch that button, even though it was somewhere inside the ship and out of his line of sight. Neat trick. I'd have to get him to show me how to do that.

Assuming he wasn't here to kill me himself.

The cargo bay ramp descended. Kyrion slowed his pace and climbed up it.

"Put me down," I protested. "I can walk onto the blasted ship by myself."

Kyrion ignored me, went to the front of the cargo bay, and set me down on the medtable. Then he stabbed his finger at me. "Lie down and get healed. I'll get us out of here."

Before I could protest, he slapped a green button on the

wall, and the cargo bay ramp zipped up. Kyrion glared at me again, then strode past me, down a long corridor, and into the flight deck at the front of the ship. He slid into the pilot's chair and started hitting buttons and pulling levers. The thrusters engaged, and the blitzer lifted off the ground.

Still sitting on the medtable, I glanced out through the windows in the cargo bay. Down below, fire was quickly spreading through the Techwave facility, and more of it was already burning than not. More explosions ripped through the sky, and the ship swung back and forth on the bumpy air currents. Kyrion cursed and hit a few more buttons, and the ride smoothed out.

I wanted to leap off the medtable, march up to the flight deck, and drop into the copilot's chair, but I couldn't summon up the energy to move, and the thought of putting weight on my twisted ankle again made me nauseated. Blood was still oozing out of my wounds, including my cut forearm. As much as it annoyed me, I did as Kyrion said, hit a button on the side of the medtable, and lay down on the smooth surface.

"Greetings," a mechanized female voice chirped in a tone that was entirely too cheerful. "Diagnostic scan to begin in five seconds. Five, four, three, two, one . . ."

A cool blue light flared, and a panel slid out of the side of the table and arched up. I tensed, but the panel smoothly arced down and fastened itself to the opposite side of the table, forming a hyperbaric chamber. A hiss sounded, and pure oxygen flooded the tube. Even with my O2 enhancement, the Magma planet's smoke and haze had still seeped into my lungs. I breathed in deeply, letting the tube's oxygen stabilize the levels in my own body. Within seconds, my lungs felt much cleaner, although the dry, chalky taste of sulfuric ash still coated my mouth.

The mechanized female voice started listing all the things that were wrong with me. It was quite a long list, and Harkin had cut me in far more places and far more times than I'd realized. The voice chirped out another cheerful warning, then robotic needles poked into my body. Some of the needles administered skinbonds, along with antibiotics and other medicines, but most of them started suturing my wounds. Despite the anesthetics to numb the pain, I still snarled as my skin was yanked this way and that and the needles stitched everything back together the way it was supposed to be. The drugs quickly took effect. Even more weariness crashed over me, and my eyes slowly drifted shut . . .

Sometime later, my eyes fluttered open. I was still lying in the hyperbaric chamber, and Kyrion was looking down through the clear plastic at me, an unreadable expression on his face. I lifted my right hand and pushed on the side of the hyperbaric chamber, but the flexible polyplastic wouldn't move.

"Turn this stupid table off, and let me out of here," I grumbled.

Kyrion leaned down a little closer. "Do you not *like* being trapped in a small space?" he drawled in a sardonic voice. "Imagine that. Or is it simply not as much fun when you're not doing it to me?"

I glared up at him and dug my fingers into the plastic, trying to rip my way free, but it remained stubbornly in place and intact.

Kyrion arched an eyebrow. "Nothing to say?"

"Let me out of here," I grumbled again. "Before I claw my way out."

He poked his index finger into the polyplastic. "Even I couldn't tear through this with my bare hands. It's much too strong for that. This chamber is airtight and has its own oxygen supply. You could suck the oxygen out of the rest of the ship, and you could still survive in there."

I tried to sit up, but he was right. The polyplastic wouldn't move a single inch. I snarled with frustration.

A sly smile spread across Kyrion's face. "It's quite amusing watching you flounder around in there."

"You'd better hope I don't figure a way out of here," I warned.

He arched an eyebrow again. "Or you'll do what? Kill me? When you're as weak as a butterfly trying to emerge from a cocoon? I don't think so."

I kept glaring at him. After a few seconds, he rolled his eyes and hit a button on the side of the medtable. The hyperbaric chamber released, and the flexible panel slid back into its hidey-hole. I sat up. My head spun around, but I gritted my teeth and swung my legs over the side of the table. Slowly, the world righted itself.

"Treatment complete. Injuries healed. Life saved," the female voice chirped again.

This time, I directed my glower down at the table. "Is it just me, or is that voice a little too pleased with itself?"

"Oh, she definitely has a superior attitude," Kyrion drawled again. "That's why I nicknamed her *Lady Quill.*"

I curled my fingers around the edge of the table to keep from staggering forward and locking them around his throat. I'd forgotten how annoying Kyrion Caldaren could be. How arrogant. How superior. How condescending.

How blasted *everything* he could be.

Still, despite my simmering anger, I couldn't help but drink him in as though he was a bottle of water and I had just stumbled out of a bone-dry desert. He was dressed in an Arrow uniform, although the dark blue fabric signified that he belonged to House Caldaren, as did the sigil of an arrow streaking upward through a cluster of stars that covered his heart. He had laid the broken hand cannon on a nearby counter, and his silver bandolier of supplies was once again slung the right way across his chest.

His longish black hair gleamed under the cargo bay's soft

lights, and his pale skin had a hint of a tan, as if he'd recently spent some time in the sun. And his eyes . . . well, his eyes were the deep, inky sapphsidian blue that had haunted my dreams for months.

Kyrion leaned back against a counter along the wall and crossed his arms over his chest, but he was so tall it still felt like he was looming over me, like a shadow I could never quite escape. Kyrion's intense gaze moved from my face down to my right shoulder, then over to my left elbow. My left forearm. My left thigh. My right shin. My right thigh.

All the places Harkin had cut me.

The wounds were gone, thanks to the medtable's skinbonds and sutures, but my clothes were ripped, and dried blood crusted each place where Harkin had hurt me, like splotchy red bull's-eyes pointing out all the pain I had endured.

Kyrion's face softened, even as something cold and volatile shimmered in his eyes. It looked a lot like rage, although I couldn't tell if it was directed at Harkin for hurting me or at me for lying to him for the last few months.

I looked away from his sharp, searching gaze and glanced around the cargo bay. I did a double take at the blitzer's surprisingly familiar interior.

"Hey. This is *my* ship. The blitzer I found on the edge of the Techwave battle. The one we used to get off Magma 7 and escape from all that blasted lava."

"*Your* ship?" Kyrion drawled in that infuriatingly arrogant voice. "*I'm* the one who flew it to Corios and spent a considerable amount of time and money remodeling it, so I would say it is now *my* ship."

I studied the interior even more closely. He *had* remodeled it. Before, the blitzer had been dull, dingy, and gray from its years of Imperium service, but now everything was bright, shiny, and polished to a high gloss. The battered cabinets and dented counters in the cargo bay had been replaced with updated versions, and the metal surfaces were so smooth and clean I could see my own reflection in them.

"Okay, I suppose it is *your* ship now," I groused.

The barest hint of a smile lifted Kyrion's lips.

I studied the new, improved cargo bay a few seconds longer, but there was no avoiding the conversation I needed to have with Kyrion, so I slid off the medtable. My legs were still a bit weak and wobbly, and I stumbled back and banged my left hand into the side of the table. A familiar pain flared, and I glanced down.

The truebond cuts in my palm—the ones that formed that eye—were a bright, vivid red, as though they were about to pop open and start oozing blood.

"What's wrong?" Kyrion asked, suspicion coloring his voice. "The medtable should have healed your injuries."

I curled my fingers into a fist, hiding the marks. "It's nothing."

"It's not *nothing*," he snapped back. "Especially since I can bloody *feel* how much your hand is throbbing. Show me. Now."

A dark, dangerous light filled his eyes, and his face was so hard that it could have been carved from stone. Kyrion dropped his arms to his sides and pushed away from the counter, but he maintained a tense, watchful stance, like a predator about to strike.

Frustration surged through me. Despite all my plans and schemes to the contrary, I had still ended up right back here with him. We weren't enemies anymore, not like we had been the first time we'd been on the blitzer, but this was still the very last place I wanted to be—for all sorts of reasons.

I blew out a breath, then opened my fingers and held my palm out where he could see it, along with the cuts.

No reaction.

Kyrion didn't move, blink, grimace, glower. He didn't even

seem to breathe. Instead, he steadfastly stared at the eye-shaped marks on my palm as though that one small symbol contained all the secrets of the galaxy.

Several more seconds ticked by in charged silence. Then he scrubbed his hands over his face, as if trying to slough off what he had just seen—irrefutable proof that the truebond still existed between us.

"How long?" he demanded. "How bloody long have you known we were still bonded?"

I flinched at his harsh, accusing tone, but I'd brought this on myself by keeping this secret. "At first, I thought the bond was broken, just like you did. After we drank those chemicals in Touma's workshop, I didn't feel the bond anymore. I didn't feel *you* anymore. Just a frozen, numb, dead space in my mind where you had been."

Kyrion jerked his head in agreement. "I felt that way too. But when did you realize the bond was still there?"

"After I killed Julieta Delano in the weapons bunker in the Kent Corp lab."

His black eyebrows shot up. "Explain."

I told him how I'd telepathically heard Julieta's thoughts and used telekinesis to grab my stormsword when she had been trying to kill me. "I did things I shouldn't have been able to do, had abilities only a powerful psion would have—that only *you* would have. I didn't think much about it in the heat of the battle, but later, when I looked back on everything that had happened, everything I had done, well, that's when I knew we were still bonded."

"And yet you didn't bother to inform me of that pertinent fact," Kyrion said in a clipped, furious tone. "Us still being bonded would have been useful to know during the last Regal ball. When Holloway ordered me to cut my own hand again and again to try to prove the bond's existence."

He flexed his fingers and held out his left palm. I let out a quiet sigh of relief. At least his hand was free of the cuts—

A red mark slashed across his skin as though drawn by an invisible laser. Then another one, then another one . . . In an instant, the same deep, red cuts crisscrossed his palm that were showing on mine. I grimaced in sympathy, but Kyrion didn't even flinch.

He regarded the wounds with a curious expression, then glanced over at my hand again. "Why did my marks disappear for all these months and yours didn't?"

"I don't know. I tried everything to heal them. Ointments, skinbonds, other medicines."

He flexed his hand. The sting of his wounds rippled through my own hand, and I bit my tongue to keep from hissing. During the past few months that we'd been separated, my perception of Kyrion's injuries and moods had faded to a cold, dull ache in the bottom of my brain, a nagging sensation I could largely ignore. But now that we were together again, his presence and emotions had roared back to the surface of my mind.

Even worse, all those sensations had intensified, and I was more aware of him than ever before. The heat of his skin. The coiled strength of his muscles. The psionic power lurking inside him like a violent storm that could boil up at any moment. And maybe worst of all, the pesky, silky threads of him that had wrapped around every single part of me.

I didn't know if absence truly made the heart grow fonder, but it certainly seemed to have strengthened our truebond.

Kyrion dropped his hand to his side. "How did you beat the truebond test?" he asked, his voice once again clipped and furious. "How did you hoodwink Holloway? How did you trick everyone in the throne room?"

I shifted on my feet. "Several months ago, right before the *Velorum* crashed, I was working in the R&D lab at Kent Corp, and an idea popped into my mind for a pair of thin, flexible, polyplastic gloves. The only gloves in the lab were thick, bulky things that made it hard to grip my tools, so I decided to create some gloves with that same level of protection but that looked like human skin and would still give me the same tactile sensation as actually touching a tool with my bare hand. I had been working on the idea off and on for several weeks. Once Holloway invited me to the Regal ball, I knew exactly how to use the gloves."

"So that night at the ball, you were wearing gloves that looked like your own skin and hid the cuts on your palm from Holloway?" Kyrion asked.

I nodded, and he barked out a harsh laugh.

"I don't know if that's brilliance or madness."

I didn't quite know myself. Either way, it had fooled Holloway and bought us both a few more months of freedom.

"But how did I get into your mindscape earlier?" he asked. "How did you drag me back in there?"

I bristled. "*I* didn't do anything. In case you've forgotten, I've spent the last several hours being experimented on by a sadistic Techwave scientist. If you wandered into my mindscape, then *you* did it of your own accord, with no help or prompting from me."

Kyrion snorted in disbelief. "I find that hard to believe, since I was sitting in my library at Castle Caldaren when a door suddenly appeared in the wall beside the fireplace, a door that led to your mindscape."

I froze. "You saw the door in your library?"

"Yes, I saw the bloody door in my library—" His eyes narrowed. "Wait. Why do you say it like that?"

I opened my mouth, but he answered his own question. "You already *knew* about the door."

His eyes narrowed a little more, and I could almost see the gears turning in his mind. "The first day you were in the library, you asked if there was a secret door that led down into the bottom of the castle."

I didn't respond, and he let out a low, vicious curse.

"You *had* been in the library before. How? Why? When were you in my castle?" He peppered me with questions.

"I've been dreaming about your castle for years," I confessed in a soft voice.

Kyrion jerked back, and his shock pulsed through my mind. *"Years?"*

I sighed, more exhaustion crashing through my body. The medtable might have healed me, but I hadn't realized how much keeping these secrets was weighing me down until right now.

"The very first time I remember seeing Castle Caldaren was the day after Nerezza abandoned me. That night, I cried myself to sleep, and I dreamed I was walking through this beautiful old castle. It was so nice and lovely and warm and safe that every night, right before I would go to sleep, I would think about it, dream about it. One night, I wound up in the library, and I loved it so much that I started going there every single night. Eventually, that door in the wall appeared, the one that leads down the spiral stairs to my mindscape."

"And you've been wandering through the castle, *my* castle, ever since?" Kyrion asked.

"Yes. Although I didn't know it was *your* castle until you brought me there after the battle on Magma 7."

"So that's why you were asking about the door in the wall. You were waiting for it to appear just like the one in your dreams. Because you had been going through it for *years*."

His harsh accusation rankled me, and I strode forward and slapped my hands on my hips.

"What are you suggesting? That I *planned* this? That I have been lying in wait ever since I was seven years old to find you and trap you into a truebond?" I gave him a disgusted look. "Please. You've said yourself that's not how truebonds work."

More icy fury filled his face, and he stepped forward,

looming over me the way he always did. "No, of course not. But you *did* plan to fool Holloway—and *me*," Kyrion said, his voice a low, dangerous growl. "That's why you wore your special gloves to the Regal ball. Because you thought Holloway might test us, and you wanted to be ready."

And just like that, all my anger and disgust drained away. He was right. I had planned to fool him.

"Yes, I deliberately fooled you, Holloway, and all the other Regals," I said in a low voice. "I didn't know what else to do."

Some of the icy fury thawed in Kyrion's face, and when he spoke, his voice was far less hostile than before. "Why?" he asked. "Why not just tell me that we were still bonded?"

Another wave of exhaustion crashed over me, along with all the worry, longing, and heartache I had been trying so hard to suppress over the last few months.

"Because you didn't want the bond," I said in a tired, bitter voice. "You *never* wanted the bond. You never wanted *me*."

I regretted the words as soon as they escaped my lips. It was bad enough that he could sense my thoughts and feelings through the bond. Now I had gone and completely cracked open my heart to him like an utter fool.

Kyrion's gaze locked with mine, and he opened his mouth. For a moment, I thought he might say . . . Well, I wasn't sure *what* I thought he might say or even what I *wanted* him to say. That he was concerned about me? That he was attracted to me? That he cared about me as much as I cared about him?

Kyrion exhaled, and his lips pressed together into a tight line. Disappointment surged through me, and I ground my teeth to keep any emotion from showing.

"It's not your fault," I said, breaking the tense, awkward silence. "It's not anyone's fault. From what Touma told us that night in his workshop, truebonds have a life and a will of their own."

"But?" he challenged.

I threw my arms out wide, encompassing the whole of the galaxy. "But I'm sick and tired of being around people who don't want anything to do with me. Of caring about people who throw me away like a piece of trash the second I'm not useful anymore. I went through that several months ago with Conrad Fawley and all those years ago with Nerezza, and I won't go through it again. That's why I fooled you and Holloway and everyone else. I gave you a chance to escape the truebond. I gave us *both* a chance to escape it."

Kyrion stiffened as though I had slapped him across the face and insulted his honor as a Regal lord. "I am *not* Conrad Fawley, nor am I Nerezza Blackwell. I would never just *abandon* you, Vesper. Not after everything we've been through together."

I shook my head, flinging off his words and the foolish hope they stirred in me. "But you came after me because of the bond. You rescued me because of the bond. Not because you *wanted* to but because you *had* to. You realized that we were still bonded, and you didn't want to risk my death affecting you, right?"

I held my breath, hoping he would contradict me. That he had rescued me because he had been concerned about *me* and not the bond we shared. But he didn't respond, and those brittle pieces of my heart cracked into even smaller, sharper shards.

"You've been right about the truebond all along," I said, once again rushing to fill in the awkward silence. "How could we ever know how much of what we feel is real? That whatever is between us is because of *our* choices and desires and not some psionic effects of the bond? You told me once that you would never let some quirk of magic dictate your fate. Well, I feel the same way." I drew myself up to my full height. "Thank you for coming to help me. I appreciate it. Truly."

"But?" he growled.

"But you can drop me off at the nearest planet and return to

Corios. I plan to get on with my life, and I suggest that you do the same."

Kyrion stared at me, his features once again cold, remote, and unreadable. He should have been jumping for joy, but instead, he eyed me as if I was a giant ice owl in a zoo that he had never seen before.

I couldn't bear the weight of his dark, steady gaze, so I gestured down at my blood-crusted clothes. "I should get cleaned up. Do you have anything I can wear?"

He tilted his head to the side. "There are some House Caldaren uniforms in the bathroom closet. First door on the left."

I headed in that direction.

"Wait," Kyrion called out.

Wary, I stopped and glanced back over my shoulder. He opened a cabinet and pulled out a bottle, along with a small packet, then came over and held them out to me.

"Electrolyte water and protein gel," he said in a gruff voice. "You need to start replacing the fluids and calories you lost in the Techwave facility."

I didn't know if his concern was genuine or if the bond had prompted it, but emotion still clogged my throat. I nodded and reached for the items. My fingers brushed up against his. For a moment, I could have sworn that Kyrion curled his fingers into mine, but in the next instant, he dropped his hand and stepped back. I clutched the bottle and packet to my chest, wishing they could shield me from all the things I felt for him.

Kyrion didn't speak, but the heavy weight of his gaze settled on my back as I left the cargo bay. My steps quickened, and I hurried down the corridor and into the bathroom.

I managed to shut the door behind me before the tears started trickling down my face.

FOURTEEN

KYRION

Vesper disappeared into the bathroom. A minute later, the soft, steady hiss of water sounded.

I exhaled, slumped down, and clutched the edge of the medtable, letting its strong, sturdy frame support me. Our conversation had shaken me more than I cared to admit, as had the way Vesper had looked at me, so hurt and defensive and so very certain I didn't want her. More than once while we'd been talking, I'd thought about showing her just how wrong she was, but I'd held back.

She was right. How could I know that my . . . concern for her was my own emotion and not a result of the truebond? That was the problem between us, that had *always* been the problem between us, and I didn't see a solution to it.

But there was nothing I could do about that right now, so I moved on to the things I could control, like seeing exactly how injured she had been.

I hit some buttons on the medtable and pulled up a diagnostic hologram of Vesper's wounds. The number of cuts that

Harkin Ocnus had inflicted on her made fresh fury flood my chest. If I ever got close to the Techwave scientist, I was going to rip his head off his body with my bare bloody hands.

But Harkin wasn't here, so I left the cargo bay and headed down the corridor. I stepped into an area that I had transformed into a library, complete with wooden shelves filled with some of my favorite books, stuffed chairs, and other comfortable furniture.

I stripped off my Arrow jacket and laid it on the holoscreen in the wooden table in the center of the library. The spy camera hidden in the House Caldaren sigil had recorded my trip into and out of the Techwave facility, and the footage flickered in the air.

I watched it all play out, but I didn't see any clues in the images. The Techwavers had been making more suits of Black Scarab armor, the same as the other facilities the Arrows and Imperium soldiers had raided over the past few months. Frustrated, I waved my hand, and the footage vanished.

"What are you doing?" Vesper asked, stepping into the library.

I stiffened at her approach. She was wearing the same sort of clothes as mine—a long-sleeved tactical shirt and cargo pants—and the dark blue material hugged her curves in all the right places. During the last Regal ball, Vesper had been as beautiful as a blue moon in her formal gown, but right now, she looked like exactly what she was: a strong, fierce warrior.

I had to clear my throat before I could answer her. "Reviewing the footage I recorded at the Techwave facility to see if I can figure out where they might be going next." I hesitated. "Perhaps you would be willing to tell me what happened? The things you heard and saw. What the guards said. Any machines or weapons you noticed. But if you don't feel like it, I understand. I know the last several hours have been . . . difficult."

Vesper snorted. "You mean because I was drugged, kidnapped, and tortured? Yeah, *difficult* is one way to describe it."

Her eyes dimmed, her shoulders drooped, and a shudder rippled through her body, but after a few seconds, she lifted her chin, reached into her pocket, and fished out a small microdot drive. "I can do a lot better than just describe things. After I escaped from Harkin's lab, I broke into General Ocnus's office, accessed his terminal, and downloaded his files."

She placed the microdot drive on the holoscreen. Dozens of files popped up, all with locked icons. I hit some buttons, trying to get past the encryption, but nothing worked, and I didn't have the expertise to crack the Techwave's code.

"I'll send the files to Daichi," I said. "He should be able to decrypt them. I'll also have him contact your friend Tivona and let her know that you're okay."

Vesper nodded. "Thank you. Tivona has to be worried sick." A pensive look filled her face. "While you're at it, please ask Daichi to access every record he can find about me, public and otherwise."

"Why?"

She grimaced. "Nerezza showed me a bunch of documents about my supposed life history, but they were all wrong. I want to examine the documents for myself and figure out who changed them and especially why."

I tapped some buttons and sent the request to Daichi, along with General Ocnus's files.

Vesper walked around the table and peered out a window set into the wall. "Where are we?"

"I had the pinpoint drive take us three jumps over from Magma 3. There are a couple of Frozon moons nearby with emergency bases for people who get stuck on broken ships, but right now, we're essentially in a dead zone."

Vesper looked at me. "Why didn't you set a course back to Corios?"

"I had different orders."

"What orders?" She frowned. "I thought you came after me because of the bond. Or was there another reason you were at the Techwave facility?"

"Holloway sent me," I replied in a smooth voice, sidestepping her question about the bond. "He received some information about your kidnapping. He told me to infiltrate the facility and kill all the Techies, men and machines alike."

Her eyes narrowed. "And what did he tell you to do with me?"

"Holloway ordered me to hold you for questioning—and then kill you."

Vesper blinked, and the velvety ribbon of her in my mind vibrated with shock. "And what did you say?"

I shrugged. "That I would do it, of course."

She eyed me, but no suspicion, worry, or fear clouded her gaze. She didn't ask any more questions, but it was obvious she trusted me *not* to kill her. Her easy acceptance soothed something deep inside me, some tension I hadn't even realized was there until this moment.

It had been a long, long time since someone had trusted me, and it surprised me how much I . . . enjoyed the feeling. Of simple trust, freely given, and with nothing asked, bargained for, or demanded in return.

Vesper's brow furrowed in thought, and she started pacing back and forth between the bookcases that flanked the walls. "Why would Holloway order you to rescue me, then turn around and kill me? It doesn't make any sense. He just made me a Regal lady a few months ago. Surely I haven't managed to piss him off enough to want me dead already."

I crossed my arms over my chest and leaned my right hip against the table. "Holloway wanted to take over Kent Corp. He didn't like you beating him to the punch or the popularity and profitability of your new brewmakers."

Vesper shook her head, making her dark brown hair swish around her shoulders. "Okay, so I screwed Holloway out of getting Kent Corp. But that's not enough reason for him to want me dead. Unless . . ."

"What?"

Worry pinched her face, and she stopped pacing. "Unless it's a test for you. To see how loyal you still are."

I nodded. "I had a similar thought. That's why I sent my official Imperium ship to land on the other side of the Techwave facility and why we are currently on this blitzer. No one knows about this ship except you, me, Daichi, and Touma."

"Why?" she asked, suspicion sharpening her voice. "What else did Holloway do?"

"He sent three other Arrows on the mission." I tapped a few buttons on the holoscreen, and an official Imperium dossier popped up and hovered over the table, along with a picture. "You already know Zane Zimmer."

Vesper's nose crinkled with disgust. "Unfortunately."

"Holloway also sent two more Arrows: Adria and Dargan Byrne."

I waved my hand, and images of the sister and brother appeared. Vesper peered at the pictures, along with the accompanying biographical information.

I knew the exact moment she read the most pertinent fact. Her head snapped up, and she looked at me with wide, surprised eyes. "The Byrnes have a truebond?"

"Yes. It makes them both much stronger and far more dangerous than the other Arrows. Even Holloway is wary of them."

Vesper frowned. "But if the Byrnes have a truebond, then why doesn't Holloway take their magic the way—"

She bit off her words, but I finished her thought. "Why doesn't he take their power the way he did to my parents?"

Vesper grimaced, then nodded.

"Because their power makes him sick."

The spy camera in my jacket had also recorded my earlier meeting with Holloway and the three Arrows. I showed Vesper how the Imperium leader had started coughing and sweating after he touched Adria and tried to siphon off her power.

Vesper circled the table, watching the footage again and again, studying it from all angles. Her eyes narrowed, and the velvety ribbon of her vibrated in my mind, as if she was summoning up and discarding one thought and theory after another.

"What makes Adria and Dargan different from your parents?" she asked, stopping on the opposite side of the table. "Why could Holloway take your parents' power but not theirs?"

"I don't know. The Byrnes' bond formed several years ago, when Dargan saved Adria from drowning in a frozen lake while we were on an Arrow mission. Although . . ."

"What?"

I shrugged, trying to ignore the uncomfortable emotions churning in my gut. "I've always wondered why Holloway didn't use the Byrnes the same way he used my parents, but I had never seen him try to siphon off their power before this morning. Perhaps it always makes him sick. Or perhaps Holloway can only absorb power from people who have a certain kind of truebond, like a romantic one instead of a familial one."

Vesper tensed, and her gaze skittered away from mine. More uncomfortable emotions churned in my gut.

I cleared my throat. "So little is known about psionic abilities in general, and even less about truebonds. I sent the footage to Daichi and Touma. Perhaps they can come up with an answer."

Vesper nodded. "If we can figure out what makes the Byrnes different, then maybe we can figure out a way to protect ourselves from Holloway. Maybe we can prevent him from ever using us against each other the way he did with your parents." She finally looked at me again. "Maybe we can find a way to stop him for good."

Hope sparked in my chest at the thought of ending Holloway once and for all, but I ruthlessly snuffed it out. Right now, I had a much more pressing concern: keeping Vesper safe.

"I'll plot a course back to Temperate 42. You'll be back at Quill Corp by late this afternoon."

"How will you explain that to Holloway?"

"I'll claim that by the time I breached the facility, you had already escaped, stolen a ship, and returned home."

A skeptical look filled her face. "Do you really think Holloway will let me go back to my regular life on Temperate 42?"

"Probably. For a little while."

She snorted. "Right up until he decides to send you to murder me again."

"Probably."

"Well, then, it's a good thing I'm not going back to Temperate 42," Vesper replied. "At least, not yet."

Suspicion filled me. "Where else would you go?"

She leaned down and tapped some buttons. A star map appeared, and Vesper stuck her fingers into the hologram and zoomed in on one part of the Archipelago Galaxy. "I'm going to Tropics 33."

"Isn't that an Erzton stronghold? One of their tourism planets?"

She nodded. "Yep. Tropics 33 was circled on a map in General Ocnus's office. Whatever the Techwave is plotting next, it's going to happen on Tropics 33."

I shook my head. "You should return to Temperate 42. Play the part of the loyal Regal lady for Holloway, and give the gossipcasts a tearful interview about your abduction."

"No," Vesper snapped. "I've been hiding out on Temperate

42 for the last three months, and what good did it do me? The Techwave kidnapped me, Harkin Ocnus tortured me, and Callus Holloway wants me dead. It's time for me to go on the offensive. Besides, the Techwave stole *my* ideas, *my* designs. I won't be able to live with myself if I don't at least *try* to figure out what their ultimate plan is, along with a way to stop them from hurting anyone else."

"You're on *my* ship," I snapped back. "Which means you go where *I* say."

She planted her hands on her hips and glared right back at me. "In case you've forgotten, I'm a Regal lady now and the head of a very powerful, wealthy corporation. I can get off your ship at the next planet and make my own way to Tropics 33. Face it, Kyrion. You can't stop me."

She was right. I doubted a black hole could stop Vesper Quill when she set her mind to something.

"Fine," I ground out the word. "We'll go to Tropics 33 and see if the Techwave shows up. And then we'll figure out what to do about Holloway."

She arched an eyebrow. "We? I thought there was no *we*."

I held my hand up so that she could see the eye I'd carved into my own palm. "Like it or not, there is still very much a *we*."

She grimaced. "We could go our separate ways again. Stay apart, like we have been for the last few months. Maybe the bond would start to fade, given enough time and distance."

My inner monster snarled at the thought of letting her go again, of not being around to protect her, but I kept my face smooth and blank.

"According to Touma, no one has ever successfully broken a truebond, so I don't think it would work." I hesitated. "Especially given how much stronger the bond feels to me now."

When the bond had first formed, the velvety ribbon that was Vesper had been nestled in a small corner of my mind. But now that ribbon was threaded throughout my entire body, and her every breath, movement, and emotion rippled back to me in waves of sensation.

"Still worried that if I die, you'll die too?" Vesper sniped.

"Oh, no," I drawled. "I already know you're going to be the death of me, Lady Vesper. I'm just hoping to delay the inevitable for as long as possible."

"Arrogant, insufferable Regal lord," she muttered.

"Sarcastic, know-it-all, genius engineer," I drawled right back at her.

Vesper's left eye twitched in annoyance, along with her fingers, as though she wanted to strangle me. Then she huffed, spun around, and stormed out of the library. Her footsteps smacked against the metal floor, but they didn't drown out her muttered curses about my existence, my interference with her plans, and what I could do with various parts of my anatomy.

Even with the pinpoint drive, it was still going to be a long, long flight to Tropics 33.

PART TWO

DREAM WORLD

FIFTEEN

VESPER

Tropics 33 was nestled between Erzton and Imperium territories, and even with pinpoint travel, it would still take us more than thirty-six hours to reach the planet. While we jumped from one point to another, then churned through the space in between, I explored the ship.

The blitzer still had all the weapons, shielding, speed, and maneuverability of a fighter ship, but the inside reminded me of Castle Caldaren. Luxe furnishings made of real stone, wood, and glass, plush rugs underfoot, paintings of Promenade Park and other Corios landmarks on the walls, cases of real paper books tucked away in little alcoves. It was by far the nicest ship I had ever been on, and strangely enough, it felt far more like home than any place I had been recently, even my own apartment on Temperate 42.

I was looking through the crates of dried food, water, and other supplies in the cargo bay when I noticed three buttons on the wall. The green, blue, and red buttons matched the ones in the corridor just beyond the cargo bay.

"What's with all the buttons?" I asked.

Kyrion was rummaging through a crate. "I didn't particularly enjoy being trapped in the cargo bay and threatened with asphyxiation and ejection into the cold embrace of deep space. So I installed some new buttons that perform the same functions as the original buttons out in the corridor. The green button opens and closes the cargo bay ramp, the blue one raises and lowers the permaglass barrier, and the red one sucks all the oxygen out of this part of the ship in case of a fire."

"Still considering killing me to break the bond, Lord Kyrion?" I snarked. "How noble of you."

"Oh, no, Lady Vesper. That spaceship has sailed, quite literally. Like it or not, we are stuck together for the foreseeable future. But lucky for you, I packed your favorite snack."

He plucked something out of the crate and tossed it in my direction. I caught the item and blanched at the strawberry protein bar. Kyrion had mocked and tempted me with the same kind of chalky, tasteless bar when we had first been trapped on the blitzer a few months ago.

I chucked the bar back at him, aiming for his head, but he easily caught it. "You're not nearly as funny as you think you are."

His low, warm laughter chased me out of the cargo bay.

Even though the medtable had healed me, I was still exhausted, so I went into one of the bedrooms and lay down, but I couldn't drift off to sleep. Grumpy, I got up an hour later and headed to the flight deck to check on our progress.

Kyrion was sprawled across the pilot's chair, his long legs stretched out to the side, staring through the windows into the blackness of space. The distant starlight gilded his black hair, even as it cast his face in shadow, and he looked every inch like the dark prince of the galaxy, as the gossipcasts had dubbed him years ago.

My heart lurched with longing, but I spun around, scurried

back into my bedroom, and shut the door. I might not be able to see Kyrion anymore, but I could still feel him. Even with several thick metal walls between us, the sticky cobweb in my mind kept pulsing, his mood tense and angry.

I resisted the urge to bang my head against the door. Being stuck on the blitzer with Kyrion was like tiptoeing around a Frozon wolf and having no idea when the fierce predator might decide to pounce on me. Or maybe I was the wolf, since my mood was just as tense and angry as his. Hard to tell.

Still, everything was fine, more or less, until that evening. I had finally managed to take a nap, although my dreams had been plagued with images of Harkin torturing me in the Techwave lab. I was still trying to shake off the dregs of the nightmares when I opened the bathroom door and came face-to-face with Kyrion.

We were opposing forces moving in different directions, and his greater size easily won that fight. I bounced off his chest and opened my mouth, but the snippy words died on my lips.

Kyrion had just showered, and his black hair was damp and mussed, as though he'd carelessly raked a hand through the thick locks rather than combing them. A shirt dangled from his hand, and his chiseled chest and sculpted abs were on full display.

I'd known that Kyrion was in excellent shape, and I'd seen his bare torso before when he'd been sparring with Zane Zimmer in the training ring at Castle Caldaren, but up close, his bulging biceps and wide expanse of muscles were even more captivating. A pair of black sleep pants were slung low on his hips, and the soft, thin fabric left little to the imagination. His feet were bare, which somehow made him even more ridiculously attractive.

My cheeks flamed. I yanked my gaze up and away from his chest, but focusing on his face wasn't any better. Kyrion was once again looming over me, his eyes glimmering like sapphsidian stars. Even worse, the sticky cobweb of him in my mind pulsed with . . . Well, I wasn't quite sure *what* the emotion was, but it intensified the burning sensation in my face, which zipped through the rest of my body.

My mouth went dry, desire exploded low in my belly, and my fingers itched with the urge to touch him. Would all those sublime muscles be as firm, hard, and warm as they looked? Or would he be cold, slick, and smooth like a statue under my fingertips? I desperately wanted to find out. For science, of course.

Kyrion peered down his nose at me. "Are you just going to stand there and stare at me, or did you have a destination in mind?"

Embarrassment doused me like a wet blanket. "I hope you didn't use up all the hot water," I groused, desperate to think about something else besides his magnificent muscles.

"Would I do that?"

"To spite me? Absolutely."

He tapped a finger on his lips and pretended to think about it. "You're right. I *would* use up all the hot water simply to inconvenience you. Then again, what with all the ogling you're doing, you could probably use a cold shower."

My mouth dropped open. "You—I—you . . ."

I croaked out some words, but my incoherent sputtering was far from the snappy, witty comeback I so desperately wanted—*needed*—right now.

Kyrion smirked, happy to have rendered me speechless, then stepped out of the doorway and sauntered down the corridor. I glared at his back, which was just as chiseled as the rest of him. Even his muscles had muscles. Arrogant, insufferable jackass.

I stomped into the bathroom and slammed the door. I drew in a breath, and Kyrion's familiar spearmint scent invaded my nose. The clean, sharp, slightly sweet aroma caused a fresh wave of heat to rush over me. I glared at the offending bottle of liquid soap sitting on the sink, but it was the only cleanser in the bathroom, and I had no choice but to carry it into the shower with me.

But the worst part was that we were both right. He had used up all the hot water, and I definitely needed a cold shower.

I let the frigid water cascade over my body as long as I could stand it, then donned some sleep clothes and went to bed. Maybe it was the scent of his spearmint soap on my skin, but this time, instead of more nightmares of Harkin, I dreamed of a bare-chested Kyrion smiling, holding out his hand, and drawing me into the shower with him. In my dream, the two of us didn't need any hot water to make the entire bathroom steam up . . .

I woke up sliding my face back and forth across my pillow like I was nuzzling his neck.

Ugh! Get a grip, Vesper.

It was just the bond, I told myself. Just our psionic abilities and pheromones and body chemistries drawing us together. Besides, we were alone on a ship. It wasn't like I had any other choices. Once again, I had only bad options, especially when it came to Kyrion Caldaren. He didn't really want me. Even if he did, it wouldn't last.

Nerezza, Liesl, and Conrad had all taught me the same painful lesson. It didn't matter what kind of relationship I had with someone. Family, friend, lover.

In the end, everyone always left me.

After a few more hours of fitful sleep, I got up early, donned a fresh House Caldaren uniform, and went down to the second deck. Kyrion had converted part of this level into a gym with treadmills, hand weights, and other equipment. Metal lockers stuffed with wooden practice swords, staffs, spears, and other weapons lined one of the walls, while the open space in the middle of the floor was covered with a thin, padded mat. The area reminded me of the training ring at Castle Caldaren.

I took off my boots and socks, picked up my stormsword, and stepped onto the mat. I slowed my breathing and quieted my mind as I flowed through a series of moves that Leandra Ferrum had shown me. The moves could be done with or without my sword, although right now, I was enjoying the solid weight of the hilt in my hand and the smooth slice of the blade through the air. Besides, I wanted to be ready if—or, rather, when—we ran into General Ocnus and the Techwave again.

An image of me chopping Harkin's head off his shoulders popped into my mind. That murderous thought brought a smile to my face, and I flowed from one move to the next . . . to the next . . . to the next . . .

I lost track of the time, but suddenly, a familiar, shadowy presence tickled my mind. I finished the latest move, lowered my sword, and turned around. Kyrion was standing in the doorway, clutching his own stormsword, as if he'd had the same idea to train.

"Care for a sparring partner?" he asked in a low voice.

I hesitated. We'd spent the past day skirting around each other, but I couldn't avoid him forever, and there was no escaping the bond between us.

I twirled my sword around in my hand. "Only if you feel like losing."

A crooked grin spread across his face, and my heart did an uncomfortable somersault.

Kyrion removed his own boots and socks, then stepped onto the mat. He rolled his shoulders and twisted his torso from side to side, loosening up. His tight tactical shirt perfectly outlined his broad shoulders and muscled chest.

"Ogling me again?" he murmured. "That seems to be a regular occurrence with you, Vesper."

Embarrassment scalded my cheeks, but I shrugged off his words. "Just sizing up the competition."

"I wasn't aware we were competing."

"Isn't everything a competition between the Arrows? It certainly seemed that way when I saw you and Zane Zimmer spar a few months ago."

Kyrion swung his sword back and forth, his strikes faster and more violent than before. "I sparred with Zane yesterday morning, right before I left for Magma 3 to find you. It took me the better part of fifteen minutes, but I finally managed to break his nose. Zane bled all over the training ring, and he was none too happy about it."

I grinned. "I would have liked to have seen that."

He cleared his throat and slowly lowered the sword to his side. "Perhaps I can show the memory to you someday . . . through your mindscape."

I froze, although my heart started hammering. My hand tightened around my own sword, and the lunarium blade pulsed a bright blue, betraying my interest. This was the first time Kyrion had ever said anything remotely positive about my mindscape and the fact that it seemed to be one of the things that connected us through the truebond. His words stirred up that pesky hope buried deep inside me, but I brushed it aside. Like me, Kyrion didn't have any other choices.

"Don't you mean my *dream world*?" I asked in a snide voice. "That's what you called it before."

"It still is your dream world. I just happen to wander through there from time to time for some reason. Although I must admit I'm curious about what is inside the door in the back of the room."

He was talking about the Door—the one that contained nothing but darkness.

"I'm not sure. Whenever I go inside that door, all I see is blackness. I feel like something is waiting inside, though." I shrugged. "Or maybe it's just the darkness in myself, all the things I've done, and all the things I will continue to do to survive."

A shadow passed over his face. "Sometimes darkness is the best friend—the *only* friend—you have. An inner monster that will never judge, betray, or abandon you, no matter all the horrific deeds you've done."

Like kill your own father. Kyrion's thought whispered through my mind, even as the sticky cobweb of him crackled with cold, as though he was sealing that memory up behind a sheet of ice.

Sympathy pinched my heart, but before I could respond, he lunged forward. Kyrion clearly didn't want to talk anymore. Neither did I. Bond or no bond, conversations like this one made me like him even more than I already did.

His stormsword glowed a dark, dangerous blue as it zipped toward my chest, but I snapped up my own weapon, easily blocking the blow. Surprise flickered across his face, although I could have sworn that sticky little cobweb in my mind pulsed with a bit of pride.

Kyrion swung his sword at me again. And then again . . . and then again . . . and then again . . .

Back and forth, we dueled across the mat, him attacking and me blocking his blows. After a particularly furious exchange that made my arms ache, Kyrion stepped back and circled me. He twirled his sword around in his hand, and the blade shimmered, as if it was mirroring his thoughts.

His eyes narrowed, and he stabbed the sword at me like an accusing finger. "You've gotten better since we last sparred on Corios. Faster, stronger, more skilled. You're not even breathing hard. How?"

I gestured at my chest. "I have an oxygen optimization

enhancement, courtesy of Kent Corp. One of the few good things about working in the R&D lab."

Kyrion huffed. "So you can breathe a little bit better and easier than the rest of us. That's *hardly* an enhancement. They might as well have given you a gold pocket watch."

I bristled. Everyone always mocked my O2 enhancement, even the other lab rats who had different, supposedly superior enhancements. "For your information, the O2 enhancement is among the most useful, statistically speaking. In certain situations, it can be much more helpful than enhanced speed and strength."

"Really? How so?"

"Forty-two percent of all deaths in and around spaceships and ports are due to a lack of oxygen," I said in a defensive voice.

He huffed again, the sound even more derisive than before. "Well, if you're ever on a ship without any oxygen, then you're probably going to die anyway, even if it is forty-two percent slower than everyone else."

I brightened. "Well, at least I would have the pleasure of watching you die first, my lord."

Kyrion rolled his eyes, then stabbed his sword at me again. "Your O2 enhancement doesn't explain why you're so much more skilled with your stormsword."

"I had an excellent teacher."

"Who?" he growled, and I could have sworn a note of jealousy rasped through his voice.

"Leandra Ferrum."

His eyebrows shot up in surprise. "You got Leandra Ferrum to train you? How? I've asked House Ferrum for trainers multiple times to help the Arrows, but they've always denied my requests."

I grinned. "I just asked nicely, something you would know absolutely nothing about."

Kyrion glowered at me, his eyes practically smoldering in his face. Ah, there was the angry Arrow and arrogant Regal lord I knew all too well.

"If you must know, I paid Leandra a not-so-small fortune. She also has several cousins on Temperate 42 whom she wanted to visit, and she enjoys flirting with Tivona. So far, the arrangement has worked out well for everyone."

Kyrion tilted his head to the side, studying me even more closely. "You've been preparing for this, haven't you? For Holloway and the Techwave to target you. What are you plotting, Vesper?"

Blast it. I'd hoped he wouldn't realize that I intended to destroy Holloway and the Techwave, but of course, he would know that I had ulterior motives. Kyrion was quite perceptive, especially when it came to Regal games, something I was still an amateur at, truth be told.

"Just making sure I know how to properly defend myself," I replied. "Something you suggested a few months ago in your library when you were whacking me with a wooden practice sword. Or have you already forgotten those lessons?"

"I haven't forgotten anything," Kyrion drawled right back at me. "Including how you always favor your right side and leave your left flank exposed."

He lunged toward my left flank. Like a fool, I turned to block him, but it was just a feint, and Kyrion spun around, tucking his sword up behind his back even as he ducked his head and avoided my strike. Then, just as quickly, he popped back upright, lashed out with his own sword, and knocked my weapon out of my hand.

I lunged for the blade, but Kyrion stepped in front of me, his sword out and up.

A smug smile stretched across his face. "Do you yield?"

I lunged to the right, still trying to reach my sword, but he blocked my path. I lunged to the left, and he followed me.

"You can't outmaneuver me, Vesper," he said in a low, mocking voice. "Leandra Ferrum might have trained you, but I've been fighting for my life for the last twenty-five years."

I ignored his crowing and kept trying to reach my sword, but he kept blocking me. Anger and frustration surged through me. We might have been sparring for fun and exercise, but I'd wanted to prove to the Arrow that I could take care of myself.

Kyrion kept crowing, and more anger surged through me. All that hot, molten, pounding anger cracked open something deep inside my body, and an incredible amount of power suddenly zipped through me, as if I were an exploding star. I snarled and instinctively snapped my hand down and out to the side to release the power—

Blue energy erupted in my palm.

I froze, staring at the pulsing mass of energy. My anger vanished, and so did the energy, fluttering away like butterflies zooming up out of my palm. I tried to catch those butterflies, but they dimmed to sparks that dropped through my open, outstretched fingers like blue raindrops. Exhaustion crashed over me, as though Kyrion and I had been fighting for hours instead of just a few minutes, and I had to lock my knees to keep from sagging down to the mat.

"What was that?" I whispered.

"You formed a psionic blade," Kyrion said in a thoughtful tone. "You shouldn't be able to do that. At least, not with your seer magic alone. Unless . . ."

"Unless what?" I asked in a guarded voice.

"Unless you were able to tap into even more of my abilities. Go beyond my surface powers of telepathy, telempathy, and telekinesis." His eyes narrowed. "Which means the truebond is even stronger than we thought."

My heart squeezed tight, although I couldn't say whether it was with fear, longing, or a touch of both. "Could your parents form psionic weapons?"

Kyrion jerked his head. "Yes. My mother could always form psi-blades, but my father didn't have that ability until after they bonded." He raked a hand through his hair, then sighed. "But over time, the ability vanished for both of them, as Holloway took more and more of their power."

"Just like I took your power a moment ago?" I asked, my words more of an accusation than a question.

He grimaced. "I didn't say that."

"But you were thinking it, right? That I'm slowly siphoning off your psionic abilities one at a time. That I'm a *leech*, just like Holloway."

He didn't respond, but a muscle ticked in his jaw. My stomach dropped like a stone. I'd said the words hoping he would refute them, but his silence spoke volumes. Was that what he truly thought of me? That I was a leech? A parasite? A burden?

Anger boiled up in my chest again, and I charged across the mat. The move took Kyrion by surprise, and I slapped his stormsword out of his hand.

"I didn't ask for this!" I yelled, slamming my hands into his chest and sending him staggering back. "I didn't plan *any* of this!"

I shoved him again, but Kyrion firmed up his stance, and I didn't even make him rock back on his heels.

"I know that!" he growled. "Don't you think I know that? I didn't ask for this either! None of it!"

I started to shove him a third time, but he grabbed my wrists and yanked me toward him. I glared up at him, and he glared down his nose at me.

"Arrogant Regal lord jackass Arrow—"

Kyrion growled, yanked me even closer, and lowered his lips to mine.

SIXTEEN

KYRION

I didn't know what happened.

One moment, Vesper and I were sparring and snarking at each other. The next, she was getting angry with me, so angry that her emotion had erupted into a psionic blade. I had been stunned when she had formed the psi-blade—stunned and proud that she was unlocking even more of her psionic potential.

And then . . . and then it had all gone to shit, and we'd started arguing. Vesper accused me of thinking she was a leech, when really, I was thinking I never should have doubted how smart, fierce, and strong she was—not for an instant. She started yelling and shoving me, and I grabbed her wrists to stop her.

The second my skin touched hers, every little thing about Vesper crystallized into super-sharp focus. The russet highlights hidden in her dark brown hair. The wavy wisps that had escaped her ponytail to frame her face. The pink flush in her cheeks. The silver flecks in her eyes that glimmered like bits of lunarium embedded in the surface of a dark blue moon.

Desire blasted through me, erupting as fast and fiercely as a Magma volcano. I didn't even think about what I was doing. I just bent my head and kissed her as though it was the most natural thing in the galaxy.

The first contact of her lips against mine sent an electric arrow zinging through my entire body, bringing with it an even deeper, tingling, almost painful awareness of her. The smoothness of her lips. The gasp of breath in her mouth. The heat of her body mixing and mingling with my own.

Vesper stiffened, as if the kiss had shocked her as much as it had shocked me. Her lips and wrists were the only parts of her that I was touching, but I was already hard and aching for her. My inner monster roared with hungry desire, and I wanted to lower her to the mat and explore every one of her strong, warm, solid curves . . .

As soon as that thought filled my mind, I tore my lips away from hers, released her wrists, and stepped back. Vesper staggered forward, as though she was a spaceship that I had unmoored from its docking station. She slowly righted herself and straightened up. She looked at me with wide eyes, as if she had never seen a monster quite like me before.

"I'm sorry," I said in a low, strained voice, fisting my fingers together to keep from reaching for her again. "I shouldn't have done that. I don't know what happened."

Before she could respond, a bitter laugh spewed out of my lips. "No, that's a lie, and not even a very good one. I lost control. But don't worry. It won't happen again."

Vesper stared at me, her chest heaving. Even with her O2 enhancement, I seemed to have kissed her senseless. Or perhaps that was just my own foolish wish and scrambled thoughts.

"Screw it," she growled.

Vesper took my face in her hands, surged forward, and kissed me.

This time, I was the one who stiffened in shock.

Her lips pressed against mine, warmer and firmer than before. This time, she was close enough that her breasts brushed up against my chest, which added to the pounding ache in my groin. I sucked in a ragged breath, and the aroma of the spearmint cleanser we'd both used flooded my nose. The scent was softer, sweeter on her, and it drew me even closer, like a mammoth butterfly buzzing over a particularly delectable blue-moon peony.

Vesper broke off the kiss and staggered back. She stopped and stared at me, her chest still heaving. Her eyes were darker and also brighter at the same time, the blue deeper and more intense, and the silver flecks hotter and more pronounced. Hunger filled her face, the same hunger that was still zinging through me in a hot, electric current.

I didn't know if I stepped toward her or she moved toward me. Or perhaps it was both of us, together, at the same time. But suddenly, we were kissing again.

I settled my hands on her waist and pulled her closer. Vesper licked at my lips, and I opened my mouth, my tongue darting out to stroke hers. She let out a low, pleased hum that made every single part of me stiffen with even more desire.

I slid my hands up her back, exploring the smooth curve of her spine the way I'd wanted to for months. Vesper stood on her tiptoes and wound her arms around my neck.

"Why . . ." she said in a breathless voice in between kisses, "do you . . . have to be . . . so blasted tall?"

"Why . . ." I growled, kissing her right back, "do you . . . have to be . . . so bloody short?"

She laughed, even as I caught her mouth with mine again.

I picked her up, and her legs locked around my waist. Even through our clothes, the wet heat of her pressed up against my dick. Vesper shuddered and rocked forward. Another growl tumbled from my lips at how bloody good she felt against me.

"I have a birth-control implant," she murmured.

"Me too," I rasped.

By this point, we were both breathing hard. Still holding her, I slowly went down on one knee, then the other. I raised my eyebrows in a silent question, and Vesper nodded. I lowered her all the way down to the mat. She dug her fingers into the front of my shirt and tugged me along with her, but I stopped myself from covering her body with my own. I had lost control before, and I wouldn't do that again, no matter how much I wanted her.

Instead, I braced my hands on the mat, my fingers just brushing the sides of her ribs, and loomed over her. I'd thought before that I had kissed her senseless, but perhaps it was the other way around. I struggled to get enough air back down into my lungs to ask if she really wanted this, if she really wanted *me*, monster and all.

"Kyr," Vesper whispered, as if she had heard my silent doubts. "Come here."

A grin spread across her face, and she tangled her fingers in my hair and tugged on my neck. An answering grin stretched across my own face, and I dipped my head toward her lips again—

Beep.

Beep-beep.

Beep.

A steady, insistent pattern of chimes rang out. Vesper and I both froze, her hand still cupping the base of my neck, my body hovering over hers, our lips inches apart.

Beep.

Beep-beep.

Beep.

The chimes rang out again and again. I stifled a groan. Daichi was pinging my tablet, and he wouldn't stop calling until I answered.

I stared down at Vesper. The silver flecks slowly dimmed

in her dark blue eyes, the passion in her gaze doused by the intrusion of the outside world. She let out a tense breath and dropped her hand from my neck. My inner monster hissed at the loss of her touch, but I leaned back on my heels.

Vesper sat up and scooted away from me, and neither one of us looked at the other as we both climbed to our feet.

"Daichi?" she asked in a low, strained voice.

"Yes."

She nodded, still not looking at me. "We should go see what he wants."

Vesper leaned down and scooped her stormsword up off the mat. The motion highlighted just how well her House Caldaren uniform hugged her curves. More desire spiked through me, and I stifled a groan.

Vesper grabbed her boots and socks, then whirled around to leave the gym. I raised my arm, wanting to take her hand in my own and pull her back against my body. Wanting to kiss her again and again until I drowned in the sensations that were still coursing through me. Wanting to lose myself in *her.*

My fingers flexed and crept a little closer toward her, but I couldn't take the final step and cross the short distance that separated us. The moment passed. Vesper didn't even see me reach for her, and she left the gym without another look.

I waited until the soft echoes of her footsteps vanished, then scrubbed my hands over my face, as if that simple motion would slough off the desire still pounding through my body.

I picked up my own stormsword and holstered the weapon to my belt. My gaze landed on the spot where Vesper and I had been. The faint outlines of our bodies were still visible in the thin mat.

As I stared at the slowly disappearing lines, I realized something.

The whole time I had been touching Vesper, I hadn't thought about the truebond. Not once, not even for the briefest moment.

Even more curious, I hadn't felt it either. It was almost like . . . the bond hadn't even been there. Like it wasn't influencing my attraction to her at all.

Before this moment, I had blamed the bond for this whole messy situation, for connecting our psionic powers and tying our fates together. And I had especially blamed the bond for all my bloody *softness* toward Vesper. All the unexpected care and concern for her thoughts, feelings, and well-being. All the rage I had felt at the sight of her being tortured, and all the slow, painful ways I wanted to torture Harkin Ocnus in return for daring to hurt her.

I'd thought those emotions were all just by-products of the truebond, that *it* was the thing that was making me care so much in the first place. But now . . . now I was wondering if it was all just Vesper herself, slowly but surely threading her way deeper and deeper into the black canyon of my heart where my inner monster had dwelled in solitude for so very long.

I kept staring at the mat. The faint outlines of our bodies were almost gone. I didn't have Vesper's seer magic, didn't have her ability to conjure up memories and watch them again and again like battle footage on a holoscreen, but her touch was burned into my brain now. Bond or not, Vesper was wrong about one thing.

I *did* want her, more than I had ever wanted anyone. Even worse, I couldn't quite drown out the voice of my inner monster, which kept whispering that my desire for her was going to be the death of us both.

SEVENTEEN

VESPER

I hurried away from the gym as fast as I could without running. If I could have run, I would have, but there just wasn't space for that. I climbed a set of tight spiral stairs to the top deck and stopped long enough to don my socks and boots. Then I did a couple of quick laps around the medtable in the cargo bay to try to work off some of the pent-up desire still hammering through my body.

When Kyrion had kissed me, I had been startled. Then shocked. And then . . . and then I had felt a whole lot of things I shouldn't have.

I blinked, and suddenly, I was in the round room of my mindscape. A door flung itself open, and I was seeing the kiss all over again. Even worse, I was *feeling* it all over again.

Kyrion's warm, firm lips. His tongue flicking against mine in a slow, seductive dance. His spearmint soap tickling my nose with its sharp, heady scent. His fingers skimming up and down my back. The coiled strength of his arms lifting me off the ground, then the hard, firm length of him nestling into the perfect spot between my thighs. Him looming over me on the mat, his eyes almost black with desire—

Crack!

My knee rammed into the side of the medtable, and the sudden spike of pain jolted me out of my mindscape and back into the real world. I cursed and hobbled around the cargo bay. I massaged the sting out of my knee, but I couldn't quite rid myself of the desire that was still simmering deep inside me.

Footsteps sounded, and Kyrion appeared at the front of the cargo bay. "I heard a noise. What happened?"

I jerked my chin at the medtable. "Stupid thing got in my way."

His lips twitched with amusement, but he had the good sense to keep his mouth shut. I massaged my knee a final time, then followed him down the corridor and into the library. The holoscreen embedded in the table was flashing and emitting the same chimes as his tablet.

"*Dream World,*" Daichi's voice echoed out of the table's speaker. "*Dream World,* come in."

I frowned. Why would he be saying that? Unless . . . I glanced over at Kyrion. "You named your ship *Dream World*?"

"I had to name it something," he replied, staring down at the holoscreen. "It seemed appropriate, given how much time we spent here together."

Kyrion naming his blitzer after my mindscape . . . Well, it made even more of those pesky feelings flood my body, especially my heart, which practically squished with softness.

No. I wrung the unwanted emotions out of my heart, then bricked it up. The name didn't mean anything, just like our kiss didn't mean anything. We had both been angry and frustrated, and each of us had a convenient set of lips that appealed to the other. Why, I bet if you put two other people in the same situation, the same result would have occurred. I should conduct an experiment at Quill Corp to confirm my theory. For science, of course.

Kyrion waved his hand over the holoscreen, and Daichi's face appeared, along with Tivona's. I stepped forward so that she could see me, although the motion put me shoulder to shoulder with Kyrion, which was far too close for comfort right now.

"Vesper!" Some of the worry eased out of Tivona's face. "You're okay!"

"*I* told you she was okay when I contacted you yesterday," Daichi said, a peevish note in his voice.

"And *I* told *you* that *I* wanted to see her for myself," Tivona snapped back.

I smiled and held my arms out wide. "As you can see, I'm fine."

A little bit more of the tension eased out of her face. "Good. I've been so worried. I got an alert on my tablet when you triggered your emergency beacon. So did the Quill Corp guards, but by the time they reached that location, you were gone." Tivona chewed on her lower lip. "I'm so sorry, Vesper. You trusted me to help keep you safe, and I failed."

I shook my head. "It's not your fault. It's mine. I thought the Techwave would bribe me, not kidnap me. There was nothing you or the guards could have done to stop them."

I told Tivona and Daichi everything that had happened in the Techwave facility, although I glossed over Harkin torturing me in his lab, since I was still coming to terms with that myself. I also shared my theory that the Techwave was planning something on Tropics 33.

"I cracked the encryption on General Ocnus's files," Daichi said. "If I didn't know better, I would say that he is planning a vacation at the Regenwald Resort."

Daichi waved his hand, and several pictures of the resort floated above the holoscreen. He was right. At first glance, the information looked harmless, as though General Ocnus had been planning a trip, but the answer to the Techwave's plot was in these files. I *knew* it was. I just had to find it, although it would take hours to sift through all this information—

Wait a second. Maybe I didn't have to sift through all the information. Maybe I just had to look at it through different eyes—General Ocnus's eyes.

My seer magic seemed to be growing, expanding, strengthening. It had shown me Liesl's reaction to Nerezza's harsh words in my mindscape and then Nerezza shooting down the *Velorum*, even though I hadn't been present for either one of those events. Maybe it would let me view the general's files the same way he had. Worth a shot.

So I drew in a deep breath, reached for my seer magic, and peered at the images through the lens of my psion power, instead of just my regular eyes. The longer and harder I looked, the more things moved and shifted on the holograms, as though I was plucking words, numbers, and images out of thin air and putting them together like the disparate parts of a brewmaker. Silver glows also appeared, highlighting even more bits and pieces of information.

My gaze zipped back and forth between everything, and a sick, sinking sensation flooded my stomach.

"What do you see, Vesper?" Kyrion asked. "Your eyes are glowing even more brightly than the holoscreen."

I shook my head and released my magic. The silver glows faded away, the floating words, numbers, and images vanished, and all the documents snapped back to the way they should be. "I'm not sure yet. Tivona, can you access the schematics on the new hand cannon in the Quill Corp mainframe? The one that's based on my design? That Rowena Kent stole and gave to the Techwave?"

"Sure," Tivona replied. "Let me pull it up . . ."

She hit several buttons and flicked through some files. The

schematics for my hand cannon appeared, along with a list of materials needed to manufacture the weapon. I pushed the schematics off to the side, then enlarged the list and swiped away all the other info except for a lone spreadsheet buried deep in Ocnus's files.

Beside me, Kyrion leaned forward and stared at the holograms with narrowed eyes, as did Daichi and Tivona from their remote locations.

"Don't you *see* it?" I asked, anger flaring in my chest. "What the bastards have done?"

Kyrion, Daichi, and Tivona all shook their heads, so I zoomed in a little more on the list and the spreadsheet. Then I stabbed my finger at first one line, then another, tagging them with red dots.

"We already knew the Techwave scientists had manufactured my hand cannon. Harkin Ocnus fired a cannon at Kyrion and me, and I saw dozens more of them in the Techwave weapons bunker," I said. "But the lab rats didn't stop with those prototypes."

Daichi's black eyebrows drew together. "What do you mean?"

"Look at the materials list for my cannon, then compare it to the Techwave spreadsheet of supplies."

Daichi leaned forward a little more, as did Tivona and Kyrion.

Tivona saw it first. She frowned and hit some buttons on her screen. "Let me run the list and the spreadsheet through Raul's sales-tracking program . . ." Her fingers stilled, and she let out a soft gasp. "Vesper, you won't believe these numbers."

"Unfortunately, I do. Raul never makes mistakes with his calculation programs." I looked at Kyrion. "Remember all those machines and conveyer belts in the factory? The Techwave wasn't just building Black Scarab armor. They were producing cannons—*my* cannons."

"How many?" Kyrion asked in a tense voice.

"Nine hundred and forty-four so far," Tivona replied in a grim voice.

Daichi let out a low whistle. "What could the Techwave do with that many cannons?"

I had to unclench my jaw to answer him. "A single hand cannon like the one Harkin shot at Kyrion and me can blast away bones, melt metal, and even cut through psionic shields. Roughly a thousand of those weapons? All firing at the same target? They could cut through much bigger, stronger energy shields, including those around ships and buildings . . ."

"The Techwave is going to use the cannons to attack the Regenwald Resort," Kyrion finished my thought.

I nodded. "Yes, although I don't know why. What's so special about the resort?"

Kyrion shrugged, while Daichi and Tivona both shook their heads. No one had an answer.

"Even if we don't know exactly why they're targeting the resort, we have to stop the Techwave before they kill the tourists and workers," I said.

"Agreed." Kyrion waved his hand, and a star map appeared, showing our blitzer zooming through space. "We should arrive at Tropics 33 early tomorrow morning galactic time. With any luck, the Techwave won't be ready to launch their attack, and we can find their base of operations."

"What about contacting the Erzton for help?" Tivona asked. "And warning them about the attack?"

"Going through official channels would take time we don't have," Kyrion replied. "Even if we did contact them, there's no guarantee the Erzton officials would believe us. Not without more proof."

The four of us discussed several more ideas, plans, and contingencies, but Daichi and Tivona were too far away to help, and it was up to Kyrion and me to thwart the impending attack.

The whole time we talked, I kept staring at the cannon schematics. Worry, fury, and disgust hammered through me at how Harkin and the other Techwave scientists had twisted my design into something truly horrific. Harkin and General Ocnus were going to pay for that.

"There's something else," Daichi said, breaking into my dark thoughts.

He waved his hand. The cannon schematics and other information vanished, and video footage appeared. "This was recorded shortly after the two of you left Magma 3."

"Where is this from?" Tivona asked.

"My official Imperium ship," Kyrion replied. "Touma set up a control program, and I used my tablet to remotely fly the ship to Magma 3 and land it near the Techwave facility."

Tivona frowned. "Why would you do that?"

Kyrion's gaze never left the footage. "Because Holloway is plotting something."

For several seconds, all that was visible was the interior of the ship, empty, still, and static. Then, in the distance, a shadow appeared, congealing into a familiar figure with blond hair, pale eyes, tan skin, and a smug smirk.

"Zane," Kyrion growled.

The video kept playing. Zane glanced around the flight deck, and his gaze fell to the camera. His lips puckered in thought, and his eyes flashed a bright silver-blue for a moment. Then he grabbed the camera and grinned into the lens.

"Clever, Kyrion," Zane murmured. "Using House Zimmer tech to spy on your own ship. Very clever."

Kyrion cursed, but Daichi held up a finger.

"Wait," he said. "There's more."

The feed went dark for several seconds, then light and sound flared to life again. The angle was a bit awkward, as though Zane had shoved the camera into a pocket on the front of his jacket, but the footage showed Dargan and Adria standing outside Kyrion's Imperium ship, with the Techwave facility burning in the background.

"He's not bloody here!" Dargan growled, swinging his sword back and forth in an annoyed motion.

Adria glanced up at the ship. "Judging from the lack of psionic echoes, Kyrion was never on this blitzer."

Dargan stabbed his sword at the still-burning facility. "Maybe one of the Techies zapped him. Maybe he's already toast inside the factory."

Zane chuckled. "Your naivety is almost charming. Kyrion Caldaren is much too stubborn to be killed in anything as clean, simple, and easy as a factory explosion."

Adria nodded. "Zane is right. Kyrion's not dead in the factory, which means he left on another ship, most likely with Vesper Quill."

She wet her lips, stepped forward, and held her hands out, skimming her palms back and forth, almost as if she was tasting the air with her fingertips. "Oh, yes," she purred. "Kyrion and Vesper left together, and the truebond between them is stronger than ever."

I froze. How could she possibly know we were bonded?

Dargan stepped up beside his sister and sniffed the air, his nostrils quivering like a bloodhound that had latched on to a fox's scent. "Oh, yeah. Holloway was right. Kyrion and Vesper are *definitely* bonded. It smells all sweet and gooey, like a marshmallow, but with burned edges. Definitely a romantic bond. It's going to be *so* much fun for us."

Adria and Dargan looked at each other and started laughing. Their gleeful chuckles made my stomach twist, even as my cheeks burned with embarrassment. They knew about the bond, and even worse, how much I cared about Kyrion. Could Dargan smell how one-sided the romantic part of the bond was? Ugh. I hoped not. That would be a whole new level of humiliation.

I didn't look at Kyrion. I didn't want him to see my feelings written all over my face, and I desperately hoped he couldn't sense them through the bond either. He tensed beside me, and the sticky cobweb in my mind pulsed, although I couldn't quite pinpoint his emotions. Concern, maybe, although it seemed to be mixed with something much softer and warmer.

"Where do you think Kyrion and Vesper went?" Zane asked. "We have to find them. Holloway is already pissed that they beat his truebond test. He'll be even more pissed if we don't deliver them as promised."

A hard fist of fear slammed into my chest and quickly morphed into sharp talons of worry that shredded my heart. Holloway had sent the three Arrows to drag us back to Corios.

Adria shrugged. "Holloway had a spy in the Techwave facility. Maybe they got out before it exploded and they know where Kyrion and Vesper are heading."

Spy? What spy? But Adria didn't reveal their name, and she pulled her tablet out of her pocket and moved away.

Zane turned toward Dargan. "Why will Vesper and Kyrion's bond be fun for you and Adria?"

A grin spread across Dargan's face. "What did you think I meant?"

"Nothing good," Zane drawled.

Dargan's grin widened. "Exactly! I've always hated Kyrion. Such a bloody arrogant dick. Always bossing all the Arrows around, even though Adria and I are much more powerful than he's ever *dreamed* of being. Kyrion thinks because he's Holloway's little pet project that he's untouchable, but I'm going to enjoy showing him otherwise."

Beside me, Kyrion stiffened, and his eyes narrowed as he glared at the footage.

Dargan ran his finger along the edge of his sword, and the lunarium blade gleamed the same stormy gray as his eyes. "While you were off getting pretty for the mission, Holloway summoned Adria and me back to the throne room for a few final instructions. He told us that we can have a little fun with Kyrion and Vesper before he sticks them in one of the palace labs and siphons off their magic. Holloway isn't going to screw around with them for years like he did with Kyrion's parents. He's planning to take all their magic at once."

My stomach twisted again, a little more violently than before, and another fist of fear slammed into my chest, driving the air out of my lungs.

"But that will kill them," Zane replied, his voice oddly flat.

Dargan clapped the other Arrow on the back. "That's the idea."

"And what do you and Adria get out of this arrangement?" Zane asked.

"People think Callus Holloway is the only one who can tap into a truebond," Dargan replied. "But if you're part of a truebonded pair, then you can feel the power of other bonded pairs around you, just like Adria and I could taste and smell Kyrion and Vesper's connection."

He glanced over to make sure his sister was still busy with her tablet, then leaned closer to Zane, as though he was revealing some great secret. "Holloway doesn't report every truebond, and the other Regals have no idea how many couples he's drained over the years. Whenever Adria and I come across a truebonded pair, we take some of their energy for ourselves before we turn them over to Holloway. It's like sinking your teeth into a juicy steak. The taste just explodes on your tongue, and it fills you up with more power than you ever imagined."

Dargan lifted his fingers to his mouth and blew a chef's kiss. Every word he said about how truebonded pairs could be used, abused, and tortured sent another nail of revulsion spiking through me, as though I was being boarded up alive in my own coffin.

Adria shoved her tablet into her pocket and came back over to Dargan and Zane. "According to Holloway's spy, Kyrion and

Vesper are most likely headed to Tropics 33. The Techwave is planning something there, and the two of them have probably decided to be brave, noble heroes and try to stop it."

Dargan snorted. "Idiots."

Adria nodded in agreement. "Idiots indeed. New orders. Holloway wants us to let Kyrion and Vesper stop whatever the Techwave is doing. Then we'll move in and capture them."

Dargan and Adria strode away, heading for their own ship in the distance. Instead of following them, Zane pulled the camera out of his pocket and flipped it around so that he was once again staring into the lens. His face was unreadable, but for the strangest reason, I could have sworn that I felt a flicker of regret from him, even though I wasn't anywhere near him, and the video had been recorded hours ago.

"See you soon, Kyrion." Zane winked at the camera. "You too, Vesper."

His hand covered the lens, and the footage cut off.

"Fuck," Kyrion muttered.

My thought exactly.

Daichi and Tivona peered at us through their respective terminal screens, worry creasing their faces. Kyrion stared at me. That sticky cobweb pulsed in my mind, and his worry, anger, and disgust matched my own.

"What do you want to do, Vesper?" he asked. "We could forget about Tropics 33 and go somewhere else. Zane, Dargan, and Adria don't know about the *Dream World,* so they wouldn't be able to track us. Neither would Holloway."

As tempting as that idea was, I couldn't just abandon the guests at the Regenwald Resort to their gruesome fate. After the *Velorum* crash, I had vowed that I would *never* stand by and watch while innocent people were hurt, not when I could do something to help them, however small it might be. So far, that vow had brought me nothing but danger, pain, and misery, but I wasn't going to break it.

I wasn't going to be like Nerezza, Conrad, the Kents, and everyone else who had used me over the years. Not in this way.

I shook my head. "No, we have to stop the Techwave. As bad as the Regals, Holloway, and the Imperium are, the Techwave is worse. Ocnus and Harkin are *worse*. They want to build a draconian, totalitarian regime. No one would be safe from them. No one would have any *freedom,* and sooner or later, we would all end up as lab experiments or stuffed into Black Scarab suits and forced to fight for the Techwave until we died."

For some reason, a bit of disappointment flashed across Kyrion's face, but he gave me a short, sharp nod.

"What about Zane, Dargan, and Adria?" Daichi asked.

"We kill them," Kyrion replied in a cold, flat tone. "And anyone else Holloway sends after us."

I nodded. "And then, when we're ready, we go back to Corios and kill that bastard ourselves."

Kyrion's eyebrows shot up, as though the venom in my voice surprised him, although his face quickly turned smooth and unreadable. The sticky cobweb of him in my mind was still and silent, and I couldn't sense what he was thinking or feeling. Neither one of us spoke, and the seconds ticked by one after another . . .

Kyrion held out his hand. I stared at his palm a moment, then stepped forward and gripped his hand. I started to give it a firm, businesslike shake, but Kyrion threaded his fingers through mine. My heart lurched at how good, how *right*, that felt, but once again, I decided not to read anything more into the motion. Instead, I squeezed his fingers, sealing this new bargain between us.

We didn't speak, but we both knew the truth—that this dangerous mission we had just assigned ourselves was most likely to end with us both captured, killed, or worse.

EIGHTEEN

VESPER

Daichi and Tivona promised to keep trying to track down the Techwave, as well as the Arrows. But for right now, all Kyrion and I could do was see what awaited us on Tropics 33.

"Vesper, I'm still digging up the information you requested," Daichi said. "I can't tell who changed your records yet, but the documents were altered quite some time ago."

I nodded, even though questions churned in my mind. "Thank you."

He nodded back to me, then looked at Kyrion. "One final update. Touma is running the tests you requested."

Kyrion's hands clenched around the edge of the table, and his body went rigid. "Holloway?"

"Yes," Daichi replied. "The results should be back soon."

Kyrion hissed out a breath between his teeth. "What about the other test?"

"Touma is running Zane's sample too. He's also combing through the Regal archives, looking for other genetic matches.

He should know more soon."

"Thank you. Keep me updated."

He tipped his head to our friends, then sliced his hand over the holoscreen, cutting the connection. Daichi and Tivona both vanished, leaving Kyrion and me alone again.

"What kind of test did you do with Holloway and Zane?" I asked.

Kyrion tensed again and stared down at the table. After a few seconds, he squared his shoulders and raised his gaze to mine. "I got samples of Zane's and Holloway's DNA before I left Corios. I asked Touma to run the samples against someone else's DNA." He paused, and when he spoke again, his voice was pitched much softer and lower than before. "Your DNA, Vesper."

Shock punched me in the chest, driving all the air from my lungs. "Why—why would you do *that*?"

But as soon as I asked the question, I knew the answer. "You want to know who my biological father is."

Kyrion nodded. "Yes, I do."

"But I told you that *I* didn't want to know. So why would *you* care so much?" Suspicion knifed through me. "This is about truebonds, isn't it? You want to know who my father is so you can see if there's a history of truebonds in his family. You're still trying to figure out why and how our bond happened."

"No. I don't care how the bond formed. Not anymore. Just like I don't care if there is a history of truebonds in your family." He hesitated. "I just . . . I wanted to find out for you, Vesper. To give you some answers."

More shock punched into my chest. "But I told you during the spring ball that I didn't want to know. That I have no desire to try to worm my way into a Regal family that would never accept me."

Kyrion shook his head. "You don't know that for sure."

Anger spurted through me, replacing my shock. "Oh, yes, I

do. Nerezza was quite chatty in the Techwave lab. She said that my father's family basically exiled her from Corios."

"Did it ever occur to you that Nerezza might have lied?" he countered.

I threw my hands up into the air. "Of course it occurred to me, but Nerezza expected Harkin to break me and the Techwave to dispose of me as soon as I fixed their new weapons. She had no reason to lie." A bitter laugh erupted from my lips, despite my best efforts to hold it back. "Nerezza didn't want me. My own *mother* didn't want me. What makes you think my father would be any different? Long-lost bastard children aren't in vogue among the Regals, Erztonians, or anyone else. It's the one accessory no House and family wants to have."

Kyrion's lips pressed together into a tight line, but he didn't dispute my words.

I glanced over at the dark holoscreen, thinking about what Daichi had said and struggling to get my seesawing emotions under control. "You're running my DNA against Holloway's, right?"

Kyrion nodded.

"Well, let's hope to all the stars and back it's not a match. Who knows what Holloway would do if I was his daughter? Probably stick me in one of his palace labs and dissect me until my magic was all used up and I went insane from the pain and trauma." I snapped my fingers. "Oh, wait. That's the same thing he wants to do to me now. See? Knowing who my biological father is changes *nothing*."

Kyrion didn't respond, although his lips flattened out into that tight, tense line again.

Another thought occurred to me, and I stabbed my finger at him. "Wait. Daichi said there have been more tests. How many people have you compared my DNA with so far?"

He shifted on his feet. "A few dozen at this point. I started with the Regals who are known to have seer abilities in their bloodlines, but so far, Daichi and Touma haven't found a match. Not so much as a distant cousin three times removed."

The depths of his betrayal flabbergasted me. Kyrion knew—*he knew*—how much Nerezza's abandonment had hurt me, and yet here he was, trying to find another family to reject me and break my heart all over again.

"I guess we're even now," I growled.

"What do you mean?"

I snapped up my left palm. The eye-shaped cuts were a bright, vivid red, as though I had squeezed my own heart between my fingers and left bloody streaks behind. "I didn't tell you that we were still bonded, and you didn't tell me that you've been trying to find my absent father. Seems as though we've both been lying to each other."

Kyrion grimaced, but once again, he didn't dispute my words. Arrogant Regal lord, thinking *he* knew what *I* wanted or what was best for me.

"You're right about one thing, though."

"What?" he asked in a low, guarded voice.

Another bitter laugh came from my lips. "There is no true care or concern with the bond. It's just magic, and it is having a grand old time screwing with both of us."

I glared at Kyrion a second longer, then whirled around and stormed out of the library.

Once again, my steps quickened, and I would have started running if I'd had the room for it. But once again, I was painfully reminded that I was stuck on this blasted blitzer with Kyrion until we reached Tropics 33.

I did a couple of laps around the medtable, going nowhere fast, and my gaze landed on the green, blue, and red buttons on the wall that controlled the cargo bay ramp, the permaglass barrier, and the oxygen level. My fingers twitched with the urge to smack the buttons, lower the permaglass barrier, and suck all the air out of Kyrion's side of the ship.

No, I decided, still glaring at the buttons. Suffocation was too quick and easy a death for him. I should shove my stormsword into his chest. Or better yet, shoot him with a blaster and watch him slowly bleed out.

I did some more laps around the medtable. After the seventh lap, I forced myself to slow down.

Despite my boiling anger, I would not—could not—ever deliberately hurt Kyrion like that. Although, if I was being completely honest, I had already hurt him by hiding the truth about the bond. I huffed. Some pair we were. Each of us was perfectly happy to lie to the other when it suited our purposes. They might have been good lies, designed to shield the other person from harm, but they still had backfired all the same.

The rest of my anger evaporated, although hurt kept grinding against my heart like it was caught in a series of geared wheels. I needed something to do, a project to occupy my hands and especially my mind until we reached Tropics 33. Maybe I could rearrange the supplies in the cargo bay, even though everything was already stowed away . . .

A gleam of silver caught my eye. The hand cannon that I'd swiped from the Techwave facility was lying on the counter where Kyrion had slung it down when we'd first boarded the blitzer. I'd been so distracted that I hadn't had a chance to study the Techwave modifications to my design.

Time to change that.

Determination surged through me, and I took the hand cannon to a maintenance area on the second, lower deck that was filled with tools and other supplies. I placed the weapon on a holoscreen. A series of 3D holograms appeared over the table, and I picked up the weapon and physically dissembled it piece by piece.

The cannon was largely the same as the one I had created at Kent Corp, the design Conrad Fawley had claimed was no good before handing it over to Rowena and Sabine Kent. Fresh anger spiked through me, but Conrad, Rowena, and Sabine were dead. They couldn't hurt me anymore, and they had suffered for their crimes against me and all the innocent people they had killed in the *Velorum* crash. Still, that bit of justice felt hollow right now.

One by one, I placed the cannon pieces on the holoscreen, creating 3D scans of each individual part. Then I zoomed in on the various pieces, comparing the holograms to the actual finished parts. I also rummaged around in the storage bins until I found some real paper, along with a gelpen, and started making notes.

The cannon featured most of my original design ideas, although Harkin and the Techwave lab rats had made a few improvements, like decreasing the barrel size and lightening the weapon's overall weight. Smart. I grumbled, wishing I'd thought of those tweaks. But there was one major difference between my original design and the Techwavers' weapon— they had changed the cannon's energy source.

Instead of a typical solar magazine, which needed to be recharged every week or so, the cannon's magazine was different. Oh, it still looked like a typical magazine, but something odd had been added to the standard solar wiring: tiny bits of pale, almost translucent stone.

Curious, I used a screwdriver to remove the magazine's clear outer casing. Next, I took a pair of tweezers, grabbed one of the tiny stones, and pulled it off a strand of solar wiring, like I was sliding a pearl off a silver necklace. I placed the stone on the holoscreen, which quickly scanned and identified it.

"Lunarium?" I muttered.

I plucked my stormsword off my belt and laid the weapon on the holoscreen next to the much smaller stone. They both had the same opalescent sheen, but the stone was much paler, and its sheen waxed and waned, as if it was a wobbly moon that was about to vanish completely. In contrast, the sword's lunarium blade maintained a high, constant luster, as though it was a steadily burning star and always contained the same amount of energy, no matter how often it was used.

I drummed my fingers on the table, making the holograms flicker, thinking back to when Harkin had fired the cannon in the Techwave facility. In the beginning, the blasts of power had been quick, steady, and incredibly strong, but the more Harkin had fired the cannon, the slower and more erratic the energy pulses had become, until the weapon had overheated. The Techwave might be using lunarium to give the cannons enough energy to cut through psionic shields, but the lunarium and the solar wiring weren't completely compatible.

I ran several simulations. No matter what variables I added, with each successive blast, the Techwave cannon grew seven percent more likely to blow up in the hands of the person shooting it than to fire at their target. The lunarium needed a stabilizing agent, some sort of stone, metal, or other substance to keep the solar wiring's energy at a steady level and stop the cannon from frying itself.

This must be the puzzle that Nerezza, Harkin, and General Ocnus wanted me to solve. Right now, their hand cannons were useful up to a certain point. But if the design flaw was fixed, and the cannons could maintain a steady level of power . . . Well, it would be hard for anyone, even a psion as powerful as Kyrion, to withstand the Techwave's weapons for long.

I studied the sword and the stone again. They weren't all that different. Both were made of lunarium, so why was the solar wiring frying so easily? What did the sword have that the cannon lacked?

I picked up my stormsword and turned it around in my hands, examining it from all angles. The hilt itself was nothing special, solid, durable silver that would withstand the fire, ice, wind, and other physical elements and psionic powers that the blade might emit. The three eye-shaped sapphsidian jewels were pretty, but they were simple decorations, just like the arrow-shaped jewel in the hilt of Kyrion's sword.

A thought popped into my mind. I set the sword down, then hit some buttons on the holoscreen and called up the site of *Celestial Stars*, one of the most popular gossipcasts in the galaxy. A few weeks ago, the gossipcast had done a puff piece on the Arrows' weapons. Tivona had loved the show, while I'd rolled my eyes in annoyance.

I found the appropriate broadcast, and the gossipcaster's cheery voice blared from the table's speakers. "And now we move on to the sword of Zane Zimmer, arguably the most handsome and eligible bachelor among the Arrows . . ."

The gossipcaster kept extolling Zane's many supposed virtues while he struck one outlandish pose after another with his sword. I waited until the video focused on his weapon, then stopped it and zoomed in.

Zane's sword was a bit larger than mine, and the hilt was covered with tiny engraved *Z*s, befitting the heir to House Zimmer. I snorted. Of course, Zane would have a weapon as obnoxious as he was. But nestled among all those *Z*s were several small pieces of sapphsidian. Excitement coursed through me, and I fast-forwarded through the rest of the gossipcast, only stopping long enough to examine the other Arrows' weapons.

Every single one of their swords, hammers, and daggers featured some sort of sapphsidian, whether it was embedded in the hilt, sparkling on the crossguard, or even touching the lunarium blade itself. The dark blue stones were the only thing all the weapons had in common.

I pumped my fist in the air in triumph. Until Harkin figured out how to stabilize the lunarium and solar wiring combination, the Techwave cannons would keep overheating.

But maybe that was the point.

Whatever their ultimate goal was, the Techwave would want to do as much damage—and kill as many people—as possible on Tropics 33. General Ocnus wouldn't care if the cannons' circuitry overheated and the weapons exploded, especially if the cannons were being wielded by empty suits of Black Scarab armor. He might even send the Scarabs into the Regenwald Resort with orders to fire their cannons *until* the weapons exploded, destroying both the Scarabs and any resistance they might encounter.

I pulled up the information Daichi had shared in the library earlier. There were no sapphsidian mines on Tropics 33, but a quick search showed that the Erzton controlled several other such mines on different planets and moons. If the Techwave ever realized that sapphsidian was the key to stabilizing their lunarium-studded magazines, then they would attack the Erzton mines just as they had been attacking Regal facilities over the past several months.

Ideas, theories, and questions spun through my mind, but I couldn't prove or answer any of them. My gaze dropped to the pieces of the hand cannon, which were strewn all over the table. What I *could* do was fix the weapon, at least enough so that it would fire again. Maybe once we got to Tropics 33, I could find some sapphsidian, add it to the solar magazine, and test my theory.

But for right now, I was determined to beat Harkin at his own game, so I started reassembling the cannon. My hands were busy, but the work was simple, and my thoughts turned back to Kyrion.

If only repairing the broken trust between us was this easy.

NINETEEN

KYRION

Vesper stormed away, but I remained in the library. Eventually, she went down to another deck and started working in one of the maintenance rooms.

Every once in a while, a muffled curse would sound, along with *cracks, bangs,* and *clang-clang-clangs* of metal striking metal. But the velvety thread of Vesper in my mind hummed with happiness, as though she was making progress on whatever she was doing.

Since it didn't seem like she was going to return to the top deck anytime soon, I went into the kitchen. Normally, I didn't think too much about what I ate, but tonight I wanted to do something special for Vesper. An apology of sorts. If food could ever truly make up for anything.

I pulled several items out of the cabinets and started rehydrating a few things, along with slicing and dicing and baking and sautéing others. Thirty minutes later, I was putting the finishing touches on the meal when Vesper stepped into the kitchen. She was carrying the hand cannon from the Techwave facility, although the device bristled with a few more parts and pieces than before. Vesper must have fixed the cannon, as well as making it more powerful, just like she did with every weapon she got her hands on.

"Going to use that on me?" I drawled.

She snorted, set the cannon down on the floor, and leaned it up against the wall. "That depends on how much you annoy me."

"Fair enough."

Her nose twitched, and she sniffed the air. "That smells good. What is it?"

I gestured over at the pot on the stove. "Heirloom tomato soup with dill and asiago cheese croutons and some hot ham-and-Swiss sandwiches. With chocolate-covered strawberries, raspberries, and blueberries for dessert."

"Fancy," she replied, although her stomach let out a telltale rumble.

She blushed and looked around the kitchen. Her gaze landed on a shiny chrome machine on the counter. "You have the new Quill Corp brewmaker, *my* brewmaker."

"Yes," I replied. "And it was worth every credit."

Her face brightened, and her pride rippled through the bond to me.

Vesper's brewmaker truly was a marvelous machine, able to make any beverage you could imagine within a matter of seconds, as well as fabricate a variety of foods. Daichi had been so impressed that he had bought one for his office and another device for his personal chambers at Castle Caldaren.

"I used your brewmaker to make some of Daichi's favorite honey-ginseng tea, although I added a squeeze of lemon and a slice of orange."

I poured some of the liquid into a glass and held it out. Vesper's fingers brushed against mine, and she took the glass and quickly stepped back, as though that simple touch had scalded her skin. Or perhaps that was just the heat warming my own fingertips.

She took a sip of the iced tea and hummed with pleasure. "This is really good. I'm surprised a mighty Regal lord such as yourself knows how to cook."

"Growing up, I fixed my own food more often than not. The servants were usually occupied with their own work, while my parents were occupied with each other. Feeding me never seemed to be high on anyone's list of priorities, so I learned to fend for myself."

A shadow passed over Vesper's face. "Feeding the students was never high on the list for the Imperium academy instructors either. If you wanted food with some actual taste and texture, instead of just a chalky protein bar or shake, you had to either buy it or make it yourself."

I tilted my head toward the table in the corner. "I made plenty if you want to join me. But if you don't, I understand. Either way, please eat something. You still need more fluids and calories to replace all those you lost at the Techwave facility."

Vesper considered the table. She hesitated, then walked over and dropped down into a chair.

I took the soup off the stove and ladled it into two bowls before sprinkling it with dill and black pepper and adding several croutons. Next, I slid the hot ham sandwiches off the griddle, the cheese oozing out the sides. I carried everything over to the table and sat down. Then Vesper and I dug into our food.

Despite the freeze-dried and other preserved ingredients, the soup had turned out surprisingly well, and the generous amounts of dill and black pepper further enhanced the tomatoes' rich, vibrant flavor. The Swiss cheese added a delightful tang to the smoky, salty ham, as did the honey mustard I'd slathered onto the thick, chewy sourdough bread. The iced tea had a delicate, refreshing blend of honey and citrus notes, while our dessert of chocolate-covered berries was dark and decadent and light and sweet at the same time.

The whole meal was rather tasty. Or perhaps it was the company that made it so. Vesper didn't speak, and neither did I, but having her on board soothed something deep inside me. I had spent so much of my life alone, had eaten so many meals alone, that it was . . . pleasant to have some company, even if that company was currently angry with me. But even more than that, I enjoyed cooking for Vesper and making sure that she had a filling meal. It was a simple thing, especially compared with all the horrors she had faced in the Techwave facility, but I hoped it comforted her in some small way.

After we finished, I pushed my empty plate aside and looked at her. "I'm sorry I didn't tell you that I was trying to find out who your father is."

Vesper sat back in her chair and considered me with cool eyes. "Why is it so important to you? It's not important to me."

"You really don't want to know?"

She sighed and twisted her empty glass around and around on the tabletop. "When I was a kid, and it became clear that Nerezza was never coming back, I used to fantasize about finding my biological father. In my daydreams, he would have no idea that I existed, and he would have been so very sorry that he didn't know me before I found him." A wry smile curved her lips. "And then he would shower me with lavish presents to make up for lost time and buy back my love."

"Would you let him?"

Her smile grew a little wider. "Of course. After he had groveled significantly enough and I had accumulated a substantial pile of presents, along with several pets. Corgi puppies and boodle kitties have always been my favorites."

We both chuckled at her light, teasing words, although her face soon turned serious again.

"But the older I got, the more I realized how unlikely that

joyous reunion was, especially among the Regals. No one wants to be confronted with the daughter they never knew existed. Or worse, confronted with the daughter they knew existed but chose to ignore."

"I'm sorry," I said in a soft voice.

Vesper shrugged. "It is what it is. I've made as much peace with it as I can."

She pushed her glass away and looked at me again. "I'm sorry too. I shouldn't have hidden the bond from you. I was trying to protect you from Holloway, the other Regals, and everyone else who would want a piece of our power. I thought it would be safer for both of us if you thought the bond was broken. I thought you would be able to move on, even if I couldn't."

Her last few words came out as a low, strained whisper. Something clenched deep inside my chest, although I couldn't say for certain what it was. "You, Vesper Quill, are a very hard person to move on from."

She smiled a little, but it was a sad, resigned expression, and the same emotions rippled along the velvety ribbon of her in my mind. "That's the problem between us, isn't it? We both want to move on, but we can't because the bond keeps dragging us back together."

I didn't want to move on from Vesper. Not anymore. But as much as I wanted to indulge my attraction to her, I just . . . couldn't. Even if I could ignore the truebond and its potential quirks, influences, and ramifications, there was no place for such softness in my life, especially not now, when Holloway had sent Zane, Adria, and Dargan to capture us.

I gestured over toward the hand cannon, which was still sitting on the floor, trying to distract Vesper and myself from our mutual melancholy. "Did you figure out how the Techwave changed your design?"

Her sadness vanished, replaced by a grim, angry expression. "Oh, yes."

We went back into the library. Vesper laid the cannon on the holoscreen, pulled up a 3D schematic of it, and told me about the adjustments the Techwave had made to her design, including the lunarium-studded solar wiring that had a tendency to overheat.

"Knowing about the lunarium power source is helpful, although it still doesn't tell us why the Techwave is heading to Tropics 33," Vesper said as she finished her explanation. "I looked at General Ocnus's files again, but my seer magic didn't point out anything else. No words, no phrases, no silver lights or telltale glows that would indicate something was important."

Her words jogged a memory in my mind. "Perhaps we don't need a magical silver glow. Perhaps all we need is the right information."

I swiped away her schematics and hit some buttons on the screen. "A few weeks ago, I asked Daichi to research which planets and moons are rich in lunarium deposits."

Vesper frowned. "Why?"

"Holloway is always looking for more lunarium. He often sends Arrows out to search for it, so I wanted to keep tabs on which planets and moons he might dispatch us to next." I hit a few more buttons, and images of burning factories and decimated buildings hovered over the table. "I also noticed something odd about the recent Techwave attacks. No matter what kind of Regal facility they strike, whether it's a metal refinery, a production plant, or a biochem lab, the Techwavers always take all the lunarium on-site. It's the only common thread that links their attacks, so I thought if Daichi could find more of it, then the other Arrows and I might be able to stake out some of the facilities that store lunarium and set a trap for the Techies."

Vesper nodded. "That makes sense. But what does that have to do with the Regenwald Resort? It's a tourist destination, and it belongs to the Erzton, not the Imperium."

"Daichi found mentions of lunarium at all the usual sites, but there was one place we both thought was a little strange." I waved my hand, and a new document appeared. "According to an old report buried in the Regal archives, there is a supposedly abandoned lunarium mine on Tropics 33."

She frowned again. "Why do you say it like that?"

"Because Holloway has spies everywhere, including on Erzton-controlled planets." I waved my hand again, and more documents and images filled the screen. "One of his spies reported that a large shipment of mining equipment was delivered to Tropics 33 last month. Why would an abandoned mine need new equipment?"

Vesper's eyes narrowed as she studied the information. "Because it's *not* abandoned. That's just a rumor the Erztonians started to keep the mine off everyone's radar."

"And now it's backfired on them. The Techwave will kill all the tourists and destroy the Regenwald Resort to hide the fact that they are really targeting the mine. But once they seize it, they'll have even more lunarium to power their new hand cannons."

We both fell silent, contemplating that horrible scenario.

"How much lunarium do you think is in the mine?" Vesper asked.

"No idea. How much do you think the Techwave needs?"

Her face scrunched up in thought, and she tapped her fingers on the cannon's barrel, as if she could pull the answer out of the weapon with the motion. "Hard to say. This cannon contains only a few small bits of lunarium, but assuming the mine is active, and it has a significant stockpile . . ." She stared off into the distance, and the silver flecks in her eyes glowed. "The Techwave could easily produce thousands, maybe even tens of thousands of weapons. With that much firepower, they might risk attacking Corios. Maybe even Crownpoint and Callus Holloway."

Tension filled me, along with a fair amount of worry. I had little regard for the other Regals and absolutely none for Holloway, but the innocent people who lived on Corios didn't deserve to suffer and die just because the Techwave wanted to topple the Imperium.

"You were right," I said. "We have to stop the Techwave now, before it's too late. Not just for the tourists at the resort but for everyone else in the galaxy."

"What about Holloway?" Vesper asked. "Somehow his Techwave spy knew that we were heading to Tropics 33, and now Zane, Dargan, and Adria are chasing us."

I shrugged. "Then we'll kill them, just like we killed the Techwave guards on Magma 3. I would rather die fighting than be Holloway's bloody battery."

Vesper nodded. "Me too. Although I wonder . . ."

"What?"

The silver flecks in her eyes brightened again. "Adria and Dargan have kept Holloway from taking their magic for years, ever since their bond formed. If they can do it, why can't we?"

I shrugged again. "I don't know what makes the Byrnes different from my parents, but we can't risk getting anywhere near Holloway. The second he gets his hands on us, he'll latch onto our power, and then we'll never be free of him."

Vesper nodded again, although the absent look on her face indicated that she was still trying to solve the problem, still trying to fix things. "You're right. We can't risk it. Still, I wonder . . ."

Her voice trailed off again. I didn't ask what she was seeing with her magic. Part of me didn't want to know.

Deep down, I had always been resigned to the idea that I would eventually be doomed to the same fate as my parents, trapped in a truebond and forced to be a power source for Holloway. At least, until he got greedy and reckless and took too much of my psion power at once and accidentally killed me. But hearing Vesper talk about Adria and Dargan as though we could somehow replicate their success in not sharing their power with Holloway . . . Well, it gave me too much bloody *hope*, when what I needed was cold, ruthless determination.

Vesper shook her head, dismissing her thought or vision or whatever it was. The silver flecks in her eyes dimmed as she focused on me again. "Promise me one thing, though."

"What?"

"That no matter what happens, we won't lie to each other anymore. Not even the good lies we think we're telling to spare the other's feelings or to keep the other safe."

"Agreed. No more lies." I paused. "Although what makes a lie *good*?"

A small, sad smile flickered across Vesper's face. "Liesl used to say that the only good lies were the ones you actually managed to believe yourself."

She started fiddling with the hand cannon, pulling out the magazine and asking the holoscreen to measure the exact amount of lunarium inside. I watched her work, thinking about her words.

Vesper was right. The only good lies were the ones you truly believed, and I had never believed any of the ones I had told myself over the past few months about how I didn't care about her.

TWENTY

VESPER

Kyrion and I worked in the library for another hour, searching for more information about the lunarium mine on Tropics 33. Then we both went to bed—separately.

I'd managed not to think about our kiss too much during dinner, but now, alone in the dark, it was *all* I could think about. Part of me wanted to slip out of bed, go down the hallway, step into Kyrion's room, and see what happened next. See where things would go, and all the passion we might share, if only for tonight.

But the morning would come all too soon, and our issues would remain the same. How we were worried that the bond was the only thing truly connecting us. How we had both lied to each other. How, deep down, we simply didn't trust each other.

As much as I wanted Kyrion, I didn't want to be with someone I didn't trust, so I grumbled and rolled over onto my side, away from the bedroom door. I closed my eyes, but it was a long, long time before I drifted off to sleep.

I woke the next morning tired and cranky, and the sensations only intensified when Kyrion and I took our seats on the flight deck. During the night, we had arrived at Tropics 33. The planet's surface was stunningly beautiful, with large swatches of vibrant emerald-green rain forest surrounded by even larger swatches of clear aquamarine water, as though the whole planet was made of sparkling jewels.

"At least it's not another Magma planet," I joked.

Kyrion snorted. "You say that now, but just wait until we're tromping through the rain forest with its excessive humidity and you're soaked with sweat. You'll be wishing we were on a bone-dry Magma planet by lunchtime."

He signaled the closest spaceport, and the blitzer started its rapid descent.

"*Dream World,* you are cleared for landing," a voice crackled over the comms system.

I grinned and sat up a little straighter. Despite everything that had happened between us, Kyrion naming his ship after my mindscape deeply pleased me.

"Don't look so bloody smug," he grumbled. "Like I said before, I had to name it something."

My grin widened.

While the blitzer sank toward the surface of the planet, Kyrion tapped on his tablet, and my own tablet chimed in response. "Here are our cover IDs. We are an extremely wealthy couple from Temperate 22 who own an import-export business and are relaxing on a tropical getaway. After we drop our bags in our rooms, we'll scope out the resort, then head over to the lunarium mine. The Erztonians give tours of it."

"How considerate of them," I murmured.

By the time I had memorized our cover story, the blitzer had landed at the spaceport. Kyrion and I shouldered our bags and strode down the cargo bay ramp. I glanced back over my shoulder. I hadn't noticed it before, but he had painted *DREAM WORLD* on the gray hull in dark blue letters. Even more curious, the space in the center of the *A* was a unique, distinctive shape—an open eye nestled in the center of the House Caldaren arrow. My heart squished yet again with all those soft, pesky feelings.

"Something wrong?" Kyrion called out.

"Of course not." I plastered a smile on my face and hurried to catch up to him.

We entered the spaceport and wound our way through several security lines and customs checkpoints. A guard ordered us to stop and scanned our tablets, checking our IDs. I held my breath, wondering if our mission was going to end right here and now and if we might be arrested—or worse. But after several long, tense seconds, the light on the guard's scanner flashed green, and he waved us on through the line.

"I had no idea Touma was so good at forging IDs," I murmured to Kyrion as we put our tablets away, picked up our bags, and left the checkpoints behind.

"Oh, no. The fake IDs are all Daichi's doing. He is quite skilled at crafting them, along with all the other electronic bits and bytes of information that make up a person's identity. Plus, he watches a lot of romance serials, and he enjoys coming up with the most outrageous backstories he can."

"So that's why my name is Baroness Ravencia Elizabeth Bertina Richter," I drawled. "I thought I recognized it from one of the serials."

Kyrion laughed, and we stepped outside. The spaceport's chilly air-conditioning vanished, and the humidity hit me like a wet, sloppy wave, as though I was wearing my clothes inside a hot running shower. Tempered silk automatically adjusted to the wearer's body heat, along with their surroundings, but the expensive fabric was no match for this environment.

Kyrion smirked. "Still glad this is a Tropics planet?"

I pulled my already sticky shirt away from my side. "Zip it, Baron Benek Darcy Kane Richter."

He laughed again, and the sound filled my ears like low, rumbling music. Despite the danger we were heading toward, Kyrion seemed lighter here than anywhere else we had been together, as if having a new persona and being on a new planet freed him from the constraints that he endured as Lord Kyrion Caldaren back on Corios. A similar lightness buoyed me.

We got into a transport, along with several other folks who were going to the resort. Unlike the transports back on Temperate 42, which were the epitome of grimy functionality, this vehicle looked brand-new, and the chrome seats practically sparkled.

I peered out through the windows. The low, squat concrete buildings and black asphalt of the spaceport quickly gave way to a lush tropical rain forest. Towering trees stretched their thick brown limbs and verdant green leaves up toward the sky, and gray vines and purple flowers wrapped around their trunks like strings of neon lights. Colorful birds swooped from branch to branch, while mammoth butterflies flitted back and forth, their wide wings shimmering an iridescent black and blue in the morning sunlight.

It was a breathtakingly beautiful paradise, which made me even more determined to stop the Techwave from destroying it.

Thirty minutes later, the transport pulled into a long, curving drive made of crushed shells that glittered like shards of rainbow glass. The centerpiece of the Regenwald Resort was a seven-story building of gleaming black wood, along with gray vines woven together in thick, tight strands. Magenta hibiscuses wider than my chest bloomed all along the vines, their petals quivering in the faint breeze and ending in sharp points that glowed with a faint, shimmering pink light. Smaller matching buildings spiraled out across the landscape, connected by permaglass walkways that overlooked swimming pools, rock-lined grottos, and other recreational areas.

I let out a low whistle of appreciation. "If all the Erztonians live like this, then I'm going to defect."

"You've never been on an Erztonian-controlled planet before?" Kyrion asked.

"Nope. This is my first time. Are they all so gorgeous?"

"Some of them are. The Erzton might control most of the galaxy's mines and minerals, but they are exceptionally responsible when it comes to their environmental impact. Erztonian laws dictate that they must always leave a place better than how they found it. For decades, this area was only used for mining, but the Erztonians transformed it into a tourist destination several years ago after the lunarium mine was supposedly played out."

The transport pulled up to the front of the resort, and a stream of workers rushed forward to collect luggage, scan tablets, and confirm reservations.

Kyrion had our luggage sent to our suite, and then we stepped into the lobby, which featured a clear permaglass floor. Fifty feet below, dozens of chefs were stirring, sautéing, and flambéing wonderful-looking dishes in an enormous chrome kitchen that was as sophisticated as any military cruiser. Next door, housekeepers were throwing towels and sheets into massive cleaners and recyclers. In the center of the lobby, the permaglass looked down over an underground pool that had been laid into the surrounding natural rock formations. Some guests had made their way down there and were lounging in long cushioned chairs, sipping drinks from hollowed-out pineapples, coconuts, and other large tropical fruits.

A bright flare of silver caught my eye, and I glanced up just in time to see someone duck behind one of the fluted amethyst columns that supported the domed wood-and-vine ceiling. Curious, I quickly rounded the column, but the figure was gone, and I only saw workers and guests moving through the lobby like normal.

"Something wrong?" Kyrion asked, stepping up beside me.

"Maybe it's weird, but I feel like someone is watching us."

He snapped to attention. "Did you get a good look at them? Was it Zane? Or Adria or Dargan?"

I shook my head. "No. I wouldn't have even noticed the figure, but my seer magic pointed them out for some reason."

Kyrion fell quiet, although tension radiated off his body as he stared out over the crowded lobby. I also kept scanning the area, but no one was paying any attention to us.

"Come on," he said. "Let's gear up in our rooms, then head over to the mine for the afternoon tour."

Kyrion headed toward the registration desk, but I glanced around the lobby again. Workers and guests kept moving through the area, but a finger of unease skittered down my spine. My seer magic kept whispering that someone was watching us, although time would tell whether they were friend—or foe.

Kyrion checked us in, and we rode an elevator to the top floor. As befitting our wealthy cover identities, he had booked a luxurious suite, and the real wood, stone, and glass furnishings were even grander than those in the lobby. No expense had been spared, except when it came to the appliances. An old Kent Corp brewmaker was squatting on the kitchen counter instead of my new, improved model. I made a mental note to ask Tivona to find out who bought the appliances for this resort. Quill Corp could make a fortune outfitting vacation spots alone.

I went into the living room in the middle of the suite. Kyrion had already unpacked his bags and laid our stormswords out on a low glass table, along with blasters, daggers, shock batons, and a couple of small metal balls that contained explosives.

"You packed all this stuff into your suitcases?" I asked.

We hadn't wanted to wear our swords into the spaceport, lest someone recognize them—and us—so Kyrion had tucked them into some secret lead-lined compartments in his bags. The Techwave cannon had been too big to hide in a suitcase, so we'd left it on the blitzer.

He pointed at the items one after another, as if counting them off on some mental checklist. "Just a few things I thought we might need."

"I would hate to see what you would pack if you thought we needed *more* weapons," I teased.

He laughed, and the sound once again pleased me. I liked making him laugh, something he didn't do nearly often enough.

Kyrion plucked his silver bandolier off the table, but instead of slinging it across his chest, he wrapped it around his waist, transforming it into a wide belt. Then he started sliding daggers into the slots, along with the marble-size explosives.

I let out another low whistle of appreciation. "You could kill a whole squad of Techwavers with your bandolier alone."

Kyrion gave me a grim smile. "That's the idea."

Next, he grabbed his stormsword, raised it up high, and tucked it over his shoulder into a hidden slot in the back of his dark blue jacket. I went around behind him. The sword was completely hidden from sight, although he could easily reach it.

"Neat trick," I said.

"Glad you approve," he replied. "Because I packed one for you too. Put on your jacket and turn around."

I did as he asked. Kyrion loomed behind me, his breath tickling my neck. He skimmed his hands over the collar of my jacket, brushing my hair aside, and I bit my tongue to hold back a shiver. Next, he slid my stormsword into the hidden slot in the back of the jacket. I reached up, back, and around, making sure that I could grab the hilt, which was sticking upright.

I turned around and faced him again. Kyrion tugged my jacket down, adjusting it into a better, more comfortable position. His hands drifted to my waist, and the warmth of his fingers soaked through the tempered silk of my shirt. He looked down at me, his eyes dark, hot, and hungry.

My heart squeezed with longing. No wonder Kyrion seemed lighter here. It would be so wonderful to be the carefree couple we were pretending to be, instead of the mismatched pair we truly were. A Regal lord and a lab rat, an Arrow and an inventor, a powerful psion and a struggling seer, forced together by extenuating circumstances and hunted by dangerous enemies.

I shook off my wistful thoughts and stepped back. Kyrion's hands fell away from my waist, although his fingers flexed and then curled into fists, as though he was stopping himself from touching me again.

"We should go," I said in a low voice.

Kyrion nodded and grabbed a few more supplies, which he tucked into his pockets. Then we left the suite.

We returned to the lobby, went outside to a raised platform, and boarded a monorail, which slowly transported us across the resort grounds. We rode past palm-tree-shaped pools filled with happy, shrieking children, as well as other, smaller, quieter pools with adults lazing on inner tubes. Some people doggedly swam laps back and forth, while others flocked to floating bars in the crystal-clear water. Some people smacked balls back and forth on stone courts, while others dodged paint lasers and hard sprays of dyed water on rope, rock, and other obstacle courses.

Hikers trudged along trails that snaked through the thick vegetation, snapping photos of the birds and butterflies that flitted back and forth above their heads. Man-sized spiders spun massive webs across some of the paths, waiting for lunch to come along and snare itself, unconcerned by the people oohing and aahing over them.

"It really is lovely," Kyrion murmured.

I could hear what he wasn't saying: that we needed to do everything in our power to keep the Techwave from killing the thousands of innocent people and animals on the resort grounds.

Thirty minutes later, the monorail pulled into a station.

A guide was waiting on the platform, and he waved his hand, drawing everyone's attention. "Howdy, folks! We are so pleased to welcome you to the Regenwald Resort. From here, you can take advantage of hiking, biking, surfing, and other activities. You can also follow me for a tour of an old lunarium mine, which we have transformed into part of the resort . . ."

Most of the guests headed for booths to rent hoverbikes, surfboards, and yoga mats, but a few followed the guide toward a massive opening in the tall rock wall at the edge of the clearing. Kyrion and I fell in step behind the other guests at the back of the tour group.

I studied all the guests, as well as the workers at the nearby booths, but everyone was either gearing up for activities or enjoying some refreshments. A few folks eyed Kyrion and me, their gazes lingering on our long-sleeved jackets and pants, clearly wondering why we weren't dressed in shorter, lighter garments. Fashionistas aside, I once again had the uneasy sense that someone was watching us.

Kyrion pulled out his tablet and swiped through a few screens. "Daichi has tapped into the resort's security feed. So far, there is no sign of Techwave activity anywhere near the resort or the mine. He'll let us know if anything changes." He hesitated. "Daichi also says there is no sign of Zane, Dargan, and Adria."

I tensed. I'd been so focused on trying to figure out who was watching us that I'd almost forgotten about the three Arrows.

Kyrion put his tablet away. "Come on. The tour group is getting away from us."

The guide gave a short safety speech about not straying

from the marked paths, and then we moved from the bright afternoon sunlight into an enormous cavern. The temperature dropped several degrees, and some of the oppressive tropical humidity faded away. I sighed with relief and pulled my sticky shirt away from my skin. Kyrion's lips twitched with amusement.

"This is why I live on a Temperate planet," I grumbled. "There's not too much of any one kind of weather."

"Corios is a Temperate planet," Kyrion replied. "You could always live there."

My gaze flew to his. Even though I was a Regal now, I had never even considered living on Corios. Kyrion grimaced and looked away, as though he'd said something he wished he hadn't.

We both fell silent as the guide escorted us deeper into the cavern, which narrowed to tunnels branching off in different directions. Our guide led us down the main center tunnel, which was wide, broad, and filled with lunarium.

Thick seams of the opalescent stone ribboned through the dark gray walls, reminding me of larger versions of the solar wiring in the Techwave's cannon. While the guide recited facts about the mine, I trailed my fingers over the stone. The lunarium was as smooth as glass, but sparks of color flickered deep inside its shiny depths—pale blue, shimmering silver, even a few bright pops of purple, pink, red, and green.

Even stranger was the sensation that emanated from the stone, like it was an opal-colored sun adding even more warmth and power to my own psionic abilities. My skin tingled, and sweat beaded on my forehead, despite the cool air. I shuddered and yanked my hand away from the lunarium, but the unusual warmth lingered in my fingers.

"As you can see," the guide continued, "the mine still contains large deposits of lunarium. However, given its low quality, the owner thought it would best serve as a tourist attraction for everyone to enjoy. Now, let's head to the next section . . ."

I turned to follow the guide, and a telltale silver flare appeared. This time, I clearly saw a figure slipping into a nearby tunnel. My seer magic whispered an urgent warning, and I darted in that direction.

"Vesper!" Kyrion hissed behind me. "What are you doing?"

Probably being a reckless idiot, but I didn't want to lose our shadow again, especially when my magic kept pointing them out. This person was important for some reason, and I wanted to know why.

The shadowy figure darted into one tunnel after another. This deep in the mine, only small floodlights were embedded in the walls, although the thick seams of lunarium added a pale, eerie glow to the surrounding stone.

The figure never slowed down or hesitated, as if they knew exactly where they were going. After a few more twists and turns, they hurried into an area without any obvious exits. Thick columns of stone twisted up to support the ceiling, creating deep shadows and plenty of places to hide.

I could sense Kyrion coming up behind me, but I ignored the questioning pulse of him in my mind. Instead, I reached up, back, and around, grabbed the hilt of my stormsword, and slid the weapon free of the hidden slot in my jacket. Then I put my back to one of the walls and crept forward, making as little noise as possible. I also reached out with my seer magic, but no more silver flares appeared. I wasn't sure if that was because the columns were blocking my view or because the figure wasn't in here anymore.

Time to find out.

I lunged forward, stabbing out with my sword and peering around the first column. Empty space greeted me. I swallowed a frustrated growl, tiptoed over to another column, and lunged forward again. More empty space.

I repeated that process over and over, working my way

around the area. I lunged around yet another column, expecting more emptiness—

Something whistled toward my head.

I ducked, and a chunk of stone zipped through the air, smacked into one of the columns, and shattered. A figure erupted from the shadows and stretched their hands out to shove me back, but I spun away, avoiding their charge.

The figure kept going, sprinting back toward the exit. I charged after them, but they were moving fast, and I wouldn't be able to catch them before they reached the main corridor. From there, they could disappear into another tunnel, and I would lose them completely—

Telekinetic power lifted the figure up and slammed them into a nearby wall. The figure bounced forward, still on their feet. They grunted and staggered to a stop.

I leaped in front of the figure, still clutching my stormsword, which was glowing a pale, faint blue in an eerie mirror of the lunarium seams in the walls. Kyrion stepped up beside me, his stormsword in his right hand and his left hand stretched out in front of him, ready to use his telekinesis again.

The figure was clad in a dark gray tactical jacket, along with matching cargo pants and boots. A helmet topped their head, hiding their features. I tensed, thinking they were a Techwaver, but a closer look revealed that it wasn't a Black Scarab helmet but something that looked like the one Kyrion sometimes donned on his Arrow missions.

I brandished my sword at the figure. "Take off your helmet and show us your face."

The figure hesitated. Kyrion growled and lifted his sword a little higher. He really was quite intimidating when he was in full-fledged Arrow mode.

The figure slowly tipped their head in surrender, then reached up and removed their helmet.

It was a woman with black hair, pale skin, and silver eyes

that had the same opalescent sheen as the lunarium in the walls. Surprise shot through me. I had only met her twice in person, but I had seen her on countless gossipcasts in recent weeks, so I recognized her immediately. So did Kyrion, who blinked several times.

Lady Asterin Armas, a member of the Erztonian nobility and the woman Kyrion had been supposed to marry.

TWENTY-ONE

KYRION

Lady Asterin Armas straightened up, her lips curving into a rueful smile. "You caught me. And here I thought I had finally mastered the art of sneaking around. My tutors would be extremely disappointed."

"What are you doing here?" I asked, my mind sorting through a dozen possible scenarios, none of them good. "Did Holloway send you?"

Her face crinkled with confusion. "Why in all the stars would Callus Holloway send me anywhere? As far as he knows, I am safely back on Sygnustern."

Sygnustern was the home planet of the Erztonians and only a few hours away from Tropics 33 by pinpoint travel.

"I'll ask the question again," I snapped. "What are you doing here?"

Vesper lowered her sword, then laid her hand on my arm. I reluctantly lowered my own sword.

Vesper studied Asterin the same way she would study a blaster, as though she was mentally disassembling the other woman, examining her inner workings, and then rebuilding Asterin in her mind. "She's a spy."

Another rueful smile spread across Asterin's face, and she tipped her head. "Guilty as charged." She arched a mocking eyebrow at me. "Is this when you do your Arrow duty and lop off my head for daring to creep along behind you?"

"That depends on who you're working for and what you're doing here," I growled.

Asterin pointed her finger at her chest. "*I* have every right to be here. This is *my* mine. The better question is what are the two of *you* doing here?" She stabbed her finger at us. "A notorious Imperium Arrow and a newly anointed Regal lady. You're both a long way from Corios."

I bit back a curse. Callus Holloway had wanted me to marry Asterin because she owned the lunarium rights on several planets and moons, and he wanted to wrest those resources away from her. Holloway had also been hoping that a bond would spark between us, since Verona and Aldrich Collier, Asterin's mother and stepfather, had a truebond.

I glanced over at Vesper, who shrugged. She didn't know what to make of Asterin following us either.

"Nothing to say?" Asterin drawled. "Pity."

She let out a low whistle. In the distance, footsteps sounded. I spun around, but a dozen guards carrying hand cannons were already streaming into the cavern. Asterin had led us into an area with no other exits. A clever trap. My estimation of her rose even higher.

The guards aimed their cannons at us, and I stepped in front of Vesper, ready to shield her from any attack.

Asterin's eyes narrowed, and her silvery gaze flicked back and forth between Vesper and me. She laughed, as if she found something highly amusing, then tucked her helmet under her arm and swept out of the cavern.

The guards jerked their weapons at Vesper and me, and

we had no choice but to sheath our swords and follow the Erztonian lady.

Asterin led us from one corridor to another. We skirted around the public areas of the mine and moved into tunnels full of workers wearing hard hats, coveralls, and gloves. Some of the workers carried complicated instruments, conducting geological surveys and other tests, but most of them were carefully aiming handheld lasers at the walls, slicing out chunks of lunarium from the surrounding stone.

I had no idea where Asterin was taking us, but so far, the guards hadn't confiscated my stormsword or the weapons hidden in my bandolier belt. My hand gripped the hilt a little tighter. The first guard who made a threatening move toward Vesper would be the first person to die.

We reached a freight elevator. Asterin stepped inside, and the guards gestured for us to follow. Asterin punched in a lengthy code on a keypad. The doors slid shut, and the elevator rose. Asterin pulled out her tablet and swiped through a few screens, but her guards never took their eyes off Vesper and me.

The guards were a mix of men and women of varying shapes and sizes. They were all dressed in dark gray coveralls as befitted miners, but they clutched their hand cannons with easy familiarity, and they didn't relax their tense, watchful stances. Not just common guards but Hammers, the elite fighting force of the Erzton. Not only would they be extremely well trained, but some, if not all, of them would have psionic abilities similar to my own powers.

Vesper and I were in trouble.

The elevator floated to a stop, and the door rattled back. Asterin stepped outside, and we went down a long corridor made of permaglass that offered a sweeping view of the tropical rain forest around the mine, as well as glimpses of the resort buildings in the distance. At the end of the glass corridor, a guard bowed to Asterin and opened a set of metal double doors.

Vesper and I followed the Erzton lady into an enormous office. Just like the corridor, the walls were permaglass, although the floor was the same dark gray stone as the tunnels. This area looked like it had been built on the very tiptop of the mine, and it resembled a glass house precariously perched atop a pile of rocks.

Thick gray rugs stretched across the floor, while the chairs and tables boasted the same black wood and gray vines that were so prevalent at the resort. A set of wind chimes hung in the corner, although they were composed of colorful stones instead of the usual metal. The chimes were still, since there was no breeze to rustle and rouse them into song, but the stones cast out rainbow prisms of color that dappled the walls like stars trapped in the permaglass. Overall, the space was comfortable without being ostentatious, unlike the luxe offices of so many Regals.

Asterin tossed her helmet down onto a chair. "Leave us."

The Hammers tipped their heads, acknowledging her order without comment, question, or complaint, indicating just how much power she had. The guards withdrew, and the last man shut the door behind him, although I could sense them lingering outside the office with my telempathy. Asterin wasn't afraid of us, which could be either a mistake on her part or an indication of how strong and protected she was in her glass fortress.

Asterin went over to a high table along the wall and picked up a pitcher full of bright orange liquid off a round metal disk. "Would you like some mango-lime-pomegranate juice? It's always kept at exactly the right temperature, thanks to my new beverage chiller." A wry smile played across her lips. "Just as Quill Corp advertises."

Vesper laughed. "Well, at least you have good taste in appliances."

"I have good taste in quality products that work exactly as they're supposed to," Asterin replied. "Not cheap shit that Regal corporations pump out en masse and pass off as being better than it really is."

One of Vesper's new brewmakers was sitting next to the disk-shaped beverage chiller. If nothing else, Asterin seemed to be a fan of Vesper's work. Perhaps this forced meeting would turn out better than I expected and not end in violence, bloodshed, pain, and death.

"Please. Sit." Asterin gestured at a nearby love seat.

Vesper went over and dropped down onto the cushions. I hesitated, then followed her.

Asterin poured three glasses of juice, set them on a silver tray, and placed the whole thing on the low table in front of Vesper and me. Then she settled herself on the opposite settee, picked up a glass, and swallowed a long gulp.

"Mmm. Cold-pressed juice truly is the best," she said. "I hope you're working on a new appliance for that."

Vesper leaned forward and grabbed her own glass. "A combination appliance, actually. A brewmaker that can cold-press fruits and vegetables into drinks, along with using the larger leftover chunks and rinds for heartier things like smoothies, soups, and stews."

"A toast to your ingenuity." Asterin raised her glass.

Vesper did the same, then the two of them looked at me.

"In Erzton society, it's a grave insult not to join your host in a toast," Asterin said in a mild voice.

Vesper let out a snort that sounded suspiciously close to a giggle. I shot her a sour glare, but I picked up the third glass.

Asterin held her glass up a second longer, then took another gulp. Vesper drank from her glass, and I did the same with mine. The juicy flavors of sweet mangoes, bright limes, and tart pomegranates burst on my tongue as though I had just sunk my teeth into the ripest, most delicious fruits. It was wonderfully refreshing, but after a few sips, I lowered the glass and set it back down on the tray. I wanted my hands free in case this meeting went sideways.

Vesper drained her juice, but Asterin cradled her glass in her hands, eyeing the two of us.

"How did you do it?" she asked.

"What?" I asked in a guarded voice.

"Convince Callus Holloway and all the other Regals that the two of you aren't bonded."

Vesper tensed, and my hands curled into fists on my lap. Asterin might think the guards stationed outside were enough to protect her, but I could easily dash my juice glass against the table, grab a broken piece, and slit her throat with it.

"Don't bother lying. My mother and stepfather have a truebond, so I am quite familiar with how they look and feel. Plus, I could tell something was wrong when Kyrion cut his hand during the truebond test during the last ball on Corios." She tilted her head to the side and studied us. "Although your bond is different from the others I have encountered."

Vesper's eyes narrowed. "You know *other* people with truebonds? Besides your mother and stepfather?"

"Oh, yes," Asterin replied. "Truebonds are not uncommon among the Erztonians, although we don't obnoxiously advertise them the way you Regals do."

"No one among the Regals advertises truebonds," I muttered.

Asterin waved away my words. "Considering all the gossipcasts I saw while I was on Corios, I would have to disagree with you, Kyrion. Especially since so many of those gossipcasts speculated about the two of *us* forming a truebond before we even got engaged. But none of that happened, and now I know why. The two of you were *already* bonded before I met either one of you at the spring ball."

"Is that what this is about?" I asked. "You're disappointed we didn't get engaged, and you didn't secure the Imperium alliance for the Erzton like your family expected?"

A merry laugh burst through her lips. "Hardly. I was *relieved* when it became apparent that your affections were engaged elsewhere. It was the perfect excuse to put off my mother and stepfather, without enduring the weight of their disappointment yet again."

Her mouth twisted, although I couldn't tell if her disgust was directed at her parents, herself, or everyone involved.

"I wore gloves," Vesper said. "To fool Holloway and everyone else. I wore thin flesh-colored gloves to hide my hands so that no one would see the cuts."

She held out her left hand so that Asterin could see the crude eye carved into her palm. Vesper nudged me with her elbow. I grumbled and held out my own left hand. Asterin frowned, her gaze moving back and forth between the respective marks.

"What is it?" I demanded. "What do you see?"

Asterin leaned back against the cushions and regarded us with a much cooler expression. "I see two Regals who slipped into my resort, my mine, with fake names under false pretenses. Two very powerful and dangerous Regals who have yet to tell me what they were doing sneaking around an Erzton facility, something that is in direct violation of the treaties between our two governments. I should ship you back to Corios at once. Given what I know about Callus Holloway's obsession with truebonds, he would give me a massive reward for turning the two of you over to him."

"That would end very badly for you," I warned in an icy voice.

Asterin stared at me, her face as cold as mine. "And it wouldn't end nearly as well or quickly for you as you think it would."

Her eyes glittered a bright silver, and power rippled off her. I couldn't tell exactly what kind of psion she was or what abilities she might have, but Asterin was strong—far stronger than I'd realized when we'd been dancing together on Corios. She was much like the lunarium in her mine, something that looked soft and pretty but had hard, hidden depths.

"Both of you, stop dishing out threats," Vesper said. "It's pointless. Especially given what is going to happen."

"What might that be?" Asterin snapped.

"The Techwave is going to attack your mine," Vesper replied.

Asterin's eyes sharpened. "Explain."

Vesper revealed everything that had happened over the past few days, including how the Techwave had kidnapped her and the clues we had uncovered about the Tropics 33 mine being their next target.

Asterin frowned. "What do they want with so much lunarium? Other minerals are worth much more, especially on the black market. And there are other mines that would be much easier targets than this one."

Vesper grimaced, and guilt rippled through the velvety ribbon of her in my mind. "The Techwave is building weapons—weapons that are based on my designs."

She told Asterin how she had been designing weapons for Kent Corp and how Rowena Kent had given the schematics to the Techwave in hopes of overthrowing the Imperium and killing Callus Holloway.

Asterin chewed on her lower lip. "Do you know when or where the Techwave might attack?"

I shook my head. "Our friends are working on it, but so far, they haven't been able to find any trace of the Techies on Tropics 33."

Asterin surged to her feet and started pacing back and forth. She clasped her hands behind her back, and her silver eyes glowed again, as though she was thinking of possible scenarios and solutions and then discarding them just as quickly. Power rippled off her again, although I couldn't tell any more about her psionic abilities than before.

She stopped and faced us. "So the two of you came here to stop the Techwave. Why risk yourselves? You could have sent a warning to the Erzton through official channels."

"That would have taken too long, and you know it," I replied.

Asterin tipped her head in agreement. "Bureaucracy is a slow, lumbering beast."

"I came here because the Techwave stole my work," Vesper said, her voice low and angry. "I wanted to use my designs to help people, but the Techwave has twisted them into something dark, ugly, and dangerous. They tried to kill me, and when that didn't work, they kidnapped me and stuck me in a lab. The Techwave scientists would have kept right on torturing me until they killed me or I broke down and did what they wanted. Those bastards are going to pay for that, along with every single person who has been helping them."

I knew she was talking about Nerezza, although she didn't mention the other woman.

"Please," Vesper said in a softer voice. "Give us a chance. Let us help you. All we want is to make sure that no one else dies."

"And get your revenge," Asterin challenged.

Vesper nodded, a fierce look on her face. "And get my revenge."

Asterin stared at Vesper, and then her gaze flicked over to me again. After several seconds of silent contemplation, she gave us both a short, sharp nod. "Very well. I'll have my guards start checking the mine, as well as the resort, for any sign of the Techwave."

Some of the tension between the three of us eased. We were all on the same side—for now.

Another sly smile curved the corner of Asterin's mouth. "As for the rest of it, well, I rather enjoy it when people get some well-deserved revenge."

TWENTY-TWO

VESPER

Asterin headed over to her desk and started making calls, alerting her people about the possibility of a Techwave attack. Kyrion went to the opposite corner, called Daichi on his tablet, and started speaking to him in a low voice.

Asterin and Kyrion had left me with nothing to do, so I roamed around the office and wound up in front of a large bookcase. Real paper books lined the shelves, a mix of romance stories and mining manuals, and I drew in a breath, inhaling that faint, musty scent I loved so much.

But the most interesting things on the shelves weren't the books—they were the rocks.

Jagged chunks of rocks perched on the shelves in neat rows. I recognized the more common stones, like amethyst, jade, and rose quartz, but I had never seen many of the others before. Some were as dull, flat, and gray as the floor, while others shimmered with even brighter neon colors than the tropical rain forest outside.

A thought occurred to me, and I leaned forward and scanned the rocks again. Tucked back in the shadows was a dark stone I hadn't noticed before. Excitement coursed through me, and I grabbed the stone and held it up to the light streaming in through the glass walls.

A piece of sapphsidian gleamed in my hand.

I turned the stone back and forth, watching the sparkling flecks of black swim around like fish trapped in the dark blue depths. In the mine, the lunarium had grown painfully hot against my skin, but the sapphsidian was surprisingly cool, as though I was clutching a chunk of frost.

Asterin finished her calls and came over to me. I started to put the stone back in its place, but she waved her hand. "Please. Look at it for as long as you like."

Her tone was polite, and she meant what she said, but I still returned the sapphsidian to its spot on the shelf. "Are these all the ores, minerals, and jewels that you mine for?"

Asterin nodded. "Most of them. I like to take a souvenir out of every mine that I work in."

"What do you know about lunarium and sapphsidian?"

"Why do you ask?" she countered.

I didn't know much about Asterin Armas, but I had liked her ever since I'd first met her when she had been hiding out in the shadows during the spring Regal ball, the same as me. Even more important, I got the sense that I could trust her. Plus, my seer magic kept painting her in that telltale silver flare, as though she was important, although to whom or for what I couldn't say.

So I shared my theory about how the sapphsidian jewels worked to stabilize the lunarium blades in stormswords and other psionic weapons and how the lack of them was why Harkin Ocnus's cannon had overheated and fried itself.

Asterin nodded again. "That makes sense. Sapphsidian is often used to shore up structures on Erzton planets, although it has been replaced by cheaper materials in recent years. But even today, sapphsidian is often used as columns and supports, especially in lunarium mines. Something about the sapphsidian balances out the more volatile nature of the lunarium, just like you are theorizing."

She gestured at Kyrion, who was still talking to Daichi on his tablet. "Much like your volatile nature balances out Kyrion's colder one, and vice versa."

I laughed. "Me? Volatile? Hardly. He's the most notorious killer in the galaxy."

"And yet you're the one trying to get revenge on the people who wronged you."

Hmm. Maybe I was more volatile than I'd realized.

I rubbed the eye that was still carved into my palm. It was inflamed and aching again. Asterin noticed the motion. I hesitated, then held my hand out where she could see it.

"Do you know why Kyrion and I have these marks? We both know the truebond is still there, so shouldn't the wounds have healed by now?"

She shrugged. "No truebond is exactly like any other. The bond and all its powers and proclivities are unique to each pair, but the wounds will probably vanish when the two of you finally accept the bond."

I frowned. "But we've both done that, more or less."

Asterin shook her head. "More or less is not the same thing as fully and completely. Your respective magics know the difference, even if your minds don't."

She stepped closer and laid her hand on my arm. When she spoke again, her voice was pitched much lower than before. "A truebond is nothing to be afraid of, even with someone like Kyrion Caldaren."

A bitter laugh burst through my lips. "Tell that to Kyrion's parents. They both died because Callus Holloway kept siphoning off their magic."

Confusion creased Asterin's face. "What do you mean?"

Kyrion was still talking to Daichi, so I quietly told Asterin what had happened to Kyrion's parents. How Holloway had taken too much of Desdemona Caldaren's magic at once, causing her to sicken and die, and how Chauncey had gone so mad from grief, rage, and the loss of his wife and their bond that he'd attacked his own son, forcing Kyrion to kill his father in self-defense.

By the time I finished, Asterin's face was dark with fury. "So that's why Holloway was so eager to see if a truebond would form between Kyrion and me. I had heard the rumors about the Caldarens, but knowing they're *true*, that Holloway really did take their power again and again until he eventually killed them . . ." Her voice trailed off, and a shiver swept through her body. "That is a fate I am happy to avoid."

Asterin might have avoided it, but it could still be my fate. Zane, Dargan, and Adria were on their way to Tropics 33 right now. What would happen when the three Arrows caught up with us? And they *would* catch up with us. I could *feel* it in my bones, as though I was watching water slowly heat up in a brewmaker and knowing it was going to boil over sooner rather than later.

"Does your mother love your stepfather?" I asked.

Asterin frowned at the abrupt change in topic. "Why would you ask that?"

I hesitated again, but she already knew so many of my secrets. What was one more at this point? "I only met Kyrion a few months ago, but somehow a bond formed between us almost immediately. Ever since then, I've been wondering how much the bond influences us, how much it might shape our decisions and especially our perceptions of each other."

Understanding dawned on Asterin's face. "Ah, you want to know if your feelings for Kyrion are genuine."

I shifted on my feet, but I didn't dispute her words. Like it or not, I *did* have feelings for Kyrion, but I wanted—*needed*—to know if they were of my own choosing.

I rubbed my head, which was aching, along with my left palm. "Yes. I don't know if my feelings are genuine. Just like I don't know when or how the bond first formed."

Asterin frowned again. "How could you not know that? Especially if you just met him a few months ago?"

I told her how I had been wandering through Kyrion's castle and library for years, long before I ever set eyes on him, either on a gossipcast or in person.

Asterin tapped her finger against her lips. "I don't know the answers to your questions, but my mother and stepfather met and fell in love, and *then* the bond formed between them. Although for you and Kyrion, it seems to be the other way around."

I scoffed. "Kyrion and I are not *in love*."

The look Asterin gave me was almost pitying. "Because you think these feelings aren't genuine, that they are just a by-product of the truebond. Right?"

I shifted on my feet again. "How can they *not* be a product of the bond? It's the only thing tying us together. Without it, we would be living separate lives on different planets."

"But would you still think about him?" Asterin asked in a soft voice. "Even if the bond wasn't connecting you, would you still wonder where he was and what he was doing? If he was having a good day? If he was safe?"

I glanced across the office. Kyrion was still talking to Daichi, his brow furrowed in concentration. Even now, when he wasn't paying the slightest bit of attention to me, my heart still quickened at the sight of him, and the low rumble of his voice sent a hum of happiness through my body.

"Then you have your answer," Asterin said. "The bond might be what first brought you and Kyrion together, and it might be a part of you both now, but it's just *one* part. It is not the *whole* of you, and it certainly doesn't control either one of you."

Her words unwound a hard knot of worry and tension deep inside my chest. "Thank you. I'll remember that."

She nodded and squeezed my arm.

"What do you know about other types of truebonds?" I asked.

"What do you mean?"

I told her about the sibling bond between Adria and Dargan Byrne and that Holloway couldn't take their magic the way he had siphoned off magic from Kyrion's parents.

Asterin's lips puckered in thought again, and she absently picked up one stone after another before setting them all back down on the shelf in a neat, precise row. "In theory, a truebond is only between the two people involved. But bonded pairs can emit a tremendous amount of psionic energy, which is how a powerful siphon like Holloway can access their magic. Maybe the Byrnes have found some way to block his power with their own. I can't really say, without seeing them in person or watching Holloway try to take their magic."

Frustration filled me. Of course, the answer—if there even was one—wouldn't be that easy to discover.

"Thank you," I said. "For everything. You've given me a lot to think about."

Asterin smiled. "A truebond can be a wonderful thing, especially between two people who genuinely care about each other. It's not something to be feared, and people like Callus Holloway shouldn't weaponize it to control other people."

The smile faded from her face, and she stepped even closer, her eyes on mine. "The Erzton treats truebonds very differently from the Imperium. If you ever need a safe haven, come to Sygnustern, and ask to speak to one of the Hammers. Just say the words *Bond of two, tried and true*, and you'll get the help you need."

Bond of two, tried and true. I repeated the phrase in my mind. Once again, Asterin's words soothed me. Something about them sounded right in a way I couldn't quite explain.

"Thank you," I repeated, flashing her a grateful smile. "That means a lot."

She nodded and smiled back at me.

Kyrion finished his call, put his tablet away, and came over to us. "Daichi is still trying to track the Techwavers, but so far, there's been no sign of them—"

BOOM!

An explosion drowned out his words, and the resulting shock wave ripped through the office, making the loose rocks on the bookshelves rattle around in a harsh warning. In the distance, through the glass walls, an orange fireball spewed into the air, along with an enormous plume of thick black smoke.

The Techwave was already here.

Asterin hurried over to her desk and yanked a blaster out of one of the drawers. Then she rushed out of the office, barking orders into her tablet. Kyrion and I drew our stormswords and followed her.

The guards outside the office had vanished, probably to check on the explosion. Asterin ran along the glass corridor, but instead of stepping inside the elevator, she shoved through a nearby door and hurried down some stairs. Kyrion and I headed after her, and our footsteps rang out in a furious cadence.

One flight, two flights, three flights, four . . .

We kept going down, down, down, and I struggled to keep up with Asterin, who flew down the steps like she was a Tropics tiger with unerring balance.

At the bottom of the steps, Asterin keyed in a code, and a

door unlocked. But instead of blindly rushing through to the other side, she stopped and looked at us.

"If your theory is right, then the attack at the resort is a diversion to draw men and resources to that area while the Techwavers breach the mine. I've told the guards to concentrate on protecting the resort guests, but I'm going into the mine to stop the Techwavers."

I glanced at Kyrion, who nodded and raised his sword a little higher. "Then we're coming with you."

Asterin held her finger up to her lips, warning us to be quiet, then opened the door and slipped through to the other side. Kyrion and I followed her.

The door led into one of the mine tunnels. The walls here were rough and uneven, instead of smooth and sculpted like the passageways we had been in before, and I got the sense this was a much older part of the mine that the tourists never saw.

Asterin moved from one tunnel to the next. Every so often, she would stop and check her tablet. I had no idea what kind of security feed she was viewing, but her lips pressed into a grim line, and she quickened her pace. Eventually, I realized the tunnels we were moving through all had one thing in common: they were sloping upward instead of going deeper underground.

We stepped into a new tunnel, which also sloped upward before leveling out. The air in this passageway was also warmer and much more humid, indicating that we were back aboveground. Fifty feet later, we rounded a corner, and the tunnel opened into an enormous cavern similar to the one Kyrion and I had come through with the tour group. Heavy equipment and battered tools squatted here and there, and it was obviously a working part of the mine.

A distinctive *clank-clank* rang out, and a Black Scarab stepped out from behind a hoverpallet and lumbered across the cavern. Asterin scurried forward and crouched down behind a stack of crates along the wall. Kyrion and I dropped down beside her, and then we all peered around the sides of the crates.

The Black Scarab stopped in the middle of the cavern, then waved its arm. More *clank-clanks* rang out, and several more Scarabs streamed into the area. The Scarabs' jerky motions indicated that they were merely machines, although more than a dozen human Techwave soldiers in spiked black armor also appeared.

"How did you know they would be here?" Kyrion whispered. "Did you spot them on your security feed?"

"No, someone is scrambling the feed, so I couldn't see them on my tablet, but most of the lunarium is stored here," Asterin replied. "It's where I would come if I wanted to steal as much lunarium as quickly as possible."

One of the Techwave soldiers tapped something on his tablet. In unison, the Black Scarabs lumbered over to the closest wall, where thick seams of lunarium were visible. A series of hydraulic *hisses* sounded, and their fingers sharpened and lengthened, transforming into wicked-looking spikes that matched the ones on the human soldiers' armor. In unison, the Scarabs punched their spiked fingers into the wall, ripping out giant pieces of stone and making thick clouds of dust swirl through the air.

A couple of Scarabs picked up the chunks of lunarium that came flying out of the wall and stacked them on a nearby hoverpallet. A few of the human soldiers monitored the Scarabs' work, while others loaded crates already packed with lunarium onto two more hoverpallets. Several soldiers were clutching hand cannons and keeping watch, although they were all facing the cavern exit and not the interior tunnel that Asterin, Kyrion, and I had used.

"We need to split up," Asterin whispered. "If we all come at them from this direction, they'll concentrate their fire and pin us down. We need to attack them from multiple sides at once, and we need to stop them here. Once they get those hoverpallets outside, it will be much harder to contain them."

"Concentrate your blaster fire on the human soldiers. Their armor is weaker, and they're easier to kill," Kyrion said. "Vesper and I will cut down the Black Scarabs with our stormswords."

"You trust me to watch your back?" I asked in a low voice. "Even though I'm not an Arrow?"

His eyes locked with mine. "I trust you more than any Arrow I've ever fought with."

Pride rushed through me at his soft, steady words, and I saluted him with my sword. Kyrion harrumphed, but a smile curved his lips.

The three of us split up. Kyrion went left, Asterin went straight ahead, and I went right.

We all scurried from one stack of crates to the next. The Black Scarabs kept ripping lunarium out of the walls, while the soldiers kept loading it onto the waiting hoverpallets. None of them noticed us creeping closer and closer.

One of the soldiers checked his tablet. "Faster! Faster!" he barked out. "The Scarabs at the resort are meeting more resistance than expected. Half of them are already down, and it won't be long before someone gets the bright idea to check the mine."

The other human soldiers picked up their speed, throwing the crates of lunarium onto the pallets. The first man hit some buttons on his tablet. In response, the Black Scarabs increased their pace, stabbing their spiked fingers into the rock wall in a rapid rhythm. Within seconds, the *clank-clank-clanks* of their jerky movements drowned out everything else.

I crept as close to one of the Black Scarabs as possible and ducked behind a machine that looked like a giant corkscrew. I looked over at Asterin, who had darted behind some machinery near the soldier who had been issuing orders. She leveled her blaster at his chest.

My gaze skipped over to Kyrion, who had also crept up behind one of the Black Scarabs.

On three. His voice whispered through my mind, and Asterin nodded, indicating that she'd heard him too. *One . . . two . . . three!*

Kyrion erupted out from his hiding place and sliced the head off a Black Scarab before the machine even realized what was happening.

I waited until the Black Scarab in front of me turned in that direction, then surged forward and swung my sword out in a vicious arc. The lunarium blade cut through the tough polymetal armor like it was made of plastipaper, and the Scarab's head flew through the air and bounced away like an oversize beach ball. The suit of armor swayed upright for another second before toppling to the ground.

The soldier with the tablet spun around. His eyes widened at the sight of the two headless suits of armor littering the cavern floor like broken toys.

"Attack!" he yelled. "We are under attack at the mine—"

Asterin stepped out from behind the machinery and shot him in the chest. The soldier screamed and went down. She kept firing her blaster, dropping soldier after soldier, while Kyrion waded through the Black Scarabs on his side of the cavern.

I charged at a second Scarab and punched my sword into its chest. The machine let out a loud, disjointed mechanical *be-ep* that sounded eerily like a human wail. I ground my teeth, yanked the blade free, and shoved that Scarab back into another one. The two machines got tangled up and went down in a heap. I chopped off the first Scarab's head, then did the same thing to the second machine.

A familiar green glow appeared in the distance. On instinct, I dove behind the closest stack of crates.

Boom!

Cannon fire hit the crates, reducing them to splinters, which zipped through the air and stung my skin like dozens of tiny polyplastic bees. I hissed and dove forward, ducking behind another stack of crates.

Boom!

These crates also disintegrated into splinters that pelted my skin.

I kept going, moving from one stack of crates to another, although as soon as I took cover, another blast of cannon fire would force me forward again. I ducked behind the last stack of crates on this side of the cavern and risked a glance back over my shoulder.

Kyrion and Asterin were still much deeper in the cavern, fighting the Black Scarabs and human soldiers. They were too far away to help me, and they would get cut down by cannon fire if they tried.

I was on my own.

"Come out," a familiar voice ordered. "Or I'll obliterate those crates, and you along with them."

I slowly stood up, my stormsword still in my hand, and moved away from the crates.

A man clutching a hand cannon was standing about twenty feet away. He was wearing a suit of spiky black armor, just like the other Techwave soldiers, and his blond hair and black eyes gleamed in the bright afternoon sunlight streaming in through the cavern entrance.

"Hello, Vesper," Harkin Ocnus purred.

TWENTY-THREE

VESPER

arkin kept staring at me, even as he jerked his head at a couple of soldiers. "Get the lunarium outside. Now!"

The men scurried over to a hoverpallet and shoved it toward the cavern entrance. I started to head them off, but Harkin waggled his cannon at me again.

"Ah, ah, ah," he said. "You stay right there, Vesper. You've already screwed up my plans enough for one day."

"Aw, did I keep you from killing innocent people and getting your hands on all the lunarium you wanted?" I clucked my tongue in mock sympathy. "General Ocnus won't like that. Your father is going to be *so* disappointed in you. More so than he already is since you haven't even figured out what's wrong with that cannon yet."

Harkin's eyes narrowed. "But you figured it out, didn't you, Vesper? Perhaps you can still be useful after all."

Kyrion and Asterin were still engaged in a furious battle with the Black Scarabs and human soldiers, and Kyrion's frustration surged through the bond.

I thought back, counting the number of times Harkin had fired his weapon. Six blasts, which wasn't as many times as he had shot at me in the Techwave facility on Magma 3.

I eyed the cannon. A faint green glow emanated from the end of the barrel. The weapon was fully charged and ready to be fired, but beads of sweat were rolling down the solar magazine and dripping onto Harkin's boots. He didn't notice the danger, though. Good.

"Come here," Harkin ordered. "Slowly. No tricks."

I eased a little closer toward him and reached for the magic flowing inside me, along with the sticky cobweb of Kyrion in my mind. Instead of examining the bond from a distance the way I usually did, I deliberately latched onto that sticky cobweb, letting its silky threads fully envelop me. In an instant, Kyrion's energy pulsed through my body, the sensation so deep, strong, and intense that it made me sway on my feet.

I steadied myself and carefully reached for that additional power. Then I flicked my left fingers, just as I had seen Kyrion do when he used his telekinesis. I wasn't sure that it would work, but a couple of loose rocks flew up off the floor and smacked into the wall. Harkin spun in that direction and fired the cannon.

Boom!

A huge piece of the wall blasted apart, shooting rocks and dust everywhere.

I sprinted toward the right. Harkin cursed, spun back around to me, and fired the cannon again.

And again . . . and again . . .

Green blasts of energy chased me through the cavern, slamming into everything around me. More of the wall disintegrated, along with barrels, tools, and mining equipment. Rocks, plastic, and metal zinged through the air and clapped together like cymbals clashing in a violent chorus. I ignored the debris and noise and kept running, still counting the blasts in my head.

Eleven, twelve, thirteen . . .

That should be enough. I stopped and whirled around.

In the distance, Kyrion cut down another Black Scarab. "Vesper!" he yelled. "Run!"

But I didn't have to run. Not anymore. I held my arms out wide, as though I was surrendering.

Harkin grinned and stepped forward, aiming at my leg. He was going to maim me, just as he'd promised back in the Techwave facility. His finger curled around the trigger, and then . . .

Pewp!

The cannon burped out an odd noise. A few weak sparks shot out of the barrel, along with a plume of green smoke. The lunarium and solar wiring had overheated, just as I'd theorized it would. Now that cannon was nothing more than a pretty paperweight.

Harkin cursed and shook the weapon, as if the violent motion would make it work again. One of the doors in my mindscape flew open, and suddenly, I was seeing another version of Harkin—the one that had taken such gleeful delight in torturing me in the Techwave lab.

Red-hot rage roared through me like a wildfire burning out of control, and I charged forward, still clutching my stormsword. Harkin cursed again, plucked a blaster off his belt, and started firing it, even as he backpedaled toward the cavern entrance.

Pew! Pew! Pew!

Green energy bolts zinged through the air. I ducked the ones I could and slapped others away with my stormsword.

"Vesper!" Kyrion yelled again behind me. "Wait! I'll help you!"

I hesitated, torn between waiting for him and giving in to my own selfish need to take down Harkin. To prove to myself that I wasn't a victim. That I would never be his experiment again.

Pew!

Harkin fired off another shot with his blaster, then turned and ran out of the cavern. I glanced back over my shoulder, but Kyrion was still dealing with the Black Scarabs, and it would take him precious time to fight through them—time that Harkin could use to escape.

More rage burned through me, blotting out everything else. Harkin wasn't getting away. Not again. Not after what he'd done to me. Not as long as I had breath left to chase him down, and with my O2 enhancement, I had enough air in my lungs for a blasted marathon.

I sprinted after him.

A dirt trail arced away from the front of the cavern, although it was much rougher and narrower than the one Kyrion and I had used with the tourist group. An exposed root scraped across my boot like a clutching hand trying to hold me back, and I had to slow down to keep from tripping over it.

Up ahead, Harkin disappeared around a bend. I yanked my boot free, charged after him, and careened around the bend—

Pew!

I stopped short and ducked as another green blaster bolt zipped through the air and slammed into a tree behind me, sending bark and leaves everywhere.

Harkin was standing off to one side of the trail. He'd dropped the hand cannon at his feet and now had both hands wrapped around his blaster. Once again, I reached for the sticky cobweb that connected me to Kyrion and snapped up my left hand. A rock flew up off the trail and slammed into Harkin's left wrist, and his blaster slipped through his fingers and tumbled to the ground. He cursed, but he had pinned himself between two large trees, and there was nowhere to run.

Harkin lunged to the side, trying to get around one of the trees, but I surged forward, and he scuttled back. I stopped in front of him, my stormsword hovering three inches away from his chest. The lunarium blade was glowing a bright neon blue, and sparks of fire were wafting off the tip and swirling through the air like hot ash.

Harkin held his hands out in a placating gesture. He wasn't wearing his kinetic gloves or his green contacts, and he looked small, soft, and much more human without the devices.

"You don't want to kill me, Vesper," he crooned. "I'm too valuable. I'm a senior member of the Techwave. I'm sure I have *something* you want. Weapons, information, access. Name your price."

I tilted my head to the side. "You know what? You *do* have something my dark little heart desires."

He wet his lips. "What? Tell me what it is, and it's yours. Anything. I promise."

"To hurt you as badly as you hurt me in your lab."

Harkin laughed, but it was a high, weak, nervous sound. "You're a scientist, Vesper. Just like I am. You know we can't make discoveries, can't achieve breakthroughs, without a little human trial and error—"

I slashed my sword across his left forearm, one of the many spots where he had cut me with a scalpel. Harkin screamed and jerked to the side, but I lashed out with my sword again, this time slicing the blade across his right thigh, another spot where he had cut me.

His head snapped up. He held his hands out again, as if asking for mercy, and sucked in a breath to scream. I stepped forward and shoved my sword straight into his chest.

"You don't get the luxury of screaming!" I hissed.

Harkin gaped at me, his mouth opening and closing, as

though he was a fish desperately trying to breathe on dry land. I snarled and shoved my sword a little deeper into his chest, then wiggled it around, just as he'd used his scalpel to probe the wounds he'd inflicted on me.

He coughed a couple of times, and a thin trickle of blood bubbled up out of his lips before sliding down his chin. I wrapped both hands around my sword and ripped the blade out of his chest. Blood misted over me like a warm fountain, but I didn't mind the sensation. Not one little bit.

Harkin stared at me a moment longer, his eyes wide and glassy with pain, then crumpled to the ground.

I towered over him, my fingers clenched around my sword, ready to stab him again, and again and again, if he so much as twitched, but he remained still. Despite my O2 enhancement, I was breathing hard, and my entire body was trembling, although I couldn't tell if it was from my rage or remembered pain or both.

Off to the right, the bushes whipped back and forth, as though caught in a violent gust of wind, even though there wasn't so much as a light breeze right now. I whirled around and snapped up my sword.

"Have I mentioned how much I hate Tropics planets?" a deep, familiar voice sniped. "All this bloody humidity *ruins* my hair."

"Shut up and keep hacking," a female voice snapped back.

The bushes whipped from side to side again. A pale blue glow flared to life, slicing a wide swath through the lush tropical greenery, and a man with blond hair and pale blue eyes stepped out onto the trail.

Zane Zimmer stopped, seeming as surprised to see me as I was to see him.

"What are you staring at?" the female voice growled again.

A woman with reddish-blond hair and gray eyes stepped out onto the trail beside him. Adria Byrne caught sight of me and surged forward—

She abruptly tripped and went down on her hands and knees. Startled, I looked at Zane, but he didn't make a move toward me. Wary, I brandished my sword at him. I had to get back to the cavern and warn Kyrion.

A hand snaked around my waist from behind. Before I could raise my sword to stab my attacker, a second hand clamped around my right wrist, pinning my arm to my side. I tried to break free, but the hands tightened, painfully bruising my skin.

I jerked my head around, looking up at my attacker. His hair was a darker red than Adria's, his skin more ruddy than rosy like hers, but his eyes were the same pale, menacing gray.

"Hello, Vesper." Dargan Byrne grinned. "We've been looking for you."

A chill slithered down my spine. The three Arrows had finally caught up to me.

TWENTY-FOUR

KYRION

"Vesper!" I yelled. "Wait! I'll help you!"

Her rage sizzled through the bond, and she sprinted out of the cavern, chasing after Harkin. She wasn't going to stop until she had killed him. Part of me applauded her ruthless determination. I would have done the same if he had tortured me, but I wanted to watch her back and be by her side when she finally ended the sadistic scientist.

I cut down another Black Scarab, removing the head from the armored suit, just as I had done to a dozen others. I started after Vesper, but another bloody machine lurched into my path, and I had to stop and decapitate it as well. Out of the corner of my eye, I spotted a human soldier creeping up on my left. I whirled in that direction—

Pew!

A blaster bolt punched into the soldier's back, sending him tumbling to the ground.

Asterin waved at me. "Go!" she shouted. "Help Vesper! I've got this!"

She spun away from me and fired her blaster, dropping another soldier. She kept firing, causing several men to take cover behind some machinery.

My gaze flicked from one enemy to another. Even with Asterin's help, I still didn't see a quick, clear path through the remaining Black Scarabs and Techwave soldiers.

Then a dim flare of silver caught my eye, centered on one of the hoverpallets squatting between me and the cavern exit. I tensed, thinking the silver flare was a weapon charging up to fire, but the glow remained soft and steady. My eyes narrowed. It wasn't a flare so much as it was . . . an outline, as though something was gilding the hoverpallet in a shimmering silver light.

I frowned. What in all the bloody stars was *that*?

But as soon as I asked the question, the answer came to me. Through the bond, Vesper could tap into my telekinesis, telepathy, and telempathy, and I must be experiencing some version of her seer power. I wasn't a brilliant engineer and genius inventor like she was, and I wasn't trying to fix a flaw in a brewmaker design, but somehow I *knew* that silver flare was showing me the way forward, showing me how to reach Vesper.

This was quite possibly the most dangerous, reckless thing I had ever contemplated, but I ran straight toward the silver flare.

Still clutching my stormsword, I sprinted past all the Black Scarabs that lumbered in my direction. These machines had been built for strength, not for speed, and I quickly outpaced them.

As I neared the hoverpallet, several soldiers popped up from behind it and aimed their blasters. I reached down, yanked one of the explosives off my belt, and thumbed the switch on the side. Then I reared my hand back and tossed the small sphere, which skittered across the top of the hoverpallet like a metallic spider and dropped off the far side. The men yelled and rushed to the left, trying to get out of the blast radius—

Boom!

The sphere detonated and tossed the hoverpallet high into the air, although just as quickly, it crashed right back down on the soldiers. A few of the men lunged out of the way, but most of them screamed, their arms and legs crushed by the heavy weight of the lunarium they'd been trying to steal.

That was the last of the soldiers, and now nothing was standing between me and the cavern exit.

A hot rush of rage pulsed through the bond, even stronger than before, quickly followed by a dark satisfaction that I knew all too well. My inner monster hummed in appreciation.

Vesper had just killed Harkin.

But her satisfaction abruptly vanished, replaced by a sharp, jangling emotion that almost knocked me off my feet.

Fear.

I gritted my teeth and staggered forward, still charging toward Vesper all the while. The fear vanished, and I was able to right myself, but I had lost precious seconds. I swallowed a frustrated snarl, tightened my grip on my sword, and ran faster.

Something was wrong.

I left the cavern behind and sprinted along the rough trail outside. My gaze snapped back and forth, searching the surrounding rain forest, but I didn't see any enemies moving through the thick, dense foliage. No Black Scarabs, no Techwave soldiers, no one.

Worry churned in my gut, keeping time with my quick steps. The excessive humidity made it seem as though I was drawing more water than air into my lungs, and a stitch sprang to life in my side, throbbing with pain and slowing my progress. Vesper was right. An O2 enhancement would have been extremely useful right now, but I shoved my discomfort aside and kept running.

I was not going to lose her now, when we were finally on the verge of . . . whatever we were on the verge of.

I rounded a curve in the trail and stopped. Harkin was sprawled across the ground, a shocked look on his face and blood all over his chest. Flies were already buzzing around the deep gashes on his arm and leg. Good for Vesper for taking that extra bit of revenge.

But that didn't explain where she was or especially her intense fear. After she had killed Harkin, she should have returned to the cavern. Unless something—or someone—had stopped her.

I glanced farther up the trail. An icy blue glow appeared in the distance, clearly visible through the dense foliage for a moment before abruptly winking out, almost like it was another flare of Vesper's power telling me which way to go.

Icy fury flooded my chest. I knew that damned color. Arrow or not, I was finally going to kill that arrogant dick.

I leaned down and scooped up Harkin's hand cannon. Then I started running again, with the cannon clutched in one hand and my stormsword in the other.

My boots slapped against the rough, uneven ground, churning up bits of dark, loamy earth. Salty sweat stung my eyes, my legs burned, as did my lungs, and that stitch in my side felt like a dagger slowly slicing through my ribs and grinding deeper and deeper into my heart, but I kept going.

There was no other option. Not when it came to Vesper.

I ran for the better part of a mile before the thick trees thinned out, ringing a large clearing. A large blitzer was parked on the tall grass, flattening it like a bizarre crop circle. My gaze zoomed across the open space, and everything else fell away—except for Vesper.

She was struggling with Dargan Byrne. Her clothes were torn and dirty, her face bloody and bruised. Adria looked on in amusement and idly twirled her stormsword around in her hand as Dargan dragged Vesper toward the blitzer. Vesper's sword was hooked to Adria's belt.

I cursed and picked up my pace, still clutching Harkin's cannon in one hand and my stormsword in the other.

Vesper couldn't have possibly heard my footsteps over the distance that separated us, but her head snapped in my direction. Our gazes locked, and her fear spiked through the bond again, along with more than a little regret, although I got the sense that emotion was for me rather than for herself.

I'm so sorry, her voice whispered in my mind. *Don't come after me. Don't fall into Holloway's trap. Don't try to save me. Please! Save yourself, Kyr.*

Kyr. My heart seized in my chest, and I quickened my pace yet again, even though I was sweating and gasping for air.

Dargan yanked Vesper off her feet and carried her up the cargo bay ramp. Adria saluted me with her stormsword, then raised her hand to her lips and blew me a mocking kiss before following Dargan up the ramp. The two of them headed deeper into the ship and vanished from sight, along with Vesper.

Zane stood at the top of the opening, his hand hovering over the button that would close the ramp. The blitzer's engines started to hum, and it was seconds away from taking off.

There was no way I could physically make it to the ship in time, so I skidded to a stop and stabbed my sword point-first into the ground. The blade wobbled back and forth like a clock pendulum, counting down the seconds I had left to save Vesper. All I had to do was prevent the ship from taking off. Then I could kill Dargan, Adria, and Zane.

I hefted the Techwave cannon in my arms and aimed it at Zane. To my surprise, he didn't try to duck out of the way. Instead, he shook his head, as if telling me not to bother.

Arrogant bastard. I aimed the weapon at his chest and pulled the trigger—

Bzzt.

Instead of a strong pulse of energy, only a few green sparks erupted from the cannon, along with a weak cough of acrid smoke. The lunarium and solar wiring had already overheated, and the weapon was fried and useless, just like Vesper had shown me back on the *Dream World*. Fuck.

Zane was still standing at the top of the cargo bay ramp, and the look he gave me was pitying, almost as if he had known the cannon wouldn't fire. But how could he have possibly known that?

Orange glows appeared, and the ship's thrusters started firing up. Desperate, I dropped the broken cannon, then stepped forward, snapped up my hand, and grabbed the ship with my telekinesis.

Zane's eyebrows shot up in surprise. He was a much stronger telekinetic than I was, but he didn't try to block my power with his own. Instead, he just shook his head, that pitying look still on his face.

The ship lifted off the ground. I snapped up my other hand and curled my fingers into claws, as though I was physically touching the cargo bay ramp. Then I yanked it down as hard as I could. Sweat streamed down my face, my heart pounded, and every muscle in my body shook from the strain, but the ship lifted a foot off the ground. Then two, then three, five, seven, ten . . .

I snarled and tightened my grip, but it was like trying to grab a dragon with a pair of pliers. Bloody mercurial magic. Where was all this storied *power* Vesper and I were supposed to have? Why wasn't the truebond helping me now when she needed it—and me—the most?

The orange glows intensified, the thrusters hummed harder, and the ship slipped out of my grip. I staggered forward and tried to latch onto it again, but my feet flew out from under me, and my knees slammed into the ground. A hard truth hammered through my heart.

I wasn't strong enough to save Vesper.

Sorry, Kyr. Zane's voice whispered through my mind, and for once, he sounded truly regretful instead of smug. *You know where we're going and what will happen next.*

Zane hit the button. He stared at me until the cargo bay ramp closed. Then, a second later, the thrusters fully engaged.

Helpless, I watched as the blitzer zoomed away—with Vesper on board.

PART THREE

TRIED AND TRUE

TWENTY-FIVE

KYRION

I was still on my knees in the clearing, staring up at the empty sky, when Asterin came running up a few minutes later.

She looked out over the flattened grass. "Oh, Kyrion. I'm so sorry."

I kept staring up at the sky, which was a beautiful, perfect blue. The shouts, screams, and sounds of blaster fire had vanished, and the rain forest was slowly returning to normal. Bright birdsong and wild animal calls cautiously trilled out again, and mammoth butterflies flitted over the colorful flowers that twined through the trees, but everything inside me was cold, numb, and dead.

Vesper was gone. On her way back to Corios—and Holloway.

I shot to my feet, spun away from the flattened grass, and stalked forward.

Asterin trotted along beside me. "Kyrion? What are you doing?"

"Going to the spaceport, getting my ship, and tracking those bastards down," I growled. "Once I catch up to them, I'm going to kill every single person who stands between Vesper and me."

Asterin stepped in front of me, and I had to pull up short to keep from bowling her over.

"Stop!" she snapped. "Don't go charging after them like a reckless idiot. You'll only get yourself killed, and Vesper too."

A dark, mirthless chuckle erupted from my lips. "Ah, but that's the irony. We won't get killed. Holloway might have some fun with us, might let others hurt us a bit, but he won't let anyone *kill* Vesper and me. Not until he's drained every single spark of our psion power."

Even as I said the words and gave voice to that awful fate, fear sliced through my gut. Suddenly, I could understand why my parents had let Holloway take their magic instead of fighting back. They had wanted to protect each other, and me too. By using their love against them, Holloway had created the perfect bloody trap, and I was as deeply snared in it as my parents had been.

Asterin stared at me, her silver eyes bright and hard. "Holloway won't let anyone kill you or Vesper? *Good.* Use that to your advantage. Give the bastard exactly what he wants, then turn his own bloody greed against him. That's the only way you're going to save Vesper, and yourself too. Not by being a stupid, reckless idiot and rushing straight into Holloway's hands."

Her words finally penetrated my rage, dread, and worry. I exhaled, raked a hand through my sweaty hair, and walled off my emotions. I couldn't be Kyr right now. No, right now, I needed to be Kyrion Caldaren, the leader of the Arrows, the most notorious killer in the galaxy, and the monster everyone feared. That was the only way I was going to reach Vesper.

I dropped my hand. "I'm sorry. You're right. Thank you."

"You're welcome." Asterin shoved her blaster onto her belt, then crossed her arms over her chest. "What do we do now?"

"*We?*"

"Yes. *We.*" She stabbed a finger at the flattened grass where Zane's ship had been. "Those arrogant bastards came to my planet, my land, my resort, and kidnapped someone who was trying to save the lives of my people. Those Arrows broke at least a dozen laws and treaties between the Imperium and the Erzton by abducting Vesper. We both know that Holloway doesn't care about treaties, so it's only fair that I go to Corios and help you steal her back from him."

Despite the situation, a grim smile tugged at my mouth. "I'm starting to like you, Lady Asterin. You are far more vicious and vindictive than you let on."

An answering smile crept across her face, and she swept into a dainty curtsy. "The feeling is mutual, Lord Kyrion. Now, let's figure out how we can save Vesper."

We returned to the resort. Thanks to the warning from Vesper and me, the Erzton Hammers had managed to stop the Black Scarabs before they had breached the main building, and none of the guests had been hurt. A small mercy, but I was happy for Asterin and her people. At least something good had come out of this whole debacle.

Two hours later, I was at the spaceport, stowing the last of Vesper's and my things on board the *Dream World*, when a loud knock banged on the hull, and Asterin strode up the cargo bay ramp.

"You ready?" she asked.

"Yes. Are you still sure you want to do this? You don't have to come with me."

A stubborn look filled her face. "Yes, I do. I owe you and

Vesper a great debt." She hesitated. "Maybe it's weird, but I feel like I *have* to come with you. Does that make any sense?"

I thought of all the times Vesper had said similar things about her own seer magic and psionic instincts. "Yes, it does."

Asterin nodded. "Good. Because I brought you some presents."

She let out a low whistle. Several guards carrying large packs boarded the ship and placed the bulging bags off to the side of the cargo bay. The guards nodded respectfully to Asterin, then left.

I gestured at the packs. "What's all this?"

"Blasters, body armor, and all the other weapons and gear I could get my hands on. I can't bring any guards to Corios," she said in an apologetic voice. "But I can equip you with everything else you need to save Vesper."

I headed toward the flight deck. "Then let's get started."

TWENTY-SIX

VESPER

It all seemed like a bad dream.

But it wasn't a dream. It was a nightmare—the worst nightmare of my life.

I'd struggled with all my might, but Dargan had pinned my arms to my sides while Adria used her telekinesis to rip my stormsword out of my hand. I'd reached for the bond, for Kyrion's power to fight back against the two psions, but Dargan had just laughed and punched me in the chest, driving the air from my lungs and badly bruising my ribs. Adria had joined in, slapping my face again and again with her telekinesis, while Zane stood off to the side, watching the brother and sister hurt me, a blank expression on his face.

I'd kept fighting, but Dargan had used his superior strength to drag me along the trail, across the clearing, and onto Zane's ship. The rage, horror, and worry on Kyrion's face when he had sprinted into the clearing and realized that the three Arrows were taking me to Holloway and his awful plans for us . . .

It made me sick deep down in a part of my heart I didn't even realize I had until that moment.

Even though I'd told Kyrion not to follow me, not to fall into Holloway's trap, I knew he wasn't going to listen. Whatever feelings he had for me, whether they were tied to the truebond or not, Kyrion would never subject me to the same horrific fate as his parents. His sense of honor wouldn't allow it. He would try to rescue me, and I had to be ready to help when he did. So for the last two hours, as the blitzer rocketed toward Corios, I'd come up with one idea after another for how I could escape, but so far, I'd discarded them all.

Try as I might, I just couldn't see a way out of this mess, not even with my magic.

"I don't get it," Dargan said, interrupting my latest thought about how I could crash the blitzer when we entered the Corios atmosphere. "Why aren't you fighting? Why aren't you trying to escape?"

I opened my eyes. I was sitting in a cushioned chair on the flight deck, a few feet away from where Zane was lounging in his own chair at the pilot controls. The name of his ship was *Pretty Boy*. Of course it was.

I lifted my hands up the scant distance they would move, given the plasticuffs looped around the chair arms. "Kind of hard to escape when you're tied down."

"Yeah, but you're not even *trying*." Dargan jerked his thumb over his shoulder. "Your stormsword is sitting right over there. You could at least *attempt* to summon it to your side and make things interesting. Not just sit there and be all quiet and boring and resigned to your fate."

He was right. My stormsword was a few feet away on a table, and the lunarium blade practically shimmered with temptation. Under normal circumstances, I could tap into my bond with Kyrion and use his telekinesis to make the weapon lift off the table and zip over into my hand. But ever since Kyrion had tried to stop the ship from taking off, the only thing I'd sensed through the bond had been his extreme exhaustion, none of his psion power, emotions, or thoughts. Worry gnawed at my heart that he'd expended too much energy trying to save me and had gravely hurt himself.

Even if I could summon up a bit of Kyrion's telekinesis, I would still be cuffed to a chair, and one of the Arrows would take my sword away before I could kill any of them with it.

"Come on, Vesper," Dargan said in a wheedling voice. "Reach for your sword. You know you want to."

I snorted. "And give you another excuse to hit me? Hard pass."

A cruel grin spread across Dargan's face. "Well, yeah. It's always so much more *fun* when the prey struggles. It makes things far more . . . *exciting*."

The sadistic purr in his voice made my stomach roil, and suddenly I was seeing another version of Dargan standing right beside the one currently in front of me. The second Dargan plucked a dagger off his belt and sliced it across my back, my arms, and my legs, as I crawled across the floor trying to escape him. I ground my teeth to hold back a shudder. That was a future I never wanted to experience.

"Given that there are three of you and one of me, the odds of me murdering you all are extremely slim. Especially when you're standing there just waiting to pounce on me like a cat on a mouse. There's no point in trying to escape. So why waste time and energy attempting it?"

Dargan huffed, as though my logic annoyed him.

"Finally, she shows some common sense," Adria drawled, striding down the corridor and stopping beside her brother.

Ever since I had returned to Temperate 42 after the last Regal ball, I had been researching truebonds, trying to learn everything I could about them, but because they were so rare, at least in the Imperium, I had never been around anyone else who'd had a bond. Over the last two hours, in between dreaming up and discarding escape and murder plans, I had been studying the Byrnes.

Psionic energy hummed between Dargan and Adria, but even more surprising was the fact that I could actually *see* it. Thick veins of pale gray energy shimmered around the two of them, as if they were connected by a series of electrical cables that let their power flow freely back and forth. It was fascinating—and disgusting.

Not only did my magic let me see their psionic connection, but it also kept giving me glimpses of all the horrific things they had done. Cutting, slicing, stabbing, hitting. The Byrnes loved hurting other people, and one victim after another paraded through my mind. The faces changed, but the sick game always remained the same. Dargan would punch someone and send them staggering over to Adria, who would slice her stormsword across their arms and legs before using her telekinesis to shove the person right back over to Dargan, so he could hit them again. Their sadistic sport went on and on and on, and the screams of their victims echoed in my ears like a scratchy song that kept repeating over and over no matter how much I wanted it to stop.

I ground my teeth to hold back another shudder and released my seer magic. The gray energy shimmering around the Byrnes vanished, as did the phantom image of a second Dargan cutting me and silently cackling with glee.

"Common sense?" I said. "Why, I've been quite sensible so far."

"Oh, please. You're still thinking about escaping." Adria pointed her index finger at my head and made a little circle with it. "I can *feel* how fast and furiously your mind is working, coming up with one doomed plan after another."

She bent down so that her face was level with mine. "Let me save you some time and energy, Vesper. Dargan and I might ostensibly be Arrows, but really, we're the two best bounty hunters in the Archipelago Galaxy. No one ever gets away from us, especially not some newbie who stumbled into a truebond a few months ago. Dargan and I have been bonded for *years*. You're no match for us, so you might as well sit back and enjoy the ride."

I glared at her. Like it or not, she was right. I was trapped.

Adria laughed at my obvious fury, then jerked her head at Dargan. Unlike the *Dream World*, which had a long corridor with rooms branching off it, this ship had a much more open floor plan, so I watched while Adria and Dargan went into the next area, which was a large gym.

She plucked a wooden staff from a rack of weapons and twirled it around in her hands. Dargan picked up another staff and did the same thing. Then the two of them started sparring for me, their literally captive audience. Despite the fury still pounding through my body, I studied them, searching for any weakness I might be able to exploit.

Thwack!

Thwack! Thwack!

Thwack!

Adria and Dargan's staffs smacked together as they attacked, dodged, and feinted. They were highly skilled, just like all the Arrows were, but their bond put them on another level. Even when doing their best to pummel each other, they flowed back and forth in quick, beautiful precision, as though sparring was simply a choreographed waltz for a Regal ball they had perfected long ago. Unleash the two of them against an opponent with their stormswords, and they would make short work of the other person, no matter how skilled and strong and how much psionic power their opponent might have.

The Byrnes kept sparring, showing no signs of tiring. Just watching them wasn't enough. I needed more information. Maybe if I could somehow touch their power, the same way

I would run my hands over a faulty appliance in the R&D lab at Quill Corp, I could learn more about their bond or, more important, why Holloway was unable to take their magic.

I cautiously reached out with my seer magic, and my fingertips instantly tingled with power, as though I had dipped them into an electric river. But whenever I tried to go deeper and latch on to the Byrnes' thoughts and feelings, those sensations would squirt away like slippery eels sliding through my hands and dropping back down into that electric river.

I bit my tongue to keep from snarling in frustration. The answer to stopping Holloway from taking Kyrion's and my power was right in front of me, close enough to see but not actually to touch and understand.

In the end, Adria was a little faster, and she knocked Dargan's staff aside, surged forward, and rested her own weapon against his throat, stopping just short of crushing his windpipe.

Dargan carefully pushed the end of her staff away. "Aw, you got me again, sis." Instead of being angry, he grinned at Adria, clearly proud of his sister for besting him.

Adria grinned back at him. "I always do. Now, go get cleaned up and get some rest before we reach Corios."

Dargan winked at me, the still-captive audience, then swaggered away. He went down a corridor, out of my line of sight. A few seconds later, a door slammed, and water started running.

Adria picked up his fallen staff and returned it to a slot on the rack, along with her own weapon.

"Aren't you afraid of going to Corios?" I asked.

She gave me a puzzled look. "Why would I be afraid of going home?"

"Because of Holloway's lust for truebonds. After he drains me and Kyrion, what's to stop him from doing the same thing to you and Dargan? Or worse, turning the two of you into his personal pets the way he did Kyrion's parents?"

Adria let out a merry laugh. She grabbed a towel off a near-by bench, wiped the sweat off her face, and tossed the towel at me. It smacked against my face and landed in my lap. Anger burned through me, but I still couldn't sense Kyrion's teleki-nesis, and I couldn't even move my hands enough to shove the smelly, damp cloth off my legs and down onto the floor. Another small, petty humiliation like all the other ones she and Dargan had inflicted on me over the past two hours.

"Callus Holloway might be a powerful siphon, but he's no threat to Dargan and me," Adria said, grabbing another towel.

"Why not?"

She wiped down her neck, then tilted her head to the side, studying me as if I'd just said something supremely stupid. "You really don't get it, do you?"

"Get what?"

Adria came over and once again leaned down so that her face was level with mine. Her gray eyes were cold and hard in her flushed face. "Holloway isn't a threat to Dargan and me because we're not afraid of him. Unlike everyone else who trembles at the mere thought of incurring his wrath and having him drain their power until they're nothing but a dry, brittle, lifeless husk."

I frowned. "Not being afraid of Holloway and his siphon magic doesn't make you brave. It just makes you reckless."

Adria laughed again, and the merry sound grated on my nerves. "And you being afraid of Holloway doesn't make you smart. It just makes you *weak*." Her nostrils flared, as though my weakness was a pungent odor that repulsed her.

I ignored her derision and thought about what she'd said. Maybe it was weird, but I felt like there was some sly, hidden message in her words, like she was openly mocking me by revealing some great secret I was too dumb to figure out. *Why* couldn't I figure it out? Why couldn't I come up with a way to escape? Or at least keep Holloway from taking my power?

Adria straightened up and tossed her second towel at me. It too smacked me in the face before dropping down to my lap. She laughed and strode away, disappearing around the same corner that Dargan had. Anger and frustration pounded through me, but all I could do was sit there and stew in silence.

"Adria is right about one thing," Zane piped up.

I ground my teeth. I'd been so focused on the Byrnes that I'd forgotten the other Arrow was still at the blitzer's controls, lounging across the pilot's chair like a smug golden dragon. I unclenched my jaw. "And what would that be?"

"You should save your energy. You're going to need it for when you officially face Holloway."

I couldn't move my arms, but my legs were free, so I swiveled the chair around to him. The sharp motion slung Adria's sweaty towels off my lap and down to the floor. "And when will that happen? The second we land?"

Zane shook his head. "Oh, no. Holloway wants to make an example out of you. I got an alert a few minutes ago. He's ordered all the Regals to meet in the Crownpoint throne room tomorrow at midnight."

He swiped something on his tablet, and images flared on the holoscreen embedded in the wall beside him.

You are cordially invited to Crownpoint Palace to celebrate the truebond of Lord Kyrion Caldaren and Lady Vesper Quill . . .

I read through the information, which looked and sounded more like a fancy wedding invitation than the execution it truly was.

"That heartless bastard," I growled. "He's going to parade us around like puppets before he takes our magic and kills us."

"Did you expect anything different?" Zane asked.

Truth be told, I *had* expected something different, for Holloway to treat us the same way he had treated Kyrion's parents. To take only a little bit of our magic at a time. To keep one of us close while sending the other out on Arrow missions.

It was far from ideal, but I'd thought it might at least give us some time to figure out a way to escape. Holloway must have realized that Kyrion and I wouldn't be as compliant as the Caldarens had been, and he didn't want to risk us slipping through his fingers again.

My chest squeezed, and my heart hammered, but I forced myself to draw in slow, deep, steady breaths. After several seconds, I was able to ignore the worst of my roiling emotions. Fear, worry, dread, panic. Adria was right. They all made me weak, which was the one thing I could not afford to be right now.

I dragged my gaze away from the holoscreen. Zane was still lounging in the pilot's chair, but his eyes were sharp and watchful, and he was far more alert than he pretended.

For a moment, I considered asking him—begging him—to help me. But then I realized that he already had, in his own way.

"Something has been bothering me."

"What?" Zane drawled. "Being separated from your beloved Kyrion? Why, I would think you would relish the chance to escape from him, if only for a little while. I can't imagine anyone who would willingly want to be around that man, what with all his cold moods and angsty brooding and especially the perpetual stick lodged up his ass." He shuddered. "I pity you, Vesper, for being forced to have a truebond with such a vile creature as Kyrion Caldaren."

Zane shuddered again, a little more dramatically than before.

"At least Kyrion doesn't pretend to be anything other than what he is," I countered. "I would much rather be bonded to someone like him, someone cold and broody and honest, than someone like *you*."

He tilted his head to the side. "And what am I like?"

"You're a blasted *fraud*," I spat out the words. "Zane Zimmer might be the golden boy, the prima donna, the arrogant diva of the Arrows, but that's not the *real* you, is it? You've created this whole swaggering persona so that people won't see the real you. In your own way, you're even more devious than Holloway is."

Zane arched a blond eyebrow. "Really? How fascinating. Tell me, how, exactly, am *I* more devious than the great Callus Holloway? Because that is a tall order."

I leaned forward and stabbed my index finger at him, although given my restraints, the motion wasn't the least bit intimidating. "This whole time, you've been pretending to help Adria and Dargan, but what you've really been doing is slowing them down."

Zane maintained his lazy, relaxed posture, although his eyes narrowed ever so slightly. "How have I been slowing them down?"

"You found the spy camera that Kyrion left on his Imperium blitzer. You spotted it immediately, and you knew exactly what it was, because you picked it up and turned it off. But then, later, when you were talking to Dargan and Adria about Holloway's plans for Kyrion and me, you turned the camera back on, even though you had to know the video footage would eventually make its way to Kyrion."

"A silly mistake on my part. Sometimes I'm just all thumbs." He held up his hands and waggled his fingers.

More anger surged through me. How had Kyrion kept from killing Zane all these years they'd been Arrows? Kyrion had far more restraint than I did. Because if I could have gotten out of this chair, I would have snatched up my sword and lopped Zane's pretty-boy head off his shoulders.

"Don't play dumb with me," I snapped. "I'm too smart for that. Just like you're too smart to accidentally turn on a camera, especially a House Zimmer spy camera. I run an R&D lab, remember? I recognized the tech."

Zane let out a low, amused chuckle. "You're right. I did deliberately turn that camera back on."

"Why?"

He shrugged. "Like Dargan said, it's no fun if the prey doesn't know you're hunting them."

"Bullshit," I countered. "You don't care about having fun with your enemies. You kill them quickly and ruthlessly and move on to the next obstacle, just like Kyrion does. The two of you are remarkably similar in that way."

This time, Zane let out a haughty, delicate sniff. "Now you're just insulting me. Kyrion Caldaren and I are *nothing* alike. We never have been, and we never will be."

"Keep telling yourself that. Maybe one day you'll even believe it. After all, the only good lies are the ones you actually believe yourself."

He tilted his head to the side again. "Where did you hear that?"

"What?"

"The part about good lies."

"It's something my cousin used to say."

Zane kept staring at me, his brow furrowed as though Liesl's old saying was more profound and important than it really was.

"You didn't answer my question," I circled back around to my original accusation. "Why did you turn that spy camera on when you knew that Kyrion and I would see the footage and realize that Holloway had sent three Arrows after us? And don't tell me it was to make the thrill of the chase more exciting. That might be true for Adria and Dargan but not for you."

He shifted in his chair, which creaked in protest. "I suppose I wanted to give you and Kyrion a sporting chance."

"Really? Is that why you tripped Adria in the rain forest?"

He shrugged again, although the tiniest wince creased his face in confirmation.

"During the last Regal ball, you said that you would do anything to eliminate Kyrion, and me too, if I got in your way. Holloway gave you the perfect opportunity to do that with this mission, but instead, you tipped us off about his plan to capture us. So what's changed between now and then?"

Zane stared at me, his lips pursing in thought. "I'm not quite sure. Something about you greatly annoys me, although I can't put my finger on exactly what it is. Other than your many lies, of course."

I bristled. "*I'm* a liar? *You're* the one hiding how clever you really are behind that shiny mane of hair, blinding smile, and diva persona."

Zane shook his head, making his hair ripple around his face. He slowly, deliberately ran his fingers through his longish golden locks, smoothing them back into place, then gave me a wide, warm smile that would have made any gossipcaster swoon. Despite the plasticuffs on my wrist, I still managed to raise my right hand high enough to flip him off.

He chuckled, although the humor swiftly faded from his face. "This is a tenuous time for the Regal Houses. We all have our own spies, and we all know the Techwave is plotting something big, something that might finally topple Holloway, despite his continued assurances that he has everything under control. Everyone is scrambling for more power, money, and resources."

"How does delivering Kyrion and me to Holloway help you get more power, money, and resources?"

Zane's eyes gleamed. "With Kyrion out of the way, Holloway will have no choice but to finally appoint me as head of the Arrows."

"And you think that will help you?" I laughed. "Please. Holloway will never give up one single *ounce* of power. Being head of the Arrows will change nothing for you in that regard."

He tipped his head, acknowledging my point. "True. But

it *will* give House Zimmer even more influence and access. Which, in turn, will help protect my father and grandmother and the members of my extended family, along with the thousands of people who work for and depend on us. You might think I'm a cruel, selfish dick, and you would be absolutely right. But I *am* doing this for a reason, Vesper. Even if it's at odds with what you want."

"Protecting your House?" I let out a disgusted snort. "That's exactly what Rowena Kent said when I threatened to expose her conspiracy to crash Imperium ships."

Zane's jaw clenched, and anger melted some of the ice in his eyes. "Unlike Rowena Kent, I actually *care* about my family and our workers. If there is one thing you should know about me, one thing that is true above all others, it's that I will do anything to protect my family—*anything*."

Even more anger blazed in his eyes, and his voice rang with conviction. He really did want to protect his father and grandmother and the other members of his House. And not to obtain more money or power or control or a higher standing among the other Regals, like Rowena Kent, but because he genuinely cared about those people.

A pang of longing spiked through my heart. If only Nerezza had loved me half as much as Zane loved his family, we might have been a real mother and daughter. I shoved that useless thought away. Zane Zimmer's hidden facets might surprise me, but he was still an arrogant, insufferable jackass.

"So you're going to sacrifice Kyrion and me to secure your own future," I didn't bother keeping the bitterness out of my voice. "You sound just like my mother."

Zane's head tilted to the side yet again, and he studied me even more closely than before. "I thought you were an orphan."

I frowned. "Who told you that?"

"House Zimmer spies, of course. My grandmother ordered them to do a deep dive into you the night you were appointed as a Regal lady. Standard operating procedure. Although you've piqued Beatrice's interest more than most. She's been reviewing files on you for the last few weeks. She even made me study the information."

He shuddered, as though reading about me had been the most boring thing ever. Oh, yes. He was most definitely an arrogant, insufferable jackass.

Zane rattled off a list of supposed facts about me, the same facts Nerezza had shown me in the Techwave facility on Magma 3. Once again, I was confronted with the knowledge that someone had gone to great lengths to conceal my identity. My mind churned, trying to figure out who it had been, but I only had one suspect—Liesl.

Back at the Techwave facility, Nerezza had claimed that her daughter had been dead for years. Then, later, on the *Dream World,* Daichi had said my personal information had been changed years ago, as though someone was coming along behind me and tidying up my existence as I moved from one academy and job to another. Liesl was the only one who would have known—or cared—enough to create such a detailed back-ground, although I had no idea how she would have accessed so many official documents. Maybe someone had helped her change them. But who? And why would Liesl concoct such elaborate lies in the first place?

Had she been trying to protect me—maybe even hide me—from Nerezza? Liesl had worked as Nerezza's right hand for years. Maybe my cousin hadn't wanted my mother to hurt me any more than she already had. Either way, Liesl was dead, so I would probably never discover the answers to my questions.

". . . and thus concludes the life of Lady Vesper Quill," Zane finished.

"Well, I hate to break it to you, but the House Zimmer spies are wrong," I said in a flat voice. "All the info about my grades at the Imperium academy and university and my various lab-rat jobs is right. But I'm no orphan. My mother is very much alive—unfortunately."

I muttered the last word, causing Zane's eyebrows to shoot up in surprise. A strange urge rose in me to tell him about how Nerezza had abandoned me for Regal riches and power, to smash his self-righteous argument about family always coming first, but I held my tongue. Zane Zimmer might have good reasons for turning me over to Holloway, but he was still going to use me to improve his own position, just like a true Regal would.

A chime sounded, and Zane checked his tablet. "The pinpoint drive is ready for the next jump. A few more jumps, and we'll be back in Imperium-controlled space."

Another wave of fear crashed over me, threatening to crush me, but I forced myself to breathe through it just like I had before.

"I hope you can figure out a way to escape, Vesper," Zane said in a soft voice. "Truly."

"Take your fake sympathy and shove it up your ass, pretty boy."

I glared at him a moment longer, then spun my chair around in the opposite direction, closed my eyes, and went back to dreaming up escape plans.

Sadly, I did not come up with any feasible way to crash the blitzer or kill Zane, Adria, and Dargan, and the next morning, we landed in the main docking bay in the tallest tower at Crownpoint. I was finally released from the chair, although a fresh set of plasticuffs was clamped around my wrists. Dargan slid my stormsword into a slot on his belt. He winked at me and patted the hilt, claiming the weapon for his own.

My hands clenched into fists, but before I could even think

about trying to grab the weapon, Adria brandished a shock baton. I flinched at the white-hot electricity crackling a few inches from my face.

"Please," she purred. "Give me a reason to use this."

I dug my nails into my palms, but there was nothing I could do. The three Arrows marched me down the ship's ramp, across the docking bay, and into an elevator. The elevator whooshed upward, causing my heart to leap into my throat. I tried to swallow it down, along with my growing dread, but I couldn't quite manage it.

The elevator floated to a stop. Dargan shoved me out of the car, and I staggered forward several steps before I was able to find my balance.

"Such a big, strong, brave Arrow, pushing around a prisoner," I said, my voice dripping with venom.

Dargan growled and raised his fist to punch me, but Zane stepped in between us.

"Holloway won't appreciate you damaging her," he said in a mild voice. "Don't do something stupid when we're right outside the throne room. Or have you forgotten we have an audience?"

He tilted his head to the side, and Dargan followed the motion over to a soldier dressed in a dark red Imperium uniform guarding the corridor. Dargan glowered at Zane, but he slowly lowered his fist. Adria rolled her eyes and moved past her brother. Dargan stomped after her.

Zane took hold of my elbow, his grip surprisingly gentle. "This way."

I wanted to jerk out of his grasp, but once again, there was nothing I could do. He led me along the corridor. At our approach, several Imperium soldiers rushed to open two double doors that stretched up to the ceiling. Adria and Dargan strode forward. Zane hesitated, as if he didn't want to be here any more than I did, but he escorted me inside.

The throne room was just as I remembered it from the last Regal ball, a cavernous space made of glossy white marble shot through with tiny seams of red. Hoverglobes bobbed up and down like oversize fireflies, adding an eerie orange tint to the copper sculptures shaped like crooked fingers and clawing hands that covered the walls, while the chandeliers overhead seemed to cast out more shadows than they banished.

Instead of regular Imperium soldiers, dozens of Bronze Hand guards clutching long bronze spears with white-hot diamond-shaped tips lined the walls. A bronze hand glimmered on each guard's breastplate, as though the metallic fingers were about to pierce their dark red armor and rip out their hearts. I shivered and looked away from them.

My gaze landed on the dais on the far side of the room. Callus Holloway was perched on his throne at the top of the steps. He too looked just as I remembered—dark brown hair with a few silver threads, tan skin, and bronze eyes. A long red jacket flowed down his body, and he cast out more of a shadow than anything else in the entire room.

A wide smile spread across Holloway's face, and he surged to his feet and hurried down the dais steps. His eagerness repulsed me.

Adria and Dargan bowed to Holloway, then moved off to the side, but Zane stayed next to me, his hand still on my elbow. He tightened his grip, almost in warning. Please. As if I didn't know exactly how much danger I was in. Still, I lifted my chin and squared my shoulders. I might be completely out of options, but I wouldn't let Holloway see how worried I was.

Holloway stopped and looked me over from head to toe, studying every little thing about me as though I was a gourmet meal that he was about to devour. My hands clenched into fists again. I longed to lunge forward and punch him, but once again, I shoved down the violent urges. Fighting would just make my situation even more precarious.

"Vesper, how lovely to see you again," Holloway purred. "And with relatively little damage. Well done, Zane."

"Hey, we're the ones who captured her—" Dargan started to protest, but Adria shoved her elbow into his stomach, silencing him.

Holloway considered the brother and sister for a moment, then strolled over to them. Dargan and Adria remained standing at attention, but their faces were wary, and unease rippled off them, tickling my psionic senses.

Holloway gave them a benevolent smile. "You're right, Dargan. You and Adria were instrumental in capturing Vesper, and you will be handsomely rewarded, the way you always are."

He rested his hand on Dargan's shoulder. Energy spiked around Holloway, and his eyes flashed a bright, sinister bronze. He curled his fingers into Dargan's shoulder like a boa constrictor wrapping around its prey. I reached out with my seer magic, watching them.

Dargan winced, and his face paled, as though he was in tremendous pain. The gray veins of energy around him flickered and dimmed, even as the same energy exploded to life around Holloway. Disgust rolled through me. Holloway truly was a fucking leech, in every sense of the word. Still, if he took Dargan's power, maybe he would ignore mine.

Adria stepped forward and laid her hand on her brother's other shoulder. Those gray veins of energy surged toward her, then back toward Holloway, as though the two of them were playing an invisible game of psionic tug-of-war with Dargan that only I could see.

Adria stepped even closer to Dargan and tightened her grip, her knuckles going white against his gray jacket. Her brother's face remained pale, but his wince vanished, and he straightened up to his full height, towering over the shorter Holloway. The gray veins of energy snapped back into place around Dargan, like an old-timey skeleton key locking away a priceless treasure behind a vault door.

The energy surrounding Holloway snuffed out, and he snatched his hand away from Dargan's shoulder and coughed as though the younger man had sucker-punched him in the throat.

My eyes narrowed, and I looked back and forth between the three of them. Holloway had tried to take their magic, but the Byrnes had fought him off, just as they had done a few days ago when the two Arrows had been in the throne room with Kyrion and Zane.

How? How was their bond different from the one between Kyrion's parents? And most important, how could Kyrion and I do what the Byrnes had just done? How could we protect ourselves from the greedy siphon?

Holloway stopped coughing and cleared his throat. "As I was saying, the two of you will be handsomely rewarded for completing this special mission."

Adria tipped her head to him. "We appreciate your generosity, my lord."

Holloway's jaw clenched at the faint note of mockery in her voice, but he spun away from the Byrnes and stalked back over to me.

Zane pressed his fingers into my elbow again in warning, or maybe sympathy, then stepped back, leaving me standing alone in my plasticuffs to face the Imperium leader.

Holloway's gaze swept over me, and his lips curled with revulsion. "After all my attempts to bond Kyrion to a Regal or Erzton lady, someone *proper,* someone *suitable*, he ends up connected to a worthless little lab rat. Why? What's so special about you, Vesper Quill?"

I shrugged. "Nothing, I suppose. Then again, villains don't think there is anything special about anyone but themselves."

Holloway laughed, and the sound scraped against my skin

like a razor. "Even your insults are lacking in wit and charm. Outside of the truebond, you are utterly useless."

I should have kept my mouth shut. Should have let his insults roll off me, but I couldn't—I just *couldn't*. Not when he was dismissing me the exact way Nerezza had done all those years ago.

"Well, this *useless* person fooled you," I snapped back. "I avoided your little truebond trap the last time I was here, and I'll find a way to escape you again, you sick, sadistic, greedy bastard."

I clucked my tongue in mock sympathy. "How very sad you are. Why, you don't even have any real power of your own. Just what you steal from other people. I would say that makes *you* the useless one."

Rage erupted in Holloway's eyes, and he surged forward, faster than a snake striking. I didn't even have time to step back, much less try to avoid him.

Holloway gripped my chin, his fingers digging painfully into my skin. He was *strong*—even stronger than Dargan—and I couldn't break his hold. He studied me a moment, then wrenched my head from side to side, shaking me like a dog would shake a rabbit in its jaws.

"Oh, yes. I can feel it now." He leaned forward, almost burying his nose in my hair. He drew in a deep breath, then let out an appreciative sigh. "Your truebond with Kyrion smells *delicious*, like a fine wine that's just been uncorked and needs a few more minutes to breathe."

I tried to jerk back, but he tightened his grip. Even worse, this . . . *power* surged off him and slammed into me. In an instant, a thousand needles plunged into my body, from the top of my head to the tips of my toes, as though I was back on the medtable on the *Dream World.*

But it was so much worse than that.

Holloway licked his lips. His bronze eyes grew brighter and

brighter, even as those needles plunged deeper and deeper, twisting into my skin, muscles, and bones. Excruciating pain blazed through my body, my heart stuttered, and cold rushed from my chest all the way out into my fingers and toes, as though my veins were filled with icy, oily sludge instead of warm blood.

Then, without warning, all those needles abruptly retracted, sucking out my magic, energy, and life and pumping it straight into Holloway.

Screams tumbled from my lips, keeping perfect time with the torrent of tears streaming down my face. My muscles spasmed, and my legs buckled, but Holloway tightened his grip on my chin, using my own stolen strength to hold my body upright.

"Not so useless now, am I, Vesper?" he hissed in my face.

I couldn't stop screaming long enough to answer him.

Off to the side, Adria watched Holloway siphon off my magic with a curious expression, as though she was witnessing a fascinating experiment, but Dargan blanched and sidled behind his sister, as if she could protect him from being Holloway's next victim. There was some clue in that, but the agonizing pain muddled my mind, and I couldn't focus on the siblings long enough to figure out what it was.

Zane stepped forward. "If I may offer a suggestion, my lord?"

"What?" Holloway growled, still gripping my chin.

"You said the truebond still needs time to strengthen to its full potential," Zane replied, his voice calm as though he was reciting known clinical facts. "Perhaps draining so much of Vesper's energy right now isn't the best course of action. Not if you want to maximize the power you get from both her *and* Kyrion during the ball tonight."

Holloway kept staring at me, his greed and lust stabbing into my body right alongside his horrid magic. He didn't want to stop. He wanted to drain me, just like he had drained

Desdemona Caldaren all those years ago. He was nothing but a greedy parasite, eager to gorge himself on as much magic as fast as possible before searching for even more.

Those invisible needles stabbed a little deeper into my body, stealing my breath. He was going to do it. He was going to kill me right here and now—

Holloway released my chin and shoved me back. I stumbled and dropped to the floor, my knees cracking against the marble. Pain spiked through my legs, but the sensation grounded me. It was a common, familiar, natural pain, not the magic-sucking slime of Holloway's siphon power.

"Get her up," he ordered.

Zane leaned down, grabbed my elbow, and pulled me upright, but once again, his motions were surprisingly gentle. He tucked me into his body the tiniest bit, and as much as I hated it, I leaned against him for support. Otherwise, I would have dropped back down to the floor.

A smile spread across Holloway's face. "Look at you, Vesper. Look how quickly you're recovering. Your bond with Kyrion must be even stronger than the one his parents had. Perhaps I'll keep the two of you alive after all." His smile twisted into a cruel sneer. "Or perhaps not."

They were both horrible fates, and try as I might, I still couldn't see a way to escape either one of them.

Holloway snapped his fingers, and two Bronze Hand guards scurried forward. "Take her away."

Zane stepped aside, and the two guards clamped their hands around my upper arms. I was still so weak that my legs buckled, and I hung between them like a limp doll that had lost its batteries.

Holloway snapped his fingers again. "Prepare her for the ball."

The Bronze Hand guards bowed to him, then dragged me backward. The hungry, greedy gleam in Holloway's eyes was the last thing I saw before the throne room doors swung shut.

TWENTY-SEVEN

KYRION

Given Asterin's influence, we didn't have any problems taking off from Tropics 33. Even though I wanted to sit in the pilot's chair and count down the minutes until we reached Corios, I forced myself to get cleaned up, eat, and get what sleep I could.

Asterin stayed in the library, communicating with her people. I had no idea what she was telling them or what she might be plotting, and I didn't care.

All I wanted was to reach Vesper before it was too late.

But the problem wouldn't be getting to her. Holloway would let me walk right into the throne room full of Bronze Hand guards. No, the problem would be trying to get away from the siphon afterward and escape the palace with our lives and our magic intact, and I had no idea how to do any of that.

The next morning, the *Dream World* reached Corios and started orbiting around the planet. From the information Daichi had sent me, no one had connected the *Dream World* to me yet, so I landed at a busy spaceport on the industrial side of the city, far from my own private port. Asterin and I both donned dark cloaks and threw the hoods up to hide our faces, then strode down the cargo bay ramp.

Daichi was waiting on the landing pad below, his tablet clutched in his hand and a worried look on his face. He did a double take when he saw Asterin, but he tipped his head to her.

Asterin looked back and forth between Daichi and me. "I'll start moving the supplies. Give you two some time to catch up."

"Thank you, Asterin," I replied.

She nodded and headed back up the ramp.

"We're clear," Daichi said. "No one tracked me here, and I hacked into the spaceport's systems and scrambled their security cameras to cover your arrival."

"How bad is it?"

He grimaced. "Holloway has decided to make an example out of you and Vesper for all the other Regals."

Daichi showed me his tablet screen. At first glance, the message looked like a standard invitation to the palace, but icy fury flooded my chest as I read through the information.

"Holloway is pretending like this is some bloody ball," I growled. "Instead of an execution."

"I'm so sorry, Kyrion," Daichi said. "I know the other Regals being there will make this even more difficult."

I massaged my pounding temples for a few seconds, then dropped my hands to my sides. I also checked the bond, just like I had done dozens of times over the past several hours.

Vesper? Can you hear me?

I called out to her telepathically, but once again, there was no reply. The velvety ribbon of Vesper was still and quiet in my mind, and I couldn't hear her thoughts or sense what she was feeling. The lack of emotion put me even more on edge.

"What do you want to do?" Daichi asked.

That was the problem. I didn't know *what* to do. I didn't have

Vesper's engineering skills, so I couldn't look at this situation and produce a solution the way she could have. I didn't know how to bloody *fix* any of this.

"I don't know," I confessed. "I don't have the faintest glimmer of a plan or even the hope of an idea right now."

Daichi squeezed my shoulder. "We'll figure something out."

I nodded with a confidence I didn't feel. "Of course."

He tilted his head toward the blitzer. "I'll go help Asterin."

Daichi walked up the cargo bay ramp. A few seconds later, his voice drifted over to me, along with Asterin's soft reply.

I turned away from the blitzer and looked to my left. In the distance, Crownpoint stretched high into the air, its chrome and glass towers glittering like fishhooks ready to snare and drag me back to Holloway. Even from here, the palace cast out a long shadow, like a black hole threatening to suck me into its depths and never let me go.

I thought of Holloway perched on his throne, peering down at Vesper and eyeing her with the same greed, lust, and hunger he had shown toward my mother, and my father too. Cold determination flared deep inside my heart, icing out my worry and dread.

Callus Holloway had forged me into an Arrow, a weapon, a ruthless killer. Now it was finally time to use all my skills, strength, and psion power against the siphon. Holloway might be a villain, but I was one too, and I grabbed onto my own darkness with both hands and held it tight, just as I had so many times before. My inner monster hummed in response, ready and eager to serve.

I still didn't know how to save Vesper, but I was damned sure going to try.

I helped Asterin and Daichi load the supplies into a private transport that Daichi had arranged. Then came the first of many questions: where to go?

I didn't dare return to Castle Caldaren. Holloway would have spies watching it, and the second I showed my face there, he would dispatch a squad of Bronze Hand guards to capture and drag me to Crownpoint. I was going to the palace, but on my own terms, not his.

Never again.

When it became apparent that I didn't have even this much of a plan, Daichi cleared his throat. "I arranged a place for us to stay. It's not the finest of accommodations, Lady Asterin, but we will be safe until we can figure out our next move."

"Please, call me Asterin," she replied. "I've spent a good portion of my life traipsing around one mine or another. I'm sure whatever accommodations you've made will be much more comfortable than that."

Daichi typed in an address in the mechanized transport, and we rode in silence, staring out through the windows and watching for spies. After a few blocks, I realized where we were going, and I breathed a little easier. Of course. I should have thought of that location myself. I needed to set my worry for Vesper aside and focus on the mission, just as I had done countless times before as an Arrow, but it was easier said than done.

Fifteen minutes later, the transport stopped in an abandoned parking garage, and Daichi, Asterin, and I got out and shouldered the bulging bags of supplies. Daichi typed in another address, sending the transport on its way, just in case anyone was tracking it. Then the three of us left the garage.

We kept to the alleys and away from the traffic cameras that covered the main streets with their plethora of nightclubs and restaurants. It wasn't hard to do. Nobody in the industrial part of the city wanted Imperium soldiers to monitor their movements, especially not the Regals who visited this area for illegal business or clandestine pleasure or both.

We zigzagged down a narrow, crooked alley and ended up in front of a sturdy metal door. No one had followed us, and I didn't sense anyone watching us with my telempathy. I nodded at Daichi, who knocked on the door once, then three more times in rapid succession, and then once more.

The door buzzed open, and we entered what was ostensibly a workshop, although it was far more cluttered than any other workshop I had ever seen. Tools, wires, broken bolts, bent nails, and loose screws fought for space on the uneven wooden shelves that hugged the walls, and even more disparate items covered the tables and chairs that were crammed into various nooks and crannies.

"What *is* this place?" Asterin asked, her eyes wide, as though she had never seen so much junk in one spot.

"My uncle Touma's workshop," Daichi explained.

We left the narrow hallway and moved into the much wider area that formed the back of the workshop. To my surprise, it was much cleaner and neater than the last time I had been here the night of the spring Regal ball.

My gaze drifted over to two chairs in the corner, where Vesper and I had downed the chemicals that we'd hoped would break the bond. Perhaps it was part of Vesper's power, or just my own memories, but suddenly, I could see her sitting in that chair, staring at me, the vial of chemicals glowing like an oblong blue moon between her fingers.

A sharp arrow of regret shot through my chest. If only I could go back to that moment, I would tell Vesper not to drink the chemicals. That it wasn't the bond I was worried about but rather all the things she stirred inside me. All the . . . concern I felt for her. All the . . . *softness*.

I hadn't wanted to admit it to myself, but I'd been so afraid that once Vesper saw the true depths and utter darkness in my heart, once she sensed it through the bond, she would reject me outright. And that, well, that would have hurt so badly that not even my inner monster could have saved me from a wound so deep.

What a bloody fool I had been.

"Daichi! Kyrion! There you are!" Touma called out.

The spelltech stepped from behind a wall of shelves. Touma was wearing his usual coveralls, although bloodred paint streaked the thick gray fabric, as though he had been moonlighting in a butcher's shop instead of fixing broken engines like usual.

Touma's gaze flicked over me, then settled on Asterin. A grin spread across his face, and he dropped into a perfect bow that would have made even the most fastidious Regal tutor proud.

"And you brought a guest," he crooned. "How wonderful! Lady Asterin. Welcome to my humble abode. I am Touma Hirano, simple spelltech, at your service."

He moved forward, gently took hold of Asterin's hand, and bowed low across her knuckles.

Asterin laughed. "Greetings, Touma."

He dropped her hand, popped back upright, and grinned at her again. "Let me introduce you to my other guests."

Other guests? My hand curled around my sword. Footsteps sounded, and two women also stepped from behind the wall of shelves. Tivona Winslow and Leandra Ferrum. I exhaled and dropped my hand from my weapon.

Tivona looked at me, worry creasing her face. "When Daichi told me that Vesper had been captured, we took the first transport to Corios. We're here to help you save Vesper. Just tell us what to do."

"Thank you. That will mean the moon to Vesper." My gaze skipped over to Leandra. "Although I'm surprised to see you here. House Ferrum has long been known for its neutrality."

Leandra shrugged. "My family has never liked Holloway,

and I am still under contract with Vesper. I will honor our agreement."

It wasn't a ringing endorsement, but at this point, I would take all the help I could get.

"Come," Touma said, gesturing at me, Daichi, and Asterin. "We've already set up a war room, of sorts."

He moved into the open space behind the shelves. Tivona and Leandra followed him, then Daichi and Asterin, with me bringing up the rear. Touma skimmed his fingers over part of the wall. A soft *click* sounded, and a hidden door popped open. Surprise filled me. He had never showed this to me before, despite the dozens of times I had visited the workshop.

We followed the spelltech down a low, long hallway that zigged and zagged just like the alley outside the workshop, then went down a flight of rickety wooden stairs. Touma keyed in a code, opening another door, and we ended up in a large space that was mostly free of clutter. Part of the area was a workshop filled with tables, tools, and wires, but there was also a kitchen, an enclosed bathroom, and a freestanding screen that cordoned off a bedroom.

"So this is where you live," I murmured. "I've always wondered. Part of me assumed you slept on a cot in a corner somewhere."

Touma's nose crinkled with comical disgust. "Of course not! The exterior workshop is just for show. To convince people, especially Imperium soldiers, that I'm not as well off as I truly am—and that there are no other exits from the building."

My gaze snagged on a large whiteboard along the wall. To my surprise, it was covered with photos and blueprints of Crownpoint, Promenade Park, and the Boulevard. Even more surprising was the bank of holoscreens next to the whiteboard, which were showing different corridors inside the palace.

I slung my bags of supplies down onto a nearby table, then went over to the screens. "You hacked into the Crownpoint security feed."

Touma clapped Daichi on the shoulder. "Thanks to my nephew's brilliance."

Daichi gave a not-so-modest shrug. "You have your talents, Uncle, and I have mine."

"Have you seen Vesper—"

Pain ripped through my body, cutting off my question. More pain exploded deep inside me, as though dozens of daggers were stabbing into my flesh from all sides at once. I wheezed in a strangled breath and staggered to the side, slamming into a table. I gripped the edge of the metal, trying to focus on its hard, smooth surface, trying to focus on something else, anything else, but the agony slicing through every atom of my being.

"Kyrion!" Daichi yelled. "Kyrion!"

He reached for me, but Asterin grabbed his arm and pulled him back.

"No!" she warned. "Don't touch him."

Daichi stopped, a worried look on his face. Touma, Leandra, and Tivona stood beside him, also clearly worried.

"Breathe, Kyrion," Asterin commanded. "Breathe through the pain. You control it. The pain does *not* control you."

I forced myself to breathe in and out in a steady, deliberate rhythm. Slowly, the pain died down to a more manageable, bearable level, but the velvety ribbon of Vesper whipped around in my mind, like a butterfly desperately trying to escape a net. Her fear surged through the bond, right along with her pain, which was much greater than my own.

"Holloway . . . is siphoning off . . . Vesper's power," I growled between breaths.

Cold fury roared through me, icing out the pain, and I straightened up, pushed away from the table, and stabbed my finger at the holoscreens. "Show me."

Daichi hesitated, then hit some buttons on his tablet. The screens flickered, and new images appeared showing the Crown-point throne room.

Holloway was clutching Vesper's chin, and his eyes brightened like bronze suns rising over the horizon, even as Vesper's paled, like blue moons about to disappear in the approaching dawn. A low snarl came from my throat, and I had to clench my hands into fists to keep from smashing the holoscreens.

Zane stepped up beside Holloway and murmured something I couldn't hear. A few more seconds passed. Holloway abruptly released Vesper, who tumbled to the floor. Zane picked her up, and some Bronze Hand guards dragged her out of the throne room.

"Where are they taking her?" I growled, still staring at the screens.

Daichi hit some buttons, and more views appeared, tracking the guards as they dragged Vesper through the corridors. Eventually, the guards stepped through a pair of double doors, which shut behind them.

"There are no cameras in that area," Daichi said in an apologetic voice.

"It's okay. I know where they took her. That area is filled with suites that Holloway reserves for special guests."

Asterin nodded. "I stayed there a few months ago when I came to Corios for the Regal balls."

I had been in that area numerous times, so I knew that the suites featured every luxury money could buy. Even though I couldn't see Vesper, my worry eased a fraction. At least the guards hadn't taken her to one of the palace labs—yet.

"What will happen to Vesper now?" Tivona asked, wringing her hands.

"Holloway will order the servants to get Vesper cleaned up," I replied. "She will be bathed and fed, then primped and pampered for the midnight ball."

"How do you know that?" Leandra asked.

"Because he's done it before," I replied in a flat voice. "There was a truebonded couple before my parents' time. My mother used to watch the footage from the Regal archives, and I've seen it too. Holloway dressed the couple up and paraded them around like puppets in front of the other Regals. Every few months, he would bring them out for everyone to gawk at before sticking them back in one of the palace labs. My mother and father would whisper about it when they thought I couldn't hear. They were worried the same thing would happen to them if they didn't cooperate with Holloway, and to me too, eventually. And now it has."

My bitter laughter bounced off the walls and quickly faded away. No one spoke, but they all shot me pitying looks. Anger sparked in my chest, and I focused on the holoscreens again so I wouldn't have to see their sympathy. Part of me appreciated their commiseration, but sympathy wouldn't help Vesper. Only ruthless action would.

Several servants entered the suite where Vesper was being held. Some carried trays of food, while others pushed racks of gowns in front of them. More disgust spiked through me every time another servant appeared. Holloway wanted Vesper to look the part of the noble lady, as if that would somehow lessen the horror of him taking her magic again, this time in front of all the other Regals.

"What if you don't go to the ball?" Leandra asked, breaking the tense silence.

Everyone looked at her in surprise, and she shrugged. "I'm not saying leave Vesper at Holloway's mercy, but if you go to the ball, you're walking straight into his trap. So what if you didn't go? That might buy us some more time to think of a way to rescue her."

I shook my head. "Not going to the ball will make Holloway even angrier. If I don't show up, he'll punish Vesper. He'll take her magic again and again because he knows that I'll feel every bloody second of it. He might even . . . drain her completely, just to hurt me that much more."

My gut twisted at the thought of Holloway killing Vesper the same way he had killed my mother, and it took me a few seconds to unclench my jaw. "I would *never* do that to Vesper. I would never let her think that I abandoned her the way her mother did. Not for one bloody *second*."

Asterin and Leandra frowned, clearly confused, but Tivona grimaced, as did Daichi and Touma. The three of them knew how cruelly Nerezza Blackwell had treated her daughter.

We all fell silent again, watching the servants come and go on the holoscreens. I gently took hold of the bond, but the velvety ribbon of Vesper was calm and quiet. She wasn't being hurt, and some of the tension inside me eased. As long as she was alive, I still had a chance to save her.

But *how*? How could I do that? How could I get us both out of a palace teeming with Imperium soldiers and Bronze Hand guards? Not to mention Zane, Adria, and Dargan, who were sure to be stationed inside the throne room.

I kept watching the screens, but one by one, the others drifted away. Asterin, Tivona, and Leandra started speaking in low voices, sorting through the supplies we had brought to the workshop. Daichi kept swiping through screens on his tablet, monitoring the palace security feeds and muttering to himself, while Touma wandered over to one of the worktables, picked up a brush, and dipped it into a can of red paint. Then he leaned forward, swiping the color onto something that looked like a headless metal horse but was probably something else entirely.

I focused on the screens again, thinking about the layout of the palace, something I had done dozens of times over the past few months as I had been searching for a way to assassinate Holloway and then escape. But this time, the situation was even more urgent and complicated, because I was trying to rescue Vesper rather than save myself.

I would happily give up my own life, as long as she escaped.

Even if I could get Vesper away from Holloway, we would

still have to contend with the Bronze Hand guards in the throne room. I could kill several of the guards but not all of them, especially if Vesper was still weak and I had to help her walk—

Thump!

Touma cursed, drawing my attention. He had knocked over the can, and red paint was rushing across the metal worktable like a river of blood. The paint sluiced off the side of the table, spattering onto a rat's nest of gleaming copper wires sitting on the floor below.

Drip, drip, drip . . .

More paint spattered onto the wires, but the vivid red color faded away, replaced by a faint silver light that I recognized as the glow of Vesper's seer magic. I frowned. Why would her power point out messy splatters of paint?

An idea flared in my mind, exploding like a new star being born. My gaze snapped from the paint over to Asterin, who was showing Tivona and Leandra some of the clear polyplastic armor she had packed. Perhaps it was Vesper's seer magic still whispering to me, or perhaps it was my own battle experience, but suddenly, I knew my idea would work.

I just *knew* it would.

Touma cursed again and reached for a rag to start wiping up the mess, but I stepped in front of him and gestured at the red paint still dripping onto the floor.

"How much more paint do you have?"

Touma glanced at Daichi, who shrugged in return. They didn't see the solution, but I did, just like Vesper would have if she'd been here.

"Several buckets of it," Touma said, answering my question. "Why?"

A grim smile curved my lips. "Because we're going to use it to save Vesper."

TWENTY-EIGHT

VESPER

Instead of a cold, sterile medical lab, the Bronze Hands took me to a suite of luxurious rooms. My plasticuffs were removed, although the guards took up positions along the walls, and several more filled the corridor outside. I didn't bother trying to bargain with them. Everyone knew the Bronze Hands were completely loyal to Holloway, and they wouldn't help me in the slightest way.

The next several hours passed in a blur. Medics injected me with skinbonds, healing the cuts and bruises Dargan and Adria had inflicted on me. Then servants appeared with trays of food. Fresh fruits, crunchy vegetables, tangy cheeses, grilled meats, decadent chocolates. Everything tasted like mush in my mouth, as did the vitamin-packed energy drinks the servants kept foisting off on me, but I downed them all without complaint. Holloway might be fattening me up to slaughter later, but I still needed to replace the nutrients he had sucked out of me if I had any chance of escaping.

In between bites and drinks, I examined the guards, the

servants, and all the fine furnishings in the suite. I might be able to brain a servant or two over the head with a porcelain vase, but that wouldn't get me past the Bronze Hands. A hard, inevitable truth squeezed my stomach, making me want to vomit all the food I had eaten.

There was no escape.

Next, I was escorted into an enormous bathroom. Once again, there was no point in protesting, although I did shoo the servants out and slam the door in their faces.

"My lady!" one of the servants yelled through the thick wood. "Your clothes are filthy! You must take a bath before the ball!"

"Yeah, yeah, I heard you the first dozen times," I muttered.

I caught sight of my reflection in the mirror that ran down one wall. Wild, tangled hair. Purple circles of exhaustion under my dull eyes. Speckles of dirt and blood on my cheeks. The servant was right. I was a grimy, filthy, blood-covered mess, so I stripped off my ruined House Caldaren uniform and climbed into a tub filled with hot water.

A reluctant groan of pleasure escaped my lips, and I sank a little deeper into the tub. Someone had scattered blue petals into the water, and a bar of matching soap sat on a nearby table. I sniffed the soap, and a sweet spearmint scent tickled my nose. My heart wrenched. It reminded me of Kyrion's cleanser on the *Dream World*.

I washed everything three times, including my hair. Every two minutes, the dirty water drained away, replaced by a fresh bath that was the perfect temperature. Even the tub itself was heated so I didn't catch a chill. Grudging respect filled me. A particularly clever invention from House Zimmer.

Eventually, I was as clean as could be, and I climbed out of the tub and donned a plush robe. But I wasn't ready to face what was coming next, so I sat down in a stuffed chair and leaned my head back against the cushion. I closed my eyes and drew in a deep breath. The lingering scent of spearmint tickled my nose again, and I thought of Kyrion . . .

I blinked, and from one moment to the next, I was in the round room of my mindscape.

"Kyr?" I asked, hope flaring in my heart. "Kyr!"

I spun around and around, the robe flapping about my legs, but he didn't appear. Even worse, his door—the one with the sapphsidian arrow streaking upward through the stone—remained shut. I tugged and tugged on that blasted door, but I couldn't open it. I also couldn't feel Kyrion through the bond right now, not the faintest wisp of him, probably due to Holloway siphoning off my magic earlier.

Frustrated, I slammed my hand up against the arrow. Maybe it was my imagination, but the sigil seemed to twitch, as though it was silently chastising me for taking my anger out on it. I glared at the arrow and started to smack it again—

Bond of two, tried and true . . .

. . . makes you weak . . .

I whirled around. Asterin's voice floated out of a nearby archway, while Adria sneered at me through another open door.

The images went on and on, with each open door showing something that had happened over the past few days. Harkin torturing me in the Techwave lab. Kyrion and me kissing in the gym onboard the *Dream World*. Asterin telling me about truebonds in her office. Adria and Dargan sparring on Zane's ship.

I started to spin away from the memories to keep searching for Kyrion, but I thought better of it, stepped forward, and watched them all. Maybe something someone had said or done would help me figure out a way to escape the palace.

The memories all played out as they had in real life, but no solutions popped into my mind. Eventually, the images rewound and started playing again, and I ended up at the Door in the back of my mindscape. I stepped into the darkness and let it wash over me, going deeper into the blackness than I ever had before. At least it was peaceful in here, unlike out in the real world, where Holloway was counting down the minutes until he could take my magic again—

My knee rammed into something, and pain spiked up my leg. I cursed, lost my balance, and staggered forward. I stretched my arms out to break my fall, and my hands landed on cool, smooth stone.

I blinked, and from one moment to the next, a pool of silver light flooded the area, as though I was standing in the middle of a moon. My hands were resting on a slab of flat stone mounted on delicate legs that resembled an odd, curved altar. My reflection glimmered in the surface of the stone, as though I was staring into a dark blue lake sprinkled with bright silver flecks. I leaned forward, my nose going down toward the surface, and my hands sank into the stone, as though I was dipping my fingertips into that chilly lake.

Startled, I snatched my hands away and scuttled back a few steps. Now that I was studying it from a distance, I realized that the stone was an enormous piece of sapphsidian studded with tiny bits of pale lunarium, as though I was looking at the most beautiful night sky I had ever seen.

A memory bloomed in my mind, something I had read years ago when I had been trying to increase my magic in hopes of winning my mother's love.

"A psionic nexus," I whispered.

Academics had different theories and names for it, but a psionic nexus was thought to be a visual representation of a psion's power, the place deep inside them where all their magic came from. A nexus could be any shape or size and made of any material, but it usually reflected some aspect of a psion's abilities. Supposedly, only the strongest psions were able to access their psi-nexuses, although the books I'd read had been vague about what, if anything, the nexuses actually *did*.

Curious, I stepped forward and skimmed my hand over the nexus. The cool blue stone rippled like water, but my searching fingers encountered one hot divot after another. I leaned forward and took a closer look. Lunarium eyes were embedded in the surface of the sapphsidian. A thought occurred to me, and I stepped back again. In fact, the entire psi-nexus was shaped like an oversize eye, just like the ones in the doors out in the main part of my mindscape.

A glimmer caught my eye, and I bent down and looked at the nearest altar leg. It too was made of sapphsidian and was mounted on a piece of arrow-shaped lunarium. I straightened up, and more lunarium arrows glittered in the sapphsidian altar, shimmering like buried treasure lost in a deep, dark ocean. The arrows matched the sigil on Kyrion's door out in the round room of my mindscape.

I frowned. If this eye-shaped psi-nexus was a visual representation of my seer magic, then why would it feature so many arrows? Did it also symbolize my truebond with Kyrion? Or some combination of our magic?

The longer I stared at the sapphsidian and lunarium, the more I realized how the stones seamlessly flowed and blended into each other, as if they were puzzle pieces that fit perfectly together. Even stranger was the sense I got from the stones, as if each one made the other stronger, sturdier, and more powerful, and they vibrated and hummed in unison like two beautiful instruments singing out a glorious symphony—

Bang!

Bang-bang!

Bang-bang-bang!

The loud noises jolted me out of my mindscape. My eyes snapped open. I was still sitting in the chair close to the bathtub. I had been so exhausted that I had fallen asleep.

"Lady Vesper?" an apologetic voice sounded. "It's time to dress for the ball."

I considered telling the person exactly what Callus Holloway could do with his blasted ball, but they were just a servant and had no more power here than I did. It wasn't right or fair to take my anger out on someone who was simply following orders and trying to survive.

"Give me a minute," I grumbled.

I got up, unlocked the bathroom door, and stepped back so that the servants could enter, but I was just going through the motions. My thoughts were still back in my mindscape, wondering what, if anything, that eye-shaped altar meant—and why I had the strangest feeling I would see it again sooner rather than later.

An hour later, I stared at my reflection in the mirror, not quite believing what I was seeing. I had expected Holloway to order me to don a ballgown, and that was exactly what I was wearing. But this was no ordinary gown—it was an exact replica of Desdemona Caldaren's wedding dress.

Desdemona's wedding to Chauncey had been broadcast live across the galaxy, and the gossipcasts often played clips of it whenever they mentioned the Regal couple. Unlike Tivona, I had never paid much attention to fashion, but even I recognized this dress.

Instead of the traditional white, the dress was a shimmering silver, with thin straps, a sweetheart neckline, and a long flared princess skirt. It would have been exceptionally beautiful if it wasn't a twisted bit of torture.

It wasn't bad enough that Holloway had already siphoned off some of my magic. Now he was playing mind games by dressing me in the same sort of gown that Kyrion's mother had worn. Holloway was reinforcing the idea that Kyrion and I were doomed to the same wretched fate as his parents, and red-hot fury filled me at how hurt Kyrion would be when he saw me in this.

But once again, there was nothing I could do. If I tried to remove the gown or the matching silver heels, the guards would shove the items right back on me again, maybe even order the servants to sew the dress to my skin. I shuddered at the idea.

The servant behind me stilled. "Is something not to your liking, Lady Vesper?" she asked in a worried voice.

I looked in the mirror at the woman, who had said her name was Inga. She looked to be in her fifties with short, dark brown hair, blue eyes, and pale skin. Inga had spent the last twenty minutes fussing with the gown, making sure it fit me just so. Maybe it was the way the light was hitting her face, but she reminded me of Liesl. My heart squeezed at the thought of my dead cousin.

"Lady Vesper?" Inga asked again.

I forced myself to smile at her. "The gown is wonderful. You've done a fantastic job tailoring it and making me look lovelier than I truly am."

Inga gave me a brief smile, but her eyes were dark and troubled. "It's easy to make someone like you look lovely."

"Someone like me?"

She gestured at herself in the mirror. "Someone who would even notice someone like me. I've worked as a stylist at the palace for more than twenty years, and I don't think any of the Regals know who I am. Not even the ones who have sat in this very chair and let me work on their hair and makeup."

Inga glanced around, but the guards standing along the wall were checking their tablets and not paying the slightest attention to us. The stylist leaned past me and picked up a bottle of foundation from the vanity table.

"You saved my son, Gunter," she whispered. "He's an Imperium soldier and was set to be deployed on one of the Kents' deathtrap ships. I hope everything works out for you, my lady."

"Thank you, Inga. I'm glad I was able to help your family."

She patted my shoulder and leaned back. Inga dabbed the foundation onto my skin, evening out my complexion, then painted my eyes and lips the same shimmering silver as the replica gown. She was copying the makeup Desdemona Caldaren had worn on her wedding day, and I had to grind my teeth to keep from knocking the bottles and powders out of her hands.

Inga used a hot iron to curl my hair into loose waves, then started pulling the locks up into a familiar style. Even my hair was going to match Desdemona's. Ugh.

"I need to add some pins to your hair, and then you'll be all set, my lady," Inga chirped in a bright voice. "I thought these pins were especially lovely, and I picked them out just for you. See?"

She held three pins out where I could see them, although she angled her body in such a way that she blocked the guards' view. Two of the pins were shaped like small, pretty butterflies, which Inga tucked into the sides of my hair. The third pin was also shaped like a butterfly, but it had a much larger top and was studded with bits of sapphsidian and blue opals that formed the creature's wings. The jewels gave way to a long, thin sheath of silver that ended in a sharp point. Less of a hairpin and more of a small dagger.

"Here," Inga crooned, ignoring my stunned look. "Let me just nestle this in your hair."

She slid the pin into the knot of hair that she had pulled around to the back of my head. Inga looked at me in the mirror again and winked. I winked back at her.

"Thank you, Inga," I replied for the guards' benefit. "You're right. The hairpins are quite lovely."

She patted my shoulder, then packed up her styling tools and makeup and left the suite. I sat in the chair, staring at my reflection in the vanity-table mirror until another guard entered the room and said it was time to go.

I got to my feet and obediently trudged after the guards, drooping my head as though I was resigned to my fate, but my heart was a bit lighter than before. I still didn't know how I could escape from the throne room, much less the palace, but at least now I had a weapon.

TWENTY-NINE

VESPER

The guards took me to an elevator, and we rode up to the top floor. The elevator floated to a stop, and the guards led me toward the throne room.

To my surprise, hundreds of Regals lined both sides of the wide corridor. They were dressed in formal jackets and beautiful gowns, and jewels flashed on their necks, wrists, and fingers, making them look like glittering peacocks strutting around a white marble menagerie.

A hush fell over the Regals as I strode past, and the servants, guards, and soldiers who were mixed in with the nobles also fell silent. I ignored the curious and pitying looks. None of these people would help me, and I would just have to help myself, the way I always did.

The Bronze Hand guards gestured for me to stop, and we all waited while several soldiers scurried forward and tugged open the throne room doors. More Regals were lined up on either side of the massive doors, as though waiting to get into an exclusive nightclub.

Zane Zimmer was close to one of the doors. He was dressed in an Arrow uniform that was the pale blue of House Zimmer. Zane's face was smooth and blank, but his fingers tapped out a quick, nervous rhythm on the silver hilt of the stormsword belted to his waist.

Standing beside him was an eighty-something woman with silver hair, rosy skin, and pale blue eyes that matched her long, billowing gown. Beatrice Zimmer, Zane's grandmother and the head of House Zimmer. Next to her was a fifty-something man clad in a pale blue jacket with the same blond hair, blue eyes, and tan skin as Zane. Wendell Zimmer, Zane's father and the second-in-command of House Zimmer.

Beatrice eyed me with wary curiosity, as if she didn't quite know what to make of me. Wendell nodded respectfully, while Zane regarded me with an unreadable expression. My fingers itched with the urge to yank the butterfly dagger out of my hair and shove it into the Arrow's heart, but I throttled my anger. Zane wasn't worth such precious energy, and I needed to save my weapon to use on Holloway.

The throne room doors finally opened. Zane was the first one through them, his swaggering stride as arrogant as ever. Beatrice and Wendell followed him, along with the rest of the Regals, servants, and guards. They all stared at me again, but no one said a word, and the only sounds were the soft *tap-tap-tap-taps* of their footsteps, along with the steady hiss of supplemental oxygen streaming out of the wall vents.

Holloway might have dubbed this a midnight ball, but everyone knew it was really an execution.

Finally, all the Regals were inside. More Bronze Hand guards came up behind me, and I had no choice but to step forward.

During the last ball, pretty flowers and ornate decorations had adorned the enormous space, along with tables filled with fancy refreshments and wall spigots that shot out colorful beverages. Tonight the space was bare and empty, except for dozens of hoverglobes that tinted the room a soft, sinister orange. The wealthier and more important Regals, including Beatrice and Wendell, had climbed spiral stairs to metal balconies that had been erected here and there, while those who belonged to the poorer, less notable Houses were sitting on cushioned bleachers that had been spaced around the throne room.

Everyone wanted the best view possible for my impending murder.

Zane was standing at the bottom of the royal dais, along with Adria and Dargan. Just like Zane, the siblings were dressed in their Arrow uniforms, the pale gray of House Byrne. Adria's stormsword dangled from her belt, while Dargan had two weapons on his belt—his stormsword along with my own. I eyed the lunarium blade, wondering how I could get my hands on it without getting cut down by the dozens of Bronze Hand guards lining the walls.

Zane checked something on his tablet, then left the throne room. He wouldn't meet my sharp, accusing gaze. Coward.

The guards gestured for me to move forward. I shut Zane out of my mind, lifted my chin, and swept through the throne room. But all too soon, I stopped at the bottom of the dais, the same spot where I had fooled Holloway and everyone else into thinking that Kyrion and I weren't bonded.

Holloway was already seated on the throne. His long red robe matched the bloody veins of color running through the white stone. He stared down his nose at me, and I looked right back at him. I would not let him see my worry. Not the smallest scrap of it.

Holloway waved his hand, calling for silence, even though the room was already deathly quiet. "We are gathered here tonight so that I might decide the punishment of Lady Vesper Quill, who attempted to hide her truebond with Lord Kyrion

Caldaren. Lady Vesper tricked many people in this room, but I had my suspicions about the veracity of the truebond test, so I set out to find the truth. For the good of the Imperium, of course."

He wasn't even going to admit that I had fooled him too. Petty bastard. Approving murmurs rippled through the crowd, and the heavy weight of everyone's speculative gazes dropped on me like a meteor plummeting from the sky. I squared my shoulders.

"How very sad that Lady Vesper conspired to deceive this court." Holloway shook his head as though I was a recalcitrant child who had broken a simple rule. "A truebond is something to be celebrated, not hidden in shame."

"The only one here who should feel shame is *you*," I called out, making my voice as loud and strong as possible. "Everyone knows you're nothing but a leech and that the only reason you're so interested in truebonds is because of the power you can take from them for yourself."

A few agreeing murmurs rang out, and Holloway's hot, angry gaze flicked left and right, like a missile seeking out targets to destroy. He slashed his hand through the air, and silence dropped over the throne room again.

"The penalty for trying to break or hide a truebond is death," he said. "Although I'm going to make an exception in your case, Lady Vesper. You will be held in the palace labs until I say otherwise."

Holloway grinned, his white teeth flashing like needles in his mouth. Instead of executing me outright, he had decided to treat me the same way he had treated Desdemona Caldaren. He was going to experiment on me for who knew how long before finally siphoning off enough of my magic at once to kill me. Terrific.

"You might have gotten away with your deception, but luckily, a source came forward and told me about your plan to thwart Regal justice," Holloway continued. "That you tried to escape the full weight and consequences of Imperium law by fleeing to a Tropics planet. For that, I want to thank them."

I frowned. What source? Who could have told Holloway that Kyrion and I were headed to Tropics 33? His spy in the Techwave? But who could that possibly be?

Holloway crooked his finger, and footsteps cracked against the marble. Like everyone else, I turned toward the source of the sound.

A shadow slinked across the floor, and a woman wearing a skintight gown covered with dark blue sequins stepped out from behind one of the columns. Her dark brown hair gleamed under the lights, as did her dark blue eyes that were so much like mine.

Lady Nerezza Blackwell.

THIRTY

KYRION

I told the others my plan for Touma's buckets of bloodred paint. At first, they doubted me, but the longer I talked, the more certain I became that it would work. Then again, it *had* to work. Failure was not an option.

Daichi and Touma offered some advice and tweaks to my plan, as did Asterin, Tivona, and Leandra. As soon as we had the rough details sketched out about who would be where and doing what, everyone split up and got to work.

The hours passed quickly, and all too soon, it was time to leave for the ball. The others had taken a break to check their supplies and weapons, but I stood in front of the holoscreens, hoping to catch a glimpse of Vesper. I didn't see her, but I did spot Adria and Dargan.

The sister and brother were in a private lounge reserved for the Arrows. Adria was relaxing on a settee, checking her tablet, while Dargan was lunging back and forth and twirling Vesper's stormsword around in his hand like a child fighting an invisible enemy. He slashed it in Adria's direction, and she jerked her hand in annoyance. Her telekinesis slapped the sword out of his fingers, and the weapon hit the floor and skittered to a stop at her feet.

Adria leaned down and picked up the sword. She gripped the blade, then slowly turned the weapon around, studying the sapphsidian eyes and other sigils embedded in the hilt.

I growled and flicked my fingers over the holoscreen, zooming in on Vesper's sword and getting a clear look at the sigils. The sapphsidian eyes were intact, as was the silver itself. Good. Those two idiots hadn't damaged her weapon.

I started to zoom back out, but Adria tilted the sword so that she was looking at the pommel and turned it around again—

Shock blasted through me, and I jerked forward and tapped my finger on the holoscreen, freezing the feed. Then I zoomed in even more on the sword, wondering if my eyes were playing tricks on me . . . but they weren't. The sigil remained exactly as it was, exactly as it had been all along, but I felt like I was seeing it for the very first time.

My shock faded away, and I turned the revelation over in my mind, studying it from all angles, just like Adria had been turning Vesper's sword around in her hands. Of course. The information made perfect sense, and it explained so many things, especially all the little ways Vesper had always reminded me of someone else, although I had never been able to put my finger on exactly who, until this moment.

A laugh burst from my mouth. Then another one, then another one. Once I started laughing, I couldn't stop, even though the mirthless chuckles shook my shoulders and made my ribs ache. The others all stopped what they were doing to look at me.

"Is something wrong?" Touma asked. "What is that awful noise? Kyrion sounds like a deranged dragon."

"I believe that is some sort of laughter," Daichi replied in a dry tone.

"Nah," Leandra chimed in. "Your uncle is right. Kyrion is cackling like a deranged dragon."

I braced a hand against my ribs, and I finally managed to stop laughing. "Oh, it's definitely laughter at the galaxy at large and the bloody ironic jokes it likes to play on us all."

Touma looked over at Daichi, who shrugged. Leandra shrugged too, while Asterin and Tivona stared at me like I'd lost my mind. But they couldn't change what I'd discovered. No one could. Not even Vesper, with her enormous ability to fix things, could alter this one stark fact.

I wondered if Vesper knew, if she had figured out the truth the same way I had. Was she stunned by the discovery? Angry? Disgusted? Or was she still in the dark? No way to know, so I set those questions aside and concentrated on the information itself—and what I could do with it.

Just because I didn't like the revelation didn't mean I couldn't weaponize it the same way Regals did with the smallest scandal. The information wasn't much in the grand scheme of things, not compared with the hundreds of Bronze Hand guards and Imperium soldiers waiting inside Crownpoint. But now I knew something that Holloway and the other Regals didn't, and I was going to squeeze every advantage out of it that I could.

"I know that look," Daichi said in a worried voice. "What are you plotting, Kyrion?"

A sharp grin spread across my face. "Oh, I have several ideas, and none of them is good."

"Ideas about what?" Tivona asked.

"Something that might help Vesper."

They all shot me curious looks, but I didn't reveal the reason for my laughter. I didn't know when or even if I would get to use the information, and I didn't want to get anyone's hopes up.

"This is your last chance to back out," I warned, looking at them all in turn. "I don't know if I'll be able to stop Holloway from taking Vesper's and my power, much less kill enough of the guards and soldiers to escape from the throne room. You're all taking a huge risk by coming with me, and if I fail, you could all be caught and executed."

Tivona stepped forward, a fierce expression on her face. "Vesper is my best friend, and I'm going to do everything in my power to save her. All I ask is that you do the same, Kyrion."

I bowed to her. "I will. I swear it."

I would do anything for Vesper, a realization that didn't startle me nearly as much as it used to. Sometime over the past few days, I had accepted my regard for her. The truebond might have brought us together, might connect us as psions, but my feelings for Vesper were all because of the person she was, not the power she had or that we might be able to have together.

Tivona nodded, satisfied by my vow. Leandra also murmured her agreement.

I turned to Asterin. "You aren't part of the Imperium. This isn't even your fight."

"I like Vesper," she replied, a grin creasing her face. "And you too, Kyrion."

Surprise rippled through me. People rarely said they liked me and meant it, but Asterin's voice rang with sincerity.

Her grin vanished, and determination filled her face. "But you're wrong. This *is* my fight. What Holloway is doing is an abomination, and he won't stop with you and Vesper. He could easily set his sights on my mother and stepfather, along with other truebonded couples in the Erzton."

Her gaze grew distant, and an image flickered off her and piqued my telepathy: a man smiling at a woman who looked like an older version of Asterin. She was right. If given the chance, Holloway would do the same thing to her mother and stepfather that he had done to my parents.

"Thank you," I replied.

Asterin's gaze cleared, and she grinned at me again.

Finally, I turned to Daichi and Touma. "The two of you have already done so much for me. Your debt was paid long ago, and you don't owe me anything."

"Thank you for saying that, even if it is complete and utter nonsense. You saved me from being executed by the Regals. I owe you my life, Kyrion." Touma clapped me on the shoulder. "Even if I didn't, you know how much I despise Callus Holloway. I'm happy to help you thwart his plan."

Daichi nodded and stepped up beside his uncle. "And you gave me a job as your chief of staff when no one else would hire me. You protected me from the Regals too. But even more important is the fact that we're friends, Kyrion, and friends help each other no matter what." He paused, and a teasing smile spread across his face. "Besides, do you know how hard it was to make a proper cup of tea before Vesper fixed my brew-maker? I owe her for that alone."

"Thank you," I replied, trying and failing to keep the raspy emotion out of my voice. "Thank you all."

Everyone nodded back at me, and then we broke apart to finish our preparations. My gaze moved from one person to the next. Tivona checking the charge on the shock baton belted to her waist. Leandra twirling her golden stormsword around in her hand. Asterin smoothing down her long skirt. Touma dabbing a final bit of silver paint onto his breastplate. Daichi swiping through screens on his tablet.

I was the leader of the Arrows, and I had led more people into battle—and to their deaths—than I cared to remember. But this was harder than any of those previous missions, because these people, our friends, were risking themselves for Vesper and me not because they had been ordered to but because they *wanted* to.

Even when my parents had been alive, I'd never had this

many true, genuine friends, which made me even more worried that I was going to get them all killed, and Vesper too, before the night was through.

Everyone completed their final checks, and then it was time to head to Crownpoint. Tivona and Leandra left first, then Asterin, and finally Daichi and Touma. I waited until they were all far away from the workshop, and then I left too.

Steering clear of the traffic and other cameras, I walked several blocks in the opposite direction from the route the others had taken, then hailed a mechanized transport. No matter what happened, I didn't want to lead Holloway and his Bronze Hand guards back to Touma's workshop.

I programmed a meandering route through the industrial side of the city, wanting to give everyone enough time to get into position. Eventually, I returned to the spaceport where the *Dream World* was still docked. Thanks to Daichi's hacking, I was able to slip through the area undetected and board the blitzer. According to the scans, no one had been near the ship since it had landed. I still double-checked for trackers, but my sweep came up clean. Good. One less thing to worry about.

I engaged the thrusters, and the blitzer lifted off the ground. I set a course for Crownpoint and pinged the palace, letting them know that I was coming. The ship zoomed toward the Boulevard, and Castle Caldaren came into view. The blue moons and stars were shining brightly overhead, and they painted the structure in a pale light that reminded me of the silvery flecks in Vesper's eyes.

For years, I had spent as little time as possible at the castle, since something around every corner reminded me of my parents and everything I had lost due to Holloway's greed. But tonight the sight of the structure steadied me. Castle Caldaren had stood against the elements and battles and everything else that had happened over the centuries, and it gave me hope that I could stand against Holloway and his horrific plans too.

I embraced that hope a moment longer, then tucked it away and unleashed my inner monster.

A few minutes later, the ship coasted through the opening and landed in the docking bay in the main tower. I hit the button to lower the cargo bay ramp, then placed my hand on the hilt of my stormsword and drew that familiar cloak of coldness around my shoulders. With my Arrow persona wrapped tightly around me, I strode down the ramp.

Zane was waiting in the docking bay, his hand on his own stormsword, with more than a dozen Bronze Hand guards spread out around him. The guards were armed with their usual spears, but the tips were glowing a soft blue instead of the usual bright white, indicating that the weapons were set to stun rather than kill. Holloway wanted me shocked into submission, not dead.

I ignored the guards and stopped in front of Zane. "Why so glum?" I drawled. "You should be happy. You're finally going to be the head of the Arrows, just like you've always wanted."

Zane shook his head. "Not like this. I never wanted this, not even for you, Kyrion."

For once, I thought he was sincere.

Zane held out his hand. "Your weapon."

I passed Zane my stormsword, which he hooked to his own belt. I'd left my blaster on the ship, along with my silver bandolier.

Zane strode away, and I fell in step beside him. The Bronze Hands closed ranks around us, and we went over to an elevator. The guards started to step inside, but Zane held out a hand, stopping them.

"He can't escape now," he said.

The guards nodded and remained outside. The elevator door

slid shut with a whisper. Zane hit the appropriate button, and the car started to rise. He leaned back against the opposite wall and crossed his arms over his chest.

"I didn't think you would come," he said. "You really do care about her, don't you?"

I mimicked his seemingly lazy pose. In so many ways, Zane and I were mirror images of each other, two sides of the same Regal coin, stamped into our respective roles and rivalries since childhood. Always pitted against each other and always ruthlessly pushing each other to excel. I supposed that was what made us such good enemies.

"Yes. I care about her. It only takes a small thing to change your whole perspective, your whole life, your whole world."

"And Vesper Quill did that for you?"

"She did. In more ways than I could possibly imagine." I stared at him. "Just like I could change your whole perspective."

Zane chuckled. "*You?* Change *my* life? How? As you pointed out earlier, I'll be the leader of the Arrows now. That's all the change I need." His tone was light, breezy even, but his lips curled with the faintest hint of disgust.

"You were right about one thing. You should have been the leader of the Arrows all along. You *would* have been the leader if Holloway hadn't made me his pet assassin. You're much better suited for the role than I am. Much better at dealing with people and politics, and much smarter than people give you credit for."

Zane tipped his head, acknowledging my points, although his eyes narrowed. "I didn't expect you to be so gracious. What are you plotting, Kyrion?"

I jerked my chin at his ice-blue jacket. "Although I've always wondered why you insist on wearing that ridiculous color. Don't you get tired of recycling all those Arrow uniforms the second you get blood on them?"

Anger flickered across Zane's face, although he maintained his relaxed pose. "Unlike you, I'm proud to wear the colors of my House, my family."

A thin smile curved my lips. "I know you are. Just as I'm proud to wear this."

I held up my hand so that he could see the eye carved into my left palm. The lines were a vivid red, as though they were on the verge of splitting open and dripping blood, but strangely enough, the wounds didn't hurt a bit.

Zane recoiled. "What is *that*?"

"The mark I carved into my hand when Holloway ordered me to conduct the truebond test during the last Regal ball. The same mark appeared on Vesper's hand, although she hid it with a special glove. The eye is Vesper's sigil. Her mindscape is full of them."

"So what?" Zane scoffed. "She's a seer. Of course she would have eyes in her mindscape. The symbolism is painfully obvious and completely unoriginal."

"You're right. Vesper is a seer, and over the past few months, she's opened my eyes to so many things."

Zane chuckled again. "Whoever knew that Kyrion Caldaren was a romantic poet at heart? You are totally mad for her, aren't you?"

In more ways than he could possibly imagine.

"*Mad* doesn't even begin to describe it. Vesper changed my life, just like I could change yours, if you're willing to listen."

Zane rolled his eyes. "This again?" He gestured around at the elevator. "In case you haven't realized it, you're trapped, Kyrion. You can't even change your own fate, so how do you think you can possibly change mine?"

I waggled my fingers, drawing his attention back to the eye carved into my palm. "I cut five marks into my skin the night of the truebond test. Five words for five cuts seems fair. Indulge me. Consider it a last request from a condemned man."

His forehead crinkled in confusion. "Did you hit your head back on Tropics 33? Because you sound concussed. There is literally *nothing* you could say, no combination of words or syllables, whether it was five or five hundred or five bloody thousand, that would change how I feel about you, that would get *me* to help *you*. I might pity you, given what Holloway had planned, but I would never disobey a direct order from him. I would *never* jeopardize my House, my family, especially not for the likes of you."

I kept staring at Zane, my hand up and steady. After a few seconds, he snorted.

"Fine. I can grant a doomed man his final wish, even if it's a foolish one. Go ahead," Zane drawled in a mocking tone, bowing low and fluttering his hand in a grand, sweeping gesture. "Tell me this great and wondrous thing that will change my life forever."

Like all the other palace elevators, this one had a security camera in the ceiling. I didn't want anyone else to hear what I had to say, so I stepped a little closer to Zane, my gaze locking with his, then reached out with my power and touched his mind.

Zane arched an eyebrow in amusement, but he didn't try to block me with his own psion power. Given our mutual disdain, the two of us rarely communicated telepathically, even in the heat of battle. But this war of words was the most important one we'd ever waged, even if he didn't realize it yet.

Still staring at him, I closed my left hand into a fist. Then, as I telepathically said the words, I slowly uncurled my fingers one by one, along with my thumb, until all five were extended out wide again.

Five words for five cuts, just like I'd promised.

Zane jerked away from the wall. His mouth gaped in shock, and his gaze zoomed over to the eye carved into my hand. He didn't say anything, but his body went rigid, and the muscles in his neck bulged with tension, as though my words had encased him in ice and he couldn't move an inch.

"See?" I murmured. "All it takes is one small thing to change your entire world."

Zane kept gaping at me as the elevator stopped. The door slid back, and I left him behind without another word.

More Bronze Hand guards were waiting outside the elevator. I ignored them and headed straight toward the throne room. After a few seconds, footsteps sounded, and Zane caught up with me. He didn't say anything as we strode along the corridor, but I could feel his mind churning, trying to make sense of my earlier words.

Far more Bronze Hand guards were lining the corridor than usual, along with Imperium soldiers, but the throne room doors were wide open. Holloway thought he had won, and he was making it as easy as possible to step into his trap before he snapped it shut behind me.

I entered the throne room. A hush fell over the crowd, and everyone looked at me, but I only had eyes for Vesper.

She was standing in the open space at the bottom of the dais, with Adria, Dargan, and several Bronze Hand guards lurking nearby. Just as I'd expected, she had been primped and poured into a silver gown that enhanced her beauty. I frowned. Her gown looked very familiar, as did the way her hair was styled . . .

Sick realization sliced through my gut, and my steps faltered. Holloway had ordered the servants to dress Vesper in a copy of my mother's wedding gown.

My gaze snapped up to Holloway on his throne, and he gave me a small, smug smile. The bastard was mocking me with my dead mother, the woman he had essentially killed in this very room.

Icy rage roared through me, freezing out my shock. I smoothed out my stride and stopped in front of the dais. Adria and Dargan clutched their weapons, as did the Bronze Hand guards, but I ignored them all and studied Vesper.

Her face was paler than normal, and the makeup couldn't quite hide the purple circles of exhaustion under her eyes, but the velvety ribbon of her was warm, strong, and vibrating with emotion. A tight knot of tension unwound in my chest. Seeing that she was alive on the security feed was one thing, but standing beside her and sensing it for myself soothed something deep inside me, even as my inner monster growled in warning, determined to protect her at any cost.

Oh, Kyr. Vesper's voice whispered through my mind, and her regret rippled through the bond to me. *I'm so sorry about the gown.*

I know. It's okay. We'll get through this—together.

"Ah, Kyrion, my boy," Holloway called out, getting up from his throne and gliding down the dais steps. "You're just in time. I was telling everyone how much help Lady Nerezza was in tracking down you and Vesper and bringing you both to justice."

Nerezza strode over to Holloway's side. She was dressed in a tight electric-blue gown with a diamond pattern that reminded me of a viper's smooth scales. Pretty to look at but poisonous to touch.

"And how did she do that?" I asked in a bored voice.

I would play Holloway's little game, for now. Every moment he blathered on was another moment the others had to get into position.

"For the last several months, Lady Nerezza has been working undercover as one of my spies," Holloway said. "On my orders, she infiltrated the Techwave, and she was the reason I was able to send Arrows to Tropics 33 to intercept Lady Vesper, as well as to protect Imperium interests and Regals who were vacationing at the Regenwald Resort during that awful Techwave attack."

All around the throne room, approving murmurs rang out at his blatant lies. The only interests Holloway had protected were his own, and he wouldn't have cared if the Techwave had killed every single Regal at the resort.

"We all owe Lady Nerezza a debt of gratitude," Holloway continued.

Nerezza smiled and nodded at his generous praise, playing the part of the gracious spy who was finally stepping out of the shadows and into the light to accept her due recognition.

Vesper laughed. The harsh, mocking sounds of her chuckles echoed off the walls. Everyone focused on her, and the smile dropped from Nerezza's lips faster than a meteor plummeting toward a planet.

Vesper stopped laughing and wiped away the tears of mirth that had gathered in the corners of her eyes. "Is that what Nerezza told you? That she's your loyal spy, risking her life to embed herself in the Techwave so she can help you thwart them? Surely you're not that much of a fucking *fool*."

Holloway's eyes glittered with anger, and he took a menacing step forward. I tensed, ready to put myself between him and Vesper, but Nerezza laid a hand on his arm. Holloway stopped and visibly reined in his anger, although he kept glaring at Vesper.

Nerezza patted his arm like a beauty taming a beast, then faced Vesper.

"I'm so sorry the Techwavers hurt you," Nerezza said in a voice that was dripping with fake sincerity. "I tried to rescue you, Vesper. Truly, I did. But the Imperium mission came first, and I had to tell Callus about the threat on Tropics 33 so that he could send Arrows to protect the Regals at the Regenwald Resort. And then, of course, when Callus told me about your betrayal, about how you were trying to hide your truebond with Kyrion, well, I had to do my duty to the Imperium and tell him where you had gone."

Vesper laughed again. "You always were good at spinning a story."

Nerezza frowned, clearly confused by Vesper's mocking familiarity, but Holloway cocked his head to the side.

"What do you mean?" he asked.

"I know what Nerezza Blackwell is capable of better than anyone," Vesper said, staring at the other woman. "And I especially know how she thinks. She might be *your* spy in the Techwave, but she's also *their* spy in the Imperium. Nerezza has always excelled at playing both sides against each other to get what she wants. The only loyalty she's ever had is to *herself.*"

"I only want to be of service to the Imperium," Nerezza countered in a soft, humble voice. "Nothing else."

"You want *power* more than anything else." Vesper spat out the words. "And you'll do anything to get it—even abandon your own daughter."

Shocked gasps rang out, and even Holloway was startled by Vesper's words. Nerezza's eyes narrowed the faintest bit, and I could feel her mind churning as she tried to think of a way to twist Vesper's words to her advantage. Slowly, the gasps died down, and everyone stared at Nerezza.

"Vesper is right," she admitted. "I did have a daughter. But tragically, she died in an accident while I was here on Corios, trying to make a better life for the two of us."

Nerezza bowed her head and clasped her hands in front of her body, striking a sad, somber pose. This time, the murmurs were more sympathetic than shocked. She truly was skilled at turning people from enemies into allies.

Vesper laughed again, the sound louder and even more mocking than before. Nerezza's head whipped up. Her sorrowful pretense cracked away, and her red lips pinched together in annoyance.

"You didn't leave your daughter behind to make a better life," Vesper continued, her voice ice-cold. "You left her behind because you didn't want the baggage of a bastard child dragging you down while you climbed the Regal ladder. Especially a child who didn't have enough psion power for you to exploit."

She spun around, addressing the Regals gathered on the balconies and bleachers. "Do you know what Nerezza truly thought about her daughter? The thing she said right before she abandoned her little girl?"

Vesper spun back around to Nerezza. "*Useless child.*"

Once again, she spat out the words, and Nerezza's forehead crinkled, as though the words were familiar but she couldn't quite place them. She froze. Her eyes widened, and her confusion cracked away, replacing by growing recognition and horror.

Vesper lifted her chin, projecting fire, fury, and strength, every inch the Regal queen that Nerezza so desperately wanted to be. "Hello, Mother."

Even more shocked gasps were followed by loud, frenzied mutters. In an instant, everyone was looking back and forth between Vesper and Nerezza. Same dark brown hair, same dark blue eyes, same straight nose and heart-shaped mouth. Once you started searching for it, the resemblance was easy to see, but Vesper was so much *more* than Nerezza—smarter, stronger, and so fierce and brave and beautiful she stole my breath.

"Nothing to say, Nerezza?" Vesper clucked her tongue in mock sympathy. "I can't believe I was stupid enough to come to Corios to find you when I was younger. You weren't worth such effort. You still aren't."

Nerezza's eyes narrowed, her nostrils flared, and her hands fisted in her skirt. She looked stunned and furious at the same time. Vesper stared at her mother a moment longer, then turned away, dismissing her completely.

Vesper looked at Holloway again. "You might think Nerezza was spying on the Techwave for you, but she's been conspiring with them for years. She was working with Rowena Kent to sabotage Imperium ships, and she fired the weapon that brought down the *Velorum*. And then, later, when Rowena was in your custody, Nerezza arranged for the other Regal lady to be poisoned. She told me so herself right before she let the Techwavers torture me on Magma 3."

More shocked gasps. Nerezza opened her mouth, but no words escaped. For once, the conniving Regal climber had been rendered speechless. More fury bloomed in her face, staining her cheeks an ugly red, and hate flashed in her eyes as she glared at Vesper.

The gasps faded away, and silence reigned once more.

Nerezza made a visible effort to get her emotions under control. She smoothed her face, released her skirt, and pivoted to Holloway. "Callus, you can't believe a word she says. Vesper Quill lied about having a truebond. Why, for all we know, *she* is the one who is secretly working with the Techwave and sabotaging the Imperium—"

Holloway waved his hand. Power rolled off him, and Nerezza's mouth snapped shut. Her eyes bulged, and she made a few strangled noises, but she couldn't overcome his telekinesis. Frustration radiated from her, along with another wave of caustic hate, this one directed at Holloway.

He made a circular motion with his index finger, and a couple of Bronze Hand guards flanked Nerezza. "We will discuss this matter later, in great detail."

His voice was casual, but Nerezza paled at the implied threat. Holloway flicked his fingers, and she staggered forward, as though an invisible hand had released her. Nerezza wheezed in a couple of breaths, her chest heaving, even as her gaze darted around the room, searching for an escape.

Holloway strode toward me. His wing tips tapped out a low,

ominous drumbeat on the white marble, and the tiny veins of red seemed to writhe under his feet. I held my position, my hands balling into fists. No matter what happened, I wouldn't let him see my fear.

Vesper started toward me, but Dargan grabbed her arm, jerking her back.

It's okay. I sent the thought to her. *I'll fight Holloway for as long as I can. You're not alone. Be ready to move.*

Vesper frowned. Once again, she started forward, and once again, Dargan yanked her back, this time using his enhanced strength to hold her in place. Anger spiked through me. If I got the chance, I was going to kill the other Arrow for putting his hands on her.

Holloway stepped in front of me, blocking my view of Vesper. "I've been waiting for this moment for a long, long time," he purred. "Ever since your weak, foolish parents died."

"Shut the fuck up," I snarled. "You might take my power, but I don't have to listen to you bloody brag about it."

Holloway shrugged. "As you wish, Kyrion. Besides, I've never been very good at waiting."

He smiled, but the expression was all teeth, and greed, hunger, and lust flitted across his face like dark storm clouds. Holloway glided forward and locked his hand around my throat. To my surprise, his fingers were cold and clammy, as if he didn't have enough life and vitality to keep his own body warm.

Then his siphon ability latched onto me, like dozens of daggers ripping into my skin, and the bastard finally made my greatest fear a reality—and took my power for his own.

THIRTY-ONE

VESPER

Kyrion let out a strangled cry and jerked back, but he couldn't break Holloway's iron grip on his neck. Despite the distance between us, I could sense Holloway's magic plunging deeper and deeper into Kyrion, piercing him just as it had pierced me. His pain erupted in my mind—so much *pain*, even more than what I had endured.

"Kyr!" I yelled. "Kyr!"

I lunged forward, wanting to help him, but Dargan's fingers dug into my upper arm, stopping me yet again. I snarled and lashed out with my other hand, trying to claw his eyes out. Dargan easily avoided my swipe, then punched me.

Pain exploded in my jaw, and the force of the blow ripped me out of his grip. I staggered back, but Dargan grabbed my arm and yanked me right back toward him again. A silver light flared around the Arrow, and for once, I knew exactly what my seer magic was telling me—that it was finally time to fight back.

I reached up, snatched the butterfly dagger out of my hair, and lashed out with the sharp point. Dargan threw his other arm up, spoiling my aim, and the dagger only stabbed into his shoulder, instead of his eye like I intended. Pity.

He yelped in surprise and released me. I whirled around and sprinted straight for Holloway and Kyrion. I needed to break Holloway's hold before he took all of Kyrion's magic—before he killed Kyrion.

"You fucking leech!" I screamed. "Get away from him!"

Holloway was so focused on Kyrion that he didn't see me coming. I put my shoulder down and rammed into him as hard as I could. Holloway's hand fell away from Kyrion's throat, and he staggered back, although some Bronze Hand guards hurried forward and caught the Imperium ruler before he hit the floor.

Kyrion gulped down one breath after another through his bruised throat, his chest heaving, the muscles in his neck tight with tension. His eyes locked with mine, and the sticky cobweb of him quivered with pain and fear, as though a pair of cold fists were slowly crushing my mind. His pain and fear matched what was pounding through my own heart.

"Guards!" Holloway yelled. "Seize them!"

Several Imperium soldiers rushed forward, while a few of the Bronze Hand guards brandished their spears at Kyrion and me. Even more fear erupted in my heart. If the soldiers latched onto us, then the guards could shock us into submission with their spears, and we would never escape Holloway—

A glimmer of gray caught my eye. Adria had drawn her stormsword. The lunarium blade was pulsing with her magic, but even more striking was the expression on her face. Adria was grinning widely, as though something about this whole situation greatly amused her. One of the doors in my mindscape flung itself open, and suddenly I was seeing another Adria standing side by side with this current version.

You being afraid of Holloway doesn't make you smart. It just makes you weak.

Adria had said that on Zane's ship when the two of us had been trading insults. I'd thought she'd just been snarking back at me, but what if there was more to her words?

What if Holloway didn't just leech magic, energy, power, life off other people? What if he could also feed off their *emotions*, like some sort of telempathic black hole? What if fear made it even easier for him to siphon off someone's power?

As soon as the idea popped into my mind, my magic kicked in, and suddenly, I could *see* how it worked. How the smallest, tiniest seed of fear could corrupt, fray, and unravel the strongest psionic power, even a truebond between two people who loved each other more than anything else, like Kyrion's parents had.

Bond of two, tried and true. This time, Asterin's voice floated through my mind. I'd thought her advice had just been a charming rhyme, a quaint password, but now I understood the truth in it and in what she had been trying to tell me, whether she realized it or not.

For the first time—the very first time—I realized that a truebond wasn't about romance or brain chemistry or pheromones or some random quirk of magic. Sure, all those things could play a part in it, especially in forming the initial connection.

But the bond itself? It was about *trust.*

It was about fully, completely, instinctively trusting the person you were bonded to. Not just with your magic but with your mind and heart too. With all your thoughts and feelings and most secret wishes and darkest desires. It was about showing someone every single part of you, bad, good, and ugly, and having them accept you as you were, just as you would accept them in return.

We can't be afraid! I sent the thought to Kyrion. *We have to believe that our bond is strong enough to defeat Holloway! That we're strong enough to defeat Holloway*—together!

Kyrion's determination pulsed through the bond, strong and

steady and buoying my own resolve. He sidestepped a soldier who lunged in his direction, but another soldier tackled him from behind, driving him down to the floor.

I started forward to help him, but a couple of Imperium soldiers charged in my direction. I dodged one of them, but the second man grabbed me around the waist. My high heels skittered on the slick marble, and we both toppled to the floor. I thrashed around, trying to escape the soldier, and the spiky shoes slid off my feet and tumbled away as though I was a princess in an old-fashioned fairy tale.

I rammed my elbow into the soldier's throat, then brought my bare foot up between us and kicked him aside. A Bronze Hand guard stepped forward and jabbed his spear downward, but I rolled away, and the weapon slammed against the floor, chipping the smooth marble.

I scrambled back up onto my hands and knees and crawled forward, trying to escape the soldiers and guards swarming toward me. A few feet away, Kyrion kicked off a soldier who was trying to shove his face against the floor. He too scrambled up onto his hands and knees and crawled forward, as desperate to reach me as I was to reach him.

"Kyr!" I yelled, stretching my right hand out toward him. "Kyr!"

"Vesper!" he yelled back, stretching his right hand out as well. "Vesper!"

My fingertips brushed against his, and a few tiny blue sparks flickered in the air, like a fire trying to sputter to life.

"No!" Holloway yelled. "Separate them! Keep them apart!"

An Imperium soldier latched onto my legs and dragged me backward, while three soldiers piled on top of Kyrion, pinning him against the floor. I snarled and swiped my hands over the marble, but I couldn't get a grip on the slick stone, much less use it to pull myself over to Kyrion.

Then a tiny bit of space wiggled its way between me and

the soldier, and he lost his hold on my legs. I kicked him in the ankle, making him grunt and stagger back into another man. A few feet away, one of the soldiers abruptly toppled off Kyrion and landed on a second man. Kyrion snarled and punched the third soldier in the throat, freeing himself from the pile of men.

I redoubled my efforts, crawling toward him even faster than before. Kyrion did the same thing, even as the Imperium soldiers and Bronze Hand guards closed ranks around us. We lunged toward each other, our hands stretching out and out and out . . .

My hand brushed Kyrion's, and I grabbed onto him . . .

He took hold of me and curled his fingers into mine . . .

I curled my fingers back into his, and we both tightened our grips as we dragged each other even closer . . .

More blue sparks flickered around us. Determination blazed in Kyrion's eyes, turning them more black than blue, and the same sensation roared through me. The sparks erupted and then immediately coalesced into thick veins of blue energy that zinged back and forth like lightning along our joined hands. The lightning arced up, brighter and hotter than before, even as shards of ice, flares of fire, and crackles of wind erupted out of the pulsing mass of energy.

I tightened my grip on Kyrion again, and he did the same to me. No one was keeping me away from him ever again—

BOOM!

The energy exploded.

Jagged forks of blue and silver lightning shot through the air, while a hard, vicious wave of telekinetic power rolled off us both. The invisible energy ripped through the room, cracking the marble floor in dozens of places, along with the dais steps and even the throne perched at the top. People screamed, and several folks slipped off the sides of the metal balconies, which were violently swaying. Imperium soldiers and Bronze Hand guards also tumbled to the floor.

The hand sculptures toppled off the walls and smashed the hoverglobes bobbing around below, causing flames to spew into the air. The metal hands crashed against the marble floor, and their copper fingers snapped off and rolled away like old-fashioned pennies. Overhead, the chandeliers whipped back and forth, and the whole tower shuddered and trembled as though it was at the epicenter of a catastrophic earthquake.

But I only had eyes for Kyrion, and he for me. We crawled even closer to each other, until I was practically sitting on his lap. He nuzzled his nose into my hair, while I buried my face against his neck and drank in his sharp, slightly sweet spearmint scent. Then, together, we rose to our feet, still holding hands and staring into each other's eyes.

Kyr.

Vesper.

Our thoughts mixed and mingled together, as did our emotions. Before, I had always thought of Kyrion as a sticky cobweb in my mind, an annoying sensation I couldn't get rid of no matter how hard I tried. But now I fully embraced the silky threads, all the cool little jagged bits and pieces of him that soothed, smoothed, and strengthened all the fiery little jagged bits and pieces of me.

It was . . . it felt . . . *amazing.*

Energy, power, emotion. It all poured from him into me and surged from me back to him again, as though we were two machines working together in perfect harmony.

"Your eyes are glowing like lunarium stars," Kyrion murmured.

"And yours look like pieces of sapphsidian, so blue they're almost black," I whispered back.

A tingling sensation swept through my left hand. I glanced down, and the eye-shaped cuts in my palm rippled once, then sank deeper into my skin and vanished completely. The cuts on Kyrion's left hand also vanished.

He grinned at me and threaded his right fingers through mine. I grinned back and swayed toward him—

"No!" Holloway screamed. "Your power is mine! Seize them! Seize them!"

All around the throne room, the Imperium soldiers and Bronze Hand guards scrambled to their feet and surged forward, surrounding Kyrion and me.

Kyrion and I stared at each other a moment longer. Then we released each other's hands and faced our enemies, still together, even though we weren't physically touching.

We didn't need to do that. Not anymore. Before, when we had been separated, Kyrion's presence had ebbed and flowed in my mind, depending on how close we were. But now I would have been able to sense him across the galaxy, just as he would have been able to sense me.

A tense silence dropped over the throne room, which had finally stopped quaking and shaking. Holloway was standing at the bottom of the dais steps, flanked by several Bronze Hand guards. Zane was near the guards, not quite with them but not separate from them either. His stormsword glowed a pale blue in his hand, and a thoughtful look filled his face.

Dargan and Adria were on the opposite side of the room. Dargan yanked the butterfly dagger out of his shoulder and tossed it aside. He snarled with anger and drew his stormsword, while Adria lifted her own weapon.

Several Regals and servants were slumped on the floor where they had fallen off the balconies, dazed expressions on their faces, but many of the Regals were still gathered on the raised platforms, clutching the metal railings for support, their faces pale with shock.

Holloway's gaze snapped back and forth between Kyrion

and me. I don't know what he saw, what his siphon magic showed him, but he blanched and took a step back. An unexpected emotion also rippled off him.

A soft laugh escaped my lips. "Can you feel that? He's afraid of us now."

Kyrion tilted his head to the side, studying the Imperium ruler. "He *is* afraid, isn't he?" A dark, vicious smile spread across his face. "Excellent."

Holloway's cheeks flushed, and his mouth opened and closed as though he were a shark out of water, desperately gasping for air. "Kill them!" he finally roared.

Dargan snarled again and charged in my direction. I flung my hand out. Telekinetic power—Kyrion's power—rolled off me and hit the Arrow, slamming him back into one of the columns. Dargan fell on his ass, clearly stunned.

I sent out another wave of telekinetic power, and my stormsword tore itself off Dargan's belt, zipped across the room, and settled into my hand. Next to me, Kyrion used his power to rip his own sword off Zane's belt.

The second the weapons were in our hands, our stormswords ignited with the combined strength of our psion power, and both blades glowed a dark blue shot through with veins of bright shimmering silver.

"Don't kill all the guards," Kyrion murmured. "Let me eliminate at least some of them."

I grinned back at him. "Funny, I was just going to say the same thing to you."

Together, we raised our swords and charged forward, taking the fight to our enemies.

THIRTY-TWO

KYRION

I sliced my stormsword across the chest of the first Bronze Hand guard who was foolish enough to attack me. The glowing lunarium blade easily sheared through his armor, and he screamed and dropped to the ground.

I grinned. That felt so good. *I* felt so bloody good.

An incredible amount of power zinged through my body, as though a medtable had injected me with a thousand tiny needles full of pure psionic energy. At this moment, I felt like I could do *anything*, even fly, if I had to.

Another guard rushed up and brandished his spear. I spun around and lashed out with my sword, cutting off the weapon's deadly tip. Another spin, and I sliced my sword across his chest the same way I had done to the first guard. The man toppled to the floor, and I stepped over his thrashing body, searching for another enemy to kill.

Vesper was also cutting down one Bronze Hand guard after another. People were screaming, and many of the Regals were stampeding toward the open doors, trying to leave. The thrashing mass of bodies created a logjam that kept more guards from entering the throne room.

I cut down another guard and whirled around. Holloway was still standing at the base of the dais, with a couple of Bronze Hands flanking him. I bared my teeth at the siphon, who scuttled back behind his men. Even more rage roared through me, and I twirled my sword around in my hand and stalked in his direction. I was finally going to end the siphon for everything he'd done to my parents—and Vesper and me too.

"Kill him!" Holloway screamed, stepping even farther back behind his guards.

The Bronze Hands brandished their spears, and the tips sparked with white-hot electricity. They had changed the settings from stun to kill, but my inner monster chuckled with amusement. That wasn't going to save them.

The guards charged forward, stabbing out with their spears, but I zigzagged back and forth between them, slicing my sword across their thighs and guts and finally their chests. The two guards dropped, and I stepped over their bodies just in time to see Holloway scurry around the broken steps, heading for the elevator hidden in the back of the dais.

I cursed. For a moment, I thought about charging after him, cutting through the elevator door, and yanking him out like a sardine from a tin can. But helping Vesper was the most important thing right now, not getting my revenge on Holloway, so I spun away from the dais.

Vesper was battling a couple of Bronze Hands, slashing her sword back and forth to fend off their stabbing spears. She cut one man's throat, then pivoted and drove her sword into the other man's chest before yanking the blade free. She glanced at me for a heartbeat, grinned, and charged at two more guards.

Several more Bronze Hands finally forced their way through the Regal logjam and flooded the throne room. A couple rushed up on Vesper's blind side, but I waved my hand, knocking them aside with my telekinesis. Then I hurried forward, attacking one guard after another, until I was right beside her.

Vesper spun one way, and I spun the other, both of us moving in perfect, deadly arcs. We ended up back-to-back, battling one guard after another.

Everything else dropped away, until all I was aware of was my sword slicing through the air. The lunarium blade spat out flashes of fire, needles of ice, and stinging gusts of wind as I sliced it across the arms, legs, and chests of the Bronze Hand guards. Vesper stayed right behind me, doing the same thing to the enemies who threatened her.

The guard in front of me dropped, dead from the long gash I'd sliced across his guts. A pale blue glint caught my eye. I whirled in that direction and whipped up my sword.

Clang!

My blade hit Zane's weapon, and hot sparks showered over us, as though we were standing in the middle of a fireworks display.

"Want to find out who's the best once and for all?" he taunted.

I hesitated, thinking about our earlier conversation in the elevator, but his jaw was clenched, and his eyes were as cold as ice.

"With pleasure!" I hissed.

I shoved him back, then went on the attack. Zane stepped up to meet me, and our swords crashed together again and again, the lunarium blades shimmering with ice and heat. I had sparred with Zane countless times over the years, and many of those exercises had bordered on outright combat, so I was as familiar with his fighting style as he was with mine.

Despite my best efforts, I couldn't wound Zane. He couldn't wound me either, but he was wearing me down, something I couldn't afford, given all the enemies still in the throne room. So I lowered my guard, just for a moment. Zane took the obvious opening, and I lunged forward and slashed my sword across his left thigh. He yelped and staggered back, his leg buckling and his knee cracking against the floor.

Something whistled through the air behind me. I whirled around and had to jerk back to keep my head from being chopped off my shoulders by Dargan. The Arrow bellowed with anger and charged forward, while Adria rushed over and attacked Vesper.

The four of us fought side by side by side by side, each battle an odd mirror image of the other. Adria and Dargan swung in unison, while Vesper and I countered the same way. Then Vesper and I attacked, and it was the sister and brother's turn to defend. All the while, our stormswords spewed out enormous blasts of fire, ice, and wind, keeping the Imperium soldiers at bay.

Adria and Dargan were just as skilled and ruthless as the Bronze Hand guards, but their truebond made them even more dangerous, the same way it did Vesper and me. Surges of strength, pulses of power, and whispers of thoughts flowed back and forth freely between the two of them, as they did between Vesper and me.

I ramped up my attacks, trying to kill Dargan. Sooner or later, Holloway would order this entire tower to be sealed off, and Vesper and I needed to escape before that happened.

Dargan increased his intensity, matching me blow for blow. Both of us were snarling, sweating, and spitting curses at each other, but neither one of us could manage to kill the other. Out of the corner of my eye, I saw Vesper slash her sword across Adria's arm, making the other woman yelp and spin away from her.

One of the Bronze Hand guards wasn't as dead as I'd thought, and he surged up off the floor and grabbed my ankle, yanking me off balance. I staggered to the side, and Dargan charged forward.

"Die, Kyrion!" he screamed.

I lifted my sword to block his attack, but I was too slow, and Dargan rammed his blade into my left side, right above my hip. White-hot pain exploded in the wound, blotting out everything else. My feet slid out from under me, and my ass hit the floor, although I managed to hold on to my sword.

Dargan towered over me. "I always knew you weren't that tough."

A grin spread across his face, and Dargan lifted his blade for a killing strike—

He screamed and arched back. Suddenly, Vesper was there, yanking her sword out of his spine and shoving it right back in again, even deeper than before.

"How do you like my sword now?" she growled.

Dargan opened his mouth, but only a strangled gasp escaped his lips, along with a few bubbles of blood. His eyes locked with mine, his gaze already going glassy with death.

Vesper yanked her sword out of his back and shoved him away. Dargan toppled to the floor right in front of Adria, whose eyes went wide with shock. She dropped to her knees, screaming and shaking her brother's shoulder, as if that would somehow wake him up.

Vesper hurried forward, leaned down, and grabbed my arm. "Kyr! We have to get out of here!"

Fire burned in my left side, but I sucked down a breath and staggered to my feet. Vesper slung her left arm around my waist, and I laid my right arm across her shoulders.

Then, together, we hurried out of the throne room as fast as we could.

This level of the palace had descended into chaos. Regals and servants were running everywhere, while Imperium soldiers were yelling and brandishing blasters and shock batons, trying to figure out where they were supposed to go and whom they were supposed to fight.

"There they are!" a familiar voice yelled. "After them!"

I glanced back over my shoulder. Zane staggered out of the throne room and into the corridor, although he was having trouble getting around all the panicked Regals who were blocking his path.

"Keep going!" I yelled at Vesper.

She tightened her grip on me and hurried forward. I forced myself to move faster, even though every step was like walking on broken glass and caused more blood to drip down my side. Dargan had injured me even more badly than I'd realized, and I was already gasping for breath. Pain flooded my body, but I walled it off behind a psionic shield, and it dimmed into a dull ache in the back of my mind. I couldn't go down again, not while Vesper needed me.

I straightened up and removed my arm from across her shoulders. Vesper glanced up at me, a questioning look on her face, but I nodded and gritted my teeth, and we kept going.

Vesper took the lead, her stormsword shining a dark, fierce blue. I limped along behind her, clutching my own sword, although my blade was barely glowing now.

In front of us, Regals and servants scattered like peony petals blown aside by a violent wind. Many flattened their backs up against the walls or hunkered down on their knees, trying to make themselves as small as possible. Even the Regals with strong psionic abilities stayed out of our way, although their eyes narrowed with speculation as we hurried by. The midnight ball hadn't turned out the way they had expected, and the evening's events would send shock waves through the Regal ranks, as well as the rest of the Imperium.

"Stop!" a soldier yelled behind us. "Stop right there!"

He charged in our direction, along with two more men.

Vesper whirled around, but the soldiers were closer to me than they were to her, and she wasn't going to be able to prevent them from tackling me.

Then a slippered foot shot out, tripping the first soldier, who went down in a heap on the floor. The other two men stumbled over the first soldier and landed on top of him, and all three men started yelling and shouting, trying to untangle themselves.

My gaze darted to the side of the corridor. Asterin winked at me, then stepped back in line with the Regals standing along the walls.

"Kyr! Let's go!" Vesper yelled.

I grinned at Asterin, then turned around and limped after Vesper.

We kept moving through the palace, trying to get far away from the throne room as quickly as possible, but guards and soldiers kept pouring in from all directions, and we had to stop and fight our way through one squad after another.

Eventually, we made it into a deserted corridor. Some of the noise and confusion faded away, and I sighed with relief. We were going to make it after all—

"There they are!" a voice yelled behind us.

Cursing, I spun around, as did Vesper. Two soldiers wearing Imperium uniforms were rushing up behind us. Vesper brandished her sword at them, and I shuffled up beside her. I didn't know how much longer I would be able to fight, but I was going to help her as long as possible—

Pew! Pew!

The two soldiers dropped to the floor, their bodies jerking with electricity as they lost consciousness. Two more soldiers moved up behind them, blasters clutched in their hands. Unlike the other soldiers, these two had a small sigil on their chests— an eye nestled in the center of an arrow. The silver symbol stood out against their painted bloodred armor.

Vesper growled and brandished her sword at the soldiers.

"It's okay," I rasped. "They're with us."

The soldiers lifted their visors, revealing their faces. Daichi tipped his head to us, while Touma held his arms out, showing off his armor, which had been among Asterin's many supplies.

"What do you think of our paint jobs?" he asked, grinning at us. "None of the Imperium soldiers gave us a second look, and it was easy for us to slip into the palace, just like Kyrion planned. Maybe I should turn my workshop into an artist's studio."

Daichi harrumphed. "If you're through congratulating yourself, Uncle, we need to move."

Touma's grin widened, but he dropped his arms and hurried down the corridor. Vesper followed him, her sword up and ready, while Daichi slung his arm around my waist and helped me forward.

"I've hacked into the security feed and scrambled all the cameras," he said. "No one should be able to track you and Vesper through the palace now."

"Thank you," I murmured. "For everything."

"In case you haven't noticed, helping you get out of trouble is one of my many job requirements as your chief of staff." Daichi grinned, his dark brown eyes gleaming in his face. "Besides, I rather enjoy being a rebellious outlaw like Touma."

I would have laughed at his dark, dry humor if it wouldn't have hurt so much.

We quickly moved from one corridor to the next. Per palace security protocols, the elevators had already been locked down, so we hurried down several sets of steps, then made our way to the main docking bay. It too had been sealed off, and a dozen men—a mix of Bronze Hand guards and Imperium soldiers— were waiting in front of the closed doors.

Touma and Vesper skidded to a halt and raised their weapons, as did Daichi and I.

The squad leader stabbed his spear toward us. "There they are! Attack! Attack! Attack!"

He charged ahead, then abruptly stopped and screamed. A gloved red hand shoved him forward, and the squad leader crumpled to the floor, bleeding out from the vicious wound in his back. Surprised, the other men scattered. A soldier wearing painted red armor stood in their midst, clutching a glowing pink stormsword. They hit a button on the side of their visor, and the red polyplastic shot up, revealing their face.

Leandra Ferrum smirked at me, then lashed out with her sword, slicing the blade across the chest of the Bronze Hand closest to her. Then the one after that . . . then the one after that . . .

Even for a psion, she moved at a dizzying speed, and she cut down three more guards in rapid succession before the rest of them even realized what was happening. The Bronze Hands yelled and screamed and tried to fight back, but mostly, they just died, one after another. Quickly, brutally, effectively. If I'd still been head of the Arrows, I would have paid Leandra whatever she wanted to get her to join the group.

In less than a minute, it was over, and only two soldiers were left. One of them charged at Leandra, but the second soldier stepped up, raised their shock baton, and stabbed it into the first soldier's back, making the man crumple to the floor. Then they hit a button on their visor, revealing another familiar face.

"Tivona!" Vesper cried out. She threw herself forward and hugged her friend.

"We need to move," Daichi repeated, staring down at his tablet. "More soldiers are on their way here." He glanced up at me. "Zane is leading them."

Of course he was. "Can you override the lockdown?"

"Here. This should help." Leandra bent down, plucked a keycard off the squad leader's belt, and handed it to Daichi.

He ran the card through the reader on the wall. The light

flashed green, but the device still wanted an override code, so Daichi started typing away on his tablet.

"Give me a minute . . ." he muttered.

I looked at the others. "As soon as the door is open, you all need to leave. Blend in with the crowd and get out of the palace as fast as you can, just like we planned."

"What about Asterin?" Tivona asked.

Vesper tilted her head to the side, and power flared in her eyes, as though she was looking at something far away. "Don't worry. Asterin can make her own way out of the palace," she murmured.

Daichi hit some more buttons. The keypad beeped, accepting his override code. He let out a loud *whoop!* of success, and the docking bay doors slid open.

Vesper looked at Tivona. "I'll contact you as soon as it's safe," she promised.

The two of them hugged again, then Leandra stepped up beside Tivona. "I'll keep her safe."

Vesper nodded. "You'd better."

Tivona smiled at Vesper, tears in her eyes, then followed Leandra down the corridor. Leandra used another guard's keycard to open a door, and the two of them vanished.

Daichi cursed, staring down at his tablet again. "Zane and the real soldiers are almost here."

"Time for us to go. I'll contact you as soon as it's safe." I echoed Vesper's promise.

Daichi squeezed my shoulder, and Touma stepped up beside his nephew. "Don't worry," the older man said, grinning at me again. "We'll be fine. We always find a way to survive."

Perhaps it was Vesper's seer power whispering to me, but somehow I knew they would.

Daichi and Touma hurried down the corridor, moving in the opposite direction of Tivona and Leandra, then opened a door and disappeared.

As soon as they were out of sight, Vesper and I entered the docking bay. Holloway had been so confident he could contain us in the throne room that he hadn't posted any guards here. A few maintenance workers were fueling some of the other ships, and they gaped as we hurried by them.

The *Dream World* was sitting in the center of the docking bay, right where I had left it, and the cargo bay ramp was still down. Almost there—

Pew! Pew! Pew!

Blaster fire erupted, zinging through the air all around me. Vesper glanced back over her shoulder, a worried look on her face.

I waved her on. "Go! Start the engines! I'll hold them off!"

She hesitated, clearly wanting to protest, but she raced up the ramp and disappeared inside the ship. I stopped at the bottom of the ramp and turned around.

More soldiers poured into the docking bay. They all aimed their blasters at me, but no more bolts zipped through the air. Holloway might have ordered his Bronze Hand guards to kill me when his own life was in danger, but now that he was safe and secure, he wanted to capture Vesper and me again. Bloody fucking coward.

"Fire!" Zane's voice rang out. "Shoot him! Don't let them escape!"

At his command, the soldiers started firing again. I gritted my teeth, lifted my sword, and deflected one bolt after another, sending them zinging right back at the soldiers. A few bolts slipped past my psionic shield and struck my arms and legs, but they were insignificant stings compared with the pounding pain in my side.

I dropped one soldier after another. Zane worked his way to the front of the group. A soldier fired at me, and I sent the bolt shooting right back at Zane. The Arrow lifted his stormsword and easily deflected the energy, a move I'd seen him do a thousand times before in both sparring bouts and actual battles.

"Give it up, Kyrion!" Zane yelled. "You'll never get off Corios alive!"

I shoved my sword onto my belt, then snapped my hand out. Zane tensed, thinking that I was targeting him, but a blaster zipped out of the fingers of the soldier standing beside him and flew over to me. The second the weapon was in my hand, I spun and fired it at a couple of fuel drums that were sitting off to the side of the docking bay.

WHOOSH!

The drums exploded with a fiery roar, making the soldiers yell and duck for cover. Even better, that first explosion set off a chain reaction, and more and more drums went up in flames like kernels of corn popping in a food fabricator.

Kyr! Let's go! Vesper's voice sounded in my mind.

I limped up the cargo bay ramp, staggered over, and hit the green button on the wall. The ramp cranked up, and the blitzer lifted off the floor.

The last thing I saw before the ramp closed and the ship shot out of the docking bay was Zane staring up at me, clutching his stormsword, even as soldiers scurried around him trying to put out the many fires I had started.

THIRTY-THREE

VESPER

I pushed the thrusters to maximum capacity, and a few minutes later, we were out of the city's airspace and rocketing through the atmosphere. No blitzers or military cruisers had been scrambled to shoot us out of the sky yet, but it was just a matter of time. I picked a random Frozon moon and engaged the pinpoint drive to take us there as soon as we were in range. Then I hurried back to the cargo bay.

Kyrion was clutching his stormsword in one hand and the wall with the other one. Blood had soaked his Arrow uniform, and the pain of his wound pulsed through the bond. Just feeling the echoes of it took my breath away, and I could only imagine how much agony he was in.

"Get on the medtable," I growled. "Right now!"

He grinned and gave me a small, weak salute with his sword. "Yes, Lady Vesper."

I wrested his stormsword out of his hand and set it on one of the counters. Then I put my arm around his waist and led him over to the medtable. Kyrion slumped down onto it, and I helped him scoot over and roll onto his back. Sweat streamed down his forehead, and his face was white with pain. I punched a button on the side of the table, and the clear plastic panel slid out and closed over him.

"Critical wound detected," the feminine voice chirped. "Immediate action needed to avoid loss of life."

A soft hiss sounded as oxygen flooded the hyperbaric chamber, and Kyrion jerked as the robotic needles punched into his skin, stitching all his organs and muscles back together. Through the bond, some of his pain eased, and I exhaled a soft, relieved breath—

Kyrion's eyes widened. "Behind you!"

I lunged to the side and threw up my hand. A blade sliced across my right forearm, making me scream and stagger back. I spun around and braced myself for another attack, but it didn't come.

Adria Byrne was standing at the front of the cargo bay, clutching her stormsword. Somehow she had gotten onto the blitzer.

Adria stared at me, although her eyes were blank, as though she was looking at something else entirely, something only she could see. She shook her head, flinging off the image, whatever it was. Her gaze sharpened again, and hate twisted her face.

"You killed him!" Adria screamed, shaking her weapon at me in a furious motion. "You killed Dargan!"

Gone was the cool, collected Arrow, and in her place was someone I didn't recognize, someone even more dangerous.

I had been in such a hurry to help Kyrion that I had left my stormsword on the copilot's chair on the flight deck, so I flung out my hand, reaching for Kyrion's sword, which was still lying on the counter.

Adria charged forward and used her own sword to slap his weapon away from me. Kyrion's stormsword hit the wall and bounced off, tumbling all the way over to the front of the cargo bay and sliding to a stop right below the three buttons on the wall.

"You killed Dargan, so I'm going to kill Kyrion. Maybe then you'll know how it feels. Maybe then you'll know how much it *hurts*," Adria hissed.

As soon as she said the words, pain exploded in my own body. Somehow I could feel *her* pain, every single bit of it, like her heart had been ripped out of her chest and replaced with shards of broken glass that scraped her insides bloody and raw with every single breath she took.

Adria was right—it hurt *so much*.

"Vesper!" Kyrion yelled. "Vesper!"

He pushed on the polyplastic panel, trying to dislodge it, but he wasn't having any success, just like when I had tried to do the same thing a few days ago.

Had it only been a few days since the battle at the Techwave facility on Magma 3? It felt like three years, and yet it hadn't been long enough with Kyrion. I'd wasted so much time worrying about the bond and whether he truly cared about me, when I should have just taken a chance and told him how I felt. I should have trusted my own instincts and feelings, instead of trying to shove them down and hide them in the cracked chasms in my heart.

I might have squandered all that precious time, but right now, at this moment, I still had a chance to protect Kyrion. So I gritted my teeth, shoved Adria's pain away, and moved forward so that I was standing between her and the medtable where Kyrion was still being treated.

"You're not touching him," I growled, my hands clenching into fists.

Adria twirled her sword around. "Maybe I've got it backward. Maybe I should kill you first, Vesper, so that Kyrion suffers." She shrugged. "I suppose it doesn't really matter either way. You're both dead."

She charged forward, but I avoided her wild, reckless swing and punched her in the face. The blow rocked Adria back and split her lip, but she smiled through the blood trickling down her chin, and a low laugh rumbled out of her mouth.

"Do you think that hurts? Nothing hurts as much as losing Dargan. *Nothing.*"

I punched her in the face again—and again and again. But she just stood there and let me hit her, laughing at each sharp, jaw-cracking blow.

Finally, I drew back, my knuckles red, raw, and stinging. Adria's face was a mess of blood and bruises, but she was still smiling and laughing.

"Is that all you've got?" She spat out a mouthful of blood. "Pathetic."

She lashed out with her sword again. I jerked away, but she still managed to cut my left thigh. I screamed and staggered backward. Adria came at me again. Desperate, I grabbed a box of protein bars off a counter and chucked it at her, but she slapped it away with her sword and telekinesis.

Back and forth through the cargo bay we fought, with me throwing every little thing I could grab to try to hold her off and her slapping them all aside and cutting me time and time again. Adria wasn't going to stop until I was dead, and Kyrion was still too injured to help me. I had to figure out some way to kill her—right now.

Desperate, my gaze zoomed around the cargo bay, flicking from one thing to another. Kyrion's sword was still sitting on the floor, but given all the deep cuts that Adria had inflicted on me, I didn't think I could grab the weapon without toppling over. So how could I stop her? How could I kill her when I didn't even have the strength to pick up a weapon? Much less stand upright long enough to wield it?

Adria drew in another breath, and more hysterical laughter erupted from her lips. I grimaced. I was really starting to hate that blasted sound, and I had no idea how she could even laugh that long, hard, and loud, unless she'd had an O2 enhancement—

An idea bloomed in my mind. Suddenly, I knew exactly what to do.

Adria stopped cackling and charged at me again. I waited until the last possible moment, then ducked her. I staggered forward, once again moving over to the opposite side of the cargo bay, where Kyrion's sword was still lying on the floor.

"Oh, no, you don't!" Adria growled.

She stepped forward and kicked the sword away from me, but I ignored the skittering blade, stumbled over to the wall, and hit the blue button there. A permaglass barrier dropped down from the ceiling, creating an airtight seal from the rest of the ship and effectively trapping me in the cargo bay with Adria and Kyrion, who was still trying to claw his way out of the tough plastic of the medtable's hyperbaric chamber.

I gulped down one deep breath after another.

"What good is that going to do you?" Adria sneered. "You just locked yourself in here with me. Idiot. You might have lived a few minutes longer if you'd tried to get into another part of the ship."

I ignored her and looked over at Kyrion. "Forty-two percent."

He frowned in confusion, but then realization dawned on his face. "No!" he yelled. "Vesper! No! Don't do it!"

I slammed my hand down onto another button—the red button.

"Oxygen purge initiated," that cheerful female voice chirped out.

A hiss sounded, and all the oxygen was sucked out of the cargo bay.

THIRTY-FOUR

KYRION

I struggled and struggled, but the needles were still stuck in my body, and I couldn't break free of the medtable's robotic grip. An electrical current zinged through the needles, making my muscles jerk and spasm.

"Please remain still until treatment is completed," the female voice admonished. "Or sedatives will be administered to ensure compliance."

Helpless, I lay there and watched while all the oxygen was purged out of the cargo bay.

Plastipapers swirled up to the vents near the ceiling, while others were drawn to similar vents close to the floor. Protein bars, empty bottles, and other loose, lightweight objects on the counters scooted around, drawn in various directions by the sudden, violent suction.

"You idiot!" Adria yelled. "You're going to kill us all!"

She tried to hit the button to reverse the process, but Vesper lunged forward and latched onto her wrists. The two of them seesawed back and forth, with Adria trying to throw Vesper aside and Vesper digging her fingers into Adria's arms to hold on.

Not only could I see her struggling with Adria, but I could also feel it through the bond. Pain pounded through Vesper's body from all the deep cuts Adria had inflicted on her.

Once again, I shoved against the polyplastic bubble of the hyperbaric chamber, just as I had a dozen times since Adria had first attacked Vesper, and once again, it didn't move a bloody inch. Next, I tried to use my telekinesis to push the button on the medtable to release the hyperbaric chamber, but my power was as weak as my body was, and it didn't work. I couldn't escape the needles or the protective bubble until the table released me.

Vesper and Adria struggled for the better part of a minute. Then Adria's movements slowed, and she opened her mouth wide, gasping for air. Vesper shoved her away, and the other woman toppled to the floor, her sword tumbling from her hand and sliding across the floor. Adria managed to get back up onto her hands and knees, but her breathing was wheezy and labored.

"Vesper!" I yelled, slapping my hand against the top of the hyperbaric chamber. "Hit the button! Reverse it! Reverse it now!"

"No . . ." Vesper rasped, swaying on her feet. "Not until . . . she's dead . . . and you're safe . . ."

Adria toppled over onto her side. Her chest heaved a few more times, then went still. Her head lolled to the side, her gray eyes fixed and still in her face.

"Vesper!" I yelled again. "Adria's down! Hit the bloody button!"

She nodded and staggered in that direction. Vesper stretched her hand out toward the red button . . . and missed. Her fingers banged up against the wall, and she slumped against the metal for support. My chest squeezed tight, although I couldn't tell if I was feeling Vesper's lack of oxygen or my own increasing dread.

Vesper looked at me, her eyes dull and dim. A ghost of a smile flickered across her face. "Saved . . . you . . . Kyr . . ."

Then her legs buckled, and she pitched to the floor.

I don't know how much time passed. Ten seconds, twenty, thirty. It felt like a bloody *eternity*, but all I could do was lie on the medtable and watch while Vesper's chest slowly went up . . . and down . . . and then stilled.

"Let me out!" I yelled, slapping my hands against the poly-plastic yet again. "Let me out of this bloody bubble!"

But the medtable didn't listen, and the needles zinged me with another, stronger current of electricity in warning. Even though every cell in my body screamed with the urge to claw my way free, I forced myself to lie still. I couldn't afford to be sedated, and the quicker I let the medtable finish its treatment, the quicker it would release me and the sooner I could get to Vesper—if it wasn't already too late.

Ten more seconds passed, twenty, thirty . . . I thought back, trying to remember everything I knew about O2 enhancements. How much did they increase a person's lung capacity? How long could Vesper survive without fresh oxygen?

"Procedure complete," the female voice said in that incessantly smug tone. "Life saved."

The robotic needles retracted from my back, and the poly-plastic bubble released itself from one side of the table and arched up over my head. I drew in a few quick, deep breaths, sucking in as much of the oxygen from the hyperbaric chamber as possible, then got to my feet.

The medtable might have saved my life, but my head was spinning from all the skinbonds and other medicines, and aches and pains still flooded my body. I shoved the discomfort away and staggered over to the wall. The oxygen purge had finished, so I hit the blue button, making the permaglass barrier shoot back up into the ceiling.

"Oxygen levels low in cargo bay," the female voice chimed out again. "Adding supplemental oxygen to that area."

A steady hiss sounded. I drew in a breath. The air was thin but breathable.

I dropped to my knees. "Vesper! Vesper!"

She wasn't breathing, so I started CPR, trying to get her lungs to work again. I pressed on her chest several times, but she didn't stir, so I picked her up and placed her on the med-table. I jabbed a button on the side, and a compartment popped open, revealing an oxygen mask. I yanked it out and placed it over Vesper's nose and mouth.

"Come on, Vesper," I growled. "Breathe!"

"No pulse detected," the mechanized voice said. "Stand clear for defibrillation."

I paced back and forth. The medtable shocked Vesper several times, trying to jumpstart her heart, but she still didn't wake up. The medtable wasn't working, so what else could I do? How could I possibly save her?

Desperate, I pressed on her chest to resume CPR, although my hands slipped on the slick fabric of her silvery wedding gown . . . I stopped and stared down at the gown. Memories of my parents flooded my mind, good, bad, ugly. But one memory rose up, clearer and more vivid than all the others—my father giving my mother some of his psion power through the truebond, trying to heal her after Holloway had taken too much of her magic.

It hadn't worked for him, but perhaps it would work for me—for *us*.

I sat down on the medtable, gathered Vesper up in my arms, and rested my cheek against hers. Then I closed my eyes and reached for the bond, for the space in my mind, heart, and body where she was. The velvety thread of her was thin, weak, and ragged, as if it was fraying away with each passing second.

Dread welled up inside me, but I pushed it down and followed the velvety thread, trying to reach deep inside Vesper to the place where her power resided . . .

Something shifted, and the whole world tilted, as though I had dropped through the bottom of the ship. My eyes snapped open. Instead of the cargo bay, I was back in Castle Caldaren, back in my library, sitting in the same chair as the last time I had been there in the real world, before I had left to find Vesper on Magma 3.

I glanced over to my right. The door was once again embedded in the wall, and I surged to my feet and hurried over to it. The knob crumbled away at my touch, but I put my shoulder down and rammed into the door, forcing it open and hurrying through to the other side. The spiral stairs swayed and shook under my frantic, pounding footsteps, and chunks of stone cracked off the railing, but I kept going. I leaped clear of the bottom of the steps just as they disintegrated.

I sprinted into the round room of Vesper's mindscape. The black vines had dried to husks, and shriveled petals were falling off the peonies like flakes of fragrant blue snow. Most of the eyes were shut, the doors were blurry outlines, and the entire area seemed far less real and solid than the last time I'd been in here. I skidded to a stop in the center of the room and whirled around and around, searching for her.

"Vesper? Vesper!"

But she wasn't in here, and I didn't see her in any of the watery images flickering in the archways. Sharp claws of fear dug into my heart. Where was she? Was she already . . . dead?

No. I shoved the thought away. Vesper wasn't dead. If she were, I wouldn't be in her mindscape. I reached out for the bond again. It was even thinner and more frayed than before, but I closed my eyes and gripped it tightly, letting it lead me to wherever she was . . .

My body spun around of its own accord, like an arrow in an old-fashioned compass pointing true north. When I opened my eyes again, I was staring at the door in the back of the room that was filled with darkness. I didn't know what was beyond that door, and I didn't bloody care, as long as it took me to Vesper.

I sprinted forward and plunged into the darkness, even though I couldn't see anything, not even the stone beneath my feet.

A faint flicker of silver caught my eye, and I veered in that direction. I ran even faster, racing toward the light, but it never seemed to get any closer, and it remained a dim beacon. Cool air gusted over my face, and the harsh echoes of my footsteps rattled away into the darkness. My lungs burned, and my left side throbbed, but I kept going, determined to find Vesper—

My body banged up against something, stopping me cold. I cursed at the delay and looked down . . .

And there she was.

Vesper was lying on a curved stone slab that reminded me of an altar, and her silver gown made her look like a mermaid floating on a dark blue lake. She was curled on her side in a protective position, as if she was trying to hold the remaining oxygen and life in her body for as long as possible.

"Vesper!"

I shook her shoulder, but she didn't stir. Even worse, she was cold to the touch, and the silvery glow surrounding her was rapidly fading away. I was no seer, and I didn't know much about mindscapes, but I had the sense that when the glow vanished, so would this place—and Vesper—so I picked her up and turned around.

Far off in the distance, I could just make out the dwindling light from the rest of her mindscape. I cradled Vesper in my arms and hurried in that direction. It seemed to take an eternity, but eventually, I rushed through the open door and back into the round room of her mindscape.

Even more of the area had disintegrated than before. I whirled around, wondering how I could get us out of here. Most of the archways had crumbled away, but one of them was still intact—a door with a sapphsidian arrow embedded in the stone.

The House Caldaren sigil—my sigil.

Still carrying Vesper, I hurried over to the door. The knob vanished before I could even reach for it, and I didn't see another way to open it. All around me, more of the mindscape crumbled away, and darkness swirled around the disintegrating edges of the room.

"Open!" I snarled, banging my shoulder into the door. "Open up! Let me through! Why is my arrow sigil even on this bloody door if you won't let me pass—"

A soft *click* sounded, like a lock opening. The door gave way, and I stumbled through the opening into the bright, blinding light on the other side . . .

The world tilted again, as though I had been sucked up in a pneumatic tube, and my eyes snapped open. Suddenly, I was back in my own body, sitting on the medtable, still cradling Vesper in my arms.

"Vesper! You have to wake up. You have to come back to me. Please. *Please.*"

But she didn't move or stir, no matter how much I pleaded with her. More dread rushed through me, but I reached for the velvety ribbon of her in my mind again. This time, instead of following it to her, as I had in her mindscape, I yanked on that ribbon, pulling her toward me. I did that again and again, even as I cupped her cheek in my hand.

"Come on," I muttered. "Wake up. Wake up, Vesper!"

I yanked on the ribbon again, even harder than before. Then again . . . then again . . .

Vesper jolted awake and sucked in a strangled breath. She clawed the oxygen mask off her face, and her eyes darted wildly from side to side. It took her several seconds to focus on me. "Kyr?"

Relief rushed through me. "It's okay," I murmured. "You're okay. You're safe now."

Her eyes darted from side to side again. "Adria?"

"Dead, thanks to you."

Vesper shuddered, and a few tears leaked out of the corners of her eyes. I gently brushed them away.

"It's okay," I repeated. "We're alive, and she isn't."

Vesper slowly sat up and glanced around curiously, as if she'd never thought she would be back here again. Then her gaze met mine. "I heard you," she rasped. "Through the bond. Calling out to me . . . begging me to come back . . . to come back to you . . ."

"Good," I drawled. "Because I would have been very bloody upset if you hadn't."

She croaked out a laugh. I held out my hand, and she curled her fingers into mine. I scooted closer and wrapped my arms around her, and she melted against me, her head resting against my chest. I buried my face in her hair, breathing in the sweet, light scent of her.

We sat like that, holding on to each other, for a long, long time.

THIRTY-FIVE

KYRION

As much as I wanted to keep holding Vesper and reassure myself that she was truly here with me, she was still bleeding from the numerous cuts Adria had inflicted on her, so I helped her lie back down on the medtable. The flexible panel closed over her, and the table went to work.

And so did I.

First, I double-checked and made sure Adria was dead. Her eyes were glassy and fixed, and her body was already going cold, so I covered her up with a tarp and went to the flight deck.

Next, I made sure the oxygen levels were normal through-out the ship, then checked our location. The pinpoint drive had flung us across space, and we were orbiting a Frozon moon. No other ships were within scanning distance. We were free from Holloway's clutches, for now.

I went into the library and turned on the holoscreen. Multiple gossipcasts blared to life.

"... shocking events of last night's Regal ball ..."

"... Kyrion Caldaren, a rogue Arrow ..."

". . . Callus Holloway is offering a substantial reward for the capture of Lord Kyrion Caldaren and Lady Vesper Quill . . ."

I scrolled through the feeds, but they were all more of the same. Holloway had declared that Vesper and I were traitors to the Imperium, and the gossipcasters were eating up his lies. My hands clenched into fists, and I wanted to smash the holoscreen to pieces. Every bounty hunter in the galaxy would be after us now, but that was a problem for later.

I switched off the gossipcasts and opened the secure private group channel that Daichi had set up for everyone before we had gone to Crownpoint. I checked the messages posted on the board, and some of the tension in my chest eased.

"How is everyone?"

Vesper was standing in the doorway. I started to go check on her, but she waved me off.

"I'm fine now. Really, I am." Her gaze fixed on the holograms floating above the table. "Tell me about the others."

"Tivona is with Leandra and her family at Castle Ferrum on Corios. They are a powerful House, with a lot of allies, and they have no love for Holloway. They'll protect Tivona." I hesitated. "Tivona has already issued a statement saying that Quill Corp had no involvement in what happened at the ball and that she personally condemns your actions."

Vesper nodded. "She's protecting herself and Quill Corp from Holloway. Good. We're going to need all the resources we can get."

I swiped over to another message. "Daichi and Touma are hiding out in one of Touma's safe houses. From the sound of things, Touma is already driving Daichi crazy."

A ghost of a smile flickered across Vesper's face. "And Asterin?"

I waved my hand, and another message appeared. "Also still on Corios. Asterin attended the ball as herself, supposedly to continue her search for a Regal husband and an alliance for her family, but so far, she's not under suspicion of anything. She should be able to leave whenever she wants. Holloway has much bigger problems to think about right now."

"Us," Vesper replied.

I showed her the gossipcasts. With every breathless report and every clip of last night's ball, Vesper's shoulders sagged a little more.

"Holloway might not have been able to take our magic, but he's *never* going to stop hunting us. He's never going to give up until he either captures or kills us both."

"I know," I replied in a low voice. "But right now, all we can do is run and hide while we try to figure things out. The two of us, together."

"Yes," she agreed. "The two of us, together."

Vesper sighed, a tired expression on her face. The same weariness swept through my own body, and we stood there in silence and watched the gossipcasts speculate about how quickly Holloway might track us down—and execute us.

Vesper and I cleaned ourselves up, then got some rest. I could have slept for days, but I got up the second I heard her stirring.

We kept circling the Frozon moon, and Vesper examined the blitzer from top to bottom, making sure everything was in working order and that Adria hadn't left any nasty surprises behind. But the ship was clean, so we wrapped Adria up in a tarp and jettisoned her body into space.

"Is it wrong that I feel sorry for her?" Vesper murmured as we watched the dead Arrow float away. "Her pain after she lost Dargan was so *intense*, like nothing I had ever experienced before, like every second without her brother was a lifetime of endless torture, misery, and agony."

Thanks to my telempathy, I had also felt Adria's pain, and

it had reminded me of the roiling emotions that had emanated from my father after my mother had died—soul-crushing grief, helplessness, rage, fear. All the things I had experienced when I thought I was losing Vesper.

Part of me had been so bloody *angry* with my father for not being able to deal with his grief, for attacking me in his drunken madness, for forcing me to kill him to protect myself. But now . . . now I understood how Chauncey had felt. Because I would have killed all the suns, moons, and stars if it would have brought Vesper back to me.

I cleared my throat and answered her question. "It's not wrong. But it was either them or us, and we chose us."

Vesper nodded, and we both watched Adria drift away until she vanished from view.

We went back to work, although we didn't speak, and a strange awkwardness crept up between us. When I had been plotting to rescue Vesper from Crownpoint, things had been so simple, so straightforward. Get her away from Holloway, and get off Corios. But now that we were safe, now that we were together, I didn't know what to do or, more important, what to say.

I knew how I felt about Vesper, but I didn't know if she returned my feelings, so I kept my thoughts to myself, even as I wondered if she could sense them surging through the bond.

An hour after we jettisoned Adria into space, we were in the cargo bay, loading fresh skinbonds and other supplies into the medtable, with the female voice chirping out instructions.

"Well," I said, closing a drawer on the side of the table. "That's it. That's the last of the repairs we need to make."

Vesper nodded and stared down at the floor rather than at me. She clearly wanted to be alone, so I headed toward the front of the cargo bay.

"Why did you come to Corios?" she asked in a low voice. "I know you didn't want me to end up like your mother . . ."

I stopped and faced her. "But?"

She swallowed. "But . . . did the bond . . . make you come?"

Surprise rippled through me. "No. Of course not. The bond didn't make me do anything. Why would you even think that?"

"Because that's what I've *always* thought, all along, from the first moment we met," she replied, her strained voice barely above a whisper. "That the bond was influencing all our actions and reactions. That it was the *only* reason we were together. Even when Asterin told me otherwise, part of me still thought that the bond was responsible for all of *this*."

She gestured back and forth between us. I opened my mouth to tell her just how wrong she was, but she cut me off.

"So you came because you knew that if Holloway drained me, then it might kill you too?"

"No."

"Then *why*?" Vesper asked, throwing her hands up into the air. "Why would you take such a stupid risk? Especially when I asked you not to?"

A harsh laugh bubbled through my lips, and I raked my hand through my hair. Even now, after everything we'd been through, she still didn't realize how I truly felt about her. Perhaps Zane had been right the day we'd been sparring in my training ring. Perhaps I really was a coldhearted bastard—but not with her, never again.

I dropped my hand, straightened up to my full height, and stared down at her. Then I confessed something I had known for months, ever since the night of the truebond test during the Regal ball.

"I would burn down the galaxy for you," I said in a soft, fierce voice. "Just for *you*, Vesper Quill. Not for anyone or anything else, and especially not for a bloody truebond."

Vesper's eyes widened, and her lips parted into a silent O.

I stood there, stiff and tall, awkwardly looming over her the way she said I always did. For once in my life, I'd laid bare the darkest desires buried deep in my heart. Now . . . now I didn't know what to do next.

Vesper slowly eased toward me as though I was a rabid beast and she didn't know how I would react to her proximity. She stopped in front of me, her body inches away from mine, so close that the sweet scent of her spearmint shampoo flooded my nose. I balled my hands into fists to keep from reaching for her.

She studied me for several long seconds, her face smooth and unreadable. Had I said too much? Revealed too much of my inner monster?

Then a smile slowly spread across her face, and the silver flecks in her eyes brightened, glimmering like tiny stars trapped inside her. "Let's burn it down together," she whispered.

Vesper stood on her tiptoes, pulled my head down to hers, and kissed me.

THIRTY-SIX

VESPER

Kissing Kyrion felt like the most inevitable thing in the galaxy.

The wildest, fiercest, hottest thing in the galaxy, a law of physics that couldn't be denied, escaped, or broken.

As soon as my lips touched his, a switch flipped deep inside me, and electricity crackled along my skin and sizzled through my body. My hands slid down to Kyrion's broad shoulders and then to his muscled chest, and I half expected white-hot sparks to shoot out of my fingertips at the contact.

I flicked my tongue against his lips, wanting to feel more of him, taste more of him. Kyrion growled, clamped his hands around my waist, and yanked me forward, so that my chest was flush against his. We kept kissing. I wrapped my arms around his neck, and he leaned forward and bent me back, almost as if we were a couple on a romance serial, and I was swooning in his arms.

I was totally swooning in his arms.

Kyrion picked me up and set me on the medtable. I started

to pull him toward me, but he stepped back out of reach.

"Are you sure about this, Vesper?" Concern creased his face, and the same emotion flickered through the bond. "You've been through a lot over the past few days. I know you're still worried about the bond and how it might be influencing you, influencing us."

"No." I shook my head. "I'm not worried about the bond anymore."

His forehead crinkled. "You're not?"

"Nope. Not at all." I hesitated, struggling to put my thoughts into words. "The bond might have initially connected us, might have been the thing that drew us together when we first met on the Imperium ship. Maybe it pointed you out to me, and me out to you. I don't know, and I don't care anymore. Mainly, what I think the truebond did was give us a chance to find each other." Emotion clogged my throat. "And I am so very glad that I found you, Kyrion Caldaren."

Kyrion stared at me, his eyes glimmering like dark blue stars. His face was unreadable, and the bond was still and quiet in my mind. I bit my lip, wondering if I'd said the right thing, if I'd convinced him just how much I cared about him, and not because of any blasted truebond but because of who he was and how much he'd come to mean to me.

Kyrion surged forward and kissed me again, his tongue plunging into my mouth. I kissed him back just as fiercely, pouring all my desire into the press of my lips and the stroke of my tongue against his, trying to show him just how much I wanted him, just how much I was burning for him.

I hooked one of my legs around his hip, drawing him even closer, and his thick, hard erection settled between my thighs. I hummed in appreciation and rocked forward, and the sticky cobweb of him in my mind pulsed in response.

"Stop squirming," he growled, bracing his hands on the medtable on either side of me.

"Then stop looming, and kiss me again," I growled right back at him.

He leaned forward, and I angled my head toward his. Right before his lips would have touched mine, Kyrion stopped and grinned down at me. "Proper looming requires a proper location."

He grabbed my waist, scooped me up off the table, spun around, and strode out of the cargo bay all in one smooth, quick motion.

"Showoff," I groused.

He laughed and kept going. I locked my legs around his waist and nuzzled my nose against his neck, drinking in his clean, sharp, spearmint scent. It made my head spin. Everything about him made my head spin.

Telekinetic power rolled off Kyrion. A door opened, and he stepped into a part of the blitzer I had never been in before: his bedroom.

He stopped and set me down on my feet. I nodded my approval.

"You're right. Proper looming *does* require a proper location." I grinned. "You know what else proper looming requires? A lot less clothing."

I unhooked my stormsword from my belt and laid it on a nearby table. Next, I toed off my boots and ripped off my socks. He mirrored my motions, then yanked his shirt up and over his head and tossed it aside, revealing the hard, solid planes of his chest.

I reached out, my fingers itching with the urge to touch him, but Kyrion shook his head, stepped back, and gestured at my shirt.

"After you, Lady Vesper," he said in a teasing tone. "Proper looming also requires fair play. Tit for tat and all that."

I huffed in annoyance, but I took off my shirt. Kyrion's fingers flexed and then clenched into fists, and heat surged through the bond, adding to the burn in my own body.

"Not so easy to just stand around, is it?" I pointed at his pants. "After you, Lord Kyrion."

He arched an eyebrow. "As you wish, Lady Vesper."

He removed his pants, along with his underwear, and was standing naked before me.

Broad shoulders, chiseled chest, sculpted abs. Once again, my fingers itched with the urge to touch him, so I stepped forward and skimmed my hands across his shoulders and down his biceps, marveling at the power coiled inside him.

"I've been dreaming about touching you for months," I confessed. "Ever since I first saw you sparring in the training ring at Castle Caldaren."

Kyrion remained tall and still, letting me continue my explorations, although a fresh wave of heat surged through the bond. I slid my fingers along his abs and started to reach lower, but he grabbed my hand.

"You're not the only one who's been dreaming about things," he said in a low, husky voice.

Kyrion trailed his fingers up my arm and along my collarbone, then circled around behind me. His left hand settled on my waist, and he stepped forward, so that his chest was plastered up against my back. He gently brushed my hair back over my shoulder and nuzzled my neck.

"Your pulse is pounding in time with mine," he murmured.

I shivered and leaned back, soaking in his warm, solid strength. Kyrion undid the magnetic clasp on my bra and slid the garment down my arms. It dropped to the floor. Next, he slid my pants and underwear down my legs. I stepped out of them and turned around so that I was facing him again.

Kyrion's hot gaze raked up and down my body, making me shiver again. "You're so lovely," he rasped. "Inside and out. Much too lovely for a monster like me."

I cupped his face in my hands. "Nonsense. I happen to adore

the monster inside you. It perfectly matches the darkness in me."

A smile spread across Kyrion's face, but it quickly faded away. His eyes darkened, and hunger pulsed through the bond, the same hunger I was feeling. Kyrion bent down and kissed me. His tongue stroked against mine, igniting a fresh wave of desire deep inside me.

Our grumbling teasing vanished, and we tumbled onto the bed together in a tangle of arms and legs. Our lips and tongues crashed together time and time again, even as our hands roamed over each other's body.

Somehow I ended up on my back with Kyrion looming over me. He nuzzled my neck again, then kissed his way down the center of my chest and took one of my nipples in his mouth. His tongue swirled around the stiff peak, tracing a hot path, then he sucked on it hard.

Electric pleasure crackled through me. I moaned and tangled my fingers in his hair, urging him on. Kyrion lavished the same attention on my other breast, and wet heat pooled between my thighs. Desire and anticipation rippled through the bond, although I couldn't tell if they were my emotions or his or both of ours mixed together.

Kyrion scooted even farther down, then braced his hands on either side of me. He wasn't touching me, but his breath was a warm tickle across my stomach. He bent down and kissed the inside of my right thigh, then my left thigh. Another shiver of anticipation swept through me.

Kyrion lifted his head. His gaze scorched into mine, his eyes almost black with desire. "I've been waiting for this moment for months," he rasped. "Wanting you for months. Ever since you left Corios after the last ball."

His confession made my heart clench and my breath hitch in my throat.

"Then stop waiting," I whispered back.

Kyrion kept his eyes on mine as he lowered his head. He paused, and I fought the urge to groan with frustration. He drew the moment out a heartbeat longer, then gave me a wicked grin and moved forward.

His tongue flicked against me in a soft, light motion. I gasped, my body trembling, even as everything inside me sparked and crackled, as though his touch was a live wire that had jolted me to life.

He kept going. First short and quick, then long and slow, all of it delicious sensation. Even more desire pulsed through the bond, until it shimmered with white-hot heat in my mind, as though every lick and suck and teasing caress was bringing him as much pleasure as it was bringing me.

"Kyr!" I gasped. "Kyr!"

He increased his tempo, and I mindlessly gasped his name over and over again while he stroked me with his tongue, then with his fingers. Those sparks and crackles melded together along with the white-hot heat in my mind, all of it bubbling up, up, up inside me like a volcano, until . . .

It exploded—and so did I.

An orgasm ripped through me, the pleasure so hot, intense, and electric that it stole my breath and left me boneless and trembling. And through it all, I could feel Kyr through our bond, riding that incredible high right along with me.

Tried and true and now, finally, together.

THIRTY-SEVEN

KYRION

Vesper moaning my name was the sexiest thing I'd ever bloody heard.

She shuddered and trembled, riding the last waves of the orgasm. Her pleasure echoed through the bond, and my inner monster rumbled in satisfaction.

I eased back up her body and planted my hands on either side of her ribs. I wanted to keep touching her, keep tasting her, keep driving her crazy with desire, the same as she was doing to me, but I held myself still and steady above her.

Vesper shuddered out another breath, then focused on me, her eyes a bright, dazzling silver. "What was it you said before?"

She slid her fingers down my chest, then took my hard, aching erection in her hand. I jerked as her fingers closed around me.

The corner of her mouth curved upward. "Oh, yes. That fair play is also part of proper looming."

Vesper ran her fingers up and down my dick. Slow, then

fast. Soft, then hard. Tingling pleasure zinged through me with every touch. My entire body tensed, and the muscles in my arms stood out in sharp relief as I struggled to hold myself steady above her and enjoy every glide of her hand against me.

Vesper stroked me a little quicker and harder, and my body trembled, swayed, and dipped, inching ever closer to hers. A few more strokes, and I couldn't stop myself from kissing her again. My lips crashed down on hers, and her satisfaction surged through the bond to me.

I grabbed her hands and lifted them up over her head. She threaded her fingers through mine, then locked her legs around my waist. Vesper rocked forward just enough to bring her amazing heat in contact with my aching dick. More pleasure zinged through me, and I groaned at how bloody good it felt.

"No more looming," she said.

"No more looming," I agreed.

I moved forward. Even though everything inside me wanted to speed up, wanted to give my inner monster the satisfaction it was so desperately craving, I forced myself to slide into her slowly, trying to make the moment last as long as possible.

I shuddered out a breath as her tight, wet heat closed around me. "Vesper . . . I can't . . . hold back . . . much longer . . ."

She surged up and kissed me. "I don't want . . . you to . . . hold back."

I drew back and then moved forward again, a little quicker than before.

She gasped and squirmed even closer to me. "Yes . . ." she murmured against my lips, her hands sliding down my arms and dropping to my shoulders. "More . . . Kyr . . ."

My hips started pumping, and I thrust into her again and again, each movement sending a shock wave of sensation shooting through my body. Vesper dug her fingers into my shoulders, her nails pricking my skin and adding to my pleasure. She slid her legs up a little higher, and I moved even deeper inside her, making us both shudder and groan.

"Kyr . . ." she rasped, and I could feel another orgasm building inside her. "Kyr!"

I surged forward again, going hard and fast now. Vesper shuddered, and pleasure zinged through her and echoed through the bond to me. I pumped my hips a final time. Stars flashed in front of my eyes, and an answering orgasm exploded deep inside me.

Together we rode that amazing high, shooting through the galaxy like twin comets trailing sparkling stardust in their wake.

Afterward, we lay on our sides, facing each other.

"What are you thinking?" Vesper murmured.

I grinned and smoothed her hair back over her shoulder. "That I spent far too much time worrying about the bloody bond when we could have been doing this."

She grinned back at me, but her eyes dimmed, and doubt tweaked the velvety ribbon of her in my mind. "Do you feel differently about me now? Since the throne room? Since we both . . . accepted the bond?"

I picked up her left hand and pressed a kiss to her palm, right where the eye had been. "Yes and no. The bond is different now. Your energy, power, emotions. They're all so much sharper, clearer, and stronger. It all feels so much . . . *easier*."

"But?"

I stared at her. "But the bond doesn't change how I feel about *you*, Vesper. The bond never had anything to do with that. I was just using it as an excuse to try to protect myself from you, from all the things I knew I could feel for you." I hesitated. "Given who I am, and especially what I did to my father, I never thought anyone could accept the darkness inside me, the monstrous things I've done in order to survive."

She cupped my cheek. "That same darkness is inside me too. Maybe that's the thing that connects us, more than any other."

I nodded, and some of the tension inside my chest eased.

She bit her lip. "But how can you know for *sure* that it's truly you and me and not just the bond making us feel this way?"

"Because I wouldn't be in this bed with you if it was only about the bond," I replied. "You really are quite extraordinary, Vesper Quill."

She tapped the end of my nose with her index finger. "So are you, Kyrion Caldaren."

I laughed. So did she, although the mood between us quickly grew serious again.

"Now that the blitzer has been repaired, we need to decide where to go next," I said. "We can't keep orbiting this Frozon moon. Sooner or later, a passing ship will spot us, and then Holloway will send a fleet of Imperium military cruisers after us."

"I've been thinking about that. I know a place we can go."

"Where?"

Vesper recounted what Asterin had said about Sygnustern, the Erzton home planet, and how everyone who had a truebond was welcome there.

I arched an eyebrow. "Even the two most wanted and notorious people in the galaxy?"

She shrugged. "I guess we'll find out."

"I guess so."

We lapsed into a comfortable silence. As much as I wanted to enjoy the moment, there was one more thing we needed to discuss. I got up, grabbed Vesper's stormsword off the table, and sat down on the edge of the bed with it.

"There's something else. Something I figured out in Touma's workshop."

"What?" Vesper asked, sitting up and scooting over beside me.

"This sigil on your sword." I tapped my finger on the *N* at the bottom of the pommel.

"Ugh! Don't remind me. I hate that Nerezza's initial is on my sword."

I shook my head. "That's the thing—it's not just an *N*."

I slowly turned the sword around, and the *N* transformed into another sigil entirely. Startled, Vesper jerked back. Her eyes locked on the new symbol, and shock and disbelief flashed across her face.

"Are you sure? That would mean . . . my *father* is . . . my *family* is . . ." Her voice trailed off, as if she couldn't even say the wretched name.

"Yes," I replied in a soft, sympathetic voice. "I sent Daichi a message earlier, asking him and Touma to confirm it with the DNA in the Regal archives . . . and they did."

Emotions cascaded through the bond, and questions whispered through Vesper's mind. So many questions about Nerezza, about her father and his family. But the longer she stared at the sigil on her sword, the more anger and disgust filled her face.

"Nerezza didn't want me, and no doubt my father and his family won't either," she muttered.

Vesper took the sword, leaned over, and shoved it under the bed as if she didn't even want to look at it right now, much less think about all the implications.

"I'm sorry. I didn't mean to upset you."

She shook her head, making her hair dance around her shoulders. "No, I'm glad you told me. At least now I know."

"But?"

She shrugged. "But it changes *nothing*."

I thought it changed a great many things, but I kept quiet. How Vesper handled the information was up to her. I would support her regardless.

I held out my hand. Relief flickered across Vesper's face. She curled her fingers into my palm, then leaned forward and brushed her lips across mine.

My inner monster roared with renewed hunger, but I forced myself to draw back. "Vesper? What are you doing?"

"We have a lot of things to figure out, and a galaxy full of enemies to avoid. But for right now, we are safe and together and sprawled across a very large and comfortable bed, and I think we should take full advantage of it."

She gently pushed on my shoulders, and I willingly fell back onto the bed. I started to flip her over, but Vesper grabbed my wrists, lifted my arms, and pinned them over my head just as I had done to her earlier. "Nope. It's my turn to loom and be on top."

I grinned. "Do your worst, Lady Vesper."

"Oh, I plan to, Lord Kyrion." Vesper grinned back at me, then lowered her mouth to mine for another kiss.

She was right. Tomorrow would be soon enough for us to start burning down the galaxy.

EPILOGUE

ZANE

"**W**hat do you mean, they're *gone*?" Holloway growled.

The Imperium soldier beside me swallowed. "Lord Kyrion's ship has already left Corios, and we haven't been able to track it. Not yet," he quickly added, after seeing Holloway's murderous glower.

"Get out of my sight, and don't come back until you've found them," Holloway growled again.

The soldier bowed his head, then scurried away as fast as he could without actually running.

Several hours had passed since the disastrous midnight ball, and Holloway's mood had further soured with every single one of them.

Dargan's body had been removed from the throne room, along with those of the Bronze Hand guards Kyrion and Vesper had killed, and a legion of servants were now on their hands and knees, trying to scrub all the blood off the cracked white marble floor. Ironically enough, the servant who was making the best progress was using a mechanical mop with a Quill Corp logo emblazoned on the handle.

I was standing at the base of the dais, leaning heavily on my right leg to protect my other side. I'd given myself a skinbond injector, so I wasn't bleeding anymore, but the wound in my left thigh still throbbed from where Kyrion had cut me with his stormsword. I idly twirled the butterfly dagger that Vesper had used to stab Dargan back and forth in my fingers. I'd scooped it up from the floor before the servants had started cleaning.

Even more anger flared in Holloway's gaze, and the chandeliers overhead flickered, indicating that he was drawing power from them, no doubt trying to soothe his bruised ego and wounded pride. After several seconds, the lights stopped flickering, although Holloway's mood remained as sour as before.

"How did this happen?" he snapped.

I shrugged. "You know exactly how it happened. You backed Kyrion into a corner, and he got the better of you."

Holloway's lips pressed into a tight line, and he leaned forward and stabbed his finger at me. "You are now the head of the Arrows, Zane, so *you* are responsible for finding Kyrion and Vesper and bringing them to me—*alive*. Cut off pieces and drag them back by their hair if you have to, but you *will* bring them back alive. That's an order."

Holloway still thought he could somehow take Kyrion and Vesper's psion power for his own, despite the fact that the two of them had decimated the throne room with their combined energy. He was even more of a fool than I'd thought, but I tipped my head.

"Yes, my lord."

He leaned forward a little more. "And if you fail, then *you'll* be the one kneeling before me instead of Kyrion, along with the rest of your family. Now, shut your insolent mouth, and get out of my sight."

I clenched my jaw, bowed to him, and exited the throne room.

There was nothing left to do at Crownpoint but clean up the mess Kyrion and Vesper had left behind, something the servants had well in hand, so I tucked the butterfly dagger into my jacket pocket and rode an elevator down to the ground floor. Dozens of gossipcast reporters were gathered on the lawn outside the palace, eagerly reporting about the events, so I slipped out a side entrance. The last thing I wanted to do right now was put on a show for them.

A shadow flitted around a column in front of me. I dropped my hand to my sword, but the shadow stepped into the light, revealing a familiar figure—Asterin Armas.

"Lady Asterin," I said, swaggering over to her. "You're here rather late, or rather early, depending on your point of view."

She lifted her chin and glared at me. "I was just cleared through security. It took *hours*, which I believe was your doing."

"More or less."

Holloway had ordered that the palace be locked down, although the order had come far too late to stop Kyrion and Vesper from escaping. The Regals and other guests had been forced to trudge down a hundred flights of stairs and then go through several security checkpoints. Standard operating procedure, which I had overseen for a variety of reasons.

"I saw you, you know," I said in a conversational tone.

"Saw me what?"

"Trip the soldier who was going to intercept Kyrion and Vesper in the corridor outside the throne room. Why, it almost looked like you did it on purpose."

Asterin's eyes narrowed. "Are you accusing me of something, Lord Zane?"

I shrugged. "You're either very clumsy or very clever, Lady Asterin. I haven't decided which one yet."

She laughed, and the harsh, mocking sound wrapped around

something deep inside me. "I could say the same thing about you. I watched you and Kyrion fight in the throne room. Why, if I didn't know better, I would say that you deliberately lowered your guard and let Kyrion cut you on purpose."

"Are you accusing me of something?"

She shrugged. "You're either an exceptionally bad warrior or an extremely good liar."

"Exceptionally bad?" I drawled. "Is that any way to talk to your future fiancé?"

Asterin snorted. "Fiancé? Please. I will *never* get engaged to you, much less actually marry you."

"Don't blame me. It's your family's plan and apparently my family's plan too."

Holloway had introduced Asterin to Kyrion at the spring ball, but when nothing had happened between them, Asterin's handler had set his sights on another Regal lord—me. Over the past few months, Asterin had visited Corios several times, and we'd been forced together at one society event after another. Every interaction between us had been genteel and polite and had made me grind my teeth in frustration.

Asterin Armas was a beautiful puzzle I couldn't quite decipher. Beatrice and Wendell thought she was exactly what she appeared to be—a lovely noble lady with perfect manners—but I thought Asterin had hidden facets, just like the lunarium she mined on all those Frozon moons.

"I don't know what your mother is like," I continued, "but my grandmother always gets what she wants."

"We'll see about that," Asterin muttered in a dark voice. "Now, if you don't have any more ridiculous questions or accusations, I'm going back to my hotel."

I bowed. Asterin snorted in derision again, then stalked away. A valet rushed forward to help her into a waiting transport. The vehicle pulled away, vanishing from view, but unease rippled through me.

I'd meant my words as a mocking joke, but as soon as they had left my mouth, a soft, familiar chime had rung in my mind. I was no seer, so I didn't have visions of the future like Julieta Delano had had, but sometimes an odd sense of certainty swept over me, and I simply *knew* things were true, even if no one believed me and there were mountains of evidence to the contrary.

And right now, every bit of my psion power was whispering that this was one of those times—that someday Asterin Armas and I *would* be engaged, whether either one of us liked the idea or not.

I hailed a transport and returned home. By the time I reached Castle Zimmer, the sun was rising over the Boulevard, my leg was throbbing even worse than before, and I was bloody exhausted. I placed my palm on the biometric scanner, and the front door unlocked with a soft click.

I went inside and walked down a long hallway, careful to keep my steps silent, so as not to wake the servants or anyone else. My path took me past Beatrice's library. Despite the early hour, a light was shining through the crack under the door. I could also sense my grandmother and my father inside, along with their mutual anger.

". . . why didn't you tell me . . ." Wendell's voice drifted through the thick wooden door.

". . . trying to protect you . . ." Beatrice answered.

". . . but I could have *done* something . . ."

". . . would have ruined our family . . ."

They kept arguing. I should have knocked on the door and told them about Holloway's orders, but I tiptoed past the library. I knew exactly what they were arguing about. I wondered when they would get around to telling me. I hoped not before I had a chance to shower and get some sleep.

I could only handle so much family drama at one time.

I headed upstairs and entered my much smaller library, housed in a tall, wide turret that overlooked the Boulevard and Promenade Park. The room was quite cluttered, and books, plastipapers, and weapons littered every available surface, but I rather enjoyed the cozy mess. And really, it wasn't a mess, since I always knew exactly where everything was.

A soft chime sounded, and I pulled my tablet out of my pocket and read the message.

I did what you asked—Inga.

Yes, she had. Inga was one of my spies inside Crownpoint and did me favors from time to time, for the right price, of course. Although in this case, she'd been happy to slip Vesper a weapon, given that Vesper had saved her son and scores of other Imperium soldiers from crashing and dying on rigged ships.

I transferred the usual credits to Inga's account, then fished the butterfly dagger out of my pocket. The blue opals and sapphsidian chips glimmered brightly, although Dargan's blood still crusted the blade. I'd have to clean that off before I returned the weapon to my mother's jewelry collection.

I suppose I wanted to give you and Kyrion a sporting chance.

I'd spouted that pithy excuse when Vesper had accused me of slowing down Adria and Dargan while the four of us had been journeying to Corios. She was right. I *had* been slowing them down. I hadn't wanted the other Arrows to leave me behind and take all the credit for the mission. If I was going to do something horrible, then I was bloody sure going to reap the rewards.

But when Holloway had siphoned off Vesper's power in the throne room, my telempathy had roared to life, and I'd felt every bit of her agony. There weren't many things I wouldn't do, few lines I wouldn't cross, but Holloway's greedy torture had sickened me.

This was the problem with having a sliver of a conscience

among the Regals and especially the Arrows. From time to time, it prompted me to do stupid things, like help a bitter enemy.

I set the dagger down on a haphazard pile of books, then plucked my stormsword off my belt and laid it beside the other weapon. The overhead lights filled in the sigils carved into the sword's silver hilt, although from this angle, the letters looked more like *N*s than the *Z*s they actually were. Strange. I had never noticed that before.

A tired sigh escaped my lips, and I trudged over to a table and loaded a pod into the brewmaker I had bought a few weeks ago, the new Quill Corp model that was so en vogue among the Regals. The device quickly spat out a hot cup of tea, which I placed on the nearby beverage chiller, also from Quill Corp.

A few seconds later, a *ding* sounded. Unlike most of the other Regals, including my grandmother and my father, I bucked tradition and preferred my tea iced and plain, rather than hot and swimming with milk, cream, and sugar. I lifted the chilled cup to my lips and took a sip. The floral flavor of the blueberries exploded on my tongue, along with faint notes of lemon. Perhaps it was an old-fashioned sentiment, but every-thing truly was better with a cup of tea, including the growing quagmire of my current predicament.

I lifted the teacup in a silent toast to the brewmaker and the beverage chiller. Vesper Quill truly was a mechanical genius, and the irony of my having so many of her appliances was not lost on me.

I sipped my tea and ambled over to one of the windows. The sun was rising over the Boulevard, painting the colorful castles in warm golden light and making them glow like rich, vibrant jewels. My gaze zoomed over to the structure at the far end of the Boulevard, catty-cornered from where I was standing.

Several Imperium soldiers were posted outside Castle Caldaren, ready to leap into action should Kyrion or Vesper appear. I snorted into my tea. The poor grunts were wasting their time. Kyrion and Vesper were long gone, and they wouldn't return to Corios until they were good and ready.

Still, the longer I looked at Castle Caldaren, the more the dark stone took on a lighter, brighter, silvery tinge, as though the rising sun was wiping away all the secrets the shadows concealed and revealing the structure's true blue color. My thoughts turned to what Kyrion had said to me in the elevator, just as they had done dozens of times over the past several hours. As much as I hated to admit it, he had been right.

One small thing *could* change your entire perspective. Even worse, it could prompt you to do all sorts of foolish, stupid, reckless things—like all the things I had done over the past several hours.

Asterin Armas had been right too. I *had* let Kyrion cut me, just as I had let him and Vesper escape from the throne room and then the docking bay. Just as I had let their friends slip through the cracks in the palace security and vanish into the night.

Just as I had used a tiny bit of my own psion power, my own telekinesis, to shove the soldiers off Vesper and Kyrion when they had been so desperately trying to reach each other in the throne room.

I had done so many things I never, ever thought I would, and it was all because of the telepathic thought Kyrion had sent to me in the elevator. Those five little words he had whispered had changed *everything*. Most people probably would have thought he was lying, but not me. The second he had spoken the words, I had *known* they were true, deep down in the bottom of my bones.

Vesper Quill is your sister.

About the Author

Jennifer Estep is a *New York Times*, *USA Today*, and internationally bestselling author who prowls the streets of her imagination in search of her next fantasy idea.

Jennifer is the author of the **Galactic Bonds, Section 47, Elemental Assassin, Crown of Shards, Gargoyle Queen**, and other fantasy series. She has written more than forty books, along with numerous novellas and stories.

In her spare time, Jennifer enjoys hanging out with friends and family, doing yoga, and reading fantasy and romance books. She also watches way too much TV and loves all things related to superheroes.

For more information on Jennifer and her books, visit her website at **www.jenniferestep.com** or follow her online on Facebook, Twitter, Instagram, Amazon, BookBub, and Goodreads.

Sign up for her newsletter at **https://www.jenniferestep.com/contact-jennifer/newsletter/**

Happy reading, everyone!

OTHER BOOKS BY JENNIFER ESTEP

THE GALACTIC BONDS SERIES
Only Bad Options
Only Good Enemies
Only Hard Problems (Zane Zimmer book)

THE SECTION 47 SERIES
A Sense of Danger
Sugar Plum Spies (holiday book)

THE ELEMENTAL ASSASSIN SERIES
FEATURING GIN BLANCO

BOOKS
Spider's Bite
Web of Lies
Venom
Tangled Threads
Spider's Revenge
By a Thread
Widow's Web
Deadly Sting
Heart of Venom
The Spider
Poison Promise
Black Widow
Spider's Trap
Bitter Bite
Unraveled

Snared
Venom in the Veins
Sharpest Sting
Last Strand

E-NOVELLAS
Haints and Hobwebs
Thread of Death
Parlor Tricks
Kiss of Venom
Unwanted
Nice Guys Bite
Winter's Web
Heart Stings
Spider and Frost (crossover novella)

THE CROWN OF SHARDS SERIES
Kill the Queen
Protect the Prince
Crush the King

THE GARGOYLE QUEEN SERIES
Capture the Crown
Tear Down the Throne
Conquer the Kingdom

THE BLACK BLADE SERIES
Cold Burn of Magic
Dark Heart of Magic
Bright Blaze of Magic

THE BIGTIME SERIES
Karma Girl
Hot Mama
Jinx

A Karma Girl Christmas (holiday story)
Nightingale
Fandemic

THE MYTHOS ACADEMY SPINOFF SERIES
FEATURING RORY FORSETI

Spartan Heart
Spartan Promise
Spartan Destiny

THE MYTHOS ACADEMY SERIES
FEATURING GWEN FROST

BOOKS
Touch of Frost
Kiss of Frost
Dark Frost
Crimson Frost
Midnight Frost
Killer Frost

E-NOVELLAS AND SHORT STORIES
First Frost
Halloween Frost
Spartan Frost
Spider and Frost (crossover novella)

OTHER WORKS
The Beauty of Being a Beast (fairy tale)
Write Your Own Cake (worldbuilding essay)